RESULTS MAY VARY

RESULTS MAY VARY

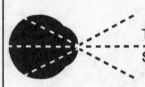

RESULTS MAY VARY

BETHANY CHASE

THORNDIKE PRESS
A part of Gale, Cengage Learning

GALE
CENGAGE Learning

Farmington Hills, Mich • San Francisco • New York • Waterville, Maine
Meriden, Conn • Mason, Ohio • Chicago

LIBRARY OF CONGRESS CATALOGING-IN-PUBLICATION DATA

Names: Chase, Bethany, author.
Title: Results may vary / Bethany Chase.
Description: Large print edition. | Waterville, Maine : Thorndike Press, 2017. |
  Series: Thorndike Press large print women's fiction
Identifiers: LCCN 2016054124| ISBN 9781410498366 (hardback) | ISBN 1410498360
  (hardcover)
Subjects: LCSH: Self-realization in women—Fiction. | Life change events—Fiction. |
  Married women—Fiction. | Marital conflict—Fiction. | Adultery—Fiction. | Large
  type books. | Domestic fiction. | BISAC: FICTION / Contemporary Women.
Classification: LCC PS3603.H37923 R47 2017 | DDC 813/.6—dc23
LC record available at https://lccn.loc.gov/2016054124

Published in 2017 by arrangement with Ballantine Books, an imprint of Random House, a division of Penguin Random House LLC

Printed in Mexico
1 2 3 4 5 6 7 21 20 19 18 17

For Allen, the original good-hearted man

For the past few years, you and I have shared the same pillow as man and wife who intended to live and grow old together, and I have become as attached to you as your own shadow.

— Lady Shigenari to Kimura Shigenari, 1615

1

We two, you know have everything before us, and we shall do very great things — I have perfect faith in us.
— Katherine Mansfield to
John Middleton Murry, May 18, 1917

There are these two little words I know, that we all know; we learn them so early that we can't remember when we did. They have a gravitational attraction to each other, I would say: the one word *love,* and the other word *story.* 'Cause you can have a story without love, sure; but when it comes to the kind of love you fall in, whether it's a slow glide or a blind plunge over the edge . . . you can't have a love without a story.

I thought I knew mine.

Adam and I had promised we would grow old together, and we had already started to. The finest creases had etched themselves into the tender skin at the corners of his

9

eyes, delicate as spider silk. They weren't visible most of the time; only in our bed, when the sunlight elbowed in on us and my eyes opened to his face. I remember brushing my fingertips against them, the morning of the day I found out, in the stillness after I switched off my alarm. I remember the little pat on the butt he gave me as I hurried out the door to work. The way he nodded when I reminded him to be ready to leave by two, so we could make it to the city on time.

Because the thing that kills me the most, when I think about that day, is how damn eager I was to get there. The three of us were spilling along the Chelsea sidewalk through the early evening warmth, dodging across Twenty-first Street in front of an oncoming delivery van, hurrying to the gallery because the opening had started twenty minutes ago and the crowd around the photographs would be starting to thicken. I was walking so fast that I stubbed the toe of my favorite wedges on a piece of fractured concrete, and the ugly scratch across the beige leather made me so *irritated,* because at that moment, it was the most upsetting thing I could imagine going wrong all evening.

I had been looking forward to it all week.

A trip into the city with Adam: the long drive from the Berkshires, down the lush green tunnel of the Taconic Parkway, then meeting up with Jonathan for this gallery opening, followed by dinner at some new restaurant in the Meatpacking District that one of Jonathan's chef buddies had opened. I could hardly wait for the people watching: the gallerinas with their sleek ponytails, and the collectors, and the wannabe collectors, and all the other art world acolytes who would be idling around the party, drifting up to and away from conversations like fireflies in my yard. I would wear my new sundress and bask in the familiar pleasure at the pride Adam took in me when we were out together. After the meal, we'd stumble home to our little walk-up apartment at one o'clock in the morning and fall asleep after some tipsy sex, lulled by the distant horns of the cabs on Ninth Avenue.

And, of course, I was excited to meet Patrick, the photographer whose show it was — I'd had a migraine the night of the party for his representation with Jonathan's girlfriend's gallery a few months back, though I'd made Adam go without me. I've thought about that, since: whether things would have turned out differently if I'd been by Adam's side that very first night. I've wondered it more than once. I've wondered what would have happened if I'd missed the night of the opening, too. But the thing about what-ifs is that you can drive yourself crazy, spinning your thoughts around and around until you're dizzy; and for all that, you only ever end up in the same place you're standing. All you can work with is what happened. What might have happened only haunts you.

So the night of Patrick's show, I was hurrying.

Beside me, Jonathan was hurrying, too; his girlfriend was going to be pissed at him for being late, because Jonathan is the kind of man you want to show off when you're dating him. *Look what I snagged! I captured him myself, from the wild.*

But Adam, I remember, was quiet. I wonder now what was shuffling through his brain as we careened toward the party. He must have been nervous. His mind must have been one long unsettled stutter of *It's going to be fine; he's not going to say anything. He has no reason to say anything. He won't say anything. He wouldn't. He won't.* I honestly believe that Adam had no idea what was about to happen, because as selfish as he is, as heedless and self-indulgent and emotionally greedy as I now know him

12

to have been, he has never actually been *mean.*

It seems strange now that I didn't notice how quiet he was being, but of course there's no reason I would have paid it any particular attention on that particular walk on that particular evening. I do remember, though, that he didn't laugh at the comment Jonathan made about Patrick's name when we spotted it on the poster in the gallery's window.

"By the way," Jonathan said, pointing at the poster, "Patrick Timothy? Alicia told me his real name is Patrick Rubinowitz. But apparently that didn't sound cool enough."

"WASP-washing one's ethnic surname is a time-honored tradition, Jonathan," I said.

"Yeah, for actors and musicians. Artists are usually a little more real than that."

"Maybe you just don't understand," I said. "Your last name is five letters long."

"True," he said, and swung open the door to the end of my marriage as I knew it.

It was quite a big deal, this opening. Patrick Timothy — or Patrick Timothy Rubinowitz, as his birth certificate would have it — was the (latest) toast of the New York art scene. Only twenty-five years old, he was being hailed as the next Mapplethorpe; in the year

13

or so since he'd started coming to people's attention, he'd been universally anointed by everybody who mattered as photography's Next Big Thing. In an artistic landscape where for so long the focus had been on what could be done with the digital, Patrick was obstinately old-school. Critics fawned over his impeccable classical technique, the richness of light in his images, the depth of contrast and range of tone he coaxed from his film. And, of course, the beauty of his compositions.

The rooms of the gallery rattled with activity. Voices and laughter ricocheted off the walls and polished concrete floor, competing in volume with the Vampire Weekend song blazing out of the speakers. The crowd was exactly as I had expected: gallery girls, their equally polished but not-quite-as-artsy friends who roamed the space like nervous gazelle, and legions of downtown chicerati in Warby Parkers and high-water trousers. Next to me, a cat-faced woman flung bangled wrists wide and exclaimed to her damp-looking assistant, "This photograph . . . is . . . *stunning. I have* to have it for the Zolkows' dining room. Saskia . . . will . . . *love it.*"

As I reached for a second glass of cold sauvignon blanc from a passing server, Jonathan poked the side of my waist. "Easy now, darlin'. Don't want you gettin' blitzed before we even make it to dinner."

I smacked his hand away and seized my wine. Jonathan has been teasing me about overdrinking for the last fifteen years, ever since the night my freshman-year roommate introduced me to vodka — cleverly concealed in cranberry juice — and my stomach rebelled several hours later by rejecting the vodka and the cranberry juice all over the floor of Jonathan's dormitory bathroom. Since my roommate had disappeared into the filthy bedroom of one of the rectangle-shaped football players with whom Jonathan had been assigned to share a suite, Jonathan was the one who shepherded me back to my room across campus and somehow, out of that ignominy, our friendship was born.

I turned to see if Adam needed another glass, but he was scanning the room for something, or someone.

"Babe, wine?"

He shook his head without looking at me. "Nah, I'm good."

"What about this photo?" I said, pointing to the one the decorator had been so enamored of. "Do you agree that Saskia . . . will . . . *love it*?"

But instead of the eager humor I'd expected to send him leaping into the game, all I saw in his face was confusion.

"Never mind," I said, and stepped closer to the photograph I had been studying. Shenanigans with his honest Jewish name aside, Patrick was extravagantly talented. The subject of his work was bodies. Sometimes his own, sometimes other people's, but, in this exhibition at least, they were all men. There were a few images of Patrick with his subjects, too — nothing played for shock value, simply snapshots of the interaction between two bodies, some more overtly sensual than others. The emphasis was on the shapes created: the contrast between two different tones of skin, or the negative space defined by the curve of a hand. Patrick presented the swells and dips and curves and ridges of the human body as a landscape, in lush black and white. Most of the images were close-ups, rendering the subject almost abstract — here the arch of a flexed calf, there the graceful terrain where the shoulder merges into the neck. I wondered: Did he already have the compositions in his mind's eye when he pressed the shutter? Or did he set the camera to keep shooting over the space of a few breaths, and then go back through the negatives to see what arrested his attention?

A voice behind me interrupted my scrutiny. "Hey, guys."

Patrick himself was standing arm in arm with Jonathan's girlfriend Alicia, or, should I say, Patrick was tolerating Alicia while she dangled off him, giggly and friendsy-wendsy. Aside from his unquestionable talent, it was easy to see why people got so worked up about him — the kid was beautiful. He had the kind of face that cried out for magazine editorials: full lips, arresting cheekbones, puppy-dog brown eyes with curving lashes, smooth tan skin. A slightly cleft chin added dimension to his otherwise regular bone structure. This was a face that could launch a thousand crushes.

There was an awkward moment while I waited for Jonathan or Adam to introduce me, then I gave up and offered my hand. "Hi, I'm Caroline, Adam's wife. It's great to finally meet you."

"I'm glad to meet you too," Patrick said. His handshake was firm, and it lingered. "You had a headache the night of the party, right?"

"I did. But I'm in fighting shape this evening," I said, lifting my wine glass briefly. "Your work is remarkable. Absolutely gorgeous."

"Agreed," said Jonathan. "Incredible stuff, man."

"Thank you," Patrick said. He was studying me so intently that my skin prickled with self-consciousness. It wasn't a sexy stare — Patrick's artwork broadcast resolute disinterest in women — but there was a curiosity about it that I wasn't expecting. The guy was looking at me like I was a foreign exchange student who'd showed up in the middle of homeroom. In a Stormtrooper outfit.

"You had a little help showing it off," whined Alicia in a way I suppose she thought was cute, and bumped her hip against him chidingly. Patrick didn't remotely strike me as the kind of gay man who calls his female friends "gurlfriend" and swaps catty observations from behind fruity cocktails, but apparently Alicia had never gotten that memo, because she was trying to make it happen. The predictable effects of Jonathan's Tennessee growl and rugged, unstudied masculinity had led me to dub him "the Panty Blaster" by the end of our freshman year — and when he got lazy, he tended to end up with physically ripe but intellectually low-hanging fruit. And then we all suffered.

"Indeed I did," Patrick said, favoring

18

Alicia with a lazy smile. His eyes drifted to Adam, like he was expecting something.

"It's great," said Adam, flicking his gaze to Patrick briefly before returning it to the gallery floor.

"Thank you, Adam," murmured Patrick, after waiting a beat to see if my husband would elaborate. "Well, if you guys will excuse me, I need to continue with the mix-and-mingle routine. Please go ahead and drink all of our wine."

After he drifted away, I resumed my study of the photographs. They really were something special. The museum where I worked, MASS MoCA in northwest Massachusetts, didn't acquire artwork for a permanent collection, but a vital part of my job as a curator was to keep my eye out for developing talent to potentially showcase in an exhibition.

"Hey, Alicia," I said, tapping her on the arm. "Can we talk a little shop for a few minutes?"

"Suuuure!" she breathed, as if I'd offered her a free first-class flight upgrade. And it belatedly occurred to me that, of course, this was why I had been invited here tonight . . . not because I was Jonathan's friend. Because I was a museum curator. And now *I* was trapped arm in arm with her as she wheeled us around the gallery, pointing out some of her favorite pieces, extolling Patrick's talent, his craftsmanship, his vision.

"You know what?" she whispered conspiratorially at one point. "There are a few other photographs I want you to see. Patrick didn't want us to put them in the main show, but I don't know why, because I think they're some of his strongest work."

My interest was piqued, as it was meant to be. "Sure, yeah, I'd love to see them."

"Come on, follow me!" she said, and towed me toward the back office of the gallery.

"Top secret," I mouthed to Adam, as she pulled me past him, and he instinctively moved as if to come with us. Just as he detached from his group, though, he was hailed by a filmmaker friend of his mother's. I smiled to myself, knowing how the unsatisfied curiosity would itch him.

Inside the storage room, the noise of the party was muffled. As I watched Alicia in her tight dress and Louboutins struggle to manhandle a couple of large, crated canvases out of the way, I almost felt bad for her, but . . . best to let her handle them. Wouldn't want to be held liable if I damaged anything.

20

"Aha!" she said, tugging forward a crate with a number of mounted, unframed photographs inside. "Here we go."

As soon as she lifted the first print out of the crate, I could tell that these were different — and I could see why Patrick had wanted to withhold them from the main show. Although, curiously, he'd had no problem turning them over to the gallery for sale. They were similar to the rest of the collection in that they were beautifully composed nudes, but these had a different character. Gone was the frozen, art-directed style of the other photographs; these were vivid, active. Full of erotic tension. As with the other images, none of these overtly depicted sex; their power derived from what was implied, yet not shown. Patrick could only have taken them in the midst of making love with his partner — the images crackled with sensuality.

"Oh wow," I said, feeling at once turned on and uncomfortably voyeuristic. Which, of course, is exactly how Patrick intended the viewer to feel. The face of his lover was cropped from all of the photos; curiosity tickled like a feather on my skin.

"I know, right?" said Alicia. "They're something."

"They are," I said. She was reaching the

21

end of the stack now. I was pretty sure none of these were going to be right for the museum — we didn't shy away from nudes, obviously, or erotic undertones, but these were probably too strong to be hung in a family-friendly museum. The photographs in the main show were better suited. But still, I wanted to see all of them. I wondered what Patrick's partner felt about these intimate images being put up for sale — if he even knew.

A burst of laughter and conversation broke my concentration as the door opened and Adam poked his head inside.

"What are you girls doing in here?" He sounded irritated, almost strained.

"I knew you couldn't wait until I came back. Alicia's showing me some of Patrick's other work," I said. "Come see."

Hesitantly, he walked forward.

"Aren't these amazing?" I said. "Probably a little too risqué for the museum, but they're so powerful."

He nodded so faintly I wasn't sure his head had even moved.

Come on, I thought. *You cannot be this weirded out by the sight of two guys together.*

Alicia pulled one more photograph from the case. It was another arresting image: Patrick's partner was leaning diagonally across the frame, his body cropped between chest and thighs. He was caught in a half-turning motion, tension pulling the side of his torso as he moved. Patrick was kissing him, just above his hip, and one of his arms was bent in a V across his partner's body, down and up. I studied the lines of Patrick's arm, the way his skin made such a bold stripe of contrast across his lover's body. The shutter had frozen him in a breathtakingly sensual moment of the kiss — I could see the negative space between his arched lips and his partner's skin.

And then, I noticed it. A little blob of a birthmark, floating under the right side of the partner's ribs, almost out of sight. As if someone had daubed him with a paintbrush, just the slightest little touch, leaving behind the shape of a checkmark.

"Hey, Adam," I said, laughing. "Check it out, this guy has a birthmark exactly like yours! Isn't that —"

But when I turned and saw my husband's face, the words piled up in my throat. He was staring at the photograph in shock, his face knotted with horror. It wasn't some other man with an oddly identical birthmark in Patrick's photograph.

It was Adam.

2

I love you *because* I love you, because it would be impossible for me not to love you.
— Juliette Drouet to Victor Hugo, 1833

One thousand times. That's how many times it must have been, at least, but probably even more, stretching over the sixteen years we had been making love to each other. Almost half our lives. A thousand times I felt him sink into my body; heard his sighing groan as he came. A thousand times I wiped his semen from between my legs: the very tangible remainder of his arousal.

A thousand times or more, starting with that very first, two months into our senior year of high school. We had spent the entire previous year exploring, all fingertips and question marks, and gradually we found ourselves wanting to know more of the

24

answers. But Adam was patient, at least back then; and perhaps even more than that, he was exacting. Our first time would not be a rushed, fumbled affair, our bodies folded into corners on the couch in the basement of his parents' brownstone. It would be deliberate, and it would be beautiful.

I let him draw me toward it slowly, sensing it was coming but not knowing when exactly it might arrive. And then, there it was: one fall weekend when his parents were out of town at a film festival, and mine had happily swallowed a tale about a visit to a barely remembered girlfriend at some college upstate. We walked hand in hand to pick up his parents' car after school, and when the garage attendant winked at me as I settled into the passenger seat, I felt my blood simmering with anticipation. Because I knew.

Adam drove us north along the Taconic, as the early falling October darkness wrapped its wings around us. We talked to each other over the soft chords of his R.E.M. CDs, and every so often he would take his eyes off the road long enough to give me a slow, sweet smile, full of promise. I had never before felt so aware of taking a step into my future. We were about to discover each other.

The air inside his parents' converted Dutchess County barn was chilly, so we hauled armloads of wood inside and built a fire in the great room while we waited for the furnace to pump heat into the space. He made a nest for us on the carpet in front of the fireplace, with old wool Pendleton blankets that smelled like winter and scratched against my bare, goosebumped skin; but I was warm, so warm, wherever he touched me.

The first time I wrapped my hand around his erection, he gasped. I knew I was the first person to touch him like this, just as he was for me, and the sheer beauty of that, it pierced me. I took in the velvety warmth of him in my hand, the startled pleasure on his handsome face that deepened as I started to stroke him, and I thought, *I want to be the only one to do this. For always.* And when he slid into me for the very first time a little while later, his hands on my face were shaking.

"You mean everything to me, Caro," he whispered. "I love you, and I swear to you, I always, always will."

He proposed the night we moved into our first apartment, a microscopic Morningside

Heights one-bedroom with paint-clotted moldings and windows that coughed in exhaust from Riverside Drive even when they were closed. We sat cross-legged on the hardwood floor, with a bottle of Trader Joe's sparkling wine and some congealing Chinese takeout between us, and talked about the future. His future, mostly. The books and the scripts he was going to write; the plays he was going to direct. The day when he would be noted publicly as simply Adam Hammond, no longer Adam Hammond, Theodore Hammond's son. He was incandescent with eagerness to dig his teeth into the city and rip off that first audacious bite.

"Wait here, okay?" he said, unfolding to upright and skating on sock feet into our bedroom. Our first, official grown-up bedroom, with the queen bed we'd been waiting six years to share. When he came back, he was practically vibrating. "Now close your eyes and hold out your hand."

I was expecting anything but a ring. Adam was a generous, creative, and deeply thoughtful gift giver, and he gave them often: every birthday, Valentine's Day, anniversary, was faithfully remembered and acknowledged. And every special occasion in between. For my college graduation a few weeks prior, he'd given me a stunning monograph on the work of Helen Franken-thaler, the artist I'd written my senior thesis about, which had been signed with a few words of congratulation by Helen herself. I had no idea how he'd gotten it; I suspected his parents had been involved. So I thought this was going to be a moving-in gift, a "Here's to finally sharing our own space without parents or roommates" celebration.

Instead, the weight that settled onto my hand belonged to a small velvet box. My breath hitched in my chest when I saw it. I couldn't move, so he did it for me, creaking open the lid to reveal the flawless solitaire inside, sparkling like a captured star.

"I was going to ask you this weekend," he said. "I had the perfect thing all planned out: a romantic walk in the park, dinner at sunset . . . but I can't wait. I've been wait-ing for six years, and I literally cannot wait one more hour. I love you more than any-thing else on earth, and I want the whole world to know it. I want to make it official. I can't imagine my life without you. . . . Please say you'll share it with me, and marry me."

The fact that he'd abandoned his plan, which had no doubt been as carefully screenwritten as the night we lost our virginity together, was a testament to the

28

strength of his emotion, and I loved him even more fiercely for it. I clasped his face in my hands, looked into his shining eyes, and said yes.

And I never looked back. Never questioned it. Not when my friends teased me, calling me a boring old fart. Not when my father ruined our post-engagement celebration with Adam's parents at their country house by confessing on the ride home that he thought I was getting married way too young.

"Care Bear, what's wrong with waiting a few more years?" he said.

"Because we've been waiting for so long already. You're acting like I just met him six months ago."

"I know it's been a long time. But that's because you started dating when you were only kids. You're still very young. You're going to change so much in your twenties, in ways you can't even imagine now. You two may grow apart from each other."

I rolled my eyes. "Ugh, Dad, we won't. If we were going to grow apart, don't you think we would have done it while we were in school two and a half hours away from each other?"

"Maybe . . . or maybe not," he said.

"Distance can be hard, but it can also hide a lot of things. You only just finished college; give yourselves a chance to get used to living together. You're going to be together regardless, so why do you need to be married?"

"Because we want to! He wants me to be his *wife,* not his girlfriend. We have complete faith in each other. And we're ready."

"But you're both going to be meeting so many new people . . . especially Adam. I just don't see what would be so terrible about putting it off for a couple of years."

"Dad, you're wasting your breath," my seventeen-year-old sister Ruby announced from the other side of the backseat. "Caroline is going to do exactly what Caroline wants. We all know that."

"Ruby, don't be rude," said our mother. "And Bernard, I don't see why you're making an issue out of this. You and I were *married* at Caroline's age, never mind engaged. She and Adam have certainly proved their commitment to each other by now. And he's such a wonderful young man, from a lovely family."

My mother's support eased the sting of my father's hesitation. She had been beside herself since the minute I'd called her, still blotting the spot on my shirt from where

Adam and I had laughingly tried to drink the Trader Joe's bubbly with our arms intertwined. Of course, she'd been saying "When you and Adam get married" for years now.

My dad sighed. "Of course he's a wonderful young man. Just think about what I'm saying, sweetheart. That's all I ask. I don't want you to ever regret this."

But by the time I finally did regret it, we were way past the point at which my father had expected us to fracture. We made it through our mid-twenties, through our late twenties, through my art history PhD and Adam's immersion in the psychotic, back-stabbing ecosystem of New York's theater world. He agreed, albeit reluctantly, to make the move to Massachusetts a few years ago, and even though we occasionally spent stretches of time as long-distance lovers when he was directing in the city, I had never worried. Adam's love for me was such an intrinsic part of him. And it was a pivotal component of his own image of himself, too: creative genius with beloved muse. I knew him better than anyone else did, or ever could, and he treasured that. Every once in a while, in the aftermath of lovemaking, he would cup my face and whisper, *I love you so much. I don't know what I would ever do without you.*

Which, it so happened, were almost the exact words he used in the fifth voicemail he left me on the night I found out about his affair. Or it might have been the sixth; I didn't know. I didn't care. I listened to all of them in the cab on the way to Jonathan's apartment, with the phone on speaker and Jonathan rubbing my arm to try to soothe me. It was a betrayal to let somebody else hear Adam's words, his pleas, his tears. But again, I didn't care. His own betrayal of me was too vast for me to comprehend; this was just a puddle of dirty slush compared to that ocean.

When the cabbie dropped us on Jonathan's street, the air held that clingy, faintly garbage-scented warmth that's particular to late summer in New York City, and the burning orange ball of the sun had yet to drop behind the tracks of the elevated subway a few blocks away. An hour ago, when that sun was only a little higher in the sky, my life, and my future, were exactly what I had always understood them to be. And now, nothing would ever mean the same to me again.

This street, for example. I'd always loved Jonathan's block, in a friendly corner of Astoria like the one I grew up in, where old Greek ladies hung their laundry from their fire escapes and gossiped on their stoops. I'd loved Jonathan's tiny studio apartment with the perpetually unmade bed shoved into one corner to make room for the dining table. But both of them were ruined for me now. They'd always be the shelter I fled to, clutching the shards of my shattered life, because I hadn't been about to head back to Adam's and my little walk-up in Hell's Kitchen. Knowing what must have gone on there, I never wanted to see that place again.

Even Jonathan was going to be different for me now. He'd been so many things to me: my closest friend, the brother I'd never had. My sounding board, my study partner, the one other person I'd known at college with blue-collar parents and a work-study job. And now he was, forever, the vector that brought Adam and his lover together. The first person I told about the affair, in choking sobs against his chest while Adam paced frantically nearby. The one who took care of me, after.

In his bathroom, I scrubbed a towel over my face one last time, and faced my reflection in the rust-edged mirror. Whenever I've been crying, my hazel eyes always look distinctly green — all that puffy pink skin around them. It's a physical trait I share with Adam, along with fair skin and opinionated dark blond hair. Before we were married, people used to mistake us for siblings on a regular basis. I used to like it. Now, even my own face was a reminder of his betrayal.

The takeout Jonathan had ordered while I showered was sitting on the counter when I walked out of the bathroom, but my stomach quivered at the mere suggestion of accepting food.

"Care, you should try to eat something," Jonathan said.

"Not gonna happen." I slumped onto his couch, picked up the remote, and started absently clicking through the limited offerings of the broadcast channels. Jonathan wouldn't spring for cable since he basically only came home to sleep.

"Yes," he said, dropping the carton of *keftedes* on the coffee table next to me and stabbing his index finger at it. "Eat."

I hissed out a sigh, popped the lid off the box, and picked a minuscule bite from one of the meatballs with the flimsy takeout fork.

"Adam came by while you were in the shower," said Jonathan. "I told him you didn't want to see him, and to leave you alone until you were ready to talk. I think he will. But he left a letter for you."

Of course he had. I spotted it, then: on the corner of the coffee table, a single sheet of folded, round-edged paper, unmistakably torn from the Moleskine notebook Adam kept with him at all times. Always the same kind, for as long as I'd known him: black cover, eight inches by five inches, ruled. There were three whole shelves of them in Adam's office at home. Usually the sanctity of the Moleskine was unbreachable; that he had been willing to tear pages from one was an indicator of his distress. An indicator, I should add, that he'd surely known I would recognize.

"Did you read it?" I said to Jonathan.

"Of course not."

"Good. That makes two of us. It would crush his little soul to know that nobody wants to read his precious fucking words."

I said it because I thought it would feel powerful, but even as my mouth made the sounds, a wave of disorientation swamped me. It wasn't like me to speak about Adam so acidly. It wasn't what we did, not even in our deepest, darkest fights. But then, he'd never hurt me enough to make me hate him before. Everything about this was uncharted territory . . . and I was lost in it.

Jonathan flopped down next to me and

35

stretched his legs out on the table. "If it makes you feel better, I laid a load of truth on him about what a despicable thing this was to do. I lit into him pretty fierce."

"Can't imagine he enjoyed that." Contrary to the stereotype about redheads having hot tempers, Jonathan goes cold-mad. I'm talking punishing, withering scorn. The bitterest medicine for a sensitive person like Adam. He must have felt about three inches tall by the time Jonathan got done with him. In spite of myself, I felt a flicker of sympathy.

Jonathan pulled his hair loose from its bun and rolled his head back and forth against the back of the couch. "No, I do not believe that he did." He stared at the ceiling for a moment, then swung his head to me again. "What are you going to do?"

"I'm going to ignore him. I think I'm probably going to keep that up for a while."

"You're gonna have to talk to him eventually."

"I'm aware of that," I snapped. "But I will when I'm damn well ready."

"Care," Jonathan said slowly, "I just have to ask." (Though I knew what he was about to ask, and really, he didn't have to.) "It's so out of the blue . . . Patrick. Did you have *any* idea?"

"You know I didn't."

"No, I mean . . . not that he was cheating, that he was . . . attracted to guys."

"Should I have? Some secret signal I missed?"

"No. I'm sorry. Just trying to make sense of it."

"*You* are? Ha." I stabbed my fork at another meatball with such force that a fragment of meat sailed out of the carton and landed with a soft *whap* noise on Adam's letter. I felt a dizzying tug of curiosity toward the letter, but I clenched my jaw until it subsided. I would not give Adam what he wanted. And besides, if his voicemails were any indication, it was probably just a bunch of beautifully worded but pointless self-flagellation.

"But no," I said. "I had absolutely no idea. I don't know if that makes it better or worse. I still can't even believe I'm having this conversation with you right now. This is somebody else's life. Other people's husbands have sleazy affairs, not . . ." My words trailed off as I realized how arrogant it sounded. *Not mine.* As if I was better than everybody else . . . as if my marriage were perfect.

Jonathan squeezed my shoulder. "Listen, you guys are gonna be fine. What he did was horrible, but you know he loves you more than anything. If anyone can pull through this, it's you two. You guys are lifers, everybody knows that."

For a long time, both of us were silent. Then he sighed.

"Christ, Patrick fucking Rubinowitz. I'm gonna have to deal with that mess at some point."

"What mess do *you* have?"

He rubbed at his bearded cheek with one palm, making the skin pucker around his eye. "Alicia."

And all of a sudden, I felt something bubbling inside me like shaken soda, something I'd usually clamped down on before: the need to be honest, when it wasn't explicitly called for. It might not be welcome, but it could do some good; and good was better than silence as far as I was concerned. "Listen, I have to tell you something, because this seems like a good night for truth — that girl, she is godawful."

Jonathan's wing-shaped eyebrows flew up his forehead, but I barreled onward. "She is, she's terrible. She's hot, and I'm sure she's fun in bed, but she's vapid and boring and shallow. *Please* dump her."

He laughed, a little uncertainly. "Well, alrighty then. Tell me how you really feel."

Which was exactly the wrong thing to say

to me in my present state of mind. "Honestly? Most of the girls you've dated since Rebecca in college have been *so awful.* Yes, including Mariah."

"I was with her for two years!"

"Yeah, and I hated her for both of them."

He narrowed his eyes at me. "Okaaaaay. I guess it's a truth party in here."

"It's been driving me insane for ages. You're too old to keep dating hot bimbos. You've got to at least *try* to find a good one."

He was working up a good head of righteous outrage, I could see it. And I deserved it. But after a few seconds of staring at me while his mind churned for a rebuttal, he abruptly surrendered to laughter, dropping his forehead into his palm.

"God help me, you're fucking right."

"I know I am."

He chuckled again. "Okay. In honor of this weird and awful night, I hereby swear" — he did Scout's Honor with his right hand — "that I, Jonathan Brast, will stop dating bimbos. And that I will try to find a good one."

"Witnessed," I said somberly, "by me, Caroline Ha—" My throat locked. I couldn't bear to form the word. My name. Adam's name.

"Shit," I whimpered.

And then Jonathan was holding me, rocking me back and forth as tears spread messily over my cheeks. The ache was eating me alive, and all I wanted to do was sink into the oblivion of sleep so I wouldn't have to feel it anymore. But I knew sleep would only get me through until tomorrow morning. As soon as I opened my eyes, the pain would be there waiting for me.

This was only the beginning.

3

My heart is full of you, none other than
you in my thoughts, yet when I seek to
say something to you not for the world,
words fail me.
— Emily Dickinson to Susan Gilbert,
June 11, 1852

At 6:06 A.M. two days later, I was facedown
in Jonathan's pillow, denying the existence
of alarm clocks and sunlight, when I heard
him set a mug down on the tiny night table
next to my head.

"Come on, Care. We've gotta get a move
on."

The words bounced slowly around my
skull. I pushed up on one elbow and glared
at him. "Get a move on where? And why
now?"

"I'm driving you back to Williamstown.
And then I have to catch the ten A.M. bus
back to the city so I can be at work by four."

41

I sank my head back into the pillow and peered at him through my one exposed eye. "Do I really have to go home?"

His smile was kind, and a little sad. "You do, darlin'. It's been fun having you here, but you're not going to figure things out binge watching *Battlestar Galactica* on my laptop."

"It's been pretty great to forget I had anything to figure out," I said.

"I know. But I think you'll feel better once you get home. Drink your tea, honey, and let's get out of here."

I sat up and drank, studying Jonathan over the edge of the mug. Why the hell, why the *ever-loving hell,* couldn't I have done what every single friend of ours in college had been vocally confident that I would do, and end my long-distance relationship with Adam so I could date Jonathan? Though no one believed me, I'd always been too in love with Adam to suffer any real twinges of attraction to Jonathan; but it hadn't escaped my notice that he was a knockout. Penetrating blue eyes and collarbone-length rusty-red hair that just begged you to run your hands through it. Fair skin so burnished with freckles it went almost golden. A jawline you could crack an egg on, currently adorned by a trim beard that — as fun as it

42

was to tease him for being a hipster — I had to admit really worked for him. And I'd seen him on enough beach trips to know he had a lot to offer in the shirtless department, if you were into that sort of thing (especially if you liked your boys inked). He had taken it as a personal challenge to be the one Southern chef in America who didn't let his pork belly roots get the better of him. And Jonathan would never, *ever* cheat.

Then again, two days ago I would have bet all the blood in my body that Adam wouldn't, either.

Usually, trips back to Massachusetts with Adam were our time to talk over the events of the weekend, molding the forms of the stories we'd collected and then baking them into fixed and hardened shapes that we'd store in our collection forever. That time I let Jonathan persuade me to eat an escargot and it took me four minutes to swallow it; the time Ruby broke the thong on her designer flip-flop and she just tucked it into her purse and walked barefoot instead of going back to her apartment.

But today, it was Jonathan driving while Adam stayed behind in the city. I had his letter tucked into the pocket of my overnight bag, still unread. It lurked there, waiting for me, like a troll under a bridge who didn't know I could see him.

The reason that Jonathan was driving, instead of me driving my own car and Jonathan tagging along for company, was that he had years ago banned me from driving any car in which he was a passenger. "You brake so hard it concusses me, and your lane changes look like you had a muscle spasm," he'd said.

Asshole. I'd learned to drive in Manhattan, for god's sake. What did he want from me?

He had to stop to piss out his coffee halfway through the drive, and I patted his head when he settled into the driver's seat again. "You look tired," I said. "Why don't you let me take the wheel?"

"That's cute, Caroline," he said, and shook the last of a mini pack of walnuts into his mouth. "How are those driving lessons coming? The ones I gave you for your thirtieth birthday?"

"You mean the worst present I've ever received?"

"Yeah, but you're spoiled. Your husband makes other guys look like toddlers whose idea of a gift is a plastic toy they just drooled on."

44

A beat after he said it, he flinched. "Shit. Sorry. Didn't mean to bring him up."

I rested my head against the window and stared out at the rippling hills on the horizon. "It's okay. It's not like I've stopped thinking about it for one second."

Somehow, we were talking around Adam the way a bereaved person and her friend might skirt the mention of their dead. And it hit me that it *felt* like a loss. He was supposed to have been with me, for every hour of the last day and a half, sitting next to me on this very drive. His absence, his silence — they were jarring and wrong. That I should be so catastrophically hurt by him, and be hurt still further by missing him after his betrayal, felt like a foreign, slimy object lodged in my chest. I wanted to stab it.

Just as Jonathan put the car into reverse, his phone rang. We both stared at it. There was only one person who would call Jonathan this early on a Sunday, and only one reason why. The troll was skulking out from under the bridge.

"What do you want me to do?" said Jonathan. "He's just going to keep calling. I think he's freaking out that you won't answer him."

"Can you just get rid of him, please?"

Jonathan stretched one eyebrow by way of

comment, but he put the car back into park and picked up the phone. "Hi, Adam."

I couldn't decipher the exact words that poured out of the speaker on Jonathan's phone, but it didn't matter: The burble of sound rang with pure frustration. And panic and worry and strain.

"She's here," Jonathan said, watching my face for guidance. "I'm taking her back home." There was a pause, then: "She doesn't want to talk to you. And she doesn't have to if she doesn't feel like it." After another moment, he turned the phone away from his mouth and spoke to me. "He says he loves you and he wants to apologize, and he says don't you want to hear what he has to say?"

God, I wanted to hear Adam's voice. The need to connect to him was like a penned wild animal, pacing, churning the dirt with its hooves. But the thought of letting that need make me crumble, in the face of a wrong I could barely begin to understand — it terrified me.

"No," I said, turning my face to the window again. "I do not."

"Boy, this brings back memories," said Jonathan an hour and a half later as he leaned, tattooed arms crossed, against the side of my car while we waited in front of Williamstown's one hotel for the bus to New York to arrive. "Sometimes I still can't believe you moved back to our college town."

Jonathan had been right that coming home would make me feel better. When we'd crested the rise leading into the last stretch toward town, some little part of me had set down its load with a sigh. That view: A broad field spread out before us, its richly carpeted green scattered with bursts of goldenrod, while in the distance, a cranberry-red barn nestled at the base of a swelling ridge of mountains, lavender against the horizon. I'd loved this particular slice of the world for fifteen straight years now, and the road that meandered along that valley, flirting with the Green River that ran along by its side, had been my way home for the past three. I defy anyone to tell me there's not something delightful about an address along a street named Green River Road.

The move to Williamstown had been 97 percent me and only 3 percent Adam, which was an unusual distribution of influence in our relationship, but I'd wanted it badly enough that I think he would have felt like too much of an asshole denying me. And since Adam was able to work from anywhere within driving distance of the city, Williamstown it was. The MASS MoCA job was fantastic, and I'd been ecstatic to get it, but the other thing was, I was just tired of living in New York. I was unique in this, among all the other NYC natives I know; most of us cling to our hectic city like caterpillars on a tree branch. But something in me yearned for someplace open and green, where I wouldn't have to share a wall or ceiling with anybody *or* their plumbing.

"I moved back to our college town," I said to Jonathan now, "but you're the guy who's planning to open a restaurant within sneezing distance of where he went to culinary school. No way, a CIA chef opening a farm-to-table place in the Hudson Valley? Who woulda thunk?"

"I should pinch you for that, but you're right," he said, flicking a piece of grass he'd been playing with onto the pavement.

"Ah, I was just teasing. You're going to do fantastic and you know it. Your food is special. And I've never seen you not own the hell out of anything you decided to do."

He squinted at the horizon. "Defining my viewpoint isn't the hard part. It's consistency that builds your reputation. I'm not going to be able to cook everything that goes out of that kitchen, which means I have to hope to god I can get a crew that's strong enough to trust. It has to be right. This is the first step to everything."

Most people I know are ahead of the curve if they have their next five years planned out; Jonathan had fifteen already charted. His dreams didn't end with a restaurant in the valley. Long-range, he was after nothing less than his own international-caliber farm hotel like Tennessee's Blackberry Farm, where he'd spent his high school years and college summers learning every facet of the luxury hospitality business. And I do mean every facet: He'd been a dishwasher, busboy, waiter, front desk attendant, prep assistant, line cook. I've always thought it was generous of the Blackberry people to keep training him on a new skill every time he showed up, rather than making him do the thing they'd paid him for the last time. I'm sure they could tell this kid from down the road was going to be a big name someday.

During the lull in conversation, the bus arrived in a puff of exhaust and squeaking brakes.

"All right, darlin', this is me," said Jonathan, pulling me into a hug. Jonathan's hugs have always felt as good as sunshine: tight but not suffocating, faintly scented of whiskey and ginger.

49

I locked my arms around his sturdy back and squeezed. "Thank you so much for taking care of me," I mumbled. "I needed it."

He kissed the side of my head. "Please. I just hate that something this shitty even happened. I meant what I said, though — you two can work through this. If you want to."

If you want to. The words lingered, long after Jonathan's bus had disappeared around the bend on southbound Route 7. They lingered as my car wheels crunched slowly along my gravel driveway, and then as I sat, while my cooling engine pinged, staring at the house I shared with Adam.

Good lord, but I loved that house. Built in 1922, it was quaint but not so old it needed constant maintenance like the slope-roofed Colonial I'd had to be talked out of by a combined team of Adam, Jonathan, and my mother. Massachusetts is the kind of place where the houses have plaques next to their front doors announcing their age, and barns with doors large enough to allow passage of an actual carriage. I'd left the city for America's old country, and I'd wanted my very own piece of history.

Shaded by a noble trio of maples on a meadow within earshot of the Green River, with its magical soundtrack of spring peepers and burbling water, our house had a deep and gracious front porch accented with a crape myrtle at each corner. The rows of multiple-paned windows that marched across most of the first floor meant that the light inside the house changed with the season. This afternoon, it was bright and green-blue with summer. It was Adam's favorite season here. I had no idea if he'd spend the rest of it with me.

If you want to. It nipped at my heels as I walked upstairs to our bedroom, and hovered over me as I lay there, precisely in the center of the same mattress that Adam and I had bought so joyfully eleven years before. Those words of Jonathan's were the first allusion I had heard, let alone uttered myself, to the fact that I might have a decision to make.

For two days, I had been nothing more than a quivering, pulsing blob of hurt — no sentient thoughts had developed so far, just one unbroken wail of pain. I hadn't even begun to consider where Adam and I might go from here. If you had asked me what I wanted, well, it was for none of this to have happened. For neither of us to have ever laid an eye on brilliant, beautiful Patrick Timothy at all.

51

Except, no. That wasn't it. I'd have to dive deeper with my wishing, down into the cold dark water where the sun didn't reach. Down to where I didn't even know what I was looking for. So far down, I was afraid to look.

My mind flicked back to the photographs: not just the one that broke everything apart, but the whole series. The way I had, cluelessly, admired the sensuality of them. Before I had realized the passion Patrick had captured had been shared with *my own motherfucking husband.*

I kicked the sheets away from my legs and tugged a pillow over my face to muffle my sobs. *Why?* Why, why, why, why, and *how?* A *man?* There was no part of my brain where it even began to make sense. Not one. He had never asked me for a threesome. I had never run across gay porn on his computer. There were no confessions about early teenage explorations, erotic dreams, surprising fantasies . . . nothing. I had been in an intense, absorbing relationship with this person since we were both sixteen years old, and not once in that time, not *once,* had he behaved like anything other than a man who wanted to have sex with women. And only women. Only me.

And our sex . . . it was good. Like in any

relationship, some times were better than others, and in the more recent years things had slowed down compared to the beginning, but that was natural, wasn't it? Nobody can sustain the level of sexual excitement they feel for their partner in the early phase of the relationship. Not over seventeen years. I had never expected to.

But had Adam? Is that what this was, he'd gotten bored? Was this even the first time? Were there others? How many? For how long? Suddenly, the room was closing in on me. Everything I'd ever counted on and trusted about my marriage, my husband, had been ripped out from under me, washed away like a bridge too flimsy for a storm.

I raised my left hand and spread my fingers. My rings glittered in the sunlight spilling through the open window: reminders of vows that had turned out to be lies. The flawless, coruscating diamond — forever! And the wedding ring . . . an *eternity* band. I remembered the priest's words from our ceremony: The rings were a symbol of unbroken unity. No beginning and no end. I wondered if Adam had even bothered taking his own ring off before he put his hands on his lover's body.

I pinched my fingers down on the rings, intending to wrench them from my hand, but they snagged on my knuckle. Or maybe, I let them snag. But one thing was for certain: If I took them off right now, I didn't know when I would put them back on again. Or if I ever would.

4

I re-read your letters the other day, & I will
not believe that the man who wrote them
did not feel them, & did not know enough
of the woman to whom they were written
to trust to her love & courage, rather than
leave her to this aching uncertainty.
— Edith Wharton to W. Morton Fullerton,
August 26, 1908

The suffocating numbness that had settled
over me since I fled the gallery with Jonathan receded slightly on Monday morning,
when I rounded the final hill on Route 2
that led into North Adams, where my
museum was, and I saw the town with all
its graceful steeples nestled against the
mountains. Relief flooded me because, as I
so often did when I saw that sight, I thought,
Yes. Yes, this had been the right thing, the
right place. The green ridges of the hills rose
against swollen purple clouds that threat-

ened rain, and the jumble of old factory buildings that made up the museum, all ruddy brick and huge creaky windows, sprawled along the Hoosic River where it ran through town. The steel letters of the museum's name that jutted from the roofline filled me with pride, every time. I loved parking my car and knowing that, within an hour, the lot would start to fill as visitors arrived — to view exhibits I had developed, artwork I had helped to showcase. Since starting at MASS MoCA, I'd busted my ass to earn a reputation as a committed and incisive curator, and my confidence in my skill sustained me. And, better still, my work made sense. My work, I could trust.

My artistic talent was modest. I knew it, had never not known it; even as a sixth grader I could tell that the drawings that my mother stuck to our fridge were nowhere near as good as those of my classmate Heisuke. Maybe I might have been second-best, but Heisuke was special. His work had *life*. With three quick twitches of his fingers, Heisuke could give you a bird, weightless on the wind; meanwhile, I could sketch for twenty minutes and produce a passable rendition of a pigeon in heart failure plunging from the sky.

Predictably, Heisuke was admitted to the

fine art program at LaGuardia High School, and, equally predictably, I was not. It frustrated me at first — that I should love artwork so much, yet remain mediocre at it despite diligent efforts at improvement. What changed everything was the day my ninth-grade class had a tour of MoMA led by a curator in a glamorously chunky turquoise necklace, and I realized that I could make a career out of loving art. Analyzing it, researching it, writing about it, but ultimately just loving it. So I took English classes at Stuyvesant instead of art classes, including the AP literature course where I met Adam. I got an art history degree from Williams, because it was the best program at a small college. PhD from Columbia, because Adam wanted to be back in New York. It had all made perfect sense, and it had all led me here.

On my way into the museum, I passed Natalie Jeremijenko's *Tree Logic* installation in the front courtyard: six young trees suspended upside down in the air, planters and all, from a framework of cables and posts. A few of their trunks had started to curve upward over time, as if to say, *Wait a minute, something isn't right here,* but even so, they leafed and turned color and thrived.

I was lucky to have my very own office, with an eight-foot-high window set into a brick wall still mottled with eighty-year-old paint. My view looked past the small fork of the Hoosic that ran beneath my window, toward the hills that hemmed the town in to the north. Usually I loved to look out of that window, but I'd spent far too much time lately sinking into my thoughts; today I was grateful for the distraction of work.

I met with the director of our children's galleries, Kidspace, about a new idea she was developing for an interactive sculpture exhibit, and then I dove into some overdue updates to my master spreadsheet for my upcoming surrealist photography exhibit. I know it's an anomaly to be a creative person who enjoys working with spreadsheets, but the delicious concreteness of a list or a chart just soothes my soul. As the day flooded past, I got swirled up into activity and almost, almost forgot that my marriage was in smithereens.

"Caroline?" The museum's director of development ("fundraising" if you like your words straightforward), Neil, was leaning through the open door of my office, one hand hooked around the doorframe. "Do you have a minute?"

"Sure." I beckoned to the pair of bony

aluminum chairs I had lifted from the equipment inventory after an event last year. It's not technically stealing if the items don't leave company property. "Make yourself comfortable."

One eyebrow quirked as he draped his long frame onto a chair, one ankle resting on the other knee. The chair creaked loudly as he settled. "I wanted to talk to you about fundraising opportunities with Crush," he said, and I gave a mental groan. Crush was a start-up founded by a fellow Williams alum and known for its eponymous, and wildly successful, family of dating apps. In fact, so successful was this start-up that it had recently gone public — to the great excitement of investors everywhere, and to the even greater excitement of every donor-funded arts organization in northwest Massachusetts. "If I'm not mistaken," said Neil, "you went to college with Diana Ramirez."

Oh yes. Indeed I had gone to college with Diana, and what a delightful experience that had been. "You're not mistaken, but I have no idea how you know that."

"Good memory," he said. "I've been looking at her for a while as a potential donor, but until the IPO I wasn't sure if she'd be worth pursuing. Fifty million shares later, she is officially worth it. So, I wanted to see if you'd be up to reaching out to her. Work the old alumni angle."

This could not possibly be happening. Not today. "Neil, I barely knew her. We certainly weren't friends. And besides, everybody's going to be chasing her. Every alum in the country has got to be crawling up her butt already, and —"

He snorted.

"Sorry. But you know what I mean."

"I do. They're going to be in there with headlamps," he said, and I did one of those big, loud, involuntary "HA!" laughs. "But," he continued, unperturbed, "that means we should be, too. I read a piece on her last week where she talked about how much she loves the Berkshires; she just bought a weekend place down near Stockbridge. So, if you're counting, that makes you an alumna of the same college, who — like her — loves the area so much that you moved back, *and* you work for a leading arts organization with deep ties to both the college and the Berkshire region." He flipped his palms up, like, case closed.

And also, the woman can't stand me, I thought. But I hated the thought of spilling tired freshman-year gossip to my co-worker; better to support my avoidance from a different angle. I leaned forward on my desk, forearms crossed. "I know. I read the same piece. The thing is, though, I'm a curator. I do my art thing and you do your fundraising thing, and I don't ever do your thing. I don't know how to do your thing. I'm not a schmoozer."

"No, you're not. Because 'schmoozer' sounds like some kind of fancy poodle mix."

I almost sprained my face trying not to laugh. I had to get him to leave me alone about this. "Seriously. I do not have the first clue how to tackle this."

"Well, you can start by putting together what you know about her, and then do some research to fill in what you're missing. Where is she from originally? What is she interested in? What are her social causes, what charities does she give to?"

"Her personally, or Crush?"

"Both. And once you've got a good picture, you can use that to create a custom-tailored menu of potential gifts. Donors want to know their money will have tangible results. So, put together a list so appealing she can't stand the thought of missing out."

Isn't this your *job?* I thought, but no sooner had my brain formed the words than he continued.

"I'll help you if you're not sure how to put it together. But I can't overstate the importance of a personal connection here, which is why I'm asking you to help get the relationship started. Just try it out. See what you can do. I know you don't have a lot of experience with this, but it's a great opportunity and we'd be fools not to throw everything we've got at it."

In the abstract, everything he said had excellent logic to it. Neil was young to be heading up a development office, but we'd lured him from the Gardner in Boston two years ago by offering him the directorship, and he'd made good on the trustees' enthusiasm in spectacular fashion ever since. If he thought I was our museum's best shot at Diana Ramirez, then he was probably right. In the abstract.

There was also the fact that his entire demeanor conveyed a serene but unbudging stubbornness. He was not going to let me out of this. "Okay," I sighed. "I'll see what I can do."

The chair squealed again as he got to his feet, and he patted it bracingly. Then he stopped in my doorway, tapped the casing as if remembering something, and pivoted back to face me. "Oh, hey, how was the Patrick Timothy show? Didn't you go this weekend?"

Hearing the name was like having my face

slapped. It took me several seconds too long to recover. "Oh. Yes. I did. It was great. Stunning, actually. The kid is the real deal."

Funny how, although I was pretty sure no one was handing out cosmic gold stars for "Be the bigger person" moments such as praising your husband's co-conspirator in cheating, I couldn't quite bury my admiration for Patrick's talent under my loathing of his greed. Even though I was certain that talent was one of the things that had made him so compelling to Adam. Like Adam, Patrick was a creator, while all I did was work with other people's creations. Was that why Adam had found him superior?

"Should we be looking at trying to exhibit him here?"

With an effort, I dragged my thoughts back to the conversation. "I heard the Whitney's all over him," I said. I had heard absolutely no such thing.

"Really?" said Neil. "Didn't think he was big enough yet for them to be interested."

"I guess he is." (He was absolutely not.) "Also, though, the images are incredible, but some of them are kinda racy," I said. "So that's a factor, too."

"Hmm," said Neil. "I saw a few in the *Times* write-up. They weren't that bad."

"You're saying that because you're an art

guy who's not threatened by images of naked human bodies. I bet you're teaching your kids the proper anatomy words, too, not stuff like 'wee-wee' and 'special place.' "

He grinned, teeth flashing white against his light brown skin. "Guilty. But, still. You know who I heard likes photography? Diana Ramirez." He rapped his knuckles against my doorframe again — *chop-chop* — and then he was gone.

For three days, I'd resisted reading Adam's letter. I hadn't wanted to give him the time and attention he craved, though the mystery of the letter's contents tormented me like a paper cut I couldn't stop touching. But my sickening revelation about Patrick's potential superiority sent me diving into my discarded overnight bag for the letter as soon as I got home from work that day. I had to know what Adam had written, why he had done what he had. And I had to know what he felt about Patrick.

I sat at the kitchen counter and opened the folded page. At the sight of my husband's familiar handwriting, memory poured down on me, as soaking heavy as rain. Letters used to be our sacred thing.

When we were in school, separated by a couple hundred miles and all the usual collegiate distractions, we would email every day, but we saved everything special for letters. Adam, of course, had started it — he hated the banality of email, preferring the old-fashioned romance of a written letter, like the missives written by Browning and Keats. And his letters were masterpieces, full of funny stories and thoughtful observations as well as romantic declarations. He narrated so beautifully that every time I read one, I could hear his voice in my ears, rolling and curving with his sentences. I'd saved every precious one of them, and he'd saved all of mine; they were nestled together in an archival storage box in the attic right at that very minute. This thing I held in my hand was, to those letters, like a mutated gene is to a pure one — related, and almost identical in many ways, yet full of dysfunction that corrupted the healthy processes of the organism.

Love — my love —
Well, having started, I can't seem to move this pen beyond that. Probably because this little brain of mine cannot seem to move its neurons beyond that. I'm all just love, love, love, like a heartbeat. You are my heartbeat.
I know you must be hungry for an-

swers, and I wish more than anything that I could give them, but I quite simply can't. I don't even understand yet why I did what I did, so I cannot hope to explain it to you. All I can do is tell you how sorry I am. I don't recognize the person who would do this thing to his beloved, his wife, his Caroline. I had never imagined what it could be like to despise myself this much; it's corrosive and foul, a film of dirty oil on the pure water that is my love for you. And I will do whatever you need to flush that water clean again.

But until you know what that is and you're ready for me to do it, I am just thinking about the love. I need you to understand that it has never faded, or grown fallow like soil that's been leached of its nutrients. It is as rich as ever, filling me up. It sustains me now, even though you can't bear the sight of me. My love is made of everything between us, every moment of every precious year, and it is still growing. It is still growing.

All my heart,

Adam

The letter made a soft *whiff* as it dropped to the counter. Well. So. That was all he had to say for himself. He loved me — but declared himself incapable of illuminating his reasons for betraying the love I'd given him for more than half our lifetime. Mainly, he wanted to remind me that he loved me. Which meant he really just wanted me to forgive him.

It was the same pattern he enacted anytime I was upset with him — poignant apology, followed by heartfelt declarations of love, with a strong implication that I shouldn't let my resentment impede our return to peace and harmony. Because in love, it wasn't worth holding a grudge over a slight. When it was something like booking plans in the city when I wanted him to attend one of my work events, I was inclined to agree with him. But infidelity?

I walked down the hall to his office, switched on the paper shredder, and fed the letter through. The growling crunch of the teeth as they ripped their way through Adam's words was very satisfying indeed.

I was ensconced in my favorite rocking chair on my back deck, watching a coral and gold sunset drain from the sky with two big glasses of Adam's prized vintage dry Riesling inside me, when my sister, Ruby, called. Because of course she would call right now.

Even under the best of circumstances, I was never fully prepared for the mental energy required by interaction with Ruby, and she had a knack for timing her infrequent calls and visits to coincide with my moments of weakness and fatigue. But I'd seen a few texts from her when I reluctantly turned on my phone this morning after my Adam-induced technology blackout, so I supposed I'd have to stop hiding.

I took a deep breath and answered the call.

"Oh my *god,* Care. Where the hell have you been? I've been trying to get ahold of you since the weekend. We were supposed to get brunch yesterday, but you never texted me back."

It was odd to realize that, as far as Ruby knew, I'd had a perfectly normal weekend, with no justifiable reason for ignoring her. Even if I'd seen the texts, what would I have said? *Sorry, can't make brunch; too busy trying to keep my organs from squirting out of this gaping wound in my chest.* "Oh, damn. I'm sorry about that."

"Did you forget? Or drop your phone in the toilet, or what?"

"I forgot. And, uh, I forgot my charger, so my phone died and I didn't see your texts. I'm sorry," I said, pronouncing each word like I was setting a bone china teacup in its

68

saucer. She couldn't notice I'd been drinking or she'd know for sure something was wrong.

"Wow. That's something I would do, that you'd scold me for. Nice going, big sis," she said, but her voice was teasing. "So anyway, we were thinking of leaving the city at two on Friday, which should put us up there around six, with traffic. Is there anything good on the roster?"

I pitched forward in my chair, my feet landing on the porch with a hard thump that yanked my rocking to a stop. Damn it — I had squelched so deep into my personal swamp that I'd completely forgotten my parents and sister were supposed to be visiting this weekend. It was their annual ritual since Adam and I moved up here: visit for opening night of one of the Williamstown Theatre Festival plays. Be squired from show to party to after-party by their playwright brother-/son-in-law. Adam loved it as much as they did, showing off his connections for my goggle-eyed family. They were arriving in four days and they had no idea Adam and I weren't speaking.

"Oh, Ruby, I meant to tell you," I said. "I think we have to cancel for this weekend. Adam —" What was the lie going to be? "Adam had to go to a thing."

69

"A thing?"

Work, brain. "A conference. Of some sort."

"On this short notice? In the middle of the festival?"

"No, he, ah, he forgot he had scheduled it. Stupid. But so, he's not here."

"Geez, a lot of forgetting going on with you two lately. You must have the tickets, though, so why can't we still come?"

Why, indeed? "I just don't see the point. With him not here, and all."

"Whatever. We're coming."

"No. Seriously. Do not come. It is not a good time."

A pause. Then: "Care, is everything okay?"

Oh, there was so much in it, that little sentence of Ruby's. Genuine concern. Worry. But there was this very, very, *very* faint note of — almost — hope? Hope that, for the first time in my well-ordered, smoothly executed life, something might not be going exactly right.

Of course, my sister would never actually wish any pain on me. But I wouldn't put it past her to feel at least a little bit glad that, for once, I had a problem. And, as it happened, the lady was in luck.

"Adam and I are having some issues," I said finally. It was a sentence I had prese-lected on the long drive back to Mas-

70

sachusetts, for the inevitable moment when I would have to tell someone.

"Oh shit, Care. I'm so sorry to hear that."

And she clearly genuinely was. A tactful person would let it rest at that, and allow me to volunteer any further detail I might wish to disclose.

"What sort of issues?" said Ruby.

I lifted my wine glass toward the light spilling from the house, and studied the way the familiar image of my kitchen window was distorted by the round glass and the liquid. "He cheated on me."

"Are you fucking kidding me?"

"Your shock is really gratifying, thank you for that," I murmured, swirling the wine.

"Because it's fucking shocking!" she yelled. "Adam adores you! Adam thinks you're the most beautiful woman ever created by God's own personal hand! He annoys the living shit out of everyone around him because he won't shut up about it!"

"Well, perhaps that's the problem."

"That he won't shut up about it?"

A firefly meandered near me, its belly glowing twice before I answered. "No. That I'm a woman."

"I don't follow," Ruby said after a moment, and it was such an oddly tentative, un-Rubylike statement that I had to laugh.

71

"Adam had an affair with a man," I said, trying the words out. But they sounded blank, incoherent, just a sequence of sounds; it was as if those words, put together, created a sentence without a meaning that my brain could recognize. I waited for an explosion of astonishment from the other end of the phone, but all I got, after a good solid couple of seconds, was:

"Oh." Then, another second or two later, "Wow."

" 'Oh, wow' is right," I said, and took another hearty glug of Riesling. When there was still nothing further forthcoming from Ruby, I continued. "So, I kicked him out. And that is why I don't want you and Mom and Dad traipsing about up here this weekend. There is no Adam, and as far as I'm concerned, there's no festival, either."

I felt an unexpected gush of relief inside me as I said it. When it came right down to it, there was little I enjoyed about the festival. All the air-kissing and hugging — it was just so phony; everyone was only there to make whatever contacts they could to advance their own careers. And the plays themselves — I always enjoyed a good Shakespeare or other classic, but somehow the ones we went to with my family were always modern pieces in the running for

"Most Pretentiously Abstract" and "Most Loathsome Characters." All of a sudden, the fact that I could skip it this year was the lone puddle of light in the dark and moldy basement of my situation.

"Well, so," began Ruby, "what are you going to do? Are you guys going to counseling?"

"Not at the present moment," I said, and I knew, if she'd been paying attention, that she would have busted me then for drinking. Ruby identified years ago that, once I get a little drunk and then realize it and decide I don't want to be, I resort to unnecessarily formal language to try to camouflage myself. It actually annoyed Adam that he hadn't been the one to discover this particular quirk; Adam liked to be considered the ultimate authority on Caroline, to the exclusion even of the people who've known me since birth. He had a seemingly endless mental catalog of my stories, traits, and linguistic tics, and whenever he caught me doing one of my Caroline Things, he would get this affectionate, indulgent, and also faintly victorious smile on his face as he called me out.

I wondered if he had a list of Patrick Things, too.

"I have no idea what I'm going to do," I said.

"And you hate it," Ruby said.

"What do you mean?"

"Care, you have the least ability to tolerate uncertainty of anyone I know."

"Oh, thanks, Ruby."

"It's not an insult; it's an observation," she sniffed.

"I am definitely going to use that comment on you someday."

"Well, fuck," said Ruby, in apt summary. "This is awful. I don't even know what to say." Then, after a moment: "So . . . you're all by yourself up there, huh?"

"Yes, and what is your next question?" A long-standing Ruby Thing is that whenever she ends a question with "huh," you can be confident she's leading you somewhere.

"How'd you like some company?"

"Like one of your foster cats? I'm still as allergic as I was last time you tried to foist one on me."

"No, I was thinking something a little bigger. How about *me*?"

Oh Christ, no. I loved my sister but the prospect of her rambunctiousness shattering my contemplative solitude was not one I could handle. All I wanted for company were the fireflies, and the cicadas whose rat-

74

tling song pulsed through the night air around my house. *Don't even bother, guys,* I wanted to tell them. *All you're gonna do is screw each other and die.*

"Oh, peanut, thank you for offering, but I'm still pretty deep in the wound-licking stage —"

"All the more reason for me to come!"

"No, I mean, I am *deep* in that stage, Ruby. Deep."

"Balls deep?" she said, before dissolving into laughter.

"You're disgusting," I said, but I was grinning.

"See? You need me."

"Ah, Rube, I just —"

"Look, I've got some wounds to lick, too, okay? We can hole up in your house together and drown our sorrows — although I sense you already got a head start on that — and we will rant about men and feel much better. It'll be awesome."

Damn it. She *had* noticed the drinking. "What sorrows do you have to drown?"

"Burqhart broke up with me. Said he felt too much pressure to propose."

Crap. Burqhart was the latest in Ruby's chain of utterly benign, utterly forgettable boyfriends. The most remarkable thing about this guy had been his name. "Well,

75

were you pressuring him?"

"Jesus, Caroline, no. I wasn't. Why would you assume I was?"

"I didn't assume. I asked you. He had to have gotten it from somewhere."

"Yeah. From the fact that his brother and his best friend just proposed to *their* girl-friends. Not from me. Unless the mere fact of my being a twenty-eight-year-old woman is a threat in and of itself."

"And you didn't talk about timelines? Hypothetical wedding or honeymoon locations?"

"What the hell? No. Why are you so convinced I did something to deserve this?"

"You deserve it for sleeping with a dude named Burqhart," I said, and swallowed another deep sip of wine.

Silence . . . then, gradually, I heard her laughing, the sound trickling out of her throat louder and louder until she couldn't pretend to hold it in any longer. Ruby can always take a joke at her expense if it's a fair one.

"See, you have to let me come. I will brighten your dreary days and give you something to laugh at."

It took me a moment to realize I was smiling, too. Really, it wasn't the worst idea in the world. Ruby and I got on each other's nerves if we spent too much time together, but two days was a manageable amount of time, and it would be nice to have another human being with me in this oppressively empty house.

"Okay. Okay! You can come. But not Mom and Dad."

"Yay! Sister time! What are you going to tell them, though?"

"I'm sticking with the business trip story for now. I have to see how it goes for the next little while before I figure out what to tell them."

"No kidding. Mom is going to *freak out*."

I groaned and shoved the thought away. I was categorically not ready to deal with my mother. "Yeah. She is. So back me up on the business trip, please."

"Yup, yup, yup. Hey, will you get all my foods for me?" said Ruby, with a six-year-old's enthusiasm. "Cocoa Puffs and Cheetos and those frozen mozzarella sticks that turn all flat and melted in the microwave?"

"You want to eat all your favorite disgusting foods in one weekend?"

"Yes," she said. "I'm embracing my breakup weight. I am diving headfirst into it. My soul will be cleansed of its sorrow by the soothing embrace of General Mills."

"Okay," I laughed, "I will get your foods.

Text me what you want."

"Thanks, sis! Look, man trouble is a shitty reason for us to get together, but we're going to have fun. I promise."

As I hung up the phone, I couldn't quite reach my sister's level of optimism that I would be able to describe any part of my life as "fun." But there was no doubt the girl could make me laugh, and that, at least, was an improvement.

5

I must confess that I have noticed a deterioration in your manner; & you are not so kind as you used to be.
— Clementine Churchill to her husband, Winston, June 17, 1940

I had known my deep-freeze silent treatment wouldn't work on Adam for long; like any force of nature, he abhorred a vacuum. So I was not surprised to find him when I arrived home from work the next day, waiting for me in our driveway in the middle of a fierce afternoon thunderstorm, in a stupid yellow hatchback with the Zipcar logo on the side.

He was in the driveway because he couldn't get inside. I'd changed the locks. I pictured him, scrambling up the front steps in the rain, only to stand on our porch dripping and confused because his key wouldn't turn. I was sure he hadn't expected me to

79

do that. It felt good to thwart him.

I was also sure he hadn't brought an umbrella with him, because checking the weather app on his phone at the beginning of the day was simply not a skill Adam had ever acquired. He relied on me to check, and to tell him anything he needed to know. I was his own personal Al Roker; just as, for any of our shared decisions or plans, I was the coordinator, the cruise director, the tour guide. *This way. Follow me.*

My heart was pumping with such sickening force that I could see the open collar of my blouse trembling when I glanced down, but I would not let Adam see that I was rattled. As calmly as if he weren't there, I killed the headlights, turned the car off, and engaged the parking brake. For all that Jonathan teases me about my driving, I have always believed in the parking brake. I popped my umbrella open and stepped out into the downpour.

I heard the thump of Adam's car door closing, and then there he was, standing in front of me. No umbrella. I honestly think I could have respected him in that moment, just the tiniest little bit, if he had only brought his own goddamned umbrella. Instead, water crashed down from the leaves of the big maple over our heads, around the ineffectual palm he held above his face. It splatted into his hair, turning it the color of wet cardboard, and ran in rivulets over his forehead and cheeks. I choked down hard on my instinct to shield him, and I choked down even harder on the love that surged inside me at the sight of him, standing in front of me in supplication. I squeezed and crushed that love until all I felt was rage.

"I have nothing to say to you," I said, clutching my umbrella handle in front of me like a shield. As badly as I wanted to understand what had happened to me, the mere fact that he was here now, ready to talk, made me want to deny him.

"Can we please go inside and talk?"

"No."

"Caroline."

I gripped the handle tighter, my sweaty palm slipping on the sleek wood. "I'm not interested."

"Sweetheart, you can't just refuse to speak to me forever."

"Watch me."

He wiped his dripping hair away from his forehead and shook a raindrop off the end of his nose. "Caroline. *Please.*"

With a sudden rush of sound, the pace of the rain spiked, the way it does just when you're thinking it cannot possibly rain any harder. The water pounded so hard on my umbrella that I could feel the vibration in the handle. I swallowed, whipped my body around so my back was to him, and walked toward the porch, my muscles tightening from the rigidity of my posture. Adam waited behind me while I collapsed my umbrella and shook it off, but I didn't reach inside my handbag for the keys. I tossed the umbrella on the floor of the porch and turned back to him, arms crossed over my chest.

"Say whatever it is you want to say, and then you're going to go."

He splayed his hands. "Seriously? I'm sopping wet, and you're going to keep me stranded out here?"

My nostrils flared. "Nobody forced you to get out of the car."

He closed his eyes and sighed. "I'm sorry. I think I got off to a bad start here."

"You pictured a *good* start to this conversation?"

When he opened his eyes again, they were brimming with tears. "Please. Please just let me tell you I am sorry. And that I love you more than anything on earth."

"Not more than you love yourself, clearly."

"I'm a selfish, worthless piece of shit. And I am so sorry. I will never be able to apologize enough for what I did to you, but I would like to spend the rest of my life trying."

Air chuffed out of me in a grotesque laugh. "Gosh, that sounds so appealing. Sixty-three years old, and still having to listen to you apologize for sticking your dick somewhere it didn't belong thirty years ago. No, thank you."

He lowered his head, the picture of abject contrition. "I know."

I pinched the bridge of my nose, trying to push back the headache I could feel building like a thundercloud. "Adam, I don't care that you're sorry. I really don't. It is the absolute minimum acceptable response to this situation, so I'm not going to give you a gold star for telling me you're *sorry* for what you did. I need — I want to know why you did it," I said, my voice breaking for the first time.

He shoved his hands in his jeans pockets and shook his head, staring out at the mist-shrouded ridge of the hills beyond the river. Rain drummed on the roof of the porch while I waited for him to speak. Finally he dropped his eyes to his feet again. "I don't know," he whispered.

"You drove all the way up here to plead your case and you can't even tell me why you cheated on me?"

He shook his head.

"Are you fucking kidding me?" I shrieked, hands thrown wide in disbelief. "Try! Just open your mouth and say something!"

"Caroline, I don't know! I don't —" He swiped a tear off his cheek with the base of his palm. "It's so messed up and confusing."

"Experimenting with a little cock confused you?"

He flinched. It always freaked him out when I used rough language. "No, it's . . . I honestly don't know how to explain."

I paused to gather myself. I knew better than this; getting information out of Adam when he didn't want to give it had to be done like coaxing a cork out of a wine bottle. The slow, careful, steady pull and then the *thwop* of release. "Okay. Let's make it easy; I'll give you yes or no questions. Was this the first time you cheated?"

"Yes."

"Was it going on for a while? It had to have been."

"Yes."

Sweat prickled my armpits as I paused to weigh my next question. But I had to know. "Do you love him?"

"No."

84

"Do you still love *me*?"

"*Yes!* I've been trying to tell you, I —"

"Aren't you attracted to me anymore?" I said, hating the way my voice trembled. I sounded like a whimpering child.

Adam stepped toward me and took my hands in his. "Oh my god, Caro. Sweetheart. Of course I am."

I forced myself to jerk my hands free. "Are you bored with me?"

"No. I'm not bored. But I think — I guess a part of me just wondered. What it would be like to be with someone else. We were together from such a young age; we never got to explore who we were with anyone other than each other."

"You don't explore *after* you're married, you son of a bitch!" I screamed, my fingernails digging into the flesh of my palms.

He threw his hands in front of him. "I know! I know. I'm not trying to defend it. You asked me why."

"So you just . . . decided to explore?"

"Not just like that. This is the part that I don't know how to explain."

"*You are a writer.* And you can't find the words?" But it was as if someone had quite literally stolen his voice. The humid air, sweet with the scent of summer rainfall, thrummed around us, but still Adam didn't

85

speak. Finally, I exhaled a weary, shuddering sigh. "You know what I want to know. Are you going to be able to tell me?"

A muscle worked in his cheek. "I'm not gay, Caroline."

"You had sex — pretty damn enthusiastically, it looked like — with a man."

"That doesn't make me gay."

"It makes you bisexual, at the very least. And since when? How did I not know this about you?"

He scowled and nudged his shoulders upward slightly. He was hunched into himself, poised in defense against me and my barrage of questions that he did not want to answer. I stared at him, at his beloved face, with the angular nose and the upper lip that was so much slimmer than the lower one, and the pronounced groove between nose and lip that was one of my favorite places to kiss. Had Patrick found that groove, too?

"I can't talk to you anymore," I said, dropping my gaze while I opened my handbag, as if my keys would be anywhere besides their dedicated side pocket. "Do you have your laptop with you in the city?"

There was a beat before he answered. "No. But what does that —"

"Okay. Then I'll get it for you. But then

86

you need to go."

"Sweetheart, no. I'm not going."

"You have to."

"Caro —"

"You have two choices. You can walk into the house when I open this door, knowing that I don't want you here and I won't speak to you, or you can turn around and drive your little rented car back to the city and leave me alone."

He spun away from me and planted his hands on the porch railing, staring out at the rain.

Without looking at him again, I let myself into the house and retrieved his laptop, cord, and mouse from his office, then stuffed them into the black nylon case that hung in its usual spot on a peg behind the door. I detoured to the laundry room to pull a dry T-shirt from the stack of folding we'd left behind in our hurry to get to the city last weekend. At the last second, I grabbed his umbrella, too — navy, with the Yale crest on it. Don't ask me why a grown-ass man still carried an umbrella with his college colors on it, because I'd asked Adam that pretty much every time I saw him with the stupid thing, and I'd never gotten a respectable answer.

I fully expected to find him in the living

room when I returned, but he was still on the porch, staring at the sheet of water that pelted down beyond the shelter of the roof. Silently, I handed him his bag; he cradled it awkwardly in one bent arm.

"Okay. You're all set." When he didn't move, I sighed. "Adam, I need you to go. That's how this is right now."

"But we have to try to fix this. Nothing will get better if you refuse to speak to me."

"Nothing will get better if I don't understand why this happened. I just asked you a couple of very important questions, and you couldn't answer them. Anything we say to each other has to start with you answering those questions."

He pressed his free hand to his eyes; tears seeped out from under his shaking fingers. "Please don't do this, Caro. I love you too much."

Adam was the only person who called me "Caro." Everyone else preferred the simple, natural "Care" if they were going to truncate my name, but not Adam. Adam liked the unusual sound, the "awkward elegance" I believe he called it, of that final *o*. It was so typical of him, to prefer the thing that was special.

And Patrick Timothy was certainly very special.

"Stop acting like I'm being cruel to you," I said. "This is all happening because of a decision *you* made. Please . . . I am begging you to leave me alone. I can't stand to have you near me right now."

He slid his hand down to his mouth and stared at me, eyes searching mine. Then he yanked his hand from his face, nodded once, and stalked across the porch and down the stairs. A minute later, I was watching the yellow car reverse way too quickly down the driveway, spitting gravel.

"Be careful!" I screamed. The highway down to New York is dangerous even on a clear, dry day; and I was so angry that I'd just sentenced my husband to drive it in tears, in a thunderstorm, in the growing dark. After listening to me spit out words as vicious as a whip to the face.

What in the name of god had he done to us?

6

Whenever we lay down together, you always told me, "Dear, do other people cherish and love each other like we do? Are they really like us?"

— A widow, to Eung-Tae Lee, June 1, 1586

Ruby blew into my house like a hurricane. My sister has always had the trait of shedding her belongings throughout a five-foot radius of her person, no matter where she is or what she's doing. No sooner had she set foot over my threshold on Friday evening than she had kicked off her leather flip-flops, tossed her handbag — so bedecked with zippers and tassels I could barely tell where the opening was — onto my entryway bench, and tipped a refrigerator-sized suitcase belly-up like a beached whale in the middle of the hallway.

"Whew! Pretty sure I blew a vein hauling that thing up your steps. Hi, Care!" Ruby said, throwing her arms around me and squeezing like she was attempting a reverse Heimlich. "Aren't you glad I'm here? This is going to be so fun!"

And suddenly, in spite of everything, I *was* glad. Ruby could be exasperating, but she was also never more than thirty seconds away from laughing — as bright and cheerful as the lemons she always smelled like. We were going to have a good weekend.

I nudged her suitcase with my toe. It solidly resisted any hint of movement. "Ruby, what do you have in here? Burqhart's dismembered body?"

"Ninety seconds inside your house and you're already mocking my pain," she said, breezing past me on her way to the kitchen. "Did you get my Bud Heavy for me?"

"I assumed you weren't serious about that, because you're not a nineteen-year-old frat boy."

She spun, hand on hip. "Caroline. Remember the plan? Achieving my rebirth in a bath of emulsifiers and flavor enhancers? The Bud Heavy is an essential part of the process."

"It's in the drink fridge," I said, then trailed after her as she went to retrieve it. I often found myself trailing after the human whirlwind that was my sister when we spent time together.

I could never quite figure out whether Ruby and I looked like each other. Where my features were more rounded, hers were pointy and elfin: upturned nose, wide mouth in a heart-shaped, sharp-chinned face. Her hair was straighter, better behaved, and, depending on the season and her mood, either blonder or darker. At the moment, it was a bright wheat blond, almost platinum, and piled into a charmingly sloppy ball on the top of her head. We both had the same general endowments in the chest area as the rest of the women in our family, to which I had always given a wholly sarcastic "Thanks, Mom," but on Ruby they were a little more manageably sized. Somehow, though, she'd stolen our dad's scrawny frame from the waist down, and though she complained extensively and often about her total absence of butt, I personally thought it well worth the trade-off when one considered how killer the girl looked in a pair of skinny jeans. Or shorts like she was wearing now, which were weirdly baggy but had an inseam the length of a matchbook. One thing Ruby and I did *not* share was our fashion sense.

"Seriously, though," I said, "why on earth did you bring so much stuff? You planning on taking up a new outdoor sport while you're here?"

She made a face like a cat who's just been dosed with a mouthful of medicine, and strolled past me without answering. I followed her to the living room, where she collapsed on the couch and popped open the beer. "I was thinking I might stay a little longer than the weekend."

"Um, how *much* longer? What is this, some kind of impromptu vacation?"

"You could say that," she murmured into her beer.

"Ruby."

She set the beer down on the side table with a deep sigh. "I got laid off."

"What? Are you serious?" I folded onto the couch next to her and propped my head on my fist.

Glumly, she nodded.

"But what the hell? I thought you were, like, the number one account manager over there."

"I was. Until my two biggest clients left for a new boutique agency that's been getting a ton of buzz lately. And which doesn't charge quite as much as we do."

"Shit. I'm sorry, that absolutely sucks."

"At least it wasn't the same *day* as I got dumped," she said, and took a deep glug of

93

beer. "I had a good forty-two hours in between."

I reached across and scritched her head with my palm the way I used to when she was little. "Man. *Fuck* this month."

"A-freaking-men."

"Did they give you a decent severance, at least?"

"They did," she sighed, rotating the beer can slowly in her palm. "They weren't total dicks about it. My boss felt horrible. It's just the rejection, you know? I busted my freaking ass for that place, and now out of nowhere it's like, *Take a hike, jerk. You're obsolete.*"

I groaned with sympathy. I couldn't imagine how I'd feel if the museum suddenly decided they didn't want me anymore. Although, apparently, since the development department seemed to have concluded I was the magic key that would unlock the coffers of Crush and spill its gold into our laps, I could be looking at a nice solid boot in the ass if I couldn't deliver. Or, at the very least, some seriously oppressive disappointment.

"So what are you going to do? Did your boss set you up with some contacts? Seems like the least he could do."

"He did. But . . . I don't know." She

94

folded her knees in front of her and wrapped her arms around them. "Whenever I think about calling up these other agencies and going in and doing the dance, I just . . . ugh. I don't want to do it. I don't want to be an account manager anymore. I've been doing some freelance graphic design and branding stuff here and there, since even before I got canned, so I'm thinking I'll stick with that for a bit and see how it goes."

"Freelance isn't going to pay your bills once the severance runs out, though."

"Not *yet,*" she said.

"I know. But remember, there's a reason why they moved you from creative to the account side."

"Yes, because they were assholes."

"And because you're phenomenal at selling," I reminded her.

"Any friendly person can sell. *I am an artist,*" she said, in a deliberately grandiose voice.

I rolled my eyes and stretched my legs out on the coffee table. There was no reasoning with her when she wasn't in the mood to hear it. "But why come up here, though? Aren't you going to need to meet with clients and whatnot?"

"Every so often, yeah; but most of it is actually sitting down and doing the work they're paying me for. I just don't want to be in the city right now. Everything reminds me of my job or stupid Burqhart or both. And it's so relaxing up here. Plus, this way I can keep you company in your time of need. Have you talked to Adam any more?" she added, after a brief pause.

"Since the monumentally inadequate conversation on Tuesday? Nope."

"Inadequate how?"

"In every conceivable way. He says he's sorry, but he won't be honest with me about why he did this. Or why . . ." My words, like my thoughts, trailed off before they approached that particular element of the situation.

"Did you have any idea?" said Ruby, charging directly toward the topic I had quite obviously veered away from.

"Why does everyone keep asking me that?" I snapped, and jumped up from the couch in search of something to cram into my mouth so maybe I could stop talking about this. So far, "everyone" had only consisted of two people, but I could already tell this was going to be my least favorite part of this conversation every single goddamn time I'd have to have it. *Didn't you suspect? Didn't you sense something was off? He was lying to you, and to himself, all along.*

You must have sensed it. Somewhere in the unsounded depths of your heart, you must have known.

As if this silence, this redaction of such an immensely important part of his identity, were my fault. As if it were *my* failure.

"Sorry," said Ruby, when I stalked back to the couch and tossed a bag of Cheetos forcefully into her lap. "Who-all is 'everyone'?"

"Jonathan," I said, through a bite of apple. "He was there when it all exploded."

"What even happened, exactly? You never told me how you found out."

With a sigh, I recounted the whole pathetic, humiliating tale. "It was the most surreal experience of my life, Rube. You remember when we drove up to see Aunt Jessie, and Dad's car slipped in the snow and we slid right off the road, and we both had that same experience of not believing it while it was happening, like, as if it was a movie we were watching or something?"

She popped a nuclear-orange Cheeto into her mouth and crunched, nodding slowly.

"Yeah. It was like that. My brain was a good three minutes behind the rest of me. I don't even remember a word Adam said after I realized. I don't remember leaving the gallery. I just remember leaning against

97

the side of the building, puking onto the sidewalk like a drunk freshman. And trying not to let it splash onto my shoes and my dress that I'd worn to look pretty for Adam, and wanting to die from the humiliation."

Ruby leaned over and rubbed my knee with her one clean hand. "I'm so sorry, Care. It's so fucking awful. And he's just such a *total* fucking pig to have done this to you."

"At least the Blaster had the sense not to make any jokes about how he always seems to get stuck taking care of me when I'm barfing," I said, and one corner of her mouth lifted.

"What does he think about it all?" she said, scuffing one foot back and forth through the shaggy wool rug.

"He thinks it sucks. Obviously."

"Yeah, but I mean, like . . . did he say anything about Adam? Like, did he ever pick up on anything?"

I gave a short huff of frustration. "No, Ruby. Nobody has ever 'picked up on' anything."

"Is he gonna try to make a play for you now?"

"What — Jonathan? Are you kidding me?"

Digging in her Cheetos bag, she shrugged. "Even if he were interested in me, *which he is not,* this is my marriage we're talking about here. Not some high school relationship on life support."

"It could be, though. I mean, it basically is. Jonathan's never known you when you weren't with Adam. I know you always said it wasn't like that —"

"Because it wasn't."

A breeze from the open window pushed a tendril of hair against her cheek, and she brushed it away. "*You* say it wasn't. I bet he'd say different. I mean, it's a no-brainer. You're a gorgeous woman, and he's obviously loved you forever. Now he's finally got his shot."

Why was she so bent on misunderstanding? "He's loved me as a friend forever. And that is *all* it is, hand to god. There are no shots being taken. If anything, he's been encouraging me to try to work through it."

Ruby grunted, unimpressed. And I wasn't particularly surprised. To say that Ruby and Adam disliked each other was an overstatement. However, it was also something of an overstatement to say they *liked* each other. I would describe it as unspokenly agreed neutrality, with occasional moments of both genuine affection and genuine loathing.

When I was younger, I thought it was jealousy, on Ruby's part. More recently, I've

99

come to understand that we all have people in our lives who inhabit different ends of our polar charges. We'd like to think that everyone we love will naturally all love each other, but it's not necessarily so; and in my case, I had a sister who was at one end of my personal spectrum and a husband who was at the other. Adam thought Ruby was flighty, giddy, and immature; she found him self-absorbed and a little pompous. In between them, I couldn't wholly deny the truth of either charge.

Though Ruby hadn't voiced her opinion, I already knew what it would be. My closest friend believed Adam and I could somehow work our way through this maze; my sister didn't even want me to try.

But before I could begin to decide what to do, there was someone else I had to talk to. I got my chance a few days later, one afternoon after work while Ruby was at an appointment with a prospective client. I had a feeling she would not approve of this particular gambit, but I had to do it. I had to know.

I was certain he would answer the call. Though he wouldn't know my number, he'd be hoping it would be somebody worth talking to. The trick was going to be keeping him on the line long enough to tell me what I wanted to know.

"This is Patrick. Who am I speaking with?"

"It's Caroline Hammond. Please don't hang up."

He paused. "I'm pretty sure that this is a conversation I don't want to be a part of. I'm going to go ahead and hang up."

"Please. I'm not calling to yell at you. Just hear me out." It burned my throat like acid — begging him — but I did it.

"So if you're not calling to yell at me . . ."

"I need a favor."

"A favor? From me?"

"I need to understand what happened. Adam won't talk about it. I need to hear it from you."

"Wow. That is not what I expected you to say. Listen . . . I have no idea why he won't talk about it, but I do know he would not be happy if I got in the middle of this."

I laughed, and it sounded like a normal laugh roughed up by a cheese grater. "Patrick. You already are."

"The thing is, I'm not. His vows have always been his problem, not mine. I'm the way he chose to break them, and that's it. So I don't want to implicate myself in making this worse for him."

"Aww, you don't want him to be mad at

you. You care about him. That's so sweet!"

I could practically taste how badly he wanted to bite back at me. And I was dying for him to. Rage was surging inside me like lava.

But he didn't. "Like I said, I don't want to get involved. So, I think it's time for me to get off the phone."

"Wait."

He paused. But I didn't have the first idea what I wanted to ask. All the questions I really wanted answered belonged to Adam. Not the ones I'd already asked him — the ones I couldn't bear to. Why did you let yourself fail me? Why was it worth it? Or was my dignity simply not a consideration for you? Let alone my love?

"Caroline?"

I sighed. "Forget it."

"Okay."

And then he was gone. No apology — but why should I have expected one? He'd known it was a shitty thing to do when he did it, and he hadn't cared then; there was no reason it should suddenly start mattering to him now.

I wondered who he thought Adam was. What parts of himself Adam had selectively presented, in his bottomless need to be adored — especially by someone as self-consciously cool as Patrick. Would I even recognize that alternate version of my husband?

Then again, there were huge chunks of my own version of Adam that I had never even suspected. A goddamned human iceberg.

I just couldn't imagine what it would be like, to be with someone who barely knew me. Who hadn't known me since I was a quiet bundle of twigs, hiding my new breasts under my dad's sweaters and writing poems about loneliness. How on earth did people get married to people they'd only known for a couple of years? Let alone a couple of years only as an adult? How could you fully love someone without having shared their life for as long as Adam and I had?

You might learn that he hates bleu cheese, but you weren't there the night he got annihilatingly sick on buffalo wings, and you didn't spend the hours from one to four A.M. slumped against the wall outside the bathroom because he was sure he was going to die and you didn't want to leave him alone with his paranoia and his bacteria. Patrick might have known that Adam's father had had a heart attack, but he hadn't seen his face when he got the news. Hadn't held him, and felt him trembling. Hadn't heard the words he mumbled into my hair the night Theodore was upgraded out of critical condition: "I don't know what would happen to me without him." Patrick might have fucked my husband, but he didn't *know* him.

And yet. He knew things I didn't. Things I didn't understand, because Adam had refused to explain them to me. What was it — exactly — that had attracted my husband so strongly? I didn't buy that "I love the person, not the plumbing" bullshit. We're not just souls drifting around in sexless bodies, like the little cherubs in *Fantasia:* The plumbing is highly relevant. When you make love to someone, no matter how poetic it might sound, you're not doing it to their *soul.*

Fingers shaking, I dialed Patrick back again.

"Caroline? You really need to —"

"Look, can I meet you to talk about this? I'm not going to attack you, and I'm not going to berate you. I just . . . want to understand."

"I don't think I can —"

"Please. Okay? Please meet me. I think I can fairly say it's the least you could do."

He sighed. "Okay. I'm around this week-end. God, I hope I don't regret this."

7

How I wanted to photograph you — the hands — the mouth — & eyes — & the enveloped in black body — the touch of white — & the throat —
— Alfred Stieglitz to Georgia O'Keefe,
June 1, 1917

Despite the array of Ruby-related detritus that quickly infiltrated every corner of my house, living with my sister turned out to be both surprisingly easy and surprisingly pleasant. Not only was it a relief to come home to a house with lights on, but my houseguest didn't seem to expect any form of entertainment beyond just sharing my company. We spent the whole of that first week eating crappy food and watching *Battlestar Galactica* on my couch. When I stopped one day to replenish our supplies at the Stop & Shop on my way home from work, I paused briefly in front of the aisle with the veggies and salad greens, gleaming with dampness from the moisture jets. And then I shrugged and headed for the frozen aisle. Cooking was something I'd done when I had a husband.

Every time I got home, Ruby would inevitably be perched on one of my counter stools, a heat-sweated beer can next to her and her bare toes wrapped around the footrest while she clicked softly on her laptop. I'd expected her to complain about the lack of air-conditioning, but she thrived in the warm, breezy air, existing only in her seemingly endless supply of oversized tank tops and loose but tiny shorts.

"Are you wearing a bra?" I said one evening, and she raised her arms and swayed. Her tank top said OH MY GOD BECKY in big block letters.

"Absolutely not. And it's freaking fantastic."

"Ouch," I said.

"Try it," she said. "I know you have to do the ladylike thing for work, but by the end of this weekend I want you to be completely feral."

"I can't. I have to go to the city on Saturday. For work," I lied, seeing the question spark in her face. "I'm not seeing Adam."

"Good," she said. "Hey, I'm about to fire

106

up the vape. You want any?"

Ruby had liked weed since she was a teenager, and now, with no particular schedule or ironclad commitments, she was partaking frequently. "I don't know how you can get work done if you're stoned all the time."

"I don't get stoned. It's just a happy little glow. Gets those creative juices flowing," she said, making a wave motion with her hands. "Did I tell you I started a blog?"

"Oh, thank god. The world was running dry on design blogs run by pretty white girls with good taste."

She flounced on the stool and angled her back to me. "You can be such a bitch, Caroline."

"I'm sorry. I didn't mean to be bitchy. It just seems like looking for a job would be a better use of your time. Or working on your portfolio site."

"Believe it or not, it's possible to do both," she said, in the patient voice of a parent explaining to a toddler. "Maybe even *smart*. The blog's a more casual format, so I can post little styled vignettes and sketches and whatnot that I wouldn't put in my main portfolio."

"All right, you know what you're doing, then. Do you want another Bud?"

She made a show of refusing to look up from her laptop, just extended one small hand and flexed her fingers like a starfish. I popped the beer open and handed it to her as I passed.

"You *should* get baked sometime," she muttered. "You could freaking use it."

I almost found myself wishing I'd taken her up on it, as a swarm of angry hornets buzzed inside me on my way to my appointment with Patrick a few days later. His notes on where to meet had been revealingly specific. Hudson River Park, the pier opposite Twenty-fourth Street. A public place, but not a restaurant or coffee shop offering refreshments, since neither of us wanted to be refreshed. Nowhere near his home, which I remembered hearing was in some artistically gritty neighborhood of Brooklyn; or at least, it had been . . . before three-quarters of his photographs from the gallery show sold out within five days of the opening. Neil from Development had said: Wasn't that remarkable? Was I sure about the Whitney wanting to work with him, because otherwise —

It was a clear, sunny afternoon in the middle of August, only two weeks since all of this began, but it felt like twice as long.

As I walked through the park to meet Patrick, people whizzed past me on every form of wheels: cyclists dressed in earnest neck-to-knees spandex, rollerbladers with their tumor-like eruptions of padding, teenagers shouting over the grinding roar of their skateboard wheels. I was almost involved in a collision from trying to avoid both a pair of joggers and a baby carriage at the same time. That's New York for you — even the parks are crowded.

I'd been debating whether Patrick would show up late or simply not at all; a passive-aggressive twenty-minutes-tardy arrival felt very much his style. But when the end of the pier came into view he was already there, leaning backward against the railing with his elbows propped against the rail on either side of him, while the sun behind him silhouetted his James Dean–esque pose. When he saw me he did one of those lifted-chin nods that guys use to greet each other.

As I drew to a stop in front of him, I traced my eyes over his face as if I were preparing to paint him. I absorbed the details of him: the crisp edge of his sideburn against his cheek; the shadow under his full lower lip. A beautiful man, no doubt about that. And with the talent to back up his looks, he was something uncommon.

Adam used to make me feel like *I* was uncommon.

Patrick tolerated my scrutiny, shifting his weight while he waited for me to speak. Finally his shoulders lifted on a breath.

"Caroline, what are you looking for?"

My brain lifted and discarded several possible responses. Answers? Reasons? The words were too simple. I set my wrists on the aluminum railing of the pier and knotted my fingers together. Amber sun gilded the surface of the river with a rippling skin of light.

"In the Old Master oil paintings, underneath the finished surface, there are layers of mistakes. First attempts at pose and texture and shadow. They got painted over, because the artist didn't like what he saw, and he wanted the finished result to look a different way. But they're there. Even though we can't see them, they're part of the painting."

He nodded. "Pentimenti."

Reeling in my grudging respect for his knowledge, I focused on the point I needed to make. "I'm trying to see those layers."

"The only person who can help you see them is Adam," he said.

"I don't think so. For one thing, he won't talk about it. But even if he did . . . I see

110

only what he chooses."

He folded his arms over his chest. "And you think it's any different with me?"

I let the last shreds of my pride drop like a paper gown at the doctor's office. "Patrick, I had no idea he was attracted to men. Seventeen years. Not one clue. Did you know that?"

"Not in so many words. But it doesn't surprise me."

"How is that possible?" I flinched at the raw pain in my voice.

"Because I'm sure he worked damn hard to make sure you wouldn't." He sighed and turned his own eyes toward the water. "Listen. I'm not the oracle of Adam, okay? I can understand why you want answers to this stuff, but the truth is, I don't even know him all that well. Definitely not better than you do. The fact that he slept with me doesn't mean he's shared anything with me besides his —" His blush, as he caught himself, made him suddenly more vulnerable than the enemy I'd been villainizing for weeks. "Sorry. I guess what I'm trying to say is, don't blow this up to be something it isn't. Just because I'm gay, that doesn't mean I know what this is all about for him."

"You know more than I do."

He shook his head from shoulder to

shoulder like a metronome. "No. I don't. All I know is that he liked to have sex with me. I don't know if I was the first; I don't know if I was the only. I definitely don't know what he liked about it compared to sleeping with you."

"He didn't tell you any of that?"

"Nope. And I really can't imagine. The one time I tried to hook up with a girl, I was fine for the hand job, but when it was my turn to reciprocate, I went soft faster than you can say sad trombone."

Treacherously, laughter spurted out of me.

"So, I can't speak to what it's like to be bi. I've known I was gay since I was ten. Out since fourteen. To understand Adam, you need to talk to Adam."

"But he won't," I said again.

"So make him. He wants you to take him back, he ought to be willing to do what you ask."

"You would think. But it's like there's a black hole surrounding the entire topic."

"Yeah. You were always a black hole, too."

An invisible fist clenched around me. "He talked about me?"

"Never. I was curious, but he always avoided mentioning you. And he'd turn the topic anytime I asked a question. I guess it made him feel guilty."

So, instead, he preferred to pretend I didn't exist.

My goodness. How silly of me to have thought I'd reached the border of my heartbreak; just look how much more room there was out here.

"Listen," said Patrick quietly after a moment, "for what it's worth . . . I am sorry. I shouldn't have gotten involved, I just . . ." His gaze drifted to the ground as his words trailed away.

I remembered suddenly that, for all his sophistication, Patrick was still only twenty-five years old. It was the kind of age where people did things like this and called it unavoidable. "Yeah. Me too. But anyway, what about you?"

His eyes narrowed and his shoulders inched inward as if tugged by an invisible fishing line. "What *about* me?"

"I'm sure you're not hurting for people to sleep with who don't have this kind of baggage. So why a married straight guy?"

His chuckle was a rusty, bitter thing. "Do you have any idea how many 'straight' guys" — he etched quote marks in the air with his fingers — "like to hit on me when they get a couple of drinks in them? Sometimes they stare at me, sometimes they try to kiss me, and sometimes they skip the niceties and just grab my dick."

Suddenly the clean, water-scented air was sour in my mouth. "So, where exactly on this spectrum of self-delusion was my husband?"

"That was the problem," he said, voice soft and underbaked. "Adam wasn't just another drunk loser."

"What was he?" I asked, trembling.

The suspended lift and drop of his shoulders told me far more than he meant it to. "He was Adam."

8

I do not think that I want to lie down in your crowded bed for bouts of therapeutic lovemaking. Loving you, I see no beauty in lopsided true love.
— Elizabeth Smart to George Barker,
September 27, 1946

"The little fucker's in love with him," I said to Jonathan an hour later, while we guzzled our second round of Sixpoints on his roof. We weren't supposed to be up there, but the six-story building afforded a great view over the rooftops of Astoria and the Manhattan skyline beyond, which naturally made it irresistible. Jonathan got busted once by his landlady for hosting a Fourth of July picnic there, but when he brought her all the leftover fried chicken and biscuits, she forgave him. He typically achieves with his food what his *darlin*'s alone cannot.

"Are you shitting me?" he said. "He told

you that, like it was *your* problem?"

I rested my head against the wall of the stair bulkhead behind us. "He didn't tell me. But it was obvious." Something else that was obvious: If Patrick had found enough to fall in love with, the affair must have been more than just sex. But how *much* more?

"Jesus Christ, what a mess," said Jonathan, pinching the skin between his eyes. "Did it at least help you to talk to him?"

"No," I said. "Patrick doesn't understand Adam any more than I do. Which I guess is a relief. I was hoping I'd get some answers, but I'm not sure I could have handled it if he'd turned out to know my own husband better than I do."

Jonathan leaned forward over his bent knees and toyed with the tab on his beer can. "You guys have always been into that. Knowing each other so well. Not that I'm an expert, seeing as I just broke up with yet another girlfriend, but . . . don't you want to keep some things to yourself sometimes?"

"What, like 'I enjoy sex with men'?"

"No, like little things. There are things it's not deceitful to keep private. I mean, aren't you allowed to have a bit of mystery still? Adam always makes those comments about you, like 'I knew you were going to say that,'

116

or telling you how you're going to react to something before you can react to it. It seems a little odd to me, to put so much emphasis on knowing everything there is to know about another person, as if they can never surprise you."

"A little odd? Thanks, Jonathan."

"Okay, not odd. But I do think it could get kind of stifling. Especially since it seems to me you never *can* know everything, anyway."

"I've never thought of it that way," I said, hugging my knees to my chest. "Knowing each other like that . . . it's always felt like one of the rewards of such a long relationship."

"It is. For sure. I just think it's possible to take it a little too far. I notice it about you and Adam because sometimes it feels like he's got you in a box. He was so shocked when you actually stood your ground about moving to Massachusetts."

"Is that how you saw it? That I stood my ground against him?"

"Well . . . yeah," he said, looking as if he already regretted the statement. "It was obvious that he didn't want to go. He expected you to turn the job down so you guys could stay in New York."

"I don't think it makes him a bad person

117

that his preference would not have been to move three hours away from all his friends and family for his wife's career."

"I didn't say he was a bad person," said Jonathan. "Especially since he did agree to move. What I'm saying is that I feel like Adam sees you as static. Like he wrote this four-hundred-page user's manual for you a long time ago, and he gets uncomfortable when you do things that don't show up in the index."

A plane roared across the sky on its way to LaGuardia while I mulled this over. "You've never mentioned this before," I said.

He shrugged, one firm shoulder shifting under his navy blue Apache Relay T-shirt. Jonathan always has the name of some band or another plastered across his chest, most of them Tennessee-based, because he's as big a chauvinist about his home state's music as he is about the food. "It was never my business. Still isn't. But I figure if you guys are going to start over, then there's probably more stuff you need to talk about than the fact that he likes guys and he cheated."

"You know what scares me?" I said, in a low voice. "I'm having a hard time envision-ing how we could start over from here. If

118

you'd asked me a month ago what I'd do if my husband cheated, I probably would have said I'd try to work through it. Adam and I have been together for so long, and built so much and shared so much . . . it would seem almost, I don't know, reckless, to turn my back on all of that because of one terrible decision. I would have said I wouldn't give up on us so easily. And a lot of me still feels like that. But every time I try to turn toward that, I keep coming back to this: *I can never fully trust him again.* And the fact that I can't let go of that scares the shit out of me, Jonathan. I haven't been by myself since I was sixteen years old. I wouldn't even know what to do or how to be. I don't know who I am without this relationship."

"I do," he said without hesitation. "I've never even known you when you weren't with him, but that doesn't matter. There's more than enough of you to stand on your own feet if you leave him. Way more than enough. I'm not worried about you at all."

I stared at him, sitting there on the roof with his ink-covered forearms looped around his knees and his hair lit up like embers by the late afternoon sun, and I started to cry. Because Jonathan *knew* me. And he loved me. Independent of himself, independent of Adam, he loved me as my

119

very own person. Nothing on earth would ever make him want to erase me. And suddenly that was the most precious thing in the world.

"Always seem to end up here," I snuffled, when he wrapped his arms around me and tucked my forehead against his neck.

"Ah, darlin'," he sighed, and squeezed me tighter.

And I don't know why I did it, because all my reasons together still didn't add up to one actual *good* one, but I guess people who've been emotionally ransacked aren't known for making the sharpest decisions. So I did it. I kissed Jonathan.

It was not a testing kiss, it was committed. I felt the prickle of his beard under my hands and the startling contrast of his soft lips against mine, and as I sank into it, his whiskey scent swirled into my brain, lulling me with its associations of safety and familiarity and total, utter trust.

After a few breathless seconds, he pulled back from me, blue eyes drilling into mine.

"Caroline? What's going on?"

"Um . . . everything?" I said, on a little trembling half laugh. "Please just let me . . ." *Let me have this,* I almost said. But I didn't. Instead I inched my face closer to his again, lips parted, asking. Asking him to forget that

120

I was still married, that he and I didn't *do* this, that we never had, that I was breaching the cardinal rule of Caroline and Jonathan with no discussion or agreement, simply because I needed him.

"This is not a good idea," he said.

I shook my head no.

"Your head is spun around every which way, honey. You know that."

I nodded.

"You still want me to kiss you."

"I need to feel wanted," I whispered. And it was okay, somehow, to let Jonathan see me that pitiful, because I couldn't imagine I'd ever trust another man this much again. Frankly, I didn't even care whether it was genuine desire or just friendship and pity that pulled him toward me, as long as he came.

"Care . . ."

"Please?"

He swallowed, then frowned. And then, sighing with something like relinquishment or acceptance or maybe both, he kissed me, one hand coming to rest on my hair like a butterfly landing on a leaf. I fitted my hands around his shoulders and leaned in to take everything he'd offer.

The air around us growled as a block's worth of air conditioners strained against the summer afternoon warmth. The kiss started out tentative but quickly intensified as his fingers sank deeper into my hair, and his other hand drifted up to cup the side of my throat, nudging me closer as he drank me up. It was such a weird mix of familiarity and strangeness, comfort and wrongness, that my neurons were firing in blaring, blurry confusion for no clear reason they could decide on. *God damn, Jonathan is an incredible kisser* was followed by *Of course he is* and then *Wait, why the hell am I kissing Jonathan?*, and then he pulled away.

"Care, this is bad," he muttered, wrist to his lips to brush away the dampness from the kiss. "This shouldn't be happening."

I wanted to pound my fists and drum my heels against the warm roof like a toddler in a tantrum.

"I'm serious. This is not the answer to anything. This is not right."

I must have looked as on the verge of a meltdown as I felt, because he sighed and cupped the back of my neck, drawing our foreheads together.

"Caroline. Honey. If things were different, I could have kissed you all day. You are beautiful, and desirable, and all of that stuff. I think Adam has lost his damn mind. But you are married to him, and whatever you decide, you have to work this out without dragging me into it. You and I are more than that."

"But you kissed me too."

"I know. I wanted to. I can't pretend I wasn't curious. Been curious for fifteen years. But I shouldn't have. We shouldn't have."

"I'm not trying to drag you into it. I just —"

"I get it," he said softly. "I really do. But this isn't the answer."

"I knoooow," I groaned, smushing my palms against my face. "I just needed something to make this hurt less."

One corner of his lips tucked up slightly into his cheek. He didn't even have to say the words, they were written all over his face. The words said, *Girl, there is no damn such thing.*

When I got home, late that night, I walked straight upstairs to the bathroom I shared with Adam, stood in front of the full-length mirror on the back of the door, and removed my clothes. When they were gone, I squared my feet to the mirror, shoved my shoulders back, and looked.

And immediately realized I had no idea what the hell I was looking for. *Oh yes, I see it clearly now; he slept with a guy because my thighs had gotten just a little bit too plump.* No. My body had been more or less the same overstatedly feminine shape for as long as Adam had known me. He liked to say I looked like a lady from a pre-Raphaelite painting: copious hair, rounded limbs — and, I assume, if one could peep under the maidens' petticoats — pronounced hips, a fluffy soufflé of a tummy, and breasts that had to be hidden under button-downs to avoid stares. The small sconces on either side of the mirror bathed my pale skin in a warm, diffuse glow. What I saw was . . . pretty.

Sexuality is a continuum — that's what we learned in my sophomore year sociology class. It was rarely as simple as checking one box or the other on the survey. But in my experience, every bisexual person I knew was a woman. The men I knew had checked their boxes with conviction and enthusiasm, and they did not tiptoe outside those four conjoining lines. So, then, did that make Adam a unicorn? Or did it make him a man who'd been lying to himself for at least the past seventeen years? Whichever it was, he clearly wasn't going to tell me.

My eyes drifted over to the towel rack by the door, where Adam's towel still hung

124

next to mine. It was one of my little weaknesses, that towel of Adam's. Such a dumb thing, but I liked it there. As if he still lived here, but was just away for a little while. As if he might come home at any moment, and step up behind me while I was brushing my teeth, and wrap his arms around me and kiss the side of my head.

God, how I missed being held. I missed the affectionate warmth of Adam's presence, the pleasure of slipping in and out of conversation with him as we moved through our days. Even the most mundane exchanges with Adam could turn into laughter with each new breath he took. It had only been two weeks, but I hadn't been apart from him for so long since college. Add in the fact that we weren't speaking — that everything between us was ruined and wrong — and his absence felt as if a part of my body had been ripped away, leaving the rest of me pulsing and raw. I kept telling myself that one way or another, it would all heal eventually, because that's what you have to tell yourself. I knew it was true. There was no other alternative.

But I wasn't looking forward to enduring it. And, even once I could crawl a little closer to normal, I wasn't looking forward to the scars.

9

I composed a beautiful letter to you in the sleepless nightmare hours of the night, and it has all gone: I just miss you, in a quite simple desperate human way.
— Vita Sackville-West to Virginia Woolf,
January 21, 1926

"So how'd it go with Adam yesterday?"

I crashed into wakefulness as Ruby's hundred and thirty-odd pounds abruptly collided with my body, one pointy elbow propelling itself into my boob. You've seen those YouTube videos of dogs waking up sleeping owners by vaulting onto their beds and pawing at them until they surface? Welcome to my sister.

"You are a terrible human being," I mumbled, pushing up on my elbows and scrubbing my face to try to scatter the sleep. "And I didn't see Adam."

126

"So what the hell were you doing there, then?"

Interrogating witnesses and making bad decisions. "I saw Patrick," I said, too morning-raw to lie. And too hungover with creeping, crawling shame to share the way I'd hit on Jonathan.

"Oh shit," she said, eyes alert with interest. "Did you rip him a new one?"

"Jesus, you're bloodthirsty. No. I did not. I was trying to find out more about him and Adam, and all I found out is that he's in love with my husband."

"Hmm," she said.

"Yeah," I sighed. The strangest thing was, though, that when I thought about Patrick now, woven in with all the hurt and the possessive rage there was a thread of sympathy. And even one of kinship. Adam was an incredibly easy person to fall in love with.

The man I'd married had this gift, unlike anyone else I knew, of listening like you were the most fascinating person he'd ever met. And it wasn't only me — I'd seen it more times than I could count, over the years, the way Adam converted strangers into friends before I'd barely struggled past "What do you do for a living?" He was fascinated by other people and their stories. And if he couldn't learn, he would invent.

At bars, parties, any activity where we were trapped with a group of strangers for a length of time, Adam had to name everyone. A look-alike, or a new nickname. He loved to draw me into it, and together we would embroider stories: these strangers' secret pasts, illegitimate children, private disappointments.

Our downstairs neighbor at the Hell's Kitchen apartment, Gregor, was obsessed with the regulation of all things in the apartment building. We sometimes had to borrow the building's ladder to change a lightbulb in our ten-foot ceiling, and if the ladder was not back in its assigned spot in the basement within a few hours, all the owners would get an email from Gregor inquiring about its return. His affinity for the ladder tortured Adam.

"Why does he need it there every single day? What does he *do* with it? Does he store his toothpaste on top of his kitchen cabinets?"

In an attempt to forestall Gregor's anxiety, Adam took to notifying him when we were borrowing it. So instead, Gregor simply addressed his concern directly to us, in the courtliest language imaginable: "Dearest Adam. Could you kindly return the ladder to the basement at your earliest convenience. Sincerely yours, Gregor."

One night, we received one of these messages on our way back from dinner at our favorite Italian place, with almost two bottles of pinot grigio sloshing around inside us. Adam, fevered with wine, paused in the hallway outside Gregor's door.

"Adam!" I giggled. "What are you doing?"

"I just want to know why," he stage-whispered back to me, raising his arm to knock. "It's eating me alive."

"Don't!" I squeaked, tugging his arm, but he swayed toward the door, chest puffing with laughter.

"Gregor," he called, in a wheedling sing-song. "Oh, Gregor . . ."

"Stop!" I said as a sliver of light showed under the door. "Seriously, let's go!"

"Gregor!"

Finally I got my arm over his shoulder and clapped my hand over his mouth, while he struggled, bellowing incoherently into my palm. And that is how Gregor found us when he swung open the door of his apartment: freeze-framed in guilty surprise, like teenagers caught toilet-papering a mailbox.

"Can I help you?" he said, looking from Adam to me and back again.

Any responses I might have been able to summon were popping like soap bubbles over my head, but Adam rallied and shoved my limp hand away from his mouth.

"The ladder," he said. "We wanted to advise you that we will return it on the morrow. You have our sincerest apologies for the inconvenience." Then he clipped his arm to his waist and sketched a solemn little half bow.

Gregor blinked, then did the same. "Good evening."

"And to you, sir," said Adam.

When the door clicked shut, we gaped at each other for a moment until I spotted the mirth quivering in his lips. "Go!" I hissed, shoving him toward the staircase before the laughter erupted, but he barely made it to the second floor landing before it was rolling out of him, deep and generous like Adam's laughter always was. When we shut our door behind us, he was wiping moisture from his eyes.

"On the morrow," I mimicked in a quasi-British falsetto. "Kind sir, we shall return it to thee anon, before the setting of the sun. . . ."

Still chuckling, he cupped my face and kissed me. "I still have so many questions!" he whispered. "Is it part of his religion? Is he a ladder worshipper? Does he rise at dawn every day and pray to the ladder?

Does he —"

I cut him off with a kiss.

Like I said: an easy person to love. But falling in love was the easy part; the work was in staying there. Feeding it and renewing it, even in the moments when his childishness or self-absorption drove me to the edge of my very last nerve. Digging in to keep our sights trained on forever — that was *my* job.

At work, I'd been avoiding thinking about my doomed-to-fail Diana Ramirez mission, but all of a sudden I was running into Neil Crenshaw constantly. Of course, he'd always been around; but as I grew itchily aware that I had devoted precisely zero consideration to how I might approach, let alone secure money from, this busy and in-demand woman I was fairly certain detested me, I swear to god I saw the man everywhere. Always with the same friendly, encouraging smile on his face.

"How's it going, Caroline?" he said, strolling into the kitchenette a few days later, while I was waiting for my burritos to finish in the microwave. (Like most of the food Ruby had gotten me hooked on over the past week and a half, they were disgusting yet delicious.) "Any thoughts on how to

131

tackle Diana?"

Thankfully, the microwave timer chose that exact moment to ding, so I occupied myself with retrieving my freshly unthawed lunch rather than meeting his eyes. "Um, it's going okay. I've been tossing around a couple of ideas, but they're not quite ready yet."

"I'm looking forward to hearing them," he said.

I angled a quick look at him. Was that the faintest current of arch humor I caught in his voice? As if he suspected the only ideas I'd been tossing concerned how best to bounce Diana lightly but firmly back into the development office's court?

But his face was interested, so I bobbed my head briskly to demonstrate my seriousness. "Great. Let me chew on it a little more and then I'll touch base with you once I've got enough to discuss."

"Sounds good," he said. "And don't feel weird about doing this. Remember what Warhol said."

" 'Business art is the step that comes after art.' Yes. I remember."

"Good. Then I don't have to bore you with the rest of it," he said, smiling, and stepped aside to let me and my burritos escape.

When I got home from work that afternoon, a sheaf of bills awaited me in the mailbox, along with the fall Boden catalog and another letter from Adam. I am aware that no one enjoys receiving bills, but for me, they have always been akin to mosquitos who brazen their way indoors: I cannot relax until they are dealt with. I think it's a holdover from my teenage years: the stack of envelopes in the wicker tray on our brown-tiled kitchen counter that grew and grew until the envelopes started sliding off the top. The tense conversations my parents never quite managed to keep as hushed as they intended; the words I overheard, like *lien* and *repossession*. These days, my bills are paid and filed the day I receive them, so I never have to think about them again.

I headed to the office and opened a window while I waited for the computer to boot up. This ancient desktop, propped on a small table in the corner, was for my use, but the room was mostly Adam's. I hadn't been in here since the day he came to see me, because it was all just too *him:* the large double bookcases groaning with his favorite reads; the smaller one crammed with his old Moleskine notebooks; the heavy antique oak desk his father had given him, at which Theodore had written his Pulitzer-winning novel. He had hoped the juju of the artifact would transfer to his son; Adam had hoped it even more. Thus far, the desk had not performed.

The notebooks seemed to pulse in my peripheral vision as if they were possessed. Adam had never really used them as personal journals; they were mainly for jotting down ideas and scene sketches, that sort of thing, but — what if? What if he'd broken his own self-established protocol and written about his affair? He'd written a few things about me from time to time, at moments of particular intensity. The thought that Adam's feelings for Patrick might have warranted exploration in his notebooks was like someone shattering a glass inside my chest.

I rolled my chair over and tapped my finger on the top edge of the last notebook, the most recent. When I tugged on it, it fell into my hand easily, softly, as if it wanted me to read it. Dread churned inside me as I began to leaf through the pages, each new expanse of paper a spray of bird shot that might knock my soft little dove of a heart out of the sky.

But in spite of my terror, there was nothing besides what belonged there: Adam's work, his ideas. Snippets of observation (*Interesting couple: the woman is a curvy rockabilly with blunt red bangs and colorful tattoo sleeves; the guy a pinched, accountant type shaped like a green bean*) and dialogue (*Texting girl giggles, "Whoops, my finger slipped"; cryogenic corporate mom next to her whispers "That's what he said"*). There were no confessions, no allusions, no personal entries at all. There was no Patrick. He might have meant *something* to Adam, but he hadn't meant more than me.

High on relief, I ran my fingers along the row of notebook spines on the shelf above: These were the journals from his high school and college years. I pulled another book toward me, the one that covered the spring and early summer leading up to our wedding day. One of the entries about me was in this volume. My fingers found the page immediately.

A letter I will never send to Caroline, he had written at the top of the page. And yet, he'd showed it to me. Partly because he wanted to share the emotion with me, and partly because he was too proud of the writing to leave it trapped unread within the pages of his notebook.

My girl, soon to be my wife . . .

I can scarcely believe it. Not because I doubted you, or doubted us, but because I'm in awe. In awe of this tremendous, breathtaking good fortune of mine. It's impudent, this luck. Impudent to have found a love like this, so young, and for it to have grown such deep and powerful roots in the unpromising soil of high school and college.

I stopped reading, laughter bubbling out of me like spring water. It was such a clean and welcome feeling to laugh without malice at something related to Adam. Because here was the thing: If I pointed out to him, even now in the midst of everything else, that he had used a metaphor concerning soil in two significant pieces of writing regarding me — this journal entry, and the letter he gave me after I discovered his affair — he would go maroon with embarrassment. Adam hated to reuse ideas, phrases, and so forth; his mind, according to him, should be a constantly rejuvenated thing, renewed by fresh turns of phrase never before assembled. The obsession could get tedious (Ruby teased him for it mercilessly), but it was *so Adam.*

All of a sudden, I missed him so badly it

136

felt like all the air had been vacuumed out of my chest.

"Sweetheart!" The naked relief in Adam's voice when he picked up the phone made my eyes sting with tears, because I felt it too. "Talk to me," he said. And I was ready to. I was so damn glad to hear his voice.

"So, I read your letter. The one you gave Jonathan."

A pause. "You hadn't read it before now?" Of course this offended him.

"I read it a while ago. I just didn't feel like talking about it before now."

"You . . . wow. Okay. And so?"

"You used another soil metaphor."

There was a long lag, as he struggled to process the fact that I hadn't directly addressed our situation. "What?"

"You compared your love to soil. And —" Helplessly, I started giggling, my shoulders twitching as I relished the sheer pleasure of laughing. "I was in the office just now, and I reread that letter you wrote in your notebook right before our wedding, and — you used soil as a metaphor then, too. Except that one was —"

" 'The unpromising soil of high school and college,' " he finished, voice rich with amusement. "Oh Christ, that's embarrassing."

137

"I knew it would kill you," I laughed.

"Guilty," he said. "Sweetheart, it's so good to hear your voice. I miss you so goddamn much. We haven't been apart this long since —"

"Since college. I know."

"So . . . how are you feeling? I know this is going to take a long time to repair. It's huge and complicated and awful. But can we please start trying? Let's just try. Let me try. That's all I'm asking for right now. Just try."

It was a lot to ask for, but it was also the simplest thing. And it was at the core of everything I had promised, ten years before: Don't give up without a fight. The fact that Adam had broken some of his own promises didn't let me off the hook for mine. Including, for example, that same promise not to fool around with someone else, even out of pure emotional desperation. I wasn't blameless myself.

This couldn't be the end.

I closed my eyes and imagined hugging my husband, the lean structure of his precious body clasped tight in my arms, and I knew the answer then. I was going to have to find a way past this devastation, because I quite simply didn't think I wanted to live without him.

"Okay," I said, the word drifting away on a rush of pure relief.

"Yes?"

"Yes," I said. "I will try."

"Caro," he said, voice impossibly tender. "Thank holy god. I can't wait to come home and see your face."

It was like hearing a note played out of tune in a beloved song. "Wait, hang on a second. I'm not ready for you to come home quite yet. I am *really fucking upset*, Adam. This is not going to get better quickly."

"Of course it's not. I know that. But why don't we meet? Just for a little while, so you can see I'm still the same person. I'm the person who's always loved you and always will."

"I'm not coming down there to see you. And I'm not ready to have you here yet."

"Then meet me in the middle somewhere. I'll figure out a place for us to go. I think it will be good for us."

The truth was, I knew my refusal to see him had been punishment as much as self-defense. It was time to let it go. "Okay. We'll meet in the middle. And I want to find us a marriage counselor, too. I think having someone to help us talk to each other is important."

"Whatever you want, sweetheart. You're

my girl. We're going to be together forever. We belong to each other. Nothing can change that."

A fist of anger punched through my good-will. "Adam. For this to work, you need to understand that what you did *did* change that. You say you belong to me, but you gave yourself to someone else. And it easily could have ended everything, forever. Your words are not aligning with the significance of what you did."

"I'm sorry," he said. "You're right."

As I set the phone on the table a moment later, I sighed. In contrast to his other only-child traits, Adam was not especially at-tached to being right; he had a tendency to agree with me quite readily during our argu-ments, just to get me over being upset. But that wasn't good enough this time. Along with everything else we had to recover from, it was clearly going to be an undertaking just to get him to *get it.* It was dawning on me, more clearly than it ever had before: Adam relied so much on the power of his words that sometimes he could use them to glide right between the sticky spider threads of what they truly meant. Another thing to discuss with the counselor, once we found one.

When I stepped out of the office, Ruby

was in her spot at the kitchen island. Her beer can froze halfway to her mouth when she saw me. "Caroline, what's that smile about?"

"I just talked to Adam. We're going to work through it."

Slowly, she lowered the beer. "What about the whole thing with Patrick being in love with him?"

"Adam doesn't love him. I can tell."

"As long as you're sure," she said, nudging the beer can along the counter with two fingertips. "I guess that means he's coming home, huh?"

"Not right away," I said. I looked across the room at the copy of *East of Eden* Adam had left on the side table mid-reread, and I could feel the smile spreading up my face like rising river water. "But yeah. He'll be home before too long."

10

You have entered into the most meaning-
ful relationship there is in all human life. It
can be whatever you decide to make it.
— Ronald Reagan to his son Michael on
the eve of Michael's marriage, June 1971

"Brace yourself. You are going to have a lot
to say about this one," I said.

"Sounds like you're the one who needs
bracing," my friend Farren said, jabbing her
plastic ice cream spoon toward me.

We were parked at a table on the broad
wooden porch of Williamstown's legendary
ice cream shop, Lickety-Split, which I have
been known to tell people is the sole reason
I moved back to my college town. It was the
kind of summer evening with which Massachusetts makes up for February: slanting
caramel sunlight and air so rich it was
practically a cocktail. Wind purred in the
trees behind the building. Farren was up to

her tonsils in a swiftly melting mountain of Purple Cow (black raspberry ice cream with white and dark chocolate chips), which she had requested be bedecked with every variety of topping, one after another, until the young clerk looked at her in concern and said, "Ma'am, I don't think there's room for any more."

"I probably do need bracing," I said, and mimed buckling my seatbelt.

"All right, dollface, let 'er rip."

I snorted. Farren was sixty-six years old and talked like a hybrid of a pompadoured Rat Packer and a nineties surfer. I'd met her a few years ago at a small gallery show she'd done in Northampton, and I'd been lobbying ever since to have her exploratory high-texture printmaking artwork featured at the museum. And although I'd been unsuccessful — so far — she still liked hanging out with me. Her rigorously enforced no-bullshit policy made her one of my very favorite people; it was what I needed right now.

"Okay. So, Adam and I have been having some trouble."

She dragged an empty chair closer and propped her small feet in their paint-spattered Crocs on it, unconcerned by the disapproving stare of the woman whose table she stole it from. The look Farren herself gave me could only be described as side-eye. "Thought you said this was going to surprise me."

"Farren!"

"You're married," she said, swirling the spoon with a flourish. "Married people have trouble. It's not exactly groundbreaking, doll."

"I guess not," I said, taken aback. Admittedly, I had expected a little more in the way of surprise. "But we're working on things. I wondered if you could give me the name of that marriage counselor in Pittsfield that Mike and Teri were seeing last year — it seemed like it was helpful."

"Not so much," muttered Farren. "He moved out a few weeks ago."

"What? No!" I yelped, with perhaps a little too much agitation, considering I'd met Farren's son all of once in my life. But he and his wife were a couple I knew who'd gone through problems and come out the other side. "What happened? I thought things had gotten better."

"She's an alcoholic," said Farren grimly. "Counseling won't do shit for that if there's no rehab. Might as well treat cancer with cold meds."

"Ugh, damn," I said. "That totally sucks.

144

What's Mike going to do?"

"He moved to Northampton and got a better job," said Farren, with a satisfied lick on her spoon. "And Tommy's in a better school. Mike's already working on me about moving down there with them, and who knows. Maybe I will. Sure can't afford the old house up here for too much longer."

"Oh no, really?"

"Yesiree, Bobbie. Unless my bank account is hiding something from me."

I felt a reflexive pinch of fear. Funny how it never quite went away. "They never do hide anything good," I said. "Well, would you still give me the counselor's info, though? I'm hoping she'll be able to help. We've got no substance problems with this one. Just garden-variety communication problems." *And a not-so-garden-variety affair.*

"Of course, doll. You have the right idea. Divorce is hell. You've got to hang in there till there's nothing left to hang from."

I blinked away the image of myself dangling stretch-armed from a sagging branch like the ubiquitous "hang in there" kitten meme. "I have to tell you, that's not quite what I expected you to say."

"Because my ex is a cheating sack of shit?"

The woman with the stolen chair huffed audibly and scooted closer to her twelve-years-old-looking son, who she seemed to sincerely believe was unfamiliar with that sort of language. This is one of the hilarious things about Farren: Because she looks essentially like a human Muppet — dewy pink skin, halo of fluffy gray curls, and a beaming smile packed with teeth — her sweet-old-lady appearance lets her skate under people's radars until she gets caught being naughty.

"Yes, and because when he left, you got together with the love of your life."

"Did your Adam fool around on you?" said Farren more quietly, excavating a large chunk of chocolate from her ice cream.

"He did," I said, and Farren shook her head.

"You can get over that," she said, mouth full of chocolate. "Lots of folks do. Frankly if there's even a chance you can, you should."

"I'm trying to. But I was prepared for you to tell me to kick the son of a bitch in the ass so hard his balls would bounce. That's why I buckled up," I said, miming the seatbelt again.

"Nah. The high road is a lonely place, girl. Unless your man is one of those mean ones that like to put their woman down and make her feel small —"

146

"He isn't," I said.

"No, he never struck me that way. But unless somebody's dealing with an ugly, hurtful kind of marriage like that, I wouldn't wish a divorce on my meanest enemy. It flips you upside down, rips you apart, and pulls out all your innards. You're lucky to come out of it feeling half the person you were before."

"So after all that, do you wish you'd stayed?"

"Nope," she said. "Worst year of my life, but it was worth it. Especially 'cause Aaron finally found his cojones and hit on me. But Bill and I, we were just plain donkey poo together."

"Donkey poo?" I laughed.

She shrugged, grinning. "I don't know. Seemed kind of small and messy. So is that the end of your big news? Pretty boring stuff, sweet cheeks. Thought you were going to tell me something exciting about that fine redheaded piece of tail you keep around. Unless that's part of the trouble?" she added, perking up.

"Oh my *god,* Farren." I blushed hot and hoped she would write it off to the missishness she liked to tease me for. "You can't call yourself a feminist and then turn around and objectify a man like that."

147

"Honey, that boy was born to be objectified. I promise you he likes it. He's lucky I didn't objectify his ass last time I saw him," she said, pinching her fingers like crab claws. "But let's back up a sec, because *you* just dodged my question."

"Um," I mumbled, cheeks flaming.

"Oh sweet baby Jesus, just tell me," said Farren. "I'm dying here."

"I may have kissed him a little bit," I muttered, and shoved Purple Cow Mountain toward her as an attempted distraction. "Eat your ice cream."

"A little bit?" she shouted. "That's not a man you kiss a little bit, that's a man you climb! And then you plant your goddamn flag, missy, you *plant your flag!*"

"Farren," I groaned, sinking lower in my chair as if it could render me invisible. "It was stupid. It was messed up, and it was a mistake. I know," I continued, after a glance at her mutinous expression. "I know it's basically a yellow card against the entire female species, but I didn't have the right to kiss him in the first place. My husband cheating on me doesn't give me a free pass to cheat back. It was an awful thing to do. And Jonathan stopped it first, anyway."

"Principles," said Farren serenely. "I like that in a man."

Principles, and plain old common sense: two things I had briefly abandoned on that warm, noisy rooftop with Jonathan. "So, are you happy now?"

"Very," she purred. "A little less interested in your future with what's-his-nuts, though. I need some vicarious excitement."

"Who says it has to be vicarious?" I said, spooning a mouthful of my own neglected ice cream. "Jonathan's single and looking. I bet he'd appreciate a mature woman with a creative soul and a good head on her shoulders."

"Don't tempt me," she said, and crab-pinched her fingers.

Firmly shoving my marriage drama onto the back burner, I resolved to tackle Diana Ramirez before Neil from Development's friendly smiles began showing signs of impatience. The problem was, I'd lived on the same hall of my freshman dorm as Diana, but I'd somehow stumbled onto her nerves during our First Days orientation, and couldn't seem to step off them the rest of the year. I was never able to identify what I'd done wrong; my entire existence simply seemed to disappoint her. Not in the kind of way whose cruelty warrants a "What the hell is your problem?" conversation; it was merely a coolness that refused to melt around the edges — even under the potentially warming effect of brushing our teeth side by side while our hallmate, a strapping pink-cheeked dude from a corn farm in Nebraska, belted ABBA's "Take a Chance on Me" in the shower. Every time I saw her, she met my eyes with this expression of faintly disgusted surprise: "Oh, that's right, *you* still live here." It's not like I was some gorgeous and obnoxiously popular chick, either; I was a smart, quiet girl who hung out in the art history building, while she was a smart, quiet girl who hung out in the computer science building. I had wanted to like her. But she hadn't wanted it back.

So, needless to say, I didn't have her contact info. But someone I knew had to know her and be willing to give me her email. She wasn't a head of state, for god's sake.

I started with Jonathan. "Didn't you sleep with her roommate?"

"I think you think I've slept with a lot more people than I actually have."

"Nope, I think I've got a pretty accurate idea."

"Well even if I had, why would I have Diana's email address? It was fifteen years ago."

150

"So you did sleep with the roommate."

He paused for an instant. "I — well, yeah."

"You're useless to me, Blaster."

"Try Ajay Shah. That guy knows everyone."

It was true. Ajay had sealed his fate as class president for infinity by spending his first two days on campus standing in the middle of the freshman quad, introducing himself to literally everyone he saw.

"Hey, what are you doing for Labor Day, by the way?" said Jonathan.

Strangely, I hadn't even thought about it. Almost three weeks of separation from Adam had been more than enough to bring home the fact that, aside from Farren, all the friends I had in Williamstown were *our* friends — other married or cohabiting couples we had met through my work or the theater festival. I hadn't confided in any of them about the state of matters in the Hammond household; the thought of being the object of other people's pity made me want to vomit.

"I don't know. Adam wants to come up, but I'm not ready yet. Maybe Ruby and I'll get our act together and try to grill something." Which, I realized as soon as I said it, was both metaphorically *and* literally serving up a big juicy hunk of meat as bait.

"Well, if you want your grilling done respectably, I can come up. My boss gave me the Saturday and Sunday off — most of the city's in the Hamptons."

I felt a rush of pure pleasure at the prospect of Jonathan's company. "Oh — yeah! Come up!"

"Will do," he said, sounding as happy as I felt.

"By the way," I said, "I guess it has to be said. . . . You won't have to bar your bedroom door. No more shenanigans from me. Adam and I are making progress. I'm seeing him this weekend to talk. And we have an appointment with a counselor in the middle of September."

"I'm so happy to hear that, darlin'," he said. "What you guys have is worth keeping. And it will be nice to cook in your kitchen one last time before he finds out I kissed you and bans me from a ten-mile radius of the place."

"I'm so sorry about that. The shenanigans. I feel awful, I —"

"Care. Honey. Don't sweat it. It's not as if I didn't enjoy it, you know?"

I did know, actually. It was exactly the fact that both of us had enjoyed it that set this confused discomfort prickling across my skin.

Though I was anticipating a struggle, class president Ajay Shah coughed up Diana's email address without so much as a squeak. Pretending I had no reason to suspect she disliked me, I wrote a warm, professional message to Diana, reintroducing myself and briefly outlining why I wanted to speak with her. Neil had said to try to create a personal connection: What was the most personal thing she and I had in common?

P.S., I wrote, it would be great to hear from you. Don't think we've spoken since the days when Jason Bratton's dirty Huskers jersey used to stink up the bathroom.

Two days later, she wrote me back. *Pretty sure that jersey got dirty enough to stand up under its own weight. Nice to hear from you. Let's chat tomorrow if that works.*

Holy crap! She sounded friendly. And far from resenting my intrusion on her time, she actually seemed . . . interested. Maybe this wasn't going to be the fool's errand I'd been convinced it would be.

I sauntered into Neil's office the next morning and sat down with elaborate decorousness in one of his guest chairs, smoothing my skirt neatly over my thighs. I clasped my palms around one knee and waited for him to finish his call.

After a moment, he tucked the phone receiver against his jaw and rotated to face me. "What's up?" he mouthed.

I shrugged and resumed gazing around his office. He had a group of framed prints arranged on one wall — blown-up images of the exhibition catalog covers we'd done in the last few years. A short but sturdy-looking fig tree glowed green in the light from the window, and there was a small flat-woven kilim rug on top of the ubiquitous gray carpet tile in the area where the guest chairs sat. The whole room had a kind of precarious tidiness to it, as if Neil had only just finished cleaning and there might, in fact, be a couple of piles of crap he simply couldn't deal with stashed behind the closed door of his closet. I liked it.

"Okay. Okay, sounds good. And thank you again. Good morning, Caroline; to what do I owe the pleasure?"

I snapped my attention back to him as I belatedly realized he had ended his phone call. "Oh. Well. I've recently been chatting over email with my new friend Diana Ramirez, and she's invited me to call her."

"That's excellent!"

"It is! But, um, now I have no idea what

I'm going to say to her."

He shrugged. "Don't try to rehearse it too much in advance. Just be yourself. Explain why you think the museum matters and why you think it should matter to her. I've heard you talk about it before — you're compelling. Try to forget that she's a big scary donor, and talk to her like one person to another."

"You make it sound so easy," I said.

"Honestly? It is. Being genuine and passionate is ninety percent of it. And remember, you're not trying to seal the deal right this second. You just want her to be interested to learn more. To come up here for a dinner, a private tour, an event with an artist. It's the first of many steps."

"Okay," I said. "I think I can do that."

"You definitely can," he said. "You got this."

Braced by his encouragement, I dialed Diana's office as soon as I got back to my desk.

"Hi there. This is Caroline H— ah, Caroline Fairley," I said, my maiden name an unexpected burst of sound in my mouth. It was nice to hear; nice to say. I hadn't said it in so long. "I'm following up on some emails I exchanged with Diana earlier in the week. She said I could go ahead and call." Caroline Fairley, clueless petitioner.

155

A few moments later, someone picked up the line. "Hi, Caroline, this is Diana."

Shit. Shit! I actually had her! What the hell did I do now? "Oh, hi, Diana; thank you for taking the time to speak with me. How are you?"

"Oh, you know . . . busy," she said, a trace of humor in her voice.

"No kidding," I said. "Just up to a few things here and there, right?"

"Just a few. So, I'm guessing somebody at your museum put you in charge of cultivating me as a donor because we went to school together, right?"

Well, then. Way to get directly to the point.

"Nailed it on the first try," I said. "I'm assuming I'm far from the only alum you've heard from since the IPO."

"And you'd be right about that."

I briefly considered passing along Neil's headlamp comment, but I had no idea if her sense of humor would absorb that or find it appalling. "I'm sure at least half of us got referred over by Ajay. You may want to consider telling that guy you've changed your email."

Her laugh was a low, rich sound. "No, it's fine. It's a good problem to have. And my assistant only forwards the things he knows I'll want to know more about."

156

"I'm excited to have made the cut, then! What makes you want to know more about MASS MoCA?"

"I don't really understand much about art, but I'm interested in things that people make with their hands. My mom is a seamstress, and I used to love to watch her sew, because when she stopped working, she had made something that didn't exist before. Everything I do is so intangible."

"Oh, I can completely understand that. But there's so much more to artwork than just craft. A good museum exhibit is even more than cool stuff to look at; it has a voice. It makes a point. That's why I think what we do at MASS MoCA is so important. Contemporary art is almost inextricable from the social and political issues of the time, and our work helps deepen people's understanding of those things. As well as offering new ways of seeing the world through the eyes of some of the most creative people out there."

"Yeah, I can imagine. That's cool — shoot, I'm sorry, I've got another call coming in — ah, and my assistant just messaged me who it is. I've been trying to catch up with this guy for weeks. I'm sorry, Caroline, I'm going to have to call you back. Have a good one, okay?"

And then she was gone. But, but, I'd made contact at least, and she did not detest me. It had even seemed to be going well, before she was summoned away from my call.

Had a good convo with Diana, I emailed to Neil. *Was going well but she had to jump off the call.*

The first of many steps, he responded.

And wasn't that just true of everything in my life these days?

11

If it is right, it happens — The main thing
is not to hurry. Nothing good gets away.
— John Steinbeck to his son Thom,
November 10, 1958

Apparently, the first of my steps back to
happiness with Adam was going to take
place outdoors. "Wear workout clothes,"
he'd said. "And a hat."

"Adam. I don't want to have an adventure.
I want to have a conversation. And that's
it."

"Adventure is overstating it."

"If you're trying to take me hiking, so help
me, I will leave you stranded in the middle
of the forest."

"It's not hiking."

"Adam . . ."

"It's an experience. Just an experience.
No gimmick. I actually think you'll enjoy
this. Just humor me."

159

And so, at ten o'clock on a hot Saturday morning in late August, I was pulling into the parking lot of the marina in Saugerties, New York, a small Hudson Valley town about halfway between Williamstown and the city. Despite Adam's refusal to give me any clues about the nature of what he had planned, the meeting location was a dead giveaway. He had chartered a sailboat for us, maybe with a lesson rolled in; but either way, there would certainly be a picnic lunch and some chilled white waiting for us on board.

The marina was located at the back corner of the town, on a deep creek that I assumed fed into the Hudson just a ways out of sight. Docked fishing skiffs and pontoon boats bobbed gently in the water in front of a row of small, colorful houses across the creek, while a group of kayaks sat in a tall rack near the launch ramp, their bright red bellies turned up to the sun. Adam was standing on a patch of lawn that sloped toward the water, deep in conversation with a bearded guy who had to be our captain for this . . . *experience*. Adam's knobby knees and furry calves protruded from the gray camouflage shorts that were his summer standard, and I swear, if my damn fool heart could have sprung itself out of my chest and

160

galloped over the grass to meet him, it would have.

Instead, I tugged my baseball cap down to try to shade my face, and gave a deliberately lukewarm wave.

"Hi, sweetheart," Adam said, reaching for my hand as I approached him. He only squeezed it briefly and let it go, though, for which I was grateful. I couldn't have handled it if he had tried to act like everything was normal. "This is Tim," he said, gesturing at the boat captain. "Tim's sister works in advertising, too, just like Ruby, only we don't think it's the same agency. Tim's sister does those screaming goat ads."

As rarely as Adam watched TV, I was willing to bet he'd never seen a screaming goat ad in his life; but he'd wanted Tim to feel proud that a stranger knew his sister's work. "Ruby lost her job," I said quietly.

"Shit, are you serious? When?"

"A couple of weeks ago." I didn't add that she'd been living with me ever since; apparently it was important to me not to let Tim the sailboat captain know that Adam and I were here trying to repair our broken marriage.

"Damn, that sucks. I'll ask around in case anybody knows someone. Well, all right, buddy, whatcha got for us today?" said

161

Adam, and Tim stepped toward the rack of kayaks. I peered behind it, as if the sailboat might be lurking there, but then Tim pulled forward a larger, double-seated kayak that was resting on the grass.

"Here she is," he said, patting the front of the big plastic shell. "Now, if you've ever taken out a single kayak before, a tandem is not a whole lot different, but . . ."

His voice slid into a rumbling drone as my brain belatedly absorbed the situation: There was no sailboat. In spite of myself, I'd sort of been looking forward to the prospect of a nice sail down the river, with the wind tugging my hair and the wake sloshing below my feet as the hull sliced through the sunlit water. Instead, I was going to be trapped inside an oversized plastic kazoo, with only my own arm power and Adam's to propel us along the river. Which, no offense to Adam, was not exactly a V-8 engine. I had been kayaking a couple of times before; it had left me with sore shoulders, a sunburn, and a raw spot on my thumb from the paddle. And this was Adam's wonderful idea?

"So remember," Tim was saying, "dig in and pull back to go forward; reverse it to stop or back up. And that's about all there is to it. Why don't you guys do a last round of sunscreen, and I'll go grab your life vests."

"Seems pretty straightforward, right?" said Adam. "I think we can handle this."

I jabbed a finger at the object resting at my feet. "What is this?"

"This is a tandem kayak. Like Tim just said. Do you want the front or the back?"

"This is not a kayak, it's a metaphor," I said. "We are literally in it together."

He beamed with pride that I'd caught on so quickly. "And we have to steer it in co-operation with each other. Completely in sync. A little push, a little pull, fighting the tide to stay on course. Battling the elements. Relying on each other —"

"OH MY GOD," I yelled. "You are ridiculous."

"I can keep going; I've got a bunch more lined up."

"No!"

"Just two little people, bobbing in the middle of a great big river . . . sure, turn your back so I can't see you laughing, that will work. Also, I love you."

It had always been an effort to stay mad at Adam, and I was horrified to find him chipping away at me even now. This was a catastrophic thing he'd done, and my anger was my only armor against the pain of it. And yet, wasn't the whole point of this sup-

163

posed to be repairing the damage?

"I'll sit in the front. I don't trust you to lead. How's that for metaphor?"

"You need me, though. You've only got one paddle."

"Shut up, Adam."

Adam's kayaking gambit had been a play of pure diabolical genius. I was trapped with him, reliant on him, and I couldn't carry on a serious conversation with him because I couldn't make eye contact unless I twisted awkwardly around in my seat.

"You're sitting stern?" Tim said to Adam, as he saw us off. "That's good, you're a little bigger. You guys will move best if you're in sync, so watch how she paddles and try to follow her lead."

"That's the plan," said the Boy Scout, kicking excitedly at his footpads inside the kayak to draw my attention to Tim's words.

"Did you pay him to say that?" I said, as we set off into the creek.

"No," said Adam. "This metaphor is actually just that damn good."

The metaphor was also good — good for Adam, that is — because this was the kind of thing we excelled at. Challenging cooperative tasks had never fazed us. We were a couple that could survive a trip to IKEA without a single cross word. I guess it was a combination of our personalities, the deep reserve of patience we kept toward each other, and Adam's unquenchable compulsion to entertain me; but the fact of it was, we just . . . got along. So while I was far from ready to forgive him, I wasn't going to make his stupid kayak trip a nightmare purely out of spite.

We followed the creek toward the river, gliding along the water with the only sounds the soft *splish* of our paddles and the occasional bird cry. Reeds swayed along the banks of the creek, and a light breeze pushed some patchy clouds across the sky, barely scattering the heat that hung in the air. As the creek opened up to the river, we passed a beautiful gable-roofed brick lighthouse at the end of a spit of land. Its tall, graceful windows looked like they had seen a thing or two in their time.

"Do you have anything to say about that?" I said, gesturing at the lighthouse with my paddle. "A beacon in the night that warns of danger? To keep sailors from crashing on unseen shoals beneath the waves?"

The kayak wobbled from side to side in the wake from a distant boat. From the stern, there was nothing but silence.

"Yeah, I thought so," I said, dipping my

165

paddle in again. "So, we're at the river. What now?"

"Let's just explore for a while."

"All right, Ahab. Tell me where you want to go."

We paddled across, then down, then back. We had a few moments of excitement when I spotted an approaching motorboat and worried we wouldn't get out of its path in time, but we dug at the water just like Tim had told us, and sped smoothly away.

"It takes more than you to scare the Hammonds!" Adam yelled at the passing boat, brandishing his paddle.

With my back to him, it was safe to smile.

It was pretty wild, floating in the middle of the Hudson. I'd grown up next door to this river, driven over it and under it more times than I could imagine, but I'd never been in it. As much as I hated to admit it, one of Adam's metaphors was right: It made me feel tiny, bobbing in my plastic kazoo amid the waves and the current, with the forested escarpment on the east bank and the blue mounds of the Catskills rising to the west. *We were here so very long before you, Caroline,* they all said. *And we will be here ever after.*

"I'm feeling my insignificance in the face of nature's majesty," I said to Adam. "What is my lesson here?"

"That if it ever gets rough out here, you're going to want somebody else to help you pull," he said quietly. "I'm good at it."

Sharp, sudden tears stung my eyes. "But you stopped pulling. You jumped ship. No, fuck that, you fucking capsized me! I need to know you will never do it again."

"Never, sweetheart. I will never do it again."

It was a promise, and like any other, it came with a choice for the person who was promised to: Believe it, or not. I dug around inside myself for the trust to believe my husband and came up only with crumbs. But at least they were something.

"I want to go back," I said, wiping my eyes with my thumbs. "I'm hot and I'm hungry and I'm incredibly tired of metaphors."

"Rear engine powering up," said Adam.

When Tim saw us approaching, he ambled across the lawn, waving. "How'd you guys do?" he said, as he caught the bow of the kayak and dragged it onto the launch ramp. "Pretty smooth working together to get around? I didn't want to tell you before you set out, but in kayak circles we like to call tandems divorce boats."

Never has a jocular wink been so poorly received.

"No divorcing in this here boat," said Adam. "Not on my watch."

As it turned out, I hadn't been completely wrong about the elements of Adam's *experience;* there actually was a picnic involved. Back across the creek toward town was a small waterfront park, with a shady slope that eased down to a beach where kids played and splashed. Adam hauled a huge cooler I'd never seen before out of the trunk of his car — not the yellow hatchback this time — and thumped it down on a picnic table with a grunt. From it, he unloaded grapes, dried apricots, a sumptuous array of cheeses and a crusty baguette to go with them, fig spread, apple chutney, a stick of my favorite spicy salami, a crisp green bottle of dry Riesling and, the finishing touch, a small bouquet of dahlias as splashy as a miniature sunset.

"Wow, the deluxe 'Make My Wife Forgive Me' package from Zabar's, huh?"

He ignored me and focused on unwrapping a wedge of Humboldt Fog. "So how come Ruby lost her job all of a sudden?"

"She lost her two biggest accounts to a competitor firm," I said. "Two days after her boyfriend dumped her."

"Oh damn, poor kid. That absolutely

168

blows. How's she holding up?"

"She's great. The boyfriend wasn't the love of her life, and she's doing some freelance work while she looks for something new. She's been staying with me, actually."

Adam shot me a quick look. He knew perfectly well what Ruby's assessment of him in the present situation would be, and how vocally she would air it. "That's nice that you guys are having some time together. I think you and I are going to need our space once I come home, though."

"I'm sure she'll be gone by then."

He offered me a slice of bread with a kingly hunk of cheese. "Have you had any luck finding a counselor?"

"Yeah — Farren gave me the name of the person her son was seeing."

This time his face came all the way up. "You told *Farren*?"

"She's my friend, so, yes. I wanted to hear what she had to say."

"Which was what?"

"That divorce is hell and I should do everything I can to stay married, including forgiving you for cheating on me."

His smile was small, wry, and completely Adam. "Please give me her address so I can send her a few skids of her favorite treat."

"Just make the Blaster hand-deliver her

next paint order in a pair of Calvins, that will do it."

At the thought of Jonathan, heat flooded my face. I was going to have to tell Adam. I had to, or I was nothing better than a hypocrite. But the problem was, if I told him now, he would turn it into *See? You cheated TOO!* As if my kissing my closest friend out of pain and soul-crushing need that Adam himself had created were equivalent to his carrying on a three-month affair because he was . . . curious.

Since I had decided to work through this with him, I'd mostly tried to push the specifics out of my mind until we had a neutral third party to help us unpack it all. But there was something that had been bothering me, itching at my mind like a scratchy tag at the back of a shirt.

I took a sip of wine to fortify myself for the question. "So, I have to ask you something."

"Sure, sweetheart," he said. Carefree. Like a man who had nothing in the world to withhold.

"I saw Patrick a couple of weeks ago, and —"

Adam's knife skidded sideways and clattered to the table. "You did *what*?"

I set my wine cup down and laced my

hands together in my lap with forced calm. "I was desperate to understand this, Adam. You refused to explain it to me even a little bit."

"Not true at all. You had no right to bring him into this."

"Me bring him in? *Me?* Would you like me to remind you why we are even discussing him in the first place?"

Adam hurled a hunk of bread toward a nearby duck, who squawked and hustled away, wings flapping indignantly. "If we're going to get past this, you're going to have to stop treating me like the bad guy, Caro. I don't want to live the rest of my life on one long guilt trip."

I bit down on the sarcastic hand slap that buzzed behind my lips. *Oh, pardon me for forgetting it is you who are the victim here.* "I understand that. And I will. But it's a little early to ask me to stop being angry."

"You need to keep punishing me?"

"Insisting you take responsibility for your actions is not punishment."

He turned back to me, eyes intent. "And asking you to be softer to me is not trying to escape responsibility. I recognize that this entire situation is my fault. I hate more than anything that I've caused you pain, and I'm doing everything I can think of to repair the damage. I'm not asking you to stop being angry. I am just asking you to choose to be kind instead of sharp. I know I deserve for you to hurt me, but all it does is add more hurt to us instead of washing it away. And I have no right to ask you, but I'm doing it anyway, because my pride doesn't mean anything to me here, and I'm terrified that I've poisoned the way you feel about me forever. I'm fucking terrified, sweetheart. Please be kind. Just kind."

I stared into my interlaced hands as if they held the answer. When I was growing up, anytime I lost patience with Ruby badly enough to merit a talking-to by my parents, my mom would lecture me with the Golden Rule, and then my dad would hit me with his version: *Kindness knows no shame.* It wasn't until years later that I discovered he'd actually stolen it from a Stevie Wonder lyric, but the truth of it was as clear as it had ever been. Jealousy and hurt will whisper excuses in your ear for almost anything you do, but acting with kindness is a choice you will never have a reason to regret. And despite the terrible mistakes he'd made, nobody deserved that generosity from me more than my husband.

I rose from my side of the bench and sat down next to Adam. He didn't reach for me or try to kiss me, but he turned his left hand palm-up on his thigh. There was the scar at the base of his thumb (slipped paring knife), and there was the glint of his wedding band. His grasp, when his fingers closed around the hand I rested in his, was firm.

He turned his face so he could kiss the side of my head. It was one of my favorite ways that he touched me. "Sweetheart?" he said softly, lips against my hair.

"Hmm?"

"What was it you wanted to ask me?"

Down at the creek, a toddler shrieked. His wild nest of sandy curls glowed golden in the sun, and a potbelly protruded above his valiant chubby legs. He jumped in the lapping water, then splashed at it with his hands again and again, squealing with delight. His father stood nearby, watching with a smile.

Do you know he's in love with you? I'd been going to ask Adam. *This affair you told me was just about attraction was also about love.*

After a somewhat uncoordinated leap, the little boy at the creek toppled over onto his bottom, and just when I thought he would erupt into tears, he looked up at his father and laughed.

And suddenly, I didn't want to hear how

Adam would have answered my question. It was the last thing I ever wanted to know.

12

I am happy in the knowledge that we are friends again, and that our love has passed through the shadow and the night of estrangement and sorrow and come out rose-crowned as of old. Let us always be infinitely dear to each other, as indeed we have been always.

— Oscar Wilde to Lord Alfred Douglas,
December 1893

I remember reading once about this dangerous little tic of human behavior called normalcy bias. What it means is that, when suddenly confronted with a threat, people often fail to respond to it appropriately at first, because their minds are busy trying to reassure them that nothing is wrong. Even with ample evidence of trouble, the brain rejects the fact that normal is gone. That popping noise in the street has got to be fireworks, even though it's the middle of the day. People will go right on believing it's fireworks until they start hearing screams.

Like I said, I thought I knew my story.

Adam had cheated, but we were fixing it. We were talking, every day more and more. Both he and I were giving concerted mental focus to the relationship in a way we had not for a very long time, and I could tell that it was helping. We were slowly dragging our wheels out of the sucking mud, and the road ahead was dry.

At no point did it occur to me that infidelity was not the cause of my problem, but rather a symptom.

Just like I've wondered what would have happened if I hadn't attended Patrick's gallery opening that clingy July night, or if Alicia hadn't shown me those other photos, I've wondered, too, what would have happened if I'd never gotten the voicemail. If the message had gone by email, instead, to its intended target.

As I walked into the house one afternoon a week or so after the kayaking expedition, the silence was shattered by the bubbling ring of a telephone: our land line, the cancellation of which had been on our household to-do list for so long that it had become a running joke. Oh, if only.

Hi there, said an unfamiliar female voice,

when the call rang through to the answering machine. *This is Frankie Berlin with the Diamond Agency, calling on behalf of Mike Diamond for A. T. Hamm. Mr. Hamm, we just got the publication payment for* Sliding Home, *and we typically send those via FedEx, but all you've got is the Manhattan P.O. address, which FedEx won't deliver to. We want to make sure we get it to you promptly, so let us know if there's another address to send to or if you want it sent regular mail. Give me a call back when you get a chance.*

I shook my head as if I had water in my ears and replayed the message, but it didn't make any more sense than it had the first time. The sensation was not unlike when Adam took me to Provence for my twenty-first birthday and I then had to get us around using only the limited resources of my rusty high school French: I could understand some of the words that people said to me, but not all of them, and my brain labored to close the gaps in comprehension with highly limited success. In this case, I understood everything this woman was talking about, but none of the details were what I expected them to be.

Adam's literary agency was Darlington Literary, a name so significant to him I could practically hear a gong sound every time he said it. It was, according to my husband, the most prestigious agency in the country, with a client roster full of hoary old names. It was also, it bears noting, Adam's father's agency; but as Adam's agent Pauline assured him when she signed him five years ago on the strength of his partially completed Very Important Novel, nepotism alone couldn't get a book published.

And indeed, she was right. The VIN, eventually completed, titled *Nothing Good Gets Away* after a passage from a letter from John Steinbeck to his teenage son, and pitched to every imprint that published high-end literary fiction, failed to sell to any of them. It was praised gloriously and rejected regretfully, but rejected it was just the same. Adam subsequently published a volume of short stories that received a glowing review in *The New York Times*, but had not yet made any real headway on another novel. It was fine, he'd said. He was enjoying plays and short fiction more these days anyway.

Never . . . not once . . . had he mentioned a project called *Sliding Home*. Not even writing it, let alone — apparently — publishing it. I had never heard of the Diamond Agency, of any agent named Mike, nor of

Adam writing under a weird pseudonym rather than his name. Fingers shaking, I reached into my purse for my phone and keyed the book's title into my search browser, and there, in bold block capitals, it was: *Sliding Home: My Journey Back to Safety,* by Richie Cabrero. And in much smaller letters underneath: "with A. T. Hamm."

Richie Cabrero, who was basically a walking punch line for late-night comedy jokes about 'roided-out baseball players? Adam had, somehow, sometime, ghostwritten a memoir for him? I backed out of the link and searched again, for A. T. Hamm this time, and two other titles popped up. One of them another celebrity memoir, and the other a *New York Times* best-selling memoir-cum-self-help-treatise from a spirituality guru I vaguely recognized from TV. And I was drenched with a sickening sense of déjà vu.

I realized, at that moment, that part of me had been waiting to hear about another infidelity. Either from Adam himself, in a gush of truth like pus released from an abscess, or from someone else. From Ruby or Jonathan, who had both said it: *Did you have any idea?*

What I had never expected to find was

something like this. Something not only secret, but so contradictory to everything I understood about Adam's work, his goals, his very personality.

"What's up, buttercup?" said Ruby, breezing in through the kitchen door as I sank to the couch with my face in my hands. "Wait, whoa, seriously, what's up?"

I raised my face and stared at her beseechingly. "Adam . . . Adam published three fucking books and didn't tell me."

She set the bucket of flowers she'd been carrying on the counter and frowned, trying to catch up to why I was so upset. "You mean, like, he self-published something?"

"No. I mean, like, my husband, who since I met him at sixteen years old has been working toward publishing a piece of literary art that's good enough to stand up to his father's, has apparently ghostwritten the memoir of a drug-addicted, steroid-abusing baseball player. As well as for some Food Network chick, and that guy who thinks you can solve every problem in your life by positive thinking."

"Jefferson Ross?"

"That's the one. He did all of this, and he never told me. He *never told me.*"

"But why on earth not?" she said, plopping down next to me and stacking her elbows on her knees.

I couldn't answer her. I felt as lost and sightless as if I'd been swallowed by a sand-storm.

Wordlessly, she handed me my phone, which I'd tossed on the coffee table when my mental whiplash had gotten too over-whelming. I pressed down on Adam's name to dial him, hoping even as I did it that he wouldn't answer. If he didn't answer, maybe I could convince myself this was a misunder-standing. The "It's not what it looks like" moment that we never had with the actual infidelity.

"Hi, sweetheart! I was just thinking about you."

Instinctively, I almost responded to the warmth in Adam's voice; my brain had been conditioned for the last seventeen years to believe that Adam being happy, Adam call-ing me "sweetheart," Adam in general, were good things. I could hear the rush of city noise behind him — a siren in the distance, someone's shout as they walked by. It was jarring to realize I had no idea where he was, what he had actually been doing for the past few weeks. Two more things I didn't know about him.

"Listen, love," he said, "hang on a minute until I can get to someplace quiet so I can talk to you."

"You can talk now," I said. "There was a message on the machine just now, from someone at the Diamond Agency about a publication payment for A. T. Hamm. Can you please explain that to me?"

Silence. There was a long, heavy silence, and then finally Adam sighed. But it wasn't a sigh of resignation or regret, it was — somehow — a sigh of long-suffering patience worn thin. "I assume, since you sound pissed rather than genuinely confused, you have already answered the question yourself."

"I know that someone named A. T. Hamm has ghostwritten three celebrity memoirs. But I'm not familiar with A. T. Hamm, or this person's work, even though his literary agency *for some reason* has my home as the contact number. This is the part I need you to explain."

He sighed again. "Jefferson Ross was the first one. I met him through someone I worked on a play with a few years back, and when he found out I was a writer he mentioned he had been working on a memoir but he needed some help to make it jell. I took a stab at it, for the hell of it, and he loved what I did, so I ended up helping him write the entire thing. Then he hooked me up with Adriana di Lorenzo, and she referred me to Richie. And there you have it."

"There I have it?" I repeated, my voice pitching upward like a kite straining at its tether. "No, Adam, I don't. You've never mentioned any of this to me. Not one single word. All I've ever heard about was plays, and stories, and *Nothing Good* — not so much as a peep that you'd been ghostwriting memoirs, for Christ's sake!"

"And why do you think that is? You should hear yourself — 'ghostwriting memoirs,' as if I'd been selling meth to middle schoolers."

"Oh, will you stop exaggerating? I have the right to be pretty fucking astonished by this! You wrote and published *three books* without telling me. You hid every step of the process, of the entire thing. You didn't share any of it with me. All this time I've been worrying, for your sake, about when you'd be ready to write another novel, and what would happen if it didn't do as well as you hoped, and meanwhile you've been making money — good money, clearly — from your writing, and you've been hiding all of it from me?"

"I wasn't hiding the money," he said quickly. "I just didn't tell you exactly what it was from. I've been putting some of it into the scholarship account, too."

Of course he had.

The scholarship account was something I admired about Adam. When we started planning to leave the city for Massachusetts, it had roughly coincided with Adam's thirtieth birthday, and this happy confluence gave his parents the idea to buy a house for us. Not only the down payment, which was not unheard-of among people we knew — the Hammonds bought the house outright. Their generosity had put us in the unusual position of being a young couple with poorly paying artsy jobs who didn't have to worry about a mortgage payment.

For my part, I was inclined to accept the generous gift for the pure good fortune it was, but Adam fretted. He insisted we had to do something to earn out this extraordinary cosmic advance, and the notion that finally struck him was a scholarship fund. He was taken with the idea of providing educational opportunities to young people whose backgrounds would not have otherwise permitted it. People like me and Jonathan, who Adam knew had only been able to attend our college by the grace of Williams's deep-pocketed financial aid endowment. But so, ever since, any extra money beyond Adam's share of our household budget went into the scholarship fund. I had never even looked at the balance; it was his project, his baby, and he was paying more than enough into our household pot to cover all of our expenses and savings goals. Though, come to think of it, there had been something of an uptick in his contributions within the last several years.

"My god, *why* didn't you tell me?" I said, suddenly exhausted. "It's such a basic thing to share with your wife. I can't begin to comprehend what would make you hide this."

"Come on, really? You can't begin to comprehend? God, you never did get it. I'll spell it out for you: Because it's not who I'm supposed to be. I'm Theodore Hammond's kid. I'm supposed to be carrying on a literary legacy, not writing memoirs for people in *Us Weekly.*"

"Then why do it?"

"Honestly? I really enjoy it. I was shocked at how much I enjoy it. Everything I've ever worked toward says I should despise this kind of thing, but I love it. I love telling other people's stories. And I like the people. Richie's got this lived-in quality about him that makes him fascinating to listen to. Jefferson is completely different in person

185

than he is on TV — he puts on a big act of being all fuzzy-wuzzy positivity, but he's a total shark. And Adriana's a screaming bitch, but it was fun as hell to somehow make her come across likable."

Each of these details scored me with a fresh slash of pain. I should have heard about these people at the time Adam was working with them, should have talked and laughed with him about them over dinner, should have read his drafts like I had with his other work. That he'd locked it away from me hurt so badly I could barely speak. "Adam, that makes perfect sense. It sounds like you were born to do this job. But you didn't think I would get that?"

"I thought you'd be disappointed," he said, stumbling on the word.

"Disappointed? That you found a niche for your writing that you're thriving in? How can you even say that?"

"Because it's kind of a bait and switch. Think about it. We spent so much time talking about our dreams when we were younger, but you're the only one of us who's actually made them come true. You've achieved every one of your goals and ended up exactly where you wanted to be. You're so certain about everything in your life, and you're *so* secure, I swear to god it's fucking

186

abnormal, Caroline. And meanwhile, you thought you were married to a serious artist, and now it turns out I'm not quite up to snuff. So no, I didn't want you to see that I didn't know what I was doing after all. I thought you'd see me as a failure."

"That's seriously what you thought I would think?" I whispered, my voice soggy with the urge to cry. "No wonder you cheated on me; you don't even know me."

"No. *You* don't know. You have no idea what it's like to need to hide part of yourself in order to be respected."

"You didn't need to hide anything from me," I said. "You just didn't trust me. Locking me out is the worst thing you could have done. Because now, I don't know you," I added, my eyes suddenly blurred over. "You've been my husband for ten years, and I do not know who you really are."

"Yes you do," he said raggedly, biting off each word. "I swear to you. You know everything that matters."

Silently I shook my head. Just a few weeks ago, I'd thought I did. But now, the weight of all the possible things that might have been concealed by this man on the other end of the line was crushing the air out of my lungs. God help me, how would I ever be able to watch him do something as basic as sending a text message again, without wondering what it said and where it was headed?

I shouldn't have asked him what I asked him next. As soon as the words spilled from my mouth, I clamped a hand to my throat as if I could somehow force them back in; put them away before he heard them. Because the answer meant everything.

"Did Patrick know about it?"

"Yeah," said Adam without hesitation, obviously expecting bonus points for telling the truth about something, "but that's because I didn't care —"

"No," I wailed. "Don't tell me that. Don't tell me you didn't care if he knew. *I* cared. *I* should have known, so I could participate and support you. I am your fucking *wife*. How do you not understand how devastating that is?"

"Caro," he whispered, catching on way, way too late.

"Don't. I don't want to hear any more. I need to go now, Adam. I need to figure out what I'm going to do."

"What you're going to do? What do you mean? This doesn't change anything."

"It changes everything," I choked out.

"No! No no no no, sweetheart, come on —"

"Is there anything else you need to share with me, before I go? I'm not talking about things you *want* to share, I mean things you *need* to share. Things you owe it to me to tell."

"No. I promise you. Please don't go."

"I have to ask you again — have you cheated on me aside from Patrick?"

"No. I swear it."

I let the words sink into me, and waited to feel a sense of certainty of their truth. But that warmth, that unquestioning trust in him that had pumped through my veins with every beat of my heart for the last seventeen years — it was gone. Without it, I felt flat; dry; blank. I felt . . . empty.

"That means literally nothing to me anymore," I said.

The very first night of our honeymoon, Adam reached across the café table and took my hand. "I can't wait till it's forty years from now," he said. "And we're back here for our anniversary, and I can annoy everyone we meet by telling them in my broken Italian that it's our fortieth year of marriage. I'll say, 'Isn't she beautiful,' and they'll say 'Yes, she is' —"

"Because they're humoring you," I said, smiling.

189

"Yes, and because they want a nice tip, but still, they'll say it. Because you will be. You're going to be so beautiful with wrinkles and gray hair."

And he meant it, too. Adam was exactly the kind of man who would see true beauty in an older woman's face, in the creases earned by time, without wishing for the bloom of her vanished youth. I had held that truth close to me, as we talked through all the things we wanted to share in our lives, all the miles we wanted to walk together.

But as we strolled, hand in hand, to our hotel, I wondered. Not everyone lives to be sixty-three. Cancer, drunk drivers, freak accidents — none of those things were known to be particular about the ages of the people they culled.

I walked next to my husband of less than forty-eight hours, feeling the warm skin and flexing joints of his fingers between mine, and I thought about the fact that one of us might die young. I thought about how it was possible one of us might be called to act upon "in sickness" rather sooner than seemed fair, and as I listened to the rumble and flow of his voice on the drifting June breeze, I was prepared to do it. The one thing that never entered my mind was that anything but death would end us.

It used to be that when I opened my eyes to his face in the morning, I smiled. My marriage, in some ways, had been as simple as that being with Adam made me deeply, deeply happy. Of course there were shared goals and long history and a thousand more complicated things; but in the morning, always, the first thing was the joy. It renewed itself, with every joke, every kiss, every kindness. I just . . . loved him. And he loved me in return, so I basked in it like a cat stretched out in a sunbeam. Adam, and his love, made me content.

And yet, he didn't feel the same. Whatever his reasons for doing what he'd done, his actions revealed a man who was restless, unsatisfied, uncertain. A man who hadn't trusted me enough to share his whole truth with me — not about who he was in bed, nor who he was in the work he cared so passionately about. None of what I'd thought I knew about him, about us, could be relied upon anymore.

It reminded me of the one and only time I'd gone scuba diving, on a trip to Mexico with Adam. It was a shallow dive among the coral reefs, in less than twenty-five feet of water, so at the end the instructor had simply signaled, grabbed our elbows, and tugged us up. Halfway up, I realized the air pressure in my ear wasn't equalizing properly as I breathed, but the instructor didn't understand my frantic waving, and when we broke the surface a few moments later I felt a pop of pain as the expanded air left my skull through a brand-new hole in my eardrum.

And then everything went sideways. With the sudden trauma to my ear, my equilibrium was unmoored, and the horizon pitched and rolled sickeningly as I flailed. The thing that brought me back was Adam. He caught my hands and planted them on his shoulders and held them there, firm and steady, until I knew which way was up.

But this time, it wasn't Adam I could ground myself with. Adam had become the horizon — the one thing I had counted on to stay in place, the line that sliced my world into up and down. I closed my eyes against the remembered vertigo, and my horizon, it just rolled and rolled and rolled.

13

It is not necessary to accept the choices handed down to you by life as you know it. . . . No one HAS to do something he doesn't want to do for the rest of his life. But then again, if that's what you wind up doing, by all means convince yourself that you HAD to do it. You'll have lots of company.

— Hunter S. Thompson to Hume Logan,
April 22, 1958

Adam and I were married at New York's Episcopal cathedral, St. John the Divine, on a warm, rainy June afternoon. Nobody wants it to rain on their wedding day, but I didn't mind a bit; in fact, that soft, friendly rain wound up being the thing I liked most about all the circumstances of the wedding itself. Aside from the dress and the groom, little else about it was what I would have chosen: the June date (I'd wanted October);

193

the Manhattan location (I would have preferred a country church in Dutchess County near the Hammonds' upstate home); the grandiosity of the whole affair. But the Hammonds were footing the bill, so I understood it was only fair to go along with what they wished. "For the honeymoon, we'll do whatever you want," Adam had promised.

At my father-in-law's request, the ceremony was performed by the same priest who had married himself and Adam's mother twenty-five years before, and baptized their infant son. I have a vivid memory of meeting Jonathan's eyes as I proceeded up the aisle: Strapped into his rented gray suit, with his bright ponytail spilling over the collar, he looked like a teenager playing dress-up, and for this brief, wild second the thought dashed through my brain of *What are we doing, why are we doing this, we are too young, this is crazy.* But then I blinked, and I looked up at Adam, who was watching me walk toward him with this smile like he was seeing the sunrise for the very first time. And then I took his hands, and the ceremony started, and all the rest of it dropped away. "What God has joined," said the priest after he had pronounced us husband and wife, "let no man put asunder."

And yet, there I was, ten years later, getting ready to put it asunder with my very own hands. Leaving would mean losing the entire narrative of my future as I thought I'd known it. And I could not even begin to imagine what might transpire in its place. But as I lay there, on that long August night when I discovered the depth of what Adam had hidden from me, the certainty calcified inside me, brittle but hard. I could not stay married to this man.

While dawn soaked slowly into the sky, I mentally replayed the wedding in reverse: releasing Adam's hands, walking backward up the aisle, getting into the car that would take me back to my parents' apartment, where I would step free of the foamy white dress that hung now in my guest room closet down the hall. Retracing my steps to the city hall marriage bureau where we filed for our license, only this time I would be filing the petition to divorce.

It turned out that New York State, somewhat sensibly I suppose, does not want you to rush out and drop divorce papers on your spouse's head without some sort of deliberate interlude of consideration. According to

195

the very informative .gov website that I spent the following evening perusing, I would have to sit out a six-month period of separation before the state would even entertain the notion of reviewing my filing. As it happened, I was already over a month into it, but even then, that was only until I could file. Lord only knew how long it would be before everything would be over.

I felt a quiver of pure fear at the word — *over* — because, quite frankly, I had never been so terrified of anything in my life. I thought of what Farren had said, about how devastating a divorce would be, and I believed it. But for the first time, I understood I had no choice. Avoiding the pain by going back to safety was not an option; my shelter had burned to the ground. And without any confidence in what it had been in the first place, all I had to rebuild with was loose and moldy straw.

My normal was gone. The marriage I'd thought I had did not exist anymore. It never really had.

I told my husband I was divorcing him in a letter.

I could try to make my reasons sound grand and dignified, I suppose. Letters had meant so much to us, after all; there was, perhaps, something a little bit fitting about that. But the truth was that I couldn't bear to say the words out loud to him. I knew, of course, that I would hear from him soon. That there would be tears. But that actual moment when it became real, when it changed from an idea that had taken shape inside me into an actual, spoken, acknowledged part of our story — into the very ending of our story, in fact — I couldn't share in it. I couldn't bear to witness the moment when he shifted, between one heartbeat and the next, from not knowing to knowing. And so, I wrote to him.

Adam —
From the first moment this all started, I've wanted to find my way to a place where we could move forward. I was prepared, with an open heart, to do it; but it's all become too much. You promised to be faithful, and you cheated. You cheated with a man, and when I asked you to explain to me what that means to you, to our marriage, you failed to even try. You hid the truth from me about your writing, your work, because you thought I would look down on you. I'll say it again — I no longer know who you really are.

I don't think you understand the impact of all of this together. You said I know everything that matters, but not only is that untrue, but the fact that so much of it was hidden until now shows a fundamental failure of trust. The two of us are supposed to know each other better than we're known by any other person on earth. And before this, I would have thought it was true. Except now I realize that I've only loved an image, not a person I completely understand. Because you never trusted me enough to fully share yourself with me.

And I think maybe I see, a little bit, why you did it. I love your father, but there's no doubt he's got a limited definition of success. But I'm not your parent; I'm your wife. For me to know you, truly know you, is far more important than for you to uphold some phony standard of perfection.

I'm crushed, and broken, and full of pain. I don't understand how and why you made these decisions, did these things that ruined us. But you did, you ruined us. I can't be married to someone I don't know and cannot trust. I can't stay in this marriage.

I sent it. And then I waited. And then he called.

Getting through the phone call was like walking through a hurricane. He called me while I was at work, four times on my cell, before giving up and calling the museum's line. I called him back from the privacy of my car. And as I looked out at the familiar surroundings while tears streamed down my face and I sobbed until I choked, the sense of dislocation was so profound it made my head spin. *How was it possible* this was actually happening?

"This isn't supposed to happen," Adam said, in a voice like stones tumbling together. "This *can't happen* to us."

"It already happened," I said. "You made it."

"I made the worst mistake of my life. Two mistakes, terrible ones. But that doesn't have to mean it's the end. It *can't* mean that. Why won't you at least try counseling?"

"Because I don't need to be counseled. I don't want to try to save the marriage anymore. I would rather be an ex-wife than a wife who can't trust her husband. I don't want to be suspicious of you for the rest of our lives. I can't live like that. And after this much concealment, I can't find the faith I'd need to have in you."

"How can you be doing this? This isn't you, Caro. This isn't like you at all. Has Ruby been telling you to leave me?"

"Don't you dare blame my sister for this," I hissed. "What makes you say this isn't like me?"

"Because it's us, love. This is *us*. I can't believe you're willing to destroy us over something like this."

"*You* destroyed it, Adam. That's the thing you keep missing here. And you're wrong that this isn't like me; that just means you misjudged me."

"I made terrible, selfish, stupid mistakes. I'm not denying that. I've damaged this marriage badly and I regret that more than anything in my life. But I know we can recover. We were making progress, *good* progress. I've built my life around you, and I will do anything to keep us together, sweetheart. I think you should, too. I think you owe it to both of us to try."

His boldness inflated my chest with pure rage. "Wrong!" I screamed. "You are not *entitled* to me, just because you love me. And not just because I love you back. You have to keep on earning that love, every day, again and again and again. I never expected perfection from this marriage, but this wasn't some dumb little fuckup; you made a choice to put someone else before me, for months, and to hide things — for *years* — which are both actions you knew goddamn well would cause me awful, awful pain. It doesn't *matter* that you didn't think I'd find out; what matters is that you recognized the disloyalty of giving what is ours to someone else, and you still did it. And you have hidden *so much more* than that from me. There is no way you can rebuild my trust. And without that, we have no future."

By the time I finished yelling I was mentally and physically exhausted, not least from the effort of stopping him from interrupting me. As soon as my lips bit off the last syllable of my final word, he was yelling back.

"You're my wife!" he shouted. "How can you just give up on me like this?"

"Because, Adam. You gave up on me," I said, in a voice as tiny as he had made me feel.

He vowed to fight me. He vowed to never sign, to keep us tied up in legal limbo until the end of time. It was all standard Adam; exactly what I had expected. The one thing I hadn't anticipated was that until the moment he opened my letter, he hadn't truly considered this was a possibility. He'd only been biding his time until he could plead his way past my resentment and my hurt. He must have thought I would forgive him anything, just because I loved him.

He wasn't alone in that, though. My mother took the news that I was divorcing Adam only slightly less poorly than Adam himself.

"Caroline Elizabeth, you cannot be serious," she breathed. "This is foolishness. Over one affair?"

Admittedly, I hadn't told her the specifics. I didn't think I could handle another round of *Did you have any idea?,* especially coming from my mother, whose concept of men who liked men was drawn wholly from sidekicks on primetime TV shows. "Mom, you sound like a politician's wife from the sixties. I happen to care extremely deeply about this one affair."

"Of course you do, darling. But it's madness to end the marriage over something like this. I'm certain Adam would never do it again."

"Really? Because I'm not."

"I am certain. I think you two clearly need to work on things, and communicate better, but once you do . . ."

I craned to reach my dusting wand onto

the top of the door casing in the guest bedroom. One of the first things I'd done to batten down the hatches for the divorce — god, that *word;* how was it now a part of my daily vocabulary? — was to let go of our housekeeper, Eileen. I loved the woman and her efforts dearly, but we'd only been able to afford her because of Adam's contributions to our budget, and I didn't find it especially fair to ask him to pay for cleaning on a house I'd banished him from. I was also sure that his eventual attorney wouldn't find it too fair, either.

"Mom, this isn't about communication. This is infidelity. And beyond that, it's dishonesty on multiple levels. I can't trust him anymore. He's been hiding parts of himself from me, and I can't stop thinking about what there is that might still be concealed. I can't spend the rest of my life wondering."

Her sigh was heavy, world-weary; unlike anything I'd ever heard from her before. My mother is a lifelong look-on-the-bright-sider who, when presented with evidence of injustice both great and small, will simply sniff, shrug her shoulders, and say, "Well, there must be a reason." But this sigh sounded . . . tired. And sad.

"Mom? Please tell me you're not about to

confess that you and Dad have cheated on each other and worked past it, because so help me God, I do not want to know."

"No, Caroline," my mother said peevishly, as if it were the most outlandish idea I could have arrived at. "We have not. But I do think you are being a bit naïve. When you marry someone, it isn't happily ever after like a fairy tale. No matter how much you love your husband, he is going to disappoint you. He is going to hurt you. And you will hurt him, too. It's what people do. Even people who love each other very, very much. The secret to staying married your whole life isn't doing everything perfectly, it's learning how to forgive."

"I don't want to forgive this, though. I can't. Some things are too big to forgive. This isn't some petty misdemeanor; this is the foundation of our marriage that we're talking about here. The basics. Don't cheat. Don't lie. Don't conceal. If I can't count on him to do those things right, then how can I count on him to do anything?"

"I don't know, darling. I just think you ought to give it another try before you throw it all out in the trash. You've given him seventeen years of your life. Don't you think that deserves the best you've got?"

■ ■ ■

But as the days passed, I only grew more entrenched. I downloaded the A. T. Hamm/ Richie Cabrero book, and reading it flooded me with fresh anger at Adam's pointless deception, because the book was *good*. It was told from Richie's point of view, of course, but I could hear Adam's voice in the cadence of the sentences, the charm of the narrative tone. My husband had tapped into a vein of wry self-deprecation in Richie's personality, and mined it for both humor and pathos that showed even the most outlandish drug-induced bender as a frightening loss of control for a man whose addiction was beginning to overpower him. In anyone else's hands, Richie's story would have been commonplace; but Adam rendered him as vividly, gloriously human, a man with good intentions who lost his way in the dark and made it back a better person.

It was a spectacular piece of work. Adam should have been proud of it, because *I* was proud, even as I was furious. He should have shared it with me — should have shared the others, too, so I could have buoyed him up and encouraged him to own this gift he had, rather than hiding it in favor of some phony pretense of literary preciousness. I should have been supporting him, not wallowing in ignorance. But he'd thought I'd be disappointed. He hadn't trusted me. He hadn't let me in.

I'd thought nothing could hurt more than the affair. I was wrong.

I officially marked the Friday before Labor Day as the end of the fifth week of my separation. New York's requirements stated simply that the marriage must have been over for at least six months and could not be saved. "Could not be saved" was something of a matter of opinion — my opinion, specifically — but the time frame was reassuringly factual. As of January 28 of next year, I would be eligible to file. It felt simultaneously way too far away and way, way too close.

"Does your lawyer need me to sign anything?" said Ruby, a couple of hairs too eagerly. She'd been unaccustomedly solemn when I told her I had decided on a divorce, and reassured me that I was doing the right thing. "I can vouch for the fact that Adam hasn't lived here since I arrived."

"Ehh, I haven't called a lawyer yet. I'm

not sure I'm ready to make it quite that official."

"But what about all the financial stuff, and the house, and —"

I cut her off with a quelling look. "Yeah. *Really* not ready to tackle that."

She shrugged. "Fair enough."

Which, I decided, was not a bad mantra for me to live by when everything I'd counted on about my relationship had been turned upside down. If anything so much as came within range of making sense — "fair enough" it would be.

14

Hang on to your hat. Hang on to your hope. And wind the clock, for tomorrow is another day.
— E. B. White to Mr. Nadeau,
March 30, 1973

"You're out of milk," said Jonathan, in a tone of bemused condemnation. "You maniacs have seven different kinds of cereal, but somehow you are *out of milk.*"

He was standing in front of my refrigerator, the doors flung wide and the whitish glow from the interior reflecting on his sharp profile and his Sugar & the Hi-Lows T-shirt.

"Let's be honest, the milk is really just a substrate," said Ruby. "Water works equally well."

"It absolutely does not, and that's disgusting. First item on your list: *milk.* Then we need to get some vegetables into you two.

You're basically one step away from scurvy."

"Arrr, me hearties," said Ruby.

"This is your fault, right?" he said, spinning to face her. "Care usually eats like a functional human being."

"Well, I've never left my husband before," I said. "Don't they say when the going gets tough, that's when you find out who you really are?"

"I don't think they were talking about breakup eating, darlin'." He closed the refrigerator doors with a sigh. "All right, let's hit the market."

Jonathan at a farmers' market is like — well, in order not to say it's like a kid in a candy store, let me say it's like a gold digger in a jewelry store. He invariably overbuys, much like he over-orders anytime we're out for a meal; he just has to try everything. But it was fun to follow him from stand to stand, laughing as Ruby mimicked his painstaking sorting through a sprawling pile of salad greens, feeling the afternoon sun on my face and the breeze toying with my hair. Just for the hell of it, I bought some beautiful amber-gold honey and a brick of homemade lavender soap. Pausing at a table overflowing with yellow, red, burgundy, and green heirloom tomatoes, I marveled at the heavy weight of them in my hand. What the hell, maybe I'd try growing a few things of my own next summer — there'd be no Adam to tease me if I screwed it up.

When we returned from the market, Ruby and I dropped the bags on the island and began unloading them, while Jonathan plugged his phone into the speaker and clicked over to the playlist he wanted. It was a long-standing rule: When he cooked, he got control of the tunes. Mouthing the lyrics to the song, he started to prep the ingredients for his marinade, moving around my kitchen like it was his own. I handed him the garlic and the thyme, which he set to work mincing, then uncapped the bottle of olive oil and glugged a healthy pour of it into his favorite stoneware mixing bowl. He liked that bowl because it was clean, white, simple. Heavy enough to stay put from its own weight, not tippy like a stainless one.

The strange and unwelcome thought pushed in that, at this point, I'd have to say I knew Jonathan better than I knew my own husband. But of course, Jonathan himself would find it creepy that I was taking inventory. I wondered what little pieces of mystery he was holding back from me, his closest friend. The fact that he'd thought about kissing me before had certainly been a new one.

It was the first time we had seen each other since that day, and things were . . . fine. We'd been friends for way too long to have our orbit misaligned by one glancing asteroid blow. We'd agreed to avoid a repeat of any weirdness in the future. Yet still it pricked at me, this physical awareness of him I'd never had before. I knew what that beautiful hair of his felt like between my fingers. Knew what my lower lip felt like when he grazed it with his teeth.

"Don't you need to measure anything?" said Ruby. "To make sure it has the right balance?"

Jonathan smiled and sliced a lemon in half, then juiced it through a strainer into the bowl. "Pretty sure I could make a grill marinade in my sleep."

"Duh, Ruby," my sister said, rolling her eyes. Ruby's ability to poke fun at herself for a flat joke or a dumb comment has always been one of my favorite traits about her. I aspire to it myself. "Here, let us help you chop the veggies," she said, grabbing an onion and diving her knife into it. Lengthwise. I took a breath and started counting.

Jonathan made it to four before he couldn't take it.

"Hey, you know what? It's better if you cut them horizontally. Like so, see? They

211

hold together better on the grill."

"Oh," said Ruby. "That makes sense." She sliced the rest of her onion into perfect quarter-inch-thick rings, then leaned forward to grab a zucchini from the farmers' market loot. "What about zucchini — do you think I can handle that?"

I made a snorting noise as Jonathan gazed at her blankly. Then he glanced from me, helplessly dissolving into giggles, to Ruby's artificially innocent smile, and shook his head.

"Assholes," he muttered. "Tell me again why I'm cooking dinner for you?"

"So we can feed your ego by praising you," Ruby said.

"Yeah, that'll do," he said, grinning. "Hey Care, pick us a bottle from Adam's stash. Something expensive."

Afternoon drifted into evening, and as the sun glazed the grass with gold between the stretching blue shadows of the trees, we sat in a row on the back porch sofa, drinking the wine while the veggies cooked on the grill. After the first bottle, Ruby went to the kitchen and emerged with a refill clutched in one fist. She plunked down into her spot to the left of me, raised the bottle, and swigged directly from it.

"Why stand on ceremony?" she said, wiping her lip as Jonathan and I gaped at her.

"Gross," I said, and Jonathan started laughing.

"What, are you worried about backwash? I heard that's not really a thing. Or maybe it was double dipping that's not really a thing. Whatever. Here, Blaster, you have some."

It dawned on me, as I lowered the wine bottle from my lips a few minutes later and passed it to Ruby, that this was the best time I'd had in a very long time. Before this visit of hers, I had forgotten what pure fun it could be to spend time with my sister. And I didn't know how I could have forgotten a thing like that, except that I had a vague but persistent feeling it had something to do with Adam.

"Care, can you grab me some plates? We're almost ready to go here." Jonathan rolled the lid of the grill back, and a deliciously scented puff of smoke billowed into the air.

But before I could snap my attention back to the present, Ruby skipped into the kitchen, then reappeared laden with plates, silverware, and my favorite vintage linen placemats and napkins. She refilled each of our wine glasses and positioned the bottle in the middle of the table with the dying sunlight illuminating its brilliant green depths.

"Wait," she muttered, and evaporated again, returning bearing a small, roughly glazed gray ceramic jar with a few stems of maroon and orange daylilies in it. I'd forgotten I even had it, let alone where I'd put it, but it looked unexpected and wonderful holding the boldly colored lilies. She placed the jar in the center of the table and then climbed onto my bench, shooting down at the table with her iPhone camera.

"Ruby, what are you doing?" I said.

"The table looks so pretty," she said, a defensive note in her voice.

"Hey, Martha Stewart, sit your butt down and eat," grumbled Jonathan, setting a plate down at the spot closest to her. "Ain't gonna cook for you again if you let my food get cold."

She dropped onto the bench and speared a hunk of swordfish with her fork. "Oh my god, this is delicious," she mumbled, eyes closed with bliss. "Seriously, Jonathan, this is amazing."

And she was right. It was heavenly. Cooked to the perfect degree of tenderness and bursting with flavor. "Blaster, you've done it again," I said, saluting him with my wine glass.

"You're gonna have to stop calling me that," he said, lifting a finger from his glass to point at me. "I'm only doing serious dating now. You're looking at a reformed man."

A small starburst of jealousy exploded inside me. "Wait, are you seeing somebody?" I squeaked. "You didn't tell me!"

"No. But when I do, it's gonna be legit."

I waited a beat, pointedly. "Yyyyyyyyokay. Whatever you say." Come to think of it, I wasn't entirely certain how I felt about the prospect of Jonathan dating someone again. I wasn't sure I minded — it's not like I was any kind of candidate — but I wasn't sure I didn't mind, either.

As the meal wound to a close, Ruby and I drooped against each other on the bench, too sleepy from wine and good food to move. Then suddenly she bestirred herself.

"Jesus Christ, enough Man Rock already," said Ruby, climbing to her feet. She marched over, yanked the speaker cable from Jonathan's phone, and plugged it into her iPhone. (The latest model, of course; Ruby prided herself on being a tech-y girl and had a full suite of Apple products, none of which exceeded the thickness of a Saltine.) The air filled with slow, loping guitar notes that intertwined and rolled over each other, one flickering off to the side while the other held steady on a repeating riff. It was aimless but sort of pleasant.

"You took off Apache Relay for the Grateful Dead?" Jonathan said.

"I need to get my mellow on. And this is the second best 'Scarlet'/'Fire' ever recorded." Ruby disappeared into the house and returned a few minutes later carrying her vaporizer and a small nugget of weed. I had no idea how she hadn't run out of the stuff already.

"Ruby, exactly how much marijuana is under my roof at the moment?"

"Never you mind," she murmured, smushing the bud into the grinder.

I watched as she twisted the grinder, then tapped the ground leaves into the chamber. "Is it enough to get me arrested?"

"It's enough to get you mellow," she said, and flashed a grin at me as she clicked the vaporizer into life. After a few minutes, she put the pipe to her mouth, inhaled deeply, then pursed her lips and aimed a jet of white vapor into the air. "You really should try some."

"What have I said to you the last four times you've offered me that?"

"You've asked me if it's going to make the house stink, and I've said no, and you've refused to try it, and I've told you you were

216

missing out. Jonathan?"

He shook his head, smiling. In fifteen years, I have never even seen Jonathan *drunk* — that is how rigidly he controls himself.

"Wow, you guys are lame," muttered Ruby. "Care, come on. Just try it. It's not going to turn you into a druggie. Live a little. Do something Adam wouldn't expect of you."

And of everything she could have said, that is the one that needled me. And she knew it. She poked the pipe in my direction, one eyebrow raised as she waited for me to take it.

"Fine."

The vaporizer was warm in my hand as I stared at it. Small and sleek, this, too, was perfectly Ruby — the dorky head-shop bongs I remembered from her college days were long gone. I put it to my lips, then hesitated. "What if I take too much?"

"You're not going to take too much. It'll be a miracle if you even get anything off it your first time."

I closed my lips around the pipe and tentatively drew, while Ruby and Jonathan watched, their faces suspended in anticipation. But when I opened my mouth to do Ruby's smoke-jet trick, the white vapor billowed freely from my lips.

217

Ruby snorted. "I knew it. Have you ever even smoked a cigarette before? This is a little harder, you've got to really drag on it. Don't just breathe it into your mouth, suck it into your lungs. Here, try again. Get ready — now drag, deep, like you're filling your whole chest up."

I did as she said, then clapped my lips shut in surprise at the sensation.

"Okay, breathe again," said Ruby, and then she crowed as I released a huge gust of vapor amid an attack of frantic coughing.

"Ohhh! There it is! You know it's a good hit if you cough like that."

"Why is this fun?" I gasped.

"Just ride it out. You'll calm down in a second. And then you will start to get happy. Jonathan, you sure you don't want to partake?" she said, flipping the vape back and forth between her fingers.

"Nah, I'm good," he said.

"Gimme," I said, and grabbed the pipe for another drag. Ruby yelped, but I batted her away. "Look, if I'm going to do some-thing, I better do it all the way. Right?"

"Yeah, but I don't want you getting too wacky your first time out."

"I thought that was the point."

I took another deep inhale, and to my relief it went down a little more smoothly this time. I rolled my head back on the couch between the other two and stared up at the night. The last of the light had just about seeped from the sky, leaving only a silvery-blue glow at the horizon, and the stars were starting to glimmer against the evening dark. The moon had drifted high above the hills beyond the river, so bright it threw shadows on the ground. Somehow, the beauty of the evening eased my gnawing awareness of Adam's absence: It felt impossible I could actually be enjoying an evening without my husband this much, but it was so wonderful to sit here with my sister and my friend and soak up the pleasure of their company.

Gradually, I slid sideways until I could rest my head on Jonathan's chest, and flung my legs across Ruby's lap. Jonathan folded his arm around my collarbones, and I wrapped one hand around his forearm and closed my eyes so I could focus on drifting. His body was radiating heat, and his skin was smooth under my hand. I could feel Ruby tapping out the looping, flickering guitar notes of the song on my shin. Everything in the world felt absolutely wonderful. If this was what weed did, then I'd have to admit I understood the attraction.

"Wow, we've been listening to this song

for an hour and a half now and Jerry hasn't even sung the first verse," said Jonathan.

"Shut up, Blaster," Ruby said.

I started giggling. "When did you get to be such a Deadhead, Rube?"

"In college. I don't know how you could have missed it."

"I was already living with Adam by then," I said.

"Oh, right. Well, it was Vincent who got me into it. Which turned out to be his only worthwhile contribution to my life."

"Ohhh, yeah, I remember Vincent. Mom *hated* Vincent."

"Mom hates all my boyfriends," she said, and took another drag on the vape.

"Not true," I said. "She's liked most of the last few. She definitely liked" — I started laughing before I even formed the first syllable of the word — "Burqhart."

"Shut up," said Ruby, but she was grinning.

"Say what, now?" said Jonathan.

"Ruby got dumped by a guy named Burqhart," I said.

"I did not get dumped," she yelped. "It was a mutual decision."

"That's not what you —"

"I want to go play in the river," my sister announced, surging to her feet so fast that my own legs went flying. I heard the pounding of her feet down the stairs from the deck to the ground, and when I sat upright there she was, standing in the middle of the back lawn, flapping her hands at us to join her. "Come on, you two! It'll be an adventure!"

Jonathan and I looked at each other and shrugged.

I rolled my jeans up to my knees and headed down the lawn. The night was slippery with moonlight, trembling with cicada song; and the grass slid cool and silky against my feet as I walked. When I reached the edge of the river, I paused, uncertain how to proceed. I knew it wasn't more than a foot or so deep here . . . didn't I? How would I know where to step? What if there were sharp rocks I couldn't see?

A few feet away, Ruby extended one leg like a ballerina and swiped the tips of her toes into the water. "Oooh! Shit, that's colder than I thought!"

Jonathan picked his way down the river-bank until the bottoms of his strong calves disappeared underwater. He waded over to where I stood and extended his hand to me. "Come on in, it's nice."

"Of course you think it's nice, Mountain Boy," yelled Ruby. " 'Look at me, I spent my childhood frolicking in the Smokies, I lost my fear of frigid water when a bear kidnapped me when I was three years old.' . . ."

"No, I find it nice because it's actually not cold," he said, not looking at her. He curled his fingers to beckon me closer. "Come on. Are you as big a wuss as your sister?"

"Screw you!" Ruby launched herself off the bank and landed with a shriek, immediately toppling over onto her hands and knees in the water. Her laughter bounced off the rippling sheet of the river and the arching tree branches above us. Shaking his head, Jonathan waded over to help her up.

Cautiously I stepped down into the river. Cold water swallowed me up to my ankles, but there was nothing sharp where I stood. I closed my eyes and curled my feet around the smooth, slippery rocks I stood on. Gradually, I grew used to the chilly water, and as I relaxed, I decided I liked its gentle tug around my legs. Ruby and Jonathan's voices mingled with the silvery gurgle of the river, and I never wanted to go back inside. Adam and I had lived here for three years; why had we never once played in the river?

After a few moments, I turned and splashed toward Ruby and Jonathan, who were standing together, heads bent in concentration. Then they both looked up as he flicked his hand, releasing a small stone that bounced four times on the surface of the still section of the water near them.

"Lookit," said Ruby, after Jonathan's stone had disappeared beneath the surface. "Tennessee here is showing me how to skip stones."

I turned my palm up, and Jonathan dropped a stone into it, smooth and wet and cool. "Try to throw it so it's almost parallel to the water. The motion with your hand is like you're throwing a Frisbee."

This was another thing I had never done before. One of the casualties of growing up in a city, I guessed. But here I was, frolicking in a moonlit river and throwing stones. I clasped the stone in my fingers, curled my arm inward, and then flung it outward. My stone arced through the air, spinning, and I held my breath as I waited for it to bounce gloriously across the water like Jonathan's had.

But then it hit the surface and sank.

"Shit," I said.

"That was a good try," said Ruby. "Here, try it again. Give her another rock."

Jonathan held his last rock out to me, suspended between his fingers, but I shook my head.

"It's okay. You do it. Show us how it's done."

He let the stone fly, and Ruby and I watched as it skidded across the water before dropping underneath it. When it vanished, we both cheered.

Suddenly, I was overwhelmed with the need to hug them. Grabbing one of them in each arm, I forced them into a triangular hug, and we huddled together like teammates.

"Thank you guys so much for coming up to be with me. I love you both a ton."

"We love you too, Care," said Ruby.

"Yeah," said Jonathan, nudging my head closer so he could kiss my temple, "we love you too."

15

You will do all sorts of things yet, and I will help you. The only thing is not to *melt* in the meanwhile.
— Henry James to Grace Norton,
July 28, 1883

The box on my doorstep should have been the first sign that I was in trouble.

I balanced it on my hip to read the label as I got the front door open. It was surprisingly heavy.

"Ruby?" I called, when I opened the door. "What on earth is this Sephora box about?"

I heard a distant shout, followed by her bare feet pelting along the upstairs hallway and down the stairs. "It came!" she panted, snatching the box from my hands and waltzing it across the room to the kitchen counter.

"What came?"

"My fun kit!" she said, beaming. "You and

225

I, sister mine, are ready to date again. And so we are going to get ourselves looking spectacular."

I watched with alarm as she stripped the packing tape from the box and dove into it. "First of all, I am categorically not ready to date. I can't even turn on my vibrator without getting angry. Second of all, you've spent the last five weeks reverting to a feral state, and now suddenly you want to look pretty again?"

"That's how it works!" she said. "You sink to the bottom, and then when you get tired of dark and murky, you push off and head for the sunlight again."

"Okay, well, you can head for the sunlight, but I'm going to stick with dark and murky for a while, thanks."

"Fine. But at least help me try some of this stuff out."

We poured ourselves some wine as Ruby unpacked her fun kit into an array of small but exuberantly colored packages all over the kitchen counter. Lotions, creams, spritzers, toners — the sheer variety of formats was baffling, let alone the types of application.

"How do you even know where to start?" I said, and she grinned.

"I don't. Here, try this," she said, shoving

a flat pink pouch toward me.

"Wrinkle-minimizing rejuvenation mask? Oh, thanks, Ruby. Or is this where you say 'It's not an insult, it's an observation' again?"

"Fine, give me the wrinkle minimizer. You take" — she rooted among the packages for a moment — "restful relaxation."

I squinted at the tiny lettering on the package. " 'Apply mask to freshly washed face. Leave on for fifteen minutes, then discard mask and massage excess product into skin.' And then what happens? All my worries float away?"

"Yes, along with all my wrinkles. Come on."

I followed her upstairs to the master bathroom, where we scrubbed our faces with a scrumptiously scented exfoliant cream before opening up the mask pouches. I got mine open first and tipped my head back to drape it onto my face, smoothing it into place as I watched Ruby fight with the package on hers. Then she raised her head and looked at me and shouted with laughter.

"Oh my god! What the hell is that thing? You look like Jason freaking Voorhees!"

I spun to face my reflection in the mirror and shrieked. She was absolutely right. The opaque, papery tissue of the mask clung in a damp white oval to my face, with sinister-looking holes for my eyes and mouth. I looked utterly deranged.

"Braaaaaaaauuuughhh," I growled, in my best attempt at whatever threatening noises Jason Voorhees might make from behind his favorite hockey mask, and Ruby squealed and stamped her feet.

"It's so insane," she wheezed. "Your mouth hole is all sideways like your face is melting off, and the flap over your nose is . . . oh my god."

"Put yours on," I giggled. "Don't leave me all alone here."

Shoulders shaking with laughter, Ruby unpeeled her mask from its wrapper and stuck it into place, and when she lowered her hands we laughed all over again because somehow, it was just as funny the second time. And then we looked at each other in the mirror and squealed and laughed again.

"Wait, wait, wait," said Ruby, skidding toward the door. "We have to get a picture of this."

She returned a minute later with her phone, and as she held it at arm's length above us while we experimented with stupid faces, I breathed in her lemony scent and wrapped my arm around her waist and squeezed, because I was just so glad she'd come to visit. And then she had to ruin it by clicking over to her Facebook app, which caused me to lunge toward her phone, shouting "RUBY ELAINE FAIRLEY, DON'T YOU DARE, don't you DARE, I will tell Mom ALL about the weed; *give me that,* you obnoxious little shit!"

I chased her down the stairs and into the kitchen, where she wheeled to face me, holding the phone in my face and wiggling her hand from side to side. I snatched it from her and read.

No such thing as natural beauty. Caroline and I heard Jason's skin stays fresh under that mask.

She'd tagged me in it, of course, but instead of running to my own phone to remove the tag, I suddenly didn't care. We looked dorky and happy and like we were having a hell of a lot of fun, and there wasn't a damn thing wrong with that.

"Nice mask," Neil said to me as he passed me in the hallway on Monday morning. "Any chance you know where I can get my hands on a really sharp machete?"

"Shut up," I mumbled. While I was busy making my little stand for social media authenticity, I'd sort of forgotten I had a few co-workers as friends on my (usually staid) Facebook page.

There was a dramatic whooshing noise behind me, as if someone was slicing a blade through the air.

"Shut *up*!" I yelled. I was absolutely not going to laugh.

"Hey, you know who I heard likes *Friday the 13th* movies? Diana —"

I slammed my office door behind me with a satisfying bang. And it was irritation, more than anything, that made me pick up the phone — so much so that I started with surprise when she actually answered.

"Hello?"

"Diana, hi. It's Caroline Fairley."

"Oh, hey, Caroline. Sorry I haven't called you back, I've been so busy —"

"I'm sure. Honestly I can hardly even imagine. But that's actually what I've been thinking about. I hate the thought of you looking at this as some sort of obligation. Why don't you come up here on a Sunday sometime? We normally open up at eleven, but I can unlock as early as nine, and then you can have the whole place to yourself. I can walk you through the exhibits, or we can just sit in the kids' galleries and play with paint."

She gave a surprised bubble of laughter. "For real?"

"For real. And if you're tired of all the wining and dining, which I'm guessing you probably are, then come over to my house for brunch. My best friend is a chef, and my one accomplishment in the kitchen was learning how to make scrambled eggs he will happily eat."

"Still buddies with Jonathan, huh? That's good to hear."

Despite the friendly words, there was a tightness in her voice that hadn't been there before. Had Jonathan neglected to tell me about mowing down Diana with his very special artillery fire? Damn that boy. I was going to kill him.

"Yeah, uh, yeah. But we can do whatever you want. Tell me what would make you feel like a guest instead of a target."

"Wow," she said after a moment. "You have no idea how appealing that is."

I did a silent, slow-motion fist pump and spun in place, tangling myself in my phone cord. "I'm glad. Tell me what date would work for you, and we'll make it happen."

"What's the name for those songs they play in baseball?" I said, leaning into the open doorway of Neil's office a few minutes later. "When the batters step up to the plate and they blast their favorite pump-up song?"

231

"Walk-up songs?" he said, grinning.

"Yes. Imagine that mine is playing right now." I swaggered into the office and swung an imaginary bat, sending an equally imaginary baseball flying over the park fence.

"I don't think Jason Voorhees really has a walk-up song. You're thinking of *Jaws*."

"Okay okay, forget the walk-up song and just ask me what I did."

"All right. What did you do?"

"Oh, I just got Diana Ramirez to agree to come up for a private tour at the end of next month, and then join me for brunch at my house afterward," I said, picking a stray thread off my cardigan with exaggerated nonchalance. "You should join, also."

Neil stretched back in his desk chair, arms behind his head. "Oho! Will you look at that? And from the woman who said she wasn't a schmoozer. Nice job, Caroline, that's great. That's fantastic, actually. It's a perfect opportunity. Personal and undemanding — you caught what would make her comfortable. Very well done."

"Thank you."

"And very gracious of you to invite her to your home. Will your husband be around, or is he the stay-in-hiding-till-they're-gone type?"

And, all of a sudden, here it was. My first

confession to the public at large. "Oh. Ah, actually, Adam won't be joining. He and I . . . well, we've split up."

"Oh, man," said Neil softly. "Damn, I am awfully sorry to hear that."

And I could tell that he was, without the slightest hint of salacious curiosity — he was just sorry. Neil, I remembered just then, had lost his wife to a sudden illness about a year and a half ago; his loss was more catastrophic than mine, and untainted by betrayal. But still, he knew what it was to lose the person you'd planned to spend your life with, the future you'd thought you'd have. He wasn't going to pity me and he wasn't going to gossip; and, unexpectedly, I didn't mind him knowing at all.

"Yeah. It's been a pretty weird couple of months."

"When did — Sorry," he said, holding his hands palms up. "Not my business."

"It's okay. End of July is when it started. It's weird, it's like half of me expects him to come home any day now, and the other half of me can barely believe that I was really married for ten years, because if I was, why on earth would we not be together now?"

Neil blew air softly through his teeth, shaking his head. "Man, do I ever know what that feels like. It does get better, eventually. That sense of alienation."

"Thank you. For telling me that, I mean." My fingers drifted to my rings, and spun them. "You're the only person I've told outside of my immediate family and my best friend. I am absolutely dreading it. To the point that it's going to be awkwardly late by the time I tell people."

He shrugged. "Do what you've got to do. Just, you know . . . try to make sure you get enough air. Don't isolate yourself too much. That's not a good place to be."

"*Divorce* is not a good place to be," I said. "But I'm okay. My sister has been visiting the last few weeks, so I'm not home alone drowning in a bowl of ramen."

"Well, if you ever do hit the ramen stage, make sure you reach out to your friends. Most people won't know what to say or do — they can get a little paralyzed — so ask them. If you want company, say so."

"Thanks, Neil. That's a good thing to hear. By the way, though . . . dare I ask what comes after the ramen stage?"

His lips moved in a faint approximation of a smile. "Not sure, actually. Still trying to figure that one out myself."

16

I never used to know anything about loneliness. Sir have you robbed me of my selfsufficiency?

— Kathleen Scott to her husband, polar
explorer Robert Scott, November 1908

In a wholly unprecedented feat, Jonathan managed to get off the Saturday following Labor Day weekend as well, and made the long drive up to visit me once more. He cooked our dinner out on the porch again, even though a light rain beaded the waiting plates stacked on the grill; the middle of September was use-it-or-lose-it season in western Massachusetts. The first crests of color had settled into the trees around the house, and the quality of the light was changing from summer-green to the golden cast of early autumn. And this time, I actually asked for Ruby's weed. It amused me to think of how astonished Adam would be.

"Okay, so don't laugh," I said to Ruby a few days later, as we sat together in companionable quiet after dinner. "But apparently there's a Grateful Dead tribute band playing in Northampton the first weekend in October, and they're supposed to be pretty good. We could go down, crash in a hotel for the night, frolic in some leaves the next day, and come home."

She looked up from painting her nails at the kitchen island and gave me a florid double take. "Excuse me, *what* did you say?"

"I know, I know."

"My sister, who never met a weepy, acoustic-guitar-playing songwriter she didn't like, wants to go see a Grateful Dead *tribute band*?"

"You should be gratified by your influence on me," I muttered, peering at the concert info on my phone. "Tickets are only twenty bucks — that's not bad. So are you just going to make fun of me, or would you actually want to go? I thought it would be a slam dunk for you."

She blew on her nails for a moment, then scrunched her mouth and nose sideways. "Actually, Care, I was thinking it's probably about time for me to go back to the city."

Dread spiraled through me at her words. Though I'd known, of course, that she wouldn't stay forever, I'd gotten used to her here. "I've grown accustomed to her face," as the lyric from *My Fair Lady* goes. And I think I had thought that whenever she did go, I would be ready for it — happy to be by myself again. I would wave her off with a light heart and a cheerful smile, thinking, *Well, that was fun, but now I'm ready to get on with it.*

I was not ready to get on with it. I felt sad, and lonely, and scared at the thought of how much sadder and lonelier I would be without my sister around. *Ramen stage, here I come.*

"Oh," I said, and words started spilling out of her.

"You're going to be totally fine. You're going to do awesome. We can still talk on the phone all the time, and I can come back on the weekends sometimes, and —"

"Jesus Christ, am I that pathetic?" I snapped. Even though, clearly, I was. I wasn't used to being needy, and I hated it. I hated that this was who I was right now. Hated that Adam had put me here and I didn't automatically know how to be strong by myself. What if I never figured it out?

"You're not pathetic," Ruby said, in the tone that people use to soothe the overly dramatic. I recognized it, because it was usually me using it on her. "You're going through something incredibly hard."

"I'm fine," I said, springing to my feet and beginning to load our dinner things into the dishwasher. "You don't need to baby-sit me. And you obviously can't stay here forever. Do you have some good prospects on jobs?"

"I'm getting pretty busy with my own clients, actually. It's amazing. People are referring me like crazy. Design*Sponge picked up a floral styling post I did, and I got a bazillion hits from it. I need to buy that woman a six-pack."

"That's fantastic, peanut. And god knows you're not going to meet the next Burqhart up in this neck of the woods."

She snorted. "I don't want to meet the next Burqhart. I wanna get me a real man, thank you very much."

"Well then," I said. "Get thee to Manhattan."

"I really will come back to visit," she said. "I don't want to completely abandon you."

"You're not abandoning me," I said, hoping if I said it that would make it feel true. "I'm a big girl."

"I know, but —"

I slapped the kitchen towel over the handle on the dishwasher and mashed the fabric down into the gap. "Ruby. I'm fine.

238

The last thing I want is you hanging out with me out of pity."

"It's not pity," she said, toying with the cuff of her sweatshirt. "Is it okay with you if I actually like hanging out with you?"

I wanted to tell her how much I'd loved having her here, but I wasn't sure how. We weren't good at this, Ruby and I. We never had been.

"I know. This has been a lot of fun."

"We haven't spent this much time together since we were kids, do you realize that? Since we were really young. Even before you left for college, all you did was hang out with Adam. And then every summer when you came home, you were inseparable. I seriously have not seen this much of you since I was eleven years old."

"That's not true," I said, but she nodded, her loose ball of golden hair wiggling on top of her head.

"Um, selective memory much? Of course it's true. It was always Adam with you. Adam this, Adam that. You were constantly spending time with him."

"Well, but . . . you and I were never the right age to 'hang out' anyway, though," I said, grasping at anything that would alleviate my sudden rush of guilt.

She bobbed her head toward one shoulder.

239

"No, you're right. Five years is a big gap when you're young. I'm not trying to blame you or anything. Just saying it's nice to get closer with you now, that's all."

She might not have been blaming me, but the more I thought about it, the more it sank in how impenetrable I must have been. Adam and I had been a couple for so long that we had become a single word: Adam-andCaroline. There was literally no space in between us.

"Yeah . . . I see what you mean. And it's been good to have you here. Really good." We shared a shy smile before I continued. "Well, since you're leaving me to my own devices, the least you can do is coach me through the rest of this."

She gnawed on a strand of her hair. "Care, the one advantage of the fact that I have failed to even approach a decent shot at marriage is that I have not yet had the chance to get divorced."

"No, but you've had breakups. You've helped friends through their breakups. You got me as far as watching bad TV, eating reprehensible food, and beautification. What's the rest of the process?"

"I'm not sure I like being pegged as a breakup expert."

"I am seeking your advice and wisdom here!"

She sighed dramatically, but I could tell it was working. Everyone likes being asked for advice, and Ruby likes it more than most.

"I don't know, just do stuff that makes you feel good about yourself. Do things that Adam never wanted to do. Blast victorious breakup songs — and no, not 'I Will Survive.' "

"All the breakup songs I know are depressing."

"Jo Dee Messina," Ruby said. "The woman is like the poet laureate of 'Later, loser' songs."

"Jo Dee Messina. Okay. What else?"

"That's all I can think of for right now. Except, as one last component under beautification — you need your nails did." She patted the counter stool next to her, then waved her other hand expansively at the group of nail polish bottles she had set up in a neat row. "What color do you want?"

Oddly, the question threw me. I wasn't used to nail polish; Adam had always preferred my hands without it. "Can you just do it clear?"

"I think you need Rum Raisin," Ruby said.

"Why even ask me?"

"To give you the illusion of free will," she

said, shaking the bottle of plummy polish back and forth. She wiggled her other fingers at me. "Gimme."

I placed my right hand in hers, mesmerized as she swept the polish across my nails in one smooth stroke after another. She was right; it looked pretty. I was fairly certain this would count as my first effort to look anything more elevated than "clean" since this whole thing began.

Ruby set my completed hand aside and gestured for the other one. Then she got halfway across and stopped.

"Hey, Care?"

"Hmm?"

She brushed her thumb gently across my fingers. "Are you really going to leave him, do you think?"

I nodded. *Are you going to leave?* was still a squishier question to answer than *Are you divorcing him?*, but I was letting myself have that. "Yeah. I am."

"What do you think about these?" she said, tapping my ring finger.

I stared. She was right. I'd taken the rings off countless times before, to wash dishes or put on lotion; but I'd always put them back on. Force of habit, I had been telling myself. I couldn't imagine what my hands would look like without them.

Careful not to smear my brand-new Rum Raisin, I pulled the rings free and set them on the counter beside me with a soft metallic clink. I stared at my hands to assess, but the sight was less jarring than I'd imagined. Because it turned out that after all, my left hand only looked just like my right one. Minus two last naked fingernails.

"Finish me up?" I said to Ruby, and she smiled.

I am mastering my love for you and turning it inwards as a constituent element of myself.

— Jean-Paul Sartre to
Simone de Beauvoir, 1926

If I'm being honest with myself, I will admit that most of the reason I moved to Massachusetts is October. In fact, I could even narrow it down to the first half of the month, when every tree in sight bursts into flame against a clear sky vibrating with sunlight. With apologies to the rest of the country, I don't see that there's a more perfect place to experience autumn than in New England. All those postcard images are real: maples stretching hundred-year-old branches over wooden houses far older still; drifts of confetti-like leaves amassing on lawns and against fences; pristine church steeples craning into skies so fiercely blue they make your eyes hurt.

There has always been something about fall that makes my nerves ring with rightness. The scents of dried leaves and woodsmoke, the taste of cider, the familiar sight of pumpkins, gourds, and flint corn: I love it all. I also love the ritual of unpacking my cold-weather garb: my sweaters with their Fair Isle patterns and chunky cable knits; the merino tights I wear with wedge-heeled pumps and Mary Janes until winter forces me to concede the end of skirt season and embark on four months of Sorel boots.

Fall used to feel like an anniversary of sorts, for Adam and me — although we married in June, it was in October that he'd kissed me for the first time, all those many years ago. And October again when we made love in a pile of blankets in front of his parents' fireplace. Although logically, the season was an ending — the end of bloom, the end of green, the end of warmth as our hemisphere slipped away from the sun — it had always made my blood race with the sense that something was starting.

As I drove to the hardware store one crisp October afternoon, the canopy of leaves above me glowing like the inside of a buttercup, I drew on that feeling. Because the empty house had grown oppressive in the week and a half I'd spent without my sister around, I had decided to fill the void with one of the items on her breakup recovery list — do the things Adam wouldn't do. In this case specifically, painting the inside of our house anything other than white.

I remembered poring over the paint deck with Adam before we moved in, fingers rifling back and forth between the cards. As per the instructions I had read in some decorating magazine, we examined the swatches under the light of our wobbly halogen floor lamp, then again by daylight. But though he accepted my insistence on evaluating the colors under different lighting, all he would ever tolerate was white. It was a warm, cozy, friendly white, not the blue-white of the snow that clung to the wooded hillside across the road in January; but white it was just the same.

This time, I was going to paint the house the way I wanted.

The clang of a bell announced my entrance into the hardware store. The guy behind the counter glanced up from his magazine (Rifles? Boobies? Or, wait — let me not make heteronormative assumptions here — leather bears?) and flicked his eyes in my direction.

"Hi there. What can I help you with?"

When I explained what I needed, he led me to the section at the back where the whole array of paint color cards spread out in ranks. I grabbed one at random: browns. With sort of a reddish cast. Five ever-so-slightly-different tints of reddish brown. And next to it, a card of infinitesimally more yellowish browns. There were *hundreds* of colors here. Now that I wasn't restricted to the whites deck, how the hell was I even going to know where to start?

"I'd suggest you try a sample," the clerk said. "Even if you think you like something, sample it on your wall first. We can mix you a pint, or you can see if the color you like is on here." He gestured to a revolving rack of small jars filled with colored paint — pre-mixed sample pots. Aha! This . . . this I could work with.

When the clerk returned to his spot at the counter, I approached the rack. My eyes landed on a pot in a tawny brown the color of homemade caramel, then another in a rich blackberry purple. I put them both in the plastic basket I'd slung over my forearm. Next I spotted my favorite color of all, the golden olive green of an empty wine bottle. Chocolate, cranberry, pear — anything that reminded me of something delicious to eat went into my basket. I hadn't the faintest idea which room I even intended what color for; I was just buying my own personal rainbow.

The heavy thump of the basket on the counter brought the clerk's head up from his magazine.

"Gracious," he said. "How many rooms you painting there?"

I set my credit card on the counter with a brisk snap. "All of them."

The bedroom was the only place to start. Partly this was because its size didn't demand the kind of mental commitment that the living area did, but that wasn't really why. This was the room where Adam and I had made love, and slept with our hearts beating close enough to knock against each other's ribs. I needed to wipe him away.

My new sheets had been a good beginning: a beige ticking stripe pattern, in soft L.L. Bean flannel, perfect for a New England girl. Buying them was almost the first thing I'd done, after Jonathan brought me home that day. Our first grown-up mattress had long since been hauled off to the dump. I had almost finished doing what I needed to feel at peace in this room; painting was the very last thing.

I spread a drop cloth out along the floor

and carefully taped its edge to the base molding of the wall opposite the bed. My habitual meticulousness was high on Adam's list of Caroline Things; if he were here, he'd tease me for this. "You're putting tiny blobs of paint on tiny brushes and rubbing them gently on the wall. You really need to hermetically seal the drop cloth?"

I dipped one of the small, spongy brushes into the first pot of paint, called Roxbury Caramel, and daubed it onto the wall, smoothing it down and out into an even rectangle. When I finished, I stepped back to get a little distance. It looked nice! It looked pretty. But I had so many other colors to test.

Next I opened the blackberry pot and the cranberry one, and laid them up in tidy rectangles in line with the caramel. As I studied them, I saw that a single wavy filament of my hair had stuck itself into the wet paint, and when I stepped toward the wall to remove it, my foot knocked into the pot of cranberry paint I'd left open on the floor. I swore and jumped backward, but thanks to my foresight with the drop cloth, there was no real harm done. Instead, as I stared down at the spilled paint, I was unexpectedly struck by how lovely it was. Richly pigmented, it seeped into a small puddle, its surface glossy in the late afternoon sunlight. I picked it up, scooping as much of the spill as I could back into the pot, then ran my finger around the edge to wipe it clean. And then I dipped two fingers inside the pot, scooped up a gout of paint, and threw it at the wall.

I didn't even realize I'd done it until I saw the paint hit the wall. It was the oddest thing. It was as if my hand had acted independent of my brain, going rogue in an instant to create an act of unpremeditated destruction. The cranberry had landed in the middle of the caramel, splattering outward from the point of impact, and as I watched, droplets began to form and ooze their way down the wall, grudgingly obeying the call of gravity. Messy as it was, the deep red glowed against the caramel, and it was beautiful — sloppy and silly, but beautiful. I put the cranberry pot down, sealed it, and reached for the blackberry.

People who don't know better think Jackson Pollock's work is random, just a haphazard landscape of splattered paint. But they couldn't be more wrong. There is structure there, and rhythm, as precisely judged as a Mozart concerto. Now, to be clear: What I did to my bedroom wall on that October afternoon was almost nothing like what Jackson did, but if he had fun with his work while he did it — well, then, that we had in common.

With my window open to the chilly, leafy-scented breeze, I blasted Jo Dee Messina's victorious breakup songs at a volume that, in New York, would have earned me a neighbor's fist pounding on the wall. It didn't even matter that I didn't especially care for country music; Ruby had been right, this woman knew what the hell she was talking about. And while I danced, and sang, and jumped around with my hands in the air, I painted. Paint after paint after paint — one handful after another, I tossed them at the wall, and something inside me flew loose every time I did. In a few places, I swiped the side of my palm through the splatter, the paint slick under my skin. Now my wall was a Franz Kline.

I painted until the square of dancing leaf shadow and light from my window had tracked its way across the room and vanished. When it grew too dim to see well, I switched on my bedside lamp and surveyed the damage. Every one of my pots was empty; there was $180 of Benjamin Moore spattered all over my bedroom wall. I had created a mad, unholy mess, but it was *my* mess. And I loved every single square inch of it.

October trickled by, one glorious stained-glass day after another, and my life without Adam began, if not to feel normal exactly, then at least to feel like less of a barrage of constant little hurts. He was still writing me letters, and I was still reading them. But I was tossing them into the recycling bin, instead of feeding them into the shredder with bloodthirsty zeal.

The long-awaited visit from Diana Ramirez was scheduled for a few days before Halloween, and I had been polishing my gallery talk and sketching out the points I wanted to make in our conversation. Neil, of course, would be doing a lot of the actual schmoozing, but he'd wanted me to stay involved, and I appreciated his confidence that I'd be an important part of the relationship. Even if, perhaps, the confidence might be a teeny bit misplaced. Under interrogation, Jonathan had sworn on his nephew's immortal soul that he'd never so much as flirted with Diana; but her voice had definitely cooled when I'd mentioned him.

The morning she arrived, the last dapples of October color clung in patches to the mountains, but mostly we were into the

tones of later fall: the smoky brown of leaf-
less trees and the heavy, impenetrable gray
of the clouds that held back the sun. Neil
waited sensibly in the vestibule behind me
while I shivered in my plum-purple duffle
coat and plaid pencil skirt outside the
museum entrance; but I'd wanted to welcome Diana with a human face amid the
sprawling complex of buildings. The leaves
had fallen off the upside-down *Tree Logic*
saplings for the season, which I always hated
because it made them look dead — it didn't
show the way they were thriving in their
unusual situation.

When I saw Diana approaching, I took a
deep breath and walked up to meet her with
my numb-fingered hand extended. Though
I barely remembered her appearance from
college, my impression was that the years
had allowed Diana Ramirez to look like
exactly what she was: a woman who'd spent
her whole life bucking expectations. Topping out at fifty-nine inches if you counted
her distressed black leather sneakers and
spiky, boyish haircut, she had full, rounded
cheeks and shrewd dark eyes. I bet there'd
been a lot of fools who'd taken the cheeks
and the stature as the measure of the
woman, and I pitied every one of them.
Because those eyes told me Diana had swat-

ted them all down like houseflies.

"Hi, Caroline," she said, shaking my hand firmly. No air-kissing for Diana. I liked that. "It's nice to see you; you look well."

"And you, too. How's the Stockbridge place? Are you mostly settled in there now?"

"Settled in? It's been done for months, but this weekend is only the second time I've gotten to use it. It still feels like some-body else's house. One of these days, I guess. Anyway, I'm glad I made it up for this. I can't believe how long it's been since I was here," she said, head swiveling as she looked around her.

"It's grown a lot. So where would you like to start — the Sol LeWitt galleries, maybe?"

She shrugged. "I don't know who that is, but sure. Sounds good."

The museum when it's empty of visitors has always been one of my absolute favorite things. It's such a unique luxury — and that morning, it was just me, Neil, Diana, and some of the greatest art of the last few decades.

Whenever I give a person or a group a tour of the collection, I can always tell whether or not I've got them. It's especially fun with high-school-age kids: 90 percent of them will be bored, checking their phones, shuffling their feet along the polished hardwood floor, but what I live for is that handful of kids who are looking around with bright, fascinated eyes. Kids like I was on that long-ago MoMA tour: wired out of their skin with the excitement of being surrounded by so much creativity.

Diana was not wired out of her skin. She was paying attention, more or less, though I caught her smothering a couple of yawns behind her hand. But she wasn't connecting with any of the artwork. And she kept glancing at her phone like it was a stopwatch timing a race. I met Neil's eyes over her lowered head, and he angled his lower lip down in the universal gesture for "Oy vey."

We took her through Sol LeWitt, through glass artist Randy Allen, and into the football-field-sized Building 5, where three enormous composite sculptures embodying the specter of climate change oozed and crawled around the cavernous, sunlit space.

"*The Island* is my favorite," Neil said to me, after Diana merely nodded in response to my explanation of the artwork. "The image of someone slowly drowning in a rising tide. It's chilling."

"Mine is *The Desert,*" I said, pointing to the dusty brown installation at the far end of the room. "If you can even call that a

favorite, you know — something so terrifying."

After a few beats of silence stretched out
between us, Diana popped her head up with
a guilty expression.

"Crap, I'm sorry," she said. "I'm addicted
to this thing. Goes with the territory, I suppose."

I smiled and nodded, even though I was
pretty sure what I'd seen in my brief glimpse
of her phone was Facebook, not an email
inbox.

"Do you want to call it a wrap for today?
You must be hungry."

"I'm about to start chewing my hand,"
she said cheerfully. "This has been fascinating, thank you, but yeah . . . I'd love a bite
to eat."

I glanced regretfully toward the rest of the
museum; I had really hoped to be able to
show her the Alex Lim installation — it was
one of my favorites. But the lady was my
guest, and my guest was hungry.

"What a lovely house," said Diana when we
arrived at my place, and the sincerity in her
voice was gratifying to hear. With this visit
of hers on the horizon, I had applied myself
to repainting in earnest, and my entire
kitchen and living area were now a warm,

forgiving greige color that perfectly matched the veins in my marble counters. I loved how *me* it was, and it felt oddly intimate, having people in this house I had recast as mine. The funny thing was, aside from painting, there hadn't been a whole lot of Adam to erase.

Diana and Neil parked themselves on the counter stools while I fired up the wood-stove and put coffee on to brew. The gloomy skies had cleared while we were inside the museum, and sunlight splashed across the counter and into the deep white farmhouse sink.

"What's Adam up to today — did you banish him so you could do work stuff?" said Diana, then frowned at my expression. "That's his name, right? Your boyfriend from college? I thought I read in the alumni magazine that you guys got married. Am I going crazy?"

"I banished him," I said with a thin smile. I was pricked by awareness that Neil, who had been studiously staring out the kitchen window throughout this exchange, knew my husband wasn't just gone for the day. I'd felt comfortable telling him about my breakup, but not this woman who'd known me and Adam as intact long before the relationship started rotting from the inside out.

"Poor guy," Diana said. "Gosh, an artist and a writer, you guys are like the ultimate creative power couple."

"I don't really make my own art," I said. "Thankfully for everyone, I figured out early that I'm way better at working with other people's. I had to do those studio classes in college as part of the major."

"I didn't know you were an artist, Care," said Neil.

"I'm not!"

"What was your medium?"

"Mediocrity," I said, and he rolled his eyes at me.

"Look. This woman is a real artist," I said to Diana, gesturing at the framed piece that hung at the end of the dining table, a collage of thickly textured musical notes printed in dark red over sheet music. "This is Farren Walker. She's a local artist who works in mixed media and high-texture printmaking."

"I have no idea what you just said," said Diana.

As I explained a bit about Farren's innovative techniques, I carefully avoided looking at Neil. I had mounted a campaign last year to have Farren and her work featured in a demonstration residency at the museum — a campaign that had been shot out of the sky by my boss, Tom, the museum director. Neil, I recalled, had given it all a regretful side-eye. Despite her engaging personality, Farren — and her lack of national media or gallery attention — were not Neil's cup of tea.

But maybe they might be Diana's. And Farren was worried about her mortgage payments.

"The amazing thing about Farren," I told Diana, "is she's sixty-six years old, and she only started making art seriously about five years ago. She used to work at a T-shirt screen-printing place over in North Adams, and she kept wondering what would happen if she could make screens with some rigidity to them, so they could be used with a thick paint that builds up texture, instead of only the flat ink. Anyway, she's phenomenal. You'd like her a lot."

"I'm sure I would," said Diana, but I knew a polite *Sure, whatever you say* when I heard it.

"It's a special point of focus for MASS MoCA to highlight a diverse group of artists," I said. "We believe that contemporary art is more than just a bunch of middle-aged white guys and Basquiat."

259

It was true — the museum did take diversity seriously, as did I personally, in my curatorial work — but as I said it to Diana it sounded awkward and limp, the verbal equivalent of an admissions catalog cover featuring an artfully multicolored group of friends lounging under a tree. Obvious bait for a woman highlighted in national media as the leading Latina entrepreneur of her generation.

"She's right about that," said Neil without missing a beat. "And, by the way, Caroline didn't just hire a preppy black guy from central casting to show up here today; I really do run the development office."

For an instant I thought my helpless whoosh of laughter was just a little too grateful, until I spotted Diana's grin. Diana's wholly genuine grin. But despite my hope that Neil's brilliant save might tip us into a productive conversation, by the time Diana got to her feet to head back to the city, I couldn't shake the feeling that the meeting had not gone exactly as I had hoped.

When I said as much to Neil, who was tracing shapes on my counter with his empty beer bottle, he shook his head.

"It takes time. It's unusual to be able to create a connection right away. We'll leave her be for a while and then follow up."

"Whatever you think is best. I'm happy to be involved where you think it's useful, but you're still Schmoozer in Chief. At least as far as this operation is concerned."

"Well, consider yourself relieved of duty, if you want. It was great to have you help establish the relationship with her, but I can take it from here. Thank you again for all your efforts."

I folded my arms over my chest and threw my weight into one hip. "Are you kicking me off the mission?"

"Just giving you an out," Neil said, smiling. "I know this wasn't exactly your thing."

I planted my palms on the counter menacingly. "No, sorry, you're stuck with me. Jason Voorhees doesn't give up on his prey after a minor setback like a spear to the face."

"Or getting pumped full of buckshot by a doomed cop," Neil said, cocking his beer bottle at me like a pistol.

I snatched it from him and tossed it into the recycling bin under the sink, but halfway to the fridge for another one, I paused. I was having fun talking with him, but the guy didn't necessarily *want* another beer; he'd been nursing the one I just threw out since after the late brunch we'd shared with

Diana. It was a Sunday afternoon, he'd been working all day, and the only thing he could possibly want was to get back home to his kids. And maybe catch the end of the football game.

"For real, though," I said, turning to face him again. "I've been enjoying this more than I expected to. I'd like to see it through to the end, whatever that will be."

"Deal," he said, popping up his hand to shake on it. "And by the way, I called this. I thought the challenge would get its hooks in you."

And he was right: I wasn't ready to be rid of Diana Ramirez just yet.

18

Beauty one could get to know and fall in love with in one hour and cease to love it as speedily; but the soul one must learn to know.
— Leo Tolstoy to Valeria Arsenev, November 2, 1856

The Monday after Diana's visit passed without event, but on Tuesday afternoon as I was getting ready to leave work, Neil called my desk line.

I pounced aggressively on the phone. "Did you hear from her?"

"No. I was checking to see if you did."

"You told me it was going to take a while!"

"Yeah, but I was still hoping you might have heard something. Hope springs eternal blah blah blah."

"I know, I know," I laughed. "Me too. But I figured I'd give her till next week and then check in."

"That sounds like a plan. Hey, listen," he said, and suddenly I was certain that whatever he was about to say had been the actual reason for his call all along. "This might be too soon for you to consider it, and if it is, then ignore me. But . . . would you ever feel like grabbing a drink after work sometime?"

I stared at the phone console in confusion, as though it were responsible for clarifying to me what exactly had happened. Did he just *ask me out*?

He gave a nervous half laugh. "Caroline?"

"Sorry," I said, struggling to recover. "Uh, sorry, you kind of caught me by surprise."

"No worries," he said instantly. "No worries at all. *I'm* sorry, I shouldn't have put you on the spot like that. Forget I said it. I'll see you tomorrow, okay? Have a good night."

The line clicked off. As I sat there holding the receiver for a good twenty seconds, staring witlessly at my computer screen, I was increasingly sure that, at the advanced age of thirty-three, I had just been asked out by a fully grown adult man for the very first time in my life. And I was also increasingly sure that I had whiffed it. My dad, no doubt, would have had some sort of on-point metaphor involving a wide receiver and a football. But any way you chose to phrase it, I had definitely screwed it up.

Neil from Development! Had asked me out! It was just so unexpected. I mean, I had recognized in the abstract that, since I'd released myself back into the wild after Adam's defection from the Vagina Republic, some sucker might eventually decide that I and my naked left hand were of interest. I just had never imagined that it would happen so soon. Or that it would be Neil who showed the interest.

And yet, I thought, he had. Rank novice though I was, even I could identify that. And I had — what had I done? Confessed that he'd completely startled me, and let him hang up before I even considered the question of whether "grabbing a drink" with him was something that held any appeal. So, I considered it now.

On the one hand, it had never even occurred to me. I'd always vaguely registered him as a good-looking guy — he had the easy smile and relentless symmetry of an L.L. Bean model, with smoky green eyes that popped against his hazelnut-brown skin — but I'd never noticed him That Way, because why would I? But I'd really enjoyed his company the other day, and throughout this whole Diana escapade for that matter. His mild personality invited me to relax when I was around him. And best of all, he'd barely known me, let alone Adam, before any of the shit had hit my personal fan. Which meant that I was pretty sure I wouldn't be required to talk about it at *all*.

Not stopping to think twice, I dialed his extension.

"What's up?" he said, sounding friendly.

"So before . . . you didn't give me a chance to answer."

"Oh! I'm sorry. Then let me ask you again. Caroline, would you ever feel like grabbing a drink after work sometime?"

"Yes, Neil, I would. That sounds lovely."

"Cool," he said, and I could hear the smile in his voice.

We decided on Thursday. I refused to let myself think about it as anything out of the ordinary; it certainly wasn't anything romantic, just a drink at a cocktail bar around the corner from the museum.

But I was surprised at how much I was looking forward to it. And then surprised again, by how much I enjoyed it.

"I promise not to talk about work if you don't," Neil said as soon as we sat down, and it was easy to stick to it. He was full of questions that delved deeper than Caroline 101, in a way that was perceptive but not intrusive ("Five years sounds like a tough gap for sisters — are you close?"), and I liked everything I learned about him in return. He'd lived in New England his whole life: grew up in Vermont, went to college in Connecticut (yes, Yale; no, he hadn't known Adam; and no, he did not still have the umbrella), grad school in Boston.

"Which makes you a Red Sox fan," I said. "That's deplorable."

"You're a Queens girl; you like the Mets, not the Yankees."

I shook my head. "Doesn't matter. It's still deplorable. Any self-respecting New Yorker hates the Red Sox."

"Well, I'm sorry to break it to you, but you're living in enemy territory."

"Don't remind me," I grumbled. "The goddamn Red Sox and the stupid Pats."

"Hey!"

"Oh come on. I do, actually, like the Giants, but even if I didn't, it wouldn't matter. The entiiiiiiiiire nation despises the freaking Patriots."

"Because they're jealous," he muttered, stretching back in his seat and crossing his arms over his chest as though the matter was closed.

I grinned. I was flirting with him. And I liked it. I liked *him*. And the more I liked him, the more I liked his full lips and his pretty eyes and his voice that ran over me like cool water on a hot day. I was a little bummed when, a few minutes later, he signaled the bartender for our tab.

"I gotta get home to the girls," he explained. "My neighbor has them for a play date, and I don't want to keep her waiting."

"How old are they again?"

"Annie's almost three, Clara's five."

"Cute," I said, straining to remember if I had ever met the girls at a museum event, but coming up blank.

"I had fun hanging out with you," he said as we folded ourselves into our coats. Getting ready to go outside in Massachusetts in November takes long enough that you can start and finish a whole new branch of conversation while it's happening.

"Me too," I said.

"Maybe dinner next week?"

"Sure. Sounds good."

"Cool," he said again. "It's a plan."

At the exact same second I said, "It's a date," and then I closed my eyes, willing the appalling social hiccup away. But when I opened them again, he was smiling like he'd just discovered an unexpectedly good toy in his Cracker Jack box.

"Yes," he said, and pushed the door open for me with one leather-gloved hand. "It is."

■ ■ ■ ■

The prospect of my first real adult date threw me for more of a loop than I could admit without shame. Only a combination of pride and indignation kept me from recruiting Ruby for help. Despite her promises, she had evaporated after her return to New York. "Look nice and be yourself" was Jonathan's helpful contribution. Because yes, I'd been desperate enough to ask him for advice. I didn't really want to think about the fact that, seeing as my last romantic interaction with a man involved throwing myself at my best friend of fifteen years because I was so freaking desperate to feel desirable to someone, it might be too soon for me to start dating. But this wasn't even "dating" yet, it was just "a date." Big difference.

And so I focused on my clothes: Should I be casual and cute in jeans and a nice top? Or should I make more of an effort? We were only going to dinner at a new restaurant that had opened in North Adams a few weeks before; I didn't want to overdo it. Finally I decided that if Neil had thought I was pretty enough to ask out in my work outfits, I might as well stay in my comfort zone — with maybe just a little hint more boob.

Jesus. This was my life now?

The evening of the date — Saturday night, like a proper date — I was still wrapped in my towel, trying to remember which direction the chick on YouTube had said I was supposed to apply my eye shadow, when Neil called.

"Hey," he said. "I am incredibly sorry to do this, but my sitter just bailed at the last minute. Would you be up for coming over here for dinner? I'll run out with the troops and grab some stuff to cook."

As his voice rumbled pleasantly in my ear, I was acutely aware that I was wearing nothing but a towel. Neil had a very nice voice. Neil had a very, very lovely voice indeed.

"Caroline?"

"Oh, um, sure," I stammered, warmth suffusing my body.

"If you'd rather reschedule, I completely understand. Just say the word."

I felt a spurt of anxiety at the thought of meeting his children. I hadn't thought I'd meet them so soon. Hadn't really thought about meeting them at all, actually.

"I don't mind, but . . . are *you* sure?"

"Well, yeah, I invited you over. You're my friend. I'm allowed to have a friend over who is a woman, right?"

It was supposed to be a rhetorical question, but he sounded unconvinced. "You are. But —"

"It's okay. Don't sweat it. Let's reschedule for some other time."

But the thing was, I'd been looking forward to seeing him. "No," I said, with awkward force. "I'll come. Same time?"

"Sure," he said, sounding relieved. He cared! He was glad I hadn't canceled!

"Okay. Send me the address and I'll see you in a little while."

Neil and his daughters lived in a large loft apartment on the top floor of one of the buildings on the main historic street in North Adams, a short drive from the museum. When he opened the door for me, smiling, I felt a flash of awkwardness — this was Neil from Development, greeting me in his home in jeans and a plaid flannel button-down, while children's voices chimed behind him and the scent of cooking filled the air — but he gave me an easy kiss on the cheek and reached out his arms for my coat.

"Guys, come greet our guest," he called, and the voices stopped. But no children were forthcoming.

Neil rolled his eyes and led the way from

the foyer. "Manners are always a work in progress, I'm afraid."

When we reached the kitchen, two small faces were turned to me, alight with interest. The girls were beautiful children, with big, curious eyes. Clara, the five-year-old, had Neil's striking eyes and watchful expression; Annie, almost three, looked more like her mother. I knew this not just by process of elimination; photos of the whole family sprawled along the wall leading to the front door. Eva Crenshaw had had eyes the color of Guinness, a head full of exuberant curls, and a warm, joyful smile. Unthinkable that someone so vibrant could have been wiped out so quickly.

I knew exactly what had happened; it was one of those stories that gnawed at you, even if the people involved were strangers. She'd started feeling unwell on a Wednesday, went to the hospital Friday. Lapsed into a coma on Saturday, and by Monday she was gone. An infection. Incomprehensible. Horrifying. I remembered signing the sympathy card for Neil, crowding my name in alongside our other co-workers'. Every signature was written with kind wishes, but they were only people's names — none of us had been able to offer any thoughts beyond the message in Hallmark script that limped across the center of the card. Because there was nothing. Just absolutely nothing you could say.

I remembered something else, too: coming home from work that day, and walking straight to Adam's office so I could hug him. It's what you do when tragedy lands close enough to brush you with its breeze; you gather your loved one close, so you can feel the thump of their heart and the sturdiness of their body while you drown in gratitude. I clutched Adam like that, and he clutched me back when I told him why.

And now look.

"Guys, this is my friend Caroline," said Neil. "She works at the museum with me." I swallowed a smile at his refusal to refer to himself as third-person "Daddy."

"Do you guys like art?" I asked, reasonably confident that this would elicit a response. All kids liked art.

Annie nodded, but Clara's expression did not change.

"Do you like painting, Annie? I like painting, too."

"I made those," she said, pointing to the wall over the dining table, which was adorned with framed artwork that had unmistakably been authored by the girls.

"No you didn't, not all of them," said Clara.

"Which ones are yours, Clara?"

Scrunching her little mouth, she pointed. "The blue one."

"That's beautiful," I said. "You both make beautiful paintings."

"I made more," said Annie. "I can show you." She made as if to hop down from her stool, but Neil stilled her with a gesture.

"We're going to eat soon, honey. You can show Caroline your paintings after dinner."

I hadn't been sure what to expect, what with the unscheduled unfamiliar children and all, but as the evening wore on I found myself thoroughly enjoying both the company of the girls and the glimpse at Neil's way with them. He didn't baby them, but talked to them like they were little adults, responding seriously to their questions and comments despite what must have occasionally been an overpowering desire to laugh. Unsurprisingly, they were bright and precocious children.

"All right, team," said Neil, getting up from the table. "Put your plates in the dishwasher, and then it's bath time and sleepy land for you. Care, I'm sorry, do you mind flying solo for a little while?"

"Not at all," I said. "Good night, ladies. It

was nice to meet you."

Unprompted, Annie suddenly cast herself at me and wrapped her sturdy little arms around my legs. "G'night," she mumbled into my thigh.

"Good night, sweetie," I said, laying my hand on her head as a dart of something sweet and sharp shot through me. Adam and I had talked about kids. We had talked about it a lot. But somehow he had never quite showed the necessary interest to shift our gear from talking to doing. I had been thinking he would speed up eventually.

Neil's face, when our eyes met briefly over Annie's head, showed a world of understanding. So much understanding I wished I hadn't looked at him at all.

19

You have a way of putting praises that makes it hard for me to walk afterward. My feet have a tendency not to touch the ground.
— William Maxwell to Sylvia Townsend Warner, April 5, 1961

After Neil took the girls to bed, I set to work clearing up after the meal. Perhaps it's the result of having spent so much time with Jonathan, but I've always felt that kitchens are three-dimensional portraits of the people they belong to. Like his office, Neil's kitchen was clean, but not particularly tidy: stray bags and boxes of food loitered at random along the counter, and the bananas in the colorful fruit bowl atop the microwave were edging past their prime. The food in the cabinets (I wasn't snooping, just trying to locate the right spots for dishes) had a very human balance between aspirationally healthy and realistically slightly less healthy, as did the fridge, which was full of vegetables, leftovers, and a well-used-looking bottle of chocolate syrup. A row of sturdy stainless canisters stood next to a fire-truck-red KitchenAid mixer; I had never known Neil to be a baker, so the mixer had to have been his wife's. There were touches of red all over the house, now that I noticed it. It must have been Eva's favorite color.

As I reached across the island to wipe up a stray patch of crumbs, I heard Neil's footsteps in the hall.

"Everybody down?" I said, turning to face him.

He smiled. "Annie's getting to be such a fighter. She used to be lights out, every time; now there's all these questions and observations." He stopped when the appearance of the kitchen sank in. "You cleaned up! You didn't have to do that."

"It was my pleasure. Thank you for the delicious meal."

He looked crestfallen. "Oh, are you heading home, then?"

"What?" I stammered. "No, I mean, I hadn't planned to yet, but —"

"Aurgh." He smeared his hands against his face, gave his head a quick shake like he had water in his ears. "I am so bad at this. I thought . . . you sounded like you were winding up to say you were going to hit the road. Anyway, please erase the last thirty seconds of conversation. Can I get you a drink? I think I might need one."

A smile teased its way out of me. "Yes. Please. What are you pouring?"

"Come take a look," he said over his shoulder, so I followed him to the bar cabinet. It was well stocked with bottles of different shapes and sizes, the gold lettering on some of them glinting in the light. *A single dad with a full bar?* I thought, until I realized. Liquor doesn't go bad. He had these before. *They* had these before. Just like *our* wine collection, which was now de facto *mine*. Was my life always going to be divided into a before and after?

In one corner, I spotted a bottle of tawny port. Adam hated the stuff; too sweet and syrupy. But I loved it after a winter meal, loved the rich caramel flavor and thicker texture. As I reached into the cabinet to grab it, the side of my breast brushed Neil's elbow. The little tingle was unexpected. And promising.

"What's that?" he asked, peering at the bottle.

"It's a dessert wine," I said. "I love that you have no idea what's in your own liquor

278

cabinet."

"I'm not a big drinker. Somebody must have brought it as a gift. It's pretty, though," he added, holding the glass I handed him up to the light.

"Well, cheers," I said, clinking my glass softly against his.

We sipped the port, still standing in the day-bright lighting of his kitchen. Silence lingered, like a bad smell. And suddenly this whole thing felt stupid. Me, on this weird quasi-date with Neil from Development, who I'd never even noticed was attractive until a week ago. And yet here we were, both of us with our lives shattered, going through the motions because it's what some well-meaning fool had told us we should do.

"Listen, maybe —" I started talking at the exact second that he did. "What?"

"You go," he said, smiling, but suddenly I didn't want to.

"No, you."

"I was just going to say, do you want to head to the other room? The couch is more comfortable than the counter. To sit on, I mean," he added, his cheeks darkening with a sudden flush.

Neil was a blusher? I'll be damned. "Sure," I said.

I followed him to the seating area at the

other side of the loft, where he popped a cord into his iPod and then, as the opening notes of *Kind of Blue* slid out from the large speakers on either side of the room, he collapsed on the couch with a happy sigh. I sat down a reasonable distance away, attempting to look relaxed but not as if I was trying to come-hither him. If indeed it was even possible to come-hither someone while wearing an office-appropriate cowl-neck sweater.

"This is good," he observed, waving his glass of port at me. "This is very, very good."

"I brought the bottle with me," I said, and he wordlessly extended his arm for a refill. Once I'd poured it for him, I did the same for myself. And now, I guessed, we talked? I had never really done this before. "Dated." I could only fumble at how this worked. "So, you like Miles Davis?" I began.

He did. He also liked Thelonious Monk, Charlie Parker, Dizzy Gillespie, Stan Getz, Lester Young, Dave Brubeck, Bill Evans, Art Tatum, and just about every other classic jazz musician I'd ever heard of. And many more that I hadn't. Neil, it turned out, *loved* jazz. When he lived in Boston during grad school, he was good enough on the saxophone that he'd earned extra money sitting in as a session player with a couple of different bands. But he categorically refused to give me a demonstration.

"It'll wake up the girls," he said. "You saw how long it took me to get Annie down!"

"I think you're chicken," I insisted. We'd been gradually working our way through the tawny port, and I was more than a little buzzed.

He shook his head. "Some other time."

"You better. You've been holding out on me this whole time! I had no idea you had anything in common with Bill Clinton."

He laughed. "Well, I'd say you've got more than a little in common with Hillary," he said.

"Publicly cheated on?" I muttered, because it's the first thing that came to mind.

He jackknifed up from the lazy sprawl he'd slid into. "Shit. No. Of course not. I meant like smart, successful. Impressive."

And to my surprise, the sting was gone as soon as it came. Wiped away by his praise. Because I could tell from the way it came tumbling out of him, he meant it. And I felt very strongly that I would like to find out more. "You think I'm impressive?"

There it was again. That subtle color in his cheeks. It was unexpectedly bewitching. "You're great at your job. I think it's fantastic how much you care about the museum.

I've always liked working with you."

Somehow that line of conversation did not go exactly where I was hoping it would go.

He leaned toward me slightly. "Oh, and Caroline?"

"Yeah?"

"I have always thought you were beautiful."

Oh, wow. This was happening. He eased toward me slowly, giving me time, giving both of us time. His dark lashes fluttered up and then down again, like moth wings. And then his lips settled over mine, lightly, and clung for an instant, and then lifted away.

Our eyes locked together, our faces only a few inches apart. The puzzled crease in his brow spelled the same disorientation I was feeling, and I gave him a tentative smile. "Good, bad, or weird?" I whispered.

He smiled back, a little sad. "Weird. But definitely not bad. I think . . . a little good. Might get better if we did it again."

I nodded, and angled my face toward him. This time, my upper lip landed directly between his, and he sucked it toward him, ever so gently. Then I felt the quick, slick streak of his tongue glide along the slippery inside of my lip, and I gasped.

He pulled away, looking anxious. "Weird?

Bad weird?"

"Good," I panted. "I didn't . . . I don't think . . . I've never been kissed exactly like that before."

"I can demonstrate again, if you would like," he said seriously.

"Yes, please," I whispered, and leaned into him for more.

And I didn't know if it was the half bottle of port that was seeping through my system, but suddenly I had caramel in my veins instead of blood. Sweet, smoky caramel. Neil was kissing me so deliberately, so thoroughly, and so expertly, that I was positive I was going to dissolve into his lap like melted butter. Adam had never kissed me like this, not even when we were teenagers and all we did was kiss; he was always firm, heavy, demanding. But this — Neil was making a leisurely meal out of me, as if I were some rare delicacy he wanted nothing other than to sample all night long. Every so often he would leave my lips to explore my eyelids, my cheeks, my ears, the underside of my jaw, but he did not once venture down my throat, and the deliberate restraint just heightened the pleasure of what he was doing. It was a long time later when we finally pulled apart for a breather.

"Wow," he said.

"Yeah," I said. "Good wow."

"So good," he said, and cupped my head for another kiss. "I didn't know how it would be. You're the first person . . . since Eva. I honestly didn't expect it to feel this good."

I shook my head. "I know. Me neither. But —" I cut myself off midsentence as he retreated. "No, everything is good. I was just going to say . . . do we care at all about the fact that we work together?"

"Ah. No. Well, personally at least, I'm way too attracted to you to give even one-eighth of a shit."

"Me neither," I said again, suddenly breathless at the fact that I was doing something I'd never imagined I would; something that, for that matter, people don't generally recommend. I, Caroline Fairley, was dating my co-worker. "I mean, me too. I mean —"

"I got it," Neil said with a sexy little smile, and pulled me into him again.

At work, we were elaborately professional. Except for the text he sent me two days later that said, *I would really like to drag you into the supply closet right now.* And the one I sent him back that said, *So why don't you?* And the fact that five minutes later, we were making out like teenagers between leftover boxes of old exhibit brochures. Our hands and mouths stayed completely PG, but the subtle pressure of his erection against me was making my head spin. It was so beautifully unmistakable that he wanted me.

At one point, he raised his head. "Hey, Caroline."

"Hmm," I said, nibbling my tingling lips.

"Can we try again for a real date soon? I would like to take you out somewhere besides my living room."

"Or the supply closet."

"Or the supply closet, yes."

A smile stole across my face. "I would like that. Although I do also like your living room. You have a very comfortable sofa."

"You are welcome there anytime," he said. But a few days later, we did manage the date.

It was such a new thing. Sitting across a restaurant table from a man I didn't know well, while the light from a single candle flickered over the pearly surface of my plate and the softly scuffed silverware, and made my glass of wine glow like a ruby. The two of us passed stories and questions and answers back and forth, back and forth. And with each tiny piece of him that I acquired, I felt almost as if I had a pencil in my hand

and I was drawing him. I'd started with the general outline, and gradually I was shading in the details of his face, stroke by stroke. Defining the shapes of his features, rendering their contours more and more precise. I'd never been so aware of *learning* someone before.

And in the midst of all the learning, I was keeping a steady mental tally of everything I shared. Neil wasn't going to be my future, but I still wanted to present myself truthfully. And *fully*. And let him do with the information, better and worse, whatever he wished.

We quickly fell into alternating, every few days, between a date out and an evening at his place. By unspoken agreement, we were keeping everything light — including the physical aspect. But I found myself thinking, with increasing urgency, about what it would be like to sleep with him. If the quality of the kissing was any indication, then dear lordy, was I in for a treat. Suddenly it seemed insane to me that I had managed to spend all of those years with Adam without even so much as wondering what another person would feel like . . . . because I was most definitely wondering now.

Neil was so much taller than Adam, for starters. Bigger in general, where Adam was slight. I had absolutely no idea what to expect from his body, but the chest and shoulders and arms I'd been feeling up through the Massachusetts-in-winter sweaters felt solid and nice. Between his spectacular kissing and his sly sense of humor, I was rapidly recalibrating my opinion of him from quiet, good-looking Neil from Development to "I had no idea you were this hot" Neil from Development. And I was very interested in my findings.

I was also curious what Neil might be thinking about *me*. This was one of the aspects of my situation for which I most fiercely resented Adam — my cluelessness about dating. Sex, I had down. Men, even, I felt to be fairly familiar territory: Sure, I'd only ever had a relationship with one of them, but it was a long relationship, and I tended to believe that many of the basic traits I understood about Adam were things that were also true of the rest of his gender. This belief was bolstered by years' worth of reports and complaints from my girlfriends about *their* men. And, of course, by spending half my own lifetime with a male best friend. Guys were just . . . guys.

But dating? As a social ritual? I had absolutely no idea where to begin, what to make of the whole dance of when to step forward and when to move back; what to say, and when to say it; and what, if you sensed that somebody didn't necessarily *want* to say something, you thought they might be trying to express via emotional semaphore instead.

I had already decided that my own approach was going to be no more complicated than total honesty, delivered on an as-needed basis. I had made Neil aware of four things: that I'd kicked Adam out after discovering his affair (as always, the important distinction was that it was me who'd done the kicking, not Adam who'd done the leaving); that the affair had been with a man; that I had decided the marriage was irrevocably over, but I was waiting out the separation period before I could file divorce papers; and that I found Neil himself very attractive. I didn't have to tell him I wasn't looking for anything serious, because any idiot could read the big red flashing sign over my head that blared BAGGAGE. That damn sign had enough wattage to power an entire city block. So to point out such an obvious thing to him bordered on insulting. And besides, the guy had lost his own wife only a year and a half ago; there was no way he was going to be up for a real relationship, either.

But still. The things I wondered. What had prompted him to ask me out? Was it just proximity? Had somebody told him it was time to get back to the pond, and he'd decided I'd be as good a guppy as anyone? Was he seeing other people? Somehow, I found the idea unpleasant. I wanted his kisses and his sleepy jazz mix and his mischievous texts to be all for me. And I didn't know what that meant.

20

I am the man you used to say you loved. I
used to sleep in your arms — do you
remember?
— Dylan Thomas to Caitlin Thomas,
March 16, 1950

There were several different people I could
have told that I was dating someone, and
for several different reasons. Adam, first of
all; and I'm sure the reasons are obvious.
Second of all: Ruby. To reassure her that I
was moving on, and making strides. Our
mother, to help convince her that I was serious about the divorce. Jonathan, simply
because he would be happy for me. Oh, and
of course, Farren — to convince her nosy,
anarchy-loving little soul that I was *not* just
waiting for the right moment with Jonathan.

The reasons I didn't tell any of those
people are probably less obvious than the
reasons I would have chosen for telling.

Instead, as November slipped toward December, I clutched my secret to myself, like a mug of warm cocoa. And every day, I missed Adam a little less.

"Have you called a lawyer yet?" said Ruby, as we chopped walnuts in my kitchen for our Thanksgiving stuffing. Due to the space constraints of both my parents' and my sister's apartments, Adam and I had hosted my family's holiday meals ever since our move to Massachusetts, and I saw no reason to alter the tradition simply because Adam was no longer involved.

"No," I said. "But I wrote up what I want for the financial settlement, so I'm ready to go once the filing date gets close enough."

My mother, drifting into the kitchen in time to catch my last words, shook her head and clucked. "I can't believe you are seriously going through with this," she said. "Honey, have you even thought through what your life is going to be like when it's final?"

"My life is going to be pretty much what it's been for the last few months, Mom."

"No," she said, swinging the bread loaf for the stuffing onto the counter with a *thwack*. "I don't think it will. You've spent the last few months in limbo, thinking about a divorce. Actually *being* divorced will be

291

different, I can promise you that. The finances, for one thing. You should have started looking for a lawyer weeks ago, if you're serious about this, because you'll need a good one to stand up to whoever his parents hire. They certainly aren't going to let you walk off with half the money they've given their son."

I watched her silver charm bracelet swing in rhythm with her hands as she cubed the bread. "I don't want half of Adam's money, anyway."

She shook a strand of gray-blond hair off her cheek and glanced up. "That's foolish, Caroline. You should be asking for half, even if you know you won't get it."

My skin rippled with revulsion. I'd always hated the opportunistic way she viewed the Hammonds' wealth. "No. I shouldn't. I want my fair share of what I paid into our assets and that's all. I didn't marry him for his money and I'm sure as hell not going to try to cash in on the way out. Now can we please talk about something else? Ruby," I said, turning to my sister, "how is the job hunt going?"

"Well, as long as you're getting ready to find someplace else to live," muttered my mom. "Because this will certainly be our last holiday in this lovely house." My mother

292

is unique among the people I know in her ability to skirt conversational markers so pointed she should have impaled herself on them. And I deeply wanted her to stop talking about this, because in spite of my bravado, I *was* a little worried about the money. I'd be able to support myself without Adam, but my mom wasn't wrong that I'd lose the house if the Hammonds wouldn't let me do a gradual buyout.

"Mom, seriously, please give it a rest," I snapped.

"The job hunt is in a holding pattern," said Ruby loudly, thumbs testily punching a text into her phone, "because, as you may recall, I have been doing quite well with my own clients and with some advertising on the blog. Or perhaps you don't recall that, seeing as you ask me the same question and I give you the same answer every time."

"I know, Rube, and that's fantastic. Really. I just think for the long term —"

"Honey, we both know this blog thing is not a serious job," said my mother. "Besides, how will you meet someone if you're holed up in your apartment all day?"

Ruby swung her head up and speared first me and then our mother with a look of utter disgust. "Oh my god. Seriously, why do I even try?" And then she whirled on the

293

balls of her feet and stomped up the stairs to the guest room, her blond knob of hair wobbling indignantly with every step. The silence following her departure was shattered by the distant but emphatic bang of her door.

Sighing, I scooped her share of walnuts onto my own cutting board and resumed my slow, steady chopping. Despite the strides we'd made during her extended visit, it was evident that Ruby and I still did not always bring out the best in each other. At least not when our mother was involved.

The one saving grace of Ruby's fits of temper has always been that they blow over fast, and the one on Thanksgiving was no exception to this rule. By the time the turkey smell really started to get good, she reappeared and proceeded to set a beautiful holiday table, using tiny white pumpkins, pale celadon gourds, and LED candles flickering in mercury glass holders that she had imported from Manhattan for the occasion. But her progress at the arrangement was considerably slowed by the fact that she was texting as if the future of the free world depended on it. Ruby has always been a phone whore, but this high a volume of traffic could only mean one thing.

"So, you gonna tell me about the guy or what?" I asked, when she ambled into the kitchen for plates.

"What guy?" she said, in a facsimile of innocence so poor that I actually laughed out loud.

"Sell that to someone who's buying," I said. "The guy. The one you've been texting since the minute you walked in here."

"Oh, that's Rashmi," she lied.

"Is it? Well, I'm thrilled to hear you and Rashmi have decided to take your friendship to the next level. And kudos on pulling off the straight act all these years, you totally had me convinced you liked di—"

"Dudes," gasped Ruby, just as our father strolled into the kitchen from the hallway behind me. "Dudes. Yeah. But, um, that's really just Rashmi. She's at her boyfriend's and his sisters are driving her nuts."

I sidled closer to her and pulled out the silverware drawer to hand her what she needed. "Come on, seriously. What's his name? Carlton? Mortimer? Eldridge?"

"Shut up, Caroline," she said, but she was smiling.

"Rube, seriously, why won't you tell me? I promise not to tease you."

"Even though your literal exact previous comment was teasing me? No. Even if there were a guy — which I am not admitting there is — sometimes it's nice to hold it to yourself a little, you know?"

She had her hands cupped together and pressed against her chest. And while it stung that she didn't want to tell me, I understood exactly what she meant. After all, I still hadn't told her about Neil — or Jonathan.

In spite of the fact that I was with my own family in my own house, it felt odder to be without Adam than I had wanted it to be. I missed him challenging my father to a duel with the electric turkey knife, and charming my mother in the kitchen with tales of the antics of the actors he'd worked with on his recent show. (Adam had a predator's eye for the vagaries of attention-addict personalities, and pilloried them mercilessly without the faintest acknowledgment that he owned such a personality himself.) I missed the way he somehow always managed, at some point in the day, to tell me he was thankful for *me*.

Given that I'd been thinking about him all day, I wasn't surprised that he called me while I lay in bed, waiting for my food coma to reach its final stages and put me to sleep.

"Happy Thanksgiving, sweetheart," he said, his voice as normal and warm as if we were merely separated by some regrettably scheduled business trip. "I missed you today."

"Happy Thanksgiving," I said. I didn't want to tell him I'd missed him, too, but even so, I was sure he already knew.

"My parents asked about you. They send their love."

"What reason did you give them?" I asked. "For us not being together."

"I told them the truth. That I had an affair."

"I appreciate that. Thank you for not pretending it was about something else."

"I didn't want to lie. I'm owning up to this."

"You didn't tell them the whole story, though, did you?"

"What does it even matter?" he said. "Honestly, Caroline. Think about it for ten seconds and tell me what essential good would have been accomplished by me telling my parents I slept with a guy."

"I think it would have been good practice for you to be honest about something uncomfortable."

"That's such a *you* way to look at this. Abstract principles that have nothing to do with how people really interact. Spoken like someone with parents who think you walk on water no matter what you do. But in *my* life, why should I share that detail? It's never going to happen again. It was a one-time thing."

"It *wasn't* a one-time thing; you were sleeping with Patrick for months."

"That isn't the point," he said loudly. "God, I am so tired of running around this track with you. It was a fluke. An aberration. I was curious and intrigued, and I acted like a stupid horny teenager. You're attaching way too much importance to the fact that it was a guy. Look, sweetheart . . . I have apologized again and again and again and again. I've told you everything there is to know. There is nothing more I can do to make this better. It's been almost four months now. When are you going to let me come home?"

I stared across the room at my Jackson Pollock wall, then craned my head to look at the others, which I had painted in my favorite dark olive green. My color. My house. My future.

"I'm not, Adam," I said, in a clear, steady voice. "I am never letting you come home again."

By the end of breakfast on Saturday, I had: 1) listened to another lecture from my mother about the foolishness of my divorce and aborted two others — admittedly, by shouting, "Mom, I do *not* want to talk about this anymore!," thus causing her to walk away in a huff; 2) witnessed my father avoiding my "Give me a hand here" stare on two separate occasions; and 3) teased an unusually recalcitrant Ruby about the identity of her mystery friend until she stowed her phone in her bag out of pure desperation to shut me up. I loved these people, but I badly needed to get them out of my space.

"You guys should probably hit the road soon if you want to get home before dark," I said, playing hard to my father's loathing of any remotely suboptimal driving condition. Jonathan likes to say I inherited my poor driving skills from my father, but that's only because he's never been in a car with my mother behind the wheel. Look, New Yorkers have too many other acquired skills to also be known as strong drivers, okay?

When I closed the door behind my family, I poured myself a mug of cider, collapsed gratefully on my couch, and reached for my phone to text Neil.

Do you want to come over for dinner tonight? My parents left early and I'm somehow willing to cook again.

Sounds awesome, Neil said. *Just spent three days with my in-laws, and — yes. Happy to pay my sitter's surge pricing.*

My heart leapt inside me like a fluffy bunny when I saw him on my doorstep, all New England wholesome in his parka and wool scarf. The kiss I pulled him into was deep and welcoming, and Neil's breath was coming fast when he finally lifted his head.

"Wow. Hello. I missed you, too."

In a burst of self-consciousness, I put my hand to my mouth, but he nipped at my fingers.

"Hey. I was pretty happy about that kiss. Anyway, what are you feeding me? I brought both kinds of wine."

"Oooh, what did you get?"

"Um," he said, lips twitching. "A red and a white?"

I laughed and kissed him again. Neil was of the tribe that bought wine according to a shifting algorithm factoring price point against the prettiness of the label — and he cheerfully admitted this fact. It was one of many things I enjoyed about him. But perhaps my favorite thing of all was his ability to equally talk for a while, or listen for a while, or pass the conversation back and forth, as a shared thing.

This evening, accompanied by a Duke Ellington mix Neil had brought along with the wine, we were mostly passing: my wacky family, his (allegedly) wackier in-laws.

"It's like the balance has been shifting somehow, ever since Eva died," he said. "She used to be so good at walking the line between what we wanted and what they wanted, and letting them think they were getting what they wanted while we were busy doing something else. But without her there, I have no buffer."

"No buffer from what?"

"Everything," he sighed. "They want us to move to be closer to them in Mississippi, never mind that *my* parents are up here, never mind that Eva never wanted to raise our kids in the South. And it's bad enough I won't take the girls to the Baptist church; the fact that I won't take them to church at all?" He mimed his skull exploding. "They're relentless."

"You know they have to be genuinely scared, though. They truly think the kids are in danger of hell if they're not exposed to the church."

He shook his head. "Then that's their problem, not mine. The girls can go to church with them when we visit, if they want to. There is no way I am taking them myself." He paused, smiling slightly. "Eva knew what she was getting into when she married me. And she was ready to take on the culture wars. It definitely would have been easier —"

"With a buffer," I finished. "I believe it. But you guys will figure it out as you go along. And remember, you have the winning card in your hand, which is that the girls live with *you.* So Eva's folks will have to get along with you if they want the girls in their lives, and however much they may fuss along the way, I promise you they know that."

"You're a smart woman," he said, eyes warm.

"I have my moments," I said, leaning over to stack his plate onto mine.

"The table looks pretty, by the way," he said, following me to the kitchen and leaning one hip against the counter behind me. "I meant to tell you. Nice Thanksgivingery."

I glanced over my shoulder at the dining table. "Oh, that's not me, that was all Ruby," I said, fitting the plates and silver into the washer before tackling the Dutch oven I had cooked our beef stew in. It had been a wedding gift from Jonathan: Le Creuset, an absurd amount of money for a twenty-three-year-old to spend. Funny that the gift would outlast the marriage.

"Ah, that makes sense. I checked out her blog once; she's really talented. The way she photographs food was making me crave stuff I don't even like."

Neil had been interested enough to look up Ruby's blog? And meanwhile I hadn't even told her about him?

Silence settled for a moment while I finished scrubbing the cast iron, then moved on to the wine goblets, carefully rinsing Cabernet residue from the gossamer-thin glass.

"Care, stop washing the dishes. It's late."

"I'm almost done. I don't want to leave these sitting here all night."

"Why not?" Neil said. "It's just a couple of glasses." He stepped close behind me and gently pulled the glass and sponge out of my hands, but he didn't let me go. Instead he kneaded my soapy hands, his fingers firm on the balls of my thumbs, the pits at the center of my palms. "Such long fingers," he said, rubbing his fingers between mine. "You would make a great pianist."

My brain was suddenly full of bubbles. I struggled to compose a sentence. "Speaking of instruments, I still want a sax demo. It sounds amazing," I said, referring to the slow swagger of vibrato brass that had filled the room. "Are you as good as this guy?"

"As Johnny Hodges on 'Jeep's Blues'? The man's a legend, baby. But I'll break it out next time you come over, I promise. Which reminds me," he continued, mouth behind my ear, "I have the sitter all night tonight. Thought it might be nice to skip my usual Cinderella routine. I have no agenda; but I did think you should be informed."

I turned my head to the side; I couldn't see him, but he could see my profile. And with his chest against my back, he could feel the way my breath had picked up. "And what should I do with this information?"

"Whatever you wish," he said, lips grazing the back of my neck. "Although I do have one or two suggestions."

"I would be very interested to hear them."

"Turn around."

Slowly, I turned to face him. "Do the suggestions involve you kissing me?"

"Every single one of them does," he murmured as he lowered his head.

It still took me by surprise, every time I touched him, how intensely attracted to him I was. Something about discovering that quiet, mild-mannered Neil was so goddamned sexy when you got him alone . . . it was like this delicious little secret that I got to keep from the rest of the world. And good god, was I ready to find out even more.

"You know, I have a few suggestions too," I said against his lips. "The tricky part is, I think they would best be accomplished upstairs."

He ran his hands deliberately down my back until he was cupping my butt, nestling me tight against him. "I think you and I must have had the exact same ideas."

We stumble-kissed our way up the stairs, but when we got to my bedroom, Neil's eyes opened just long enough to snag on my Jackson Pollock wall. "What happened here?"

I shrugged. "Therapy."

The chuckle that vibrated against my ear was rich with affection, and for a moment I pulled back. What were we doing? Was this too much, too fast? "Are you sure we should be —" I started, but he cut me off with a kiss.

"Yes," he muttered. "We should."

"I just want — I just have to put it out there that it's going to be weird. For both of us. I mean, good weird, but —"

"Does this feel weird?" he asked, sliding his tongue lightly along my collarbone.

"Mmm. No."

"This?" Teeth scraping the base of my throat, making me gasp.

"No."

"Then stop talking."

Once, not long after Adam and I got engaged, Jonathan confessed to me that he couldn't see himself ever getting married, because he didn't know how he could give up the thrill of being with a new person. I told him that once he met the right girl, his heart would start to be more compelling than his dick. Because, of course, I was the ultimate authority on monogamy and commitment.

But now, with Neil, I finally got it. Nothing we were doing was mechanically different from anything Adam and I had ever done, but because it was Neil and it was the first time, all of my nerve endings were buzzing. It just *felt* different: different pace, different pressure in his touch, different ways of coaxing the little sighs and moans out of me.

With palms and fingers and lips and tongue, I measured the countless ways *he* was different. Darker coloring, broader shoulders, deeper chest, longer and more muscular legs; I added them all to the tally of things that were new. That Adam was not, or had never seen, or would never know about my life. About me.

Like the cry that shivered out of my throat

306

when I finally sank onto Neil's body, savoring the pressure as he filled me and we began to move. And the moans I couldn't control, every time we slid together, their pitch creeping up as he pulsed his hips up harder, pressed me closer. The fact that right now Neil was fucking me better than Adam had in *years* — that it was so good I could barely stand it, could barely drag air into my gasping lungs.

The pathetic irony of Adam's infidelity was that he had always been so deeply possessive of *me,* so as a supersonic boom of an orgasm roared through me, sending my fingers biting into Neil's shoulders, all I could think about was how viciously I wished my husband could see this. Me, panting with pleasure from another man's touch. It would fucking destroy him, and I wanted it to.

Neil came a minute after I did, and I watched, eating up his ragged gasp and the way his handsome face twisted as he moved inside me. As it subsided, his eyes flickered open. And for one long, suspended heartbeat, disorientation was splashed across his face, chased quickly by pain. I was not who he had expected to see.

It was such an impossible tangle, the four people there in that room that night.

■ ■ ■

Sometime later I woke, chilled. The spot next to me was empty and felt like it had been for a while.

I found Neil downstairs. He was sitting in a chair next to the dining room window, back curved like a bow, arms folded on the sill. A mug listed sideways in one hand. When he heard my feet on the stairs, he gave me a wisp of a smile, then turned back to the window again. My brain skittered for something to say, but I didn't have any references for this kind of situation. No sense asking how he was feeling; pain pulsed around him like an electrical storm. Any of the easy, empty platitudes that hovered on my tongue would have been a desecration.

I pulled a chair next to him and peered into his mug to see if he needed a refill.

"Cider? Really?"

This time, his smile had a little life. "It's friendlier than booze."

I gave him a skeptical eyebrow, but plucked it away from him for a sip. The sweet flavor made me think of orchards in October, pulling fruit from the tree, the crisp snap as I took a bite. "You're right."

He nodded. I wondered if he had a lot of

nights like this, or if this apple cider was just about tonight.

I wrapped my arms around my knees and stared out into the yard. It was a curiously still night — not so much as a whisper of movement among the branches of the trees down by the river. Their edges were blurred with a thin smear of mist in the wan moonlight. No motion was visible beneath the ice that crusted the river's surface.

We sat that way, not speaking, for a long time. I didn't try to touch him, just sat there with him in the darkness, my shoulders next to his and the warmth of my breath making tiny blossoms of fog on the cold glass of the window. I hated that I had nothing to offer him besides the cider. But sometimes, I figured, just not being alone was exactly what was needed.

Maybe it was half an hour that I kept vigil with Neil; maybe more. The radiator clicked and hissed into the silence, then fell quiet. In the stillness that descended, I realized I was shivering, so I creaked to my feet and cupped my hand around the back of Neil's neck.

"Come back to bed when you're ready. I think it will feel a little better in the morning."

Before I could move away, he uncoiled a

little, reached toward me, and slowly wound his arms around my hips, gathering me closer so his cheek pressed against my belly. I curved my hands around his close-shaven head, massaging circles on his scalp. He pulled back to look at me, and teased apart the seam of my robe, opening a narrow stripe of naked skin to the chilly air. Then he leaned forward again and pressed a kiss to that little rounded hill right below my belly button.

"Caroline," he said softly. It was a question and an invocation and an apology. And I answered the only way I could have, pulling the robe open wider so he could slide his hands inside and warm them.

21

I feel foolish and happy as soon as I let myself think of you.
— Honoré de Balzac to Countess Ewelina Haska, January 19, 1834

The next time I woke, it was from a clinging kiss on the back of my shoulder blade. Followed by another, then another. I groaned, dragged my hair out of the way, and rolled over. Neil was sitting on the edge of the bed next to me, smiling, already fully dressed.

"I've got to get home to my keepers," he said.

I smiled, struggling not to resent that he had to go so early, when all I wanted was to spend the day in bed with him. After the rocky start last night, he'd seemed determined to demonstrate that the real live woman in his hands was of very great interest indeed, and I'd fallen asleep quivering

311

and exhausted. But I was already ravenous for him again.

He was, it turned out, put together beautifully under his sweaters. He had the look of a former athlete — he'd rowed in college and grad school — who had taken care of himself well: He wasn't ripped, but he had shape where it was nice to have shape, and a flat belly with an appealing dusting of hair. Farren, no doubt, would call him something like a tall drink of water, or — even worse — some appalling metaphor involving chocolate that would make me want to die from inappropriateness.

Neil leaned in to kiss me and, close up, the bright sunlight revealed that his eyes were a more complex color than I'd ever realized — dark olive green, banded with a ring of gray at the edge of the iris, and sparks of topaz-gold around the pupil. It made me think of butterfly wings.

"I guess I'll see you tomorrow," I said. "Where we will be super professional all day and definitely not think about sex at all."

He gave a sexy little chuckle and sank his hand into my hair for a deep, breath-stealing kiss. I was so dazed it took me almost a full minute to process the words he tenderly murmured when he lifted his head.

"Did you just ask me if I ever heard from

Diana Ramirez?" I yelled, and he rocked backward on my bed, laughing.

"Just keeping things professional," he said, getting to his feet. "Hey. Will you be up for sleeping over at my place on Saturday? Since, you know, we're sleeping together now and all."

I pulled the covers up to my chin and glared at him. "Only if you promise not to mention Diana Ramirez in bed again ever in your misbegotten life."

"Deal," he said, offering his hand to shake on it. But at the last second he tugged my hand closer and kissed the backs of my fingers. "See you later, baby," he said, knocked his knuckles against my door casing, and left.

When he had gone, I yanked my covers all the way up over my face and burrowed under their soft, flannelly weight. For some reason, the word that came to mind was the one that had popped into my head when I first discovered Neil's vulnerability to blushing: bewitching. The damn man was bewitching. Because I was most certainly bewitched.

We did, as it turned out, finally hear from Diana Ramirez that week. She responded to one of my follow-ups, which had variously taken the form of one unanswered phone call, one email with a link to Farren's website, and comp tickets to an upcoming musical performance at the museum. This time, she was responding to the tickets: "Thanks!" Exclamation point smiley face.

"How do you put up with this shit all the time?" I fumed, from the guest chair in Neil's office.

He shrugged and tossed his pen in the air like a juggler. "Patience, girlhopper. Give her till January before you give up on her. Nobody can pay attention to anything around the holidays."

I squinted at him in sudden suspicion. "Do you say 'Patience, girlhopper' to your daughters?"

The pen spun into the air again. "Maybe."

"You realize they have no idea what you're talking about, right?"

"They definitely don't," he agreed. "But by the way," he said, launching the pen into flight once more.

"Yes?"

"I also call them 'baby.'"

The next Saturday was the first big snowstorm of the winter, and after calling my neighbor to reconfirm for the third time that he did, in fact, remember the substantial amount of money I had paid him in October to plow my driveway for the season, I tossed my canvas duffel in my backseat and headed to Neil's. It always amazes me how, much like people say happens to women with childbirth, those of us with northern winters have forgotten the pain of them by June, and greet the return of snow in December with dewy-eyed amnesiac joy.

Or, then again, maybe that was just me.

But it was so unearthly *pretty*. Inconvenient and even dangerous as they were, it was impossible to hate the fluffy crystals that tumbled out of the flat gray sky, covering fields and roads and rooftops with a pure and lovely coat of white, and decking every bare tree branch in sight with frosting. Heavy snowstorms were one of the only times I missed New York, because there, they turned the city silent; but up here, it was always quiet. My car was a warm, solitary pod of sound that whirred over white velvet roads to North Adams, where I found the Crenshaws in the midst of a snowball fight on the sidewalk in front of their building.

Neil waved one shearling-gloved hand when he saw me straggling toward them. "Guys," he called. "Caroline is here; that means it's time to go inside and start dinner."

Predictably, this was greeted with howls of protest, but after some stern negotiations, Neil was able to wrangle his snow-maddened children inside and into their apartment, where they shed hats and gloves and boots and small puffy coats in an astonishingly rapid near-biological process that reminded me strongly of Ruby.

Basic principles of fairness told me that I shouldn't pick a favorite between Neil's daughters, but it was impossible for it not to be Annie. Aside from her having a sunnier and more affectionate personality than her sister, she was cartoon cute, with immense dark eyes, round cheeks, and hair that projected in two downy puffballs on either side of her head. She liked to sit next to me when I shared meals with them, and would swing her foot against the table leg incessantly until Neil told her to stop it — whereupon she would simply start again two minutes later. One time, in an attempt to head off the reprimand I could see gathering in Neil's face like a storm cloud, I had simply reached down and wrapped my hand around Annie's ankle. Which she thought was the most hilarious thing in the world. The "Make Caroline Catch Me" game had taken on a life of its own by this point, and showed no signs of becoming less amusing to either of us.

This evening, though, I had been trying to draw Clara out by asking her about her Thanksgiving visit from her grandparents, but while she answered my questions politely, she just clearly . . . didn't want to talk.

"Did you have fun at Thanksgiving, Clara?"

"Yes."

"What did you do?"

"Nana and Poppy visited us."

"Where do Nana and Poppy live?"

"Mississippi."

And so forth. Stubbornly, I pressed on; there had to be something I could ask this child that would spark her interest.

"So how about Christmas? That's only a few weeks away now. Are you excited about that?"

"I hate Christmas," she said, pushing a rejected chunk of potato around the perimeter of her plate. "And I hate Thanksgiving. Everyone is so sad since Mommy died."

"Hey," said Neil softly, leaning over to wrap his arm around her. "We're not always sad, baby. Sometimes we are, and that's okay. But sometimes we don't feel as sad, and that's okay too. Mommy wouldn't want us to be sad all the time. She wouldn't want you and Annie to be sad at all. Nana and Poppy and I, sometimes we can't help being sad, but we have a lot to be happy about, too. Like you two."

My eyes stung, and, lacking anything better to do with myself, I glanced at Annie, who was staring at her father with a furrowed brow. Moving stealthily while she was distracted, I pounced my hand onto her foot, making her shriek with laughter, so much so that a half-chewed mouthful of green beans spilled onto her shirt.

"Sorry," I mouthed to Neil, suddenly anxious that it hadn't been the right thing to do. Who was I to break into this family's conversation about their loss? But he just shook his head, smiling. And then he handed me a napkin for Annie's green beans.

Later, after the house was still and dark and Neil had amply reconfirmed his qualifications in the bed department, he snuggled me against him as our skin cooled; but after a minute, the rib cage under my arm was rising and falling steadily in time with the breath that stirred the hair by my ear. I had thought it was an Adam thing, crashing hard into sleep immediately following an orgasm, but maybe it was just a guy thing. I peered at the dark smudges of his lashes resting against his cheeks, and smiled.

Outside, the snow was falling even more heavily now, and the dense white cloud cover reflected the orange glow of the street lamps into the room. A plow rattled down the street outside the building, and Neil started awake.

"Mmm. Dozed off," he said, and inched forward to kiss me. "It's so nice to have you here. And I'm glad for you to spend more time with the girls."

"I'm glad too," I said.

"I saw your face before. At Clara, saying that Eva had died. I told them that. I told them exactly that . . . that Mommy got sick with a terrible disease, and it made her body stop working, and that's why she's gone. I told them that we will always love her, and remember her, and remember how much she loved us, but I didn't tell them she's watching over us from heaven. I told them that she's gone. My in-laws were not happy with me, but what was I going to say?"

I nodded, but my uncertainty must have shown in my face.

"Okay, I can see you don't like that, either. I'm curious: What do you think I should have said?" His tone was conversational, not defensive, but I still knew I was way out of my depth.

"Neil, I couldn't even begin to have the right to an opinion about that."

He shrugged. "I'm asking. That gives you the right."

"I don't —"

"Let's look at it another way. Do you believe in God? I don't care if you were raised to believe. I mean do you now, personally, believe in the existence of God?"

I only had to think about it for a minute before I answered. "Not really. I guess I believe it's possible, but no, I don't actively think there is one. At least, not according to what any of the religions say."

He nodded. "Okay. And do you believe in an afterlife?"

"I don't know. Again, I'm not sold on the whole thing with the choirs of angels and Jesus on the big golden armchair, but it seems impossible to me that when we die, we're just gone. I mean, there are so many examples, millions of them, of ordinary everyday people, many of whom aren't even religious, and they talk about sensing the presence of loved ones who are gone. I guess . . . I guess maybe that's what I would have said. Not that she was in heaven, but that . . . they'd always carry her spirit inside them. So that they could still feel close to her."

He brushed my cheek with his knuckles. "That's a beautiful thought. And I wish I could believe in it, I really do. But I know better."

"How?"

"I told you I didn't have siblings because it's easier to explain that way, sometimes, without getting into everything . . . but I had an older brother, Jason. He died when I was eleven and he was fourteen. Leukemia. If I could tell you the times I tried to feel his presence around me . . . tried to talk to him and feel like he was listening . . . we even had an honorary seat and a moment of silence for him at our wedding. And that's all it was: silence and an empty chair."

I stroked his throat, aching. The cruelty of living could steal your breath sometimes, it really could. "Neil, I'm so sorry."

"So the thing is, I know. I *know* there's nothing left of Eva for them to feel, other than what we do ourselves to keep her memory alive. I don't see the benefit of telling them otherwise. I won't lie to my kids. I won't. Not about death, not about heaven, not about Eva."

The air in the room was too taut, too

silent. I wanted to pull him back into the present. "What about Santa Claus?"

He laughed. "There's been some confusion about that," he admitted. "Last year I got a letter from one of the moms, accusing me of ruining Christmas for the rest of her daughter's life because Clara told her Santa was actually just her mommy and daddy."

"Oh boy."

"I believe the word used to describe me was 'joyless.' "

"Nice thing to say to a man who just lost his wife."

"Yeah, well." He rolled onto his back and rested one wrist on his forehead. "I've been wondering if I should reconsider my approach on that one. I don't know what the answer is. I don't know what any of the answers are."

"Nobody does."

"No, I mean, I seriously don't. It scares the shit out of me. I'm raising girls. Two girls! What the hell do I know about raising girls?"

"You're doing a phenomenal job."

"But none of the hard stuff has hit. They're small enough that the boys haven't started acting like dickheads yet; but they will. And I've got these two tiny women that I have to teach to be strong, and to stand up for themselves, and respect themselves, and to not text people photos of their boobs or sleep with boys to get approval." He ran a hand over his scalp. "I have to talk to them about their vaginas, Caroline! And their periods! How the hell am I supposed to talk to a young girl about her period?" he demanded, hands flung wide with entreaty.

I couldn't help it; I started giggling. The panic in his voice. I pulled his face toward me and kissed him. "You are going to do great. Seriously. You're already teaching them most of it, and as for the sex stuff . . . did Eva have any sisters?"

He made a wry face. "Yeah, but Rose is . . . let's just say a sex discussion with Rose is not going to be any less embarrassing than one with me."

"Well, you still have some time to figure it out. If all else fails, you can buy them one of those books, throw it in the room with them, and lock the door."

"Believe me, that's about what I'm planning on," he said.

"Just as long as you give them the talk way before you even think they'll need it. I think dads tend toward a certain . . . inaccuracy about that sort of thing."

He flipped onto his side again, facing me. "How old were *you*?"

"The first time I had sex?"

He nodded.

"Seventeen."

He pursed his lips, clearly torn between the sense that this was perfectly normal for the grown woman he was sleeping with, yet alarmingly young-sounding for either of his daughters.

"It was fine," I assured him, grinning. "*I* was fine. Hell, we even got married. Although, actually, scratch that. Maybe marrying the first guy you sleep with isn't such a sterling idea."

He leaned in to kiss me, like he always did whenever I made some deprecating remark about my marriage. "I don't think I knew that about you," he said. "I knew you were together a long time, but high school, wow."

"Yeah. Adam cited that as one of the reasons he imploded. *He never got to explore who he was without me, let alone with another person.*" I heard the bitter, mocking tone of my voice and I despised it. "Anyway, he's exploring now." I paused for a moment, but remembered the promise I had made to myself, and, though unspoken, to Neil: total truth. "It was Patrick, by the way. That Adam had the affair with."

Neil blinked, twice. "Who's Patrick?"

"Patrick Timothy. Rubinowitz," I added,

as a matter of spite. "I found out about it at the gallery opening when I realized the guy Patrick was kissing in one of his photos had a very familiar birthmark."

"Shit," Neil said softly. "No wonder you didn't want to try to exhibit him." He shifted closer and pressed a lingering kiss to my shoulder. "I have to tell you, I thought about you a couple of times. Before we were dating."

"You thought about me? What does that mean?"

"In the sexy way," he said, a soft laugh in his voice. He trailed more kisses down my arm. "Like, I saw you at work looking hot, and then I went home and jerked off while I thought about having sex with you."

Surprise and self-consciousness flushed my skin with heat, but he kept going. "The first time, I hated myself for thinking of someone else instead of Eva. It felt like a betrayal. And then I came in the next day and there you were again. Laughing, and talking to me. I'd always thought you were so beautiful, and then your sister posted that cute photo of you two with your Jason masks, and I realized I just *liked* you. And for the first time it felt like maybe it was better . . . if I didn't think about sex with Eva. Because here was someone who was actually alive."

I cupped my palm against his cheek and kissed him, slow.

He eased me back onto the pillow to give himself better access to what he wanted. "I obviously never expected to have the opportunity to act on it," he said, resuming his chain of kisses along my shoulder. "I would never have wished for Adam to do what he did. But since he did do it . . ."

The thought of Adam felt very distant now. "I agree with you," I said. "Since he did do it, I am enjoying a lot of benefits."

"I'm very happy to be your silver lining," he said, and lowered his head to kiss me in earnest.

"Daddy?"

The tiny voice brushed against me in my sleep, like a soap bubble. "Daddy," it peeped again, and I groaned in protest, but Neil was already stirring. The room was still dark. The doorknob rattled, but didn't turn, and I barely had time to feel grateful for Neil's foresight in locking it before the voice outside escalated into a panicked wail.

"I'm right here, baby, just hang on a second," he called, whipping his jeans up his legs and tugging on his T-shirt, but the door rattled harder and the wailing intensified.

"Sorry," he whispered to me with a pained grimace, then opened the door to the small banshee melting down in the hallway. He pulled it closed again behind him, but I could still hear his voice as he soothed her.

"Clara, sweetheart, I'm right here. I'm right here, I've got you."

"I couldn't find you, Daddy!" she sobbed. "Where did you go?"

I flinched. Oh, how that must have raked him.

"Sweetheart, I didn't go anywhere, I was just asleep. I woke up as soon as you called me. And here I am, see?"

"But I couldn't get to you, I couldn't find you."

"Baby, that's only 'cause I locked the door," he explained. "I was right on the other side, like I am every night. Like I will be always. Now, what's wrong? Why did you come to get me?"

"I made the bed wet again," she snuffled.

"Is that all? That's no big deal, baby. Come on, let's go find you some clean sheets."

The crisis seeming to have been averted, I sighed out my breath and sagged back onto my pillow. The malevolent red numbers on

Neil's alarm clock stated it was 5:54 in the morning. I had no idea what to do. Should I get up and help him? He seemed to have it well under control, but I felt a little useless just lying there.

A few minutes later, he shuffled back into the room, scuffing a hand over his head and yawning. "Clara's back down, but now Annie's up. And when Annie's up, she stays up. So that means I'm up," he said, leaning across the bed to kiss me. "But you should stay here. I'll try to keep her quiet so you can sleep."

"Okay."

"Oh, and Caroline?" he said as he straightened. "As much as I love having you naked in my bed, PJs would probably not be a bad decision."

I stared at him and slowly shook my head. "Neil, I didn't bring PJs to your house."

"Right," he said, nodding once as if remembering something. "Of course you didn't." He crossed to his dresser and pulled out a T-shirt and a pair of plaid flannel PJ bottoms.

"Plaid," I muttered as they landed in my lap. "Damn New Englander."

"Damn New Yorker," he said. "You think the plaid is bad? I could have given you my

Brady jersey." He winked at me as the door closed behind him.

22

I'd like to paint you, but there are no colors, because there are so many, in my confusion. . . .
— Frida Kahlo to Diego Rivera

I woke again to an explosion of giggles as a herd of very small elephants thundered barefoot down the hallway.

"Annie, your turn!" A squeal, then more giggling. Then more elephants.

I squinted one eye at the clock: 7:37. It was still pretty painful, considering we hadn't gone to sleep until after two, but at least the sun was up.

As I extracted myself from under the covers, I heard Neil's voice.

"Guys! I told you, no running. You can play in your room, but you cannot play out here."

"But whyyyyyy?" It had to be Clara.

"Because I said so. Enough."

The sounds drifted away again, but I was up. I needed some sort of sweatshirt, though: Neil's apartment was chilly now that winter had really settled in. I creaked open a likely looking drawer in the big dresser from which he'd retrieved my PJs, and grinned at what greeted me inside. Gray sweaters, navy sweaters, oatmeal sweaters: The drawer was overflowing with rugged, manly wool. I grabbed the first one off the heap and tugged it over my head. The cuffs were so long they covered my fingertips.

Neil was nowhere in sight when I emerged from his bedroom, so I followed the sounds of muffled laughter down the hall toward the girls' room. The door was ajar, so I knocked and nudged it open a little further. Annie and Clara were sitting in the middle of a large, colorfully striped rug, their Disney dolls strewn around them like victims of a shipwreck.

"Hey, ladies, whatcha doing?" I said.

"We're playing princesses," announced Annie. "Wanna play?"

"Sure," I said, settling cross-legged on the floor. Presumably Neil would reappear before long from wherever he'd gone and rescue me.

"Here, you be Belle," said Annie, thrust-

331

ing a yellow-gowned brunette toward me. I thought of King Kong with Fay Wray in his fist.

I retrieved Belle from her, but I wasn't sure what precisely one was supposed to *do* when playing princesses, and Annie did not give immediate direction. I studied Belle, who had some severely snarled hair and a permanent expression of dimwitted surprise. Well, I knew what to do with the hair, at least.

"Do you have a brush, so I can brush out her hair?" I asked Annie, but it was Clara who passed it to me, unsmiling.

I tackled Belle's bedhead in silence for a few minutes while Annie chattered. She and Clara seemed to be setting up some sort of tea party for the dolls, and I couldn't help noticing that amid a passel of blondes and redheads, and a couple of brunettes with a hint of a tan, there was only one princess who looked like these two little girls. And not only that, but pinned on the wall above the twin beds on either side of the room were posters of the ethereally blond heroine of the latest merchandise juggernaut disguised as a children's movie. I was absolutely certain that Neil, understandably, despised it, and equally certain that, if Annie and Clara were anything like my other

332

friends' kids collectively, the noble intentions he must have started with had been slowly but helplessly ground down by the glacier-like weight of his daughters' craving for princesses. There was something adorable about that.

I could sense Clara watching me, so I offered her a friendly smile, but the only response was a frown. It was such a peculiar sensation to look at her — her beautiful eyes and the shape of her face were so familiar, it was all Neil — but the hostility made her a stranger.

"Did you sleep here in our house last night?" asked Clara after a while.

Ruh-roh. "Oh . . . um, yes, I did," I said.

"You weren't in the office room," she said. "And I didn't see you on the couch where Uncle Colin sleeps when he stays over. Where did you sleep?"

I pressed down on my panic, reminding myself that this wasn't an inquisition; she was just a little girl and she was curious because I had apparently spent the entire night in her apartment and she had no idea where I had been. I didn't see a way to lie, or a reason to. "Oh, well . . . I, uh . . . . I slept in your daddy's bedroom."

The frown deepened. "But that's Daddy's room."

"It is, you're right. But he said it was okay for me to sleep there." God damn it, where the hell was Neil?

"That used to be Mommy's room, too. Why did Daddy let you sleep in Mommy's room?"

I was losing ground, quickly. "You know, I think . . . I think maybe that's something you should talk about with your daddy. And he can tell you about it."

"What's something she should talk about with me?" said Neil, appearing in the doorway and crossing his arms with a lazy smile. I had never been happier to see him.

"Why *she* slept in you and Mommy's room," announced Clara, landing hard on each angry syllable.

"Oh, that's easy," said Neil. He swept some of the flotsam and jetsam out of his way until there was room for him to sit down next to her. "Caroline is my sleepover friend."

"Your sleepover friend?"

"Yeah." He selected one of the other abandoned dolls — I think it might have been Ariel the mermaid — and started fastidiously straightening her outfit. "You know how some of the older girls have their friends come and stay over at their house for the night?"

"Yeah . . ."

"And they sleep in their rooms so they can talk about stuff?"

"Yeah . . ."

"So that's why Caroline slept over. And every once in a while, I sleep over at her house, too. We're sleepover friends." As he delivered this coup de grâce, he shot me such an intimate smile that I was sure steam had to be rising from my skin.

"Daddy, can I have a sleepover friend?" asked Annie.

"Sure you can, sweetheart, when you're a little older."

And exactly how MUCH older depends on which sort of sleepover friend we're talking about, I thought, unable to repress a smirk.

"All right, princesses," said Neil. "It's Sunday morning, and you know what Sunday morning means —"

"Pancakes!" shouted Annie, leaping to her feet and charging out the door, her doll dangling wildly from her hand. Clara followed behind, laughing, her concerns about my lurking behavior apparently forgotten for the time being.

"Nice save, sleepover friend," I said, shimmying against Neil for a kiss as his arm slipped around my waist.

He grinned. "Oh, I had that one ready. I

335

knew that was going to come up sooner rather than later."

"Pretty *and* smart," I said, between little nibbling kisses. "And they said it couldn't be done."

He gave my flannel-clad butt one last lingering rub, then herded me toward the door. "Come on. Pancake time."

Sunday pancakes, it turned out, were something of an event in the Crenshaw household. Until Neil told them to knock it off, the girls ran laps around the kitchen island like it was the hippodrome; then, once quelled, they sat in their spots at the counter and chattered at him nonstop. He'd clicked on his iPod — a bright, infectiously rhythmic Cuban band this time — and he was punctuating his movements around the kitchen in time to the music. I don't think he even realized he was doing it, but it was cute as all hell. And the actual pancakes themselves were no ordinary pancakes — these were made with lemon juice and ricotta cheese, moist and delicious, drizzled with maple syrup from a farm in Vermont a few miles from where he'd grown up.

"Daddy makes us different pancakes every single week," bragged Clara. "These ones are my favorite, but I also like the pumpkin ones —"

336

"Chocolate chip!" bellowed Annie.

"And blueberry, and banana, and cinnamon apple . . ."

"Wow, Neil," I said, but the extensive repertoire was only part of the reason I was so impressed. He'd created this ritual for them, so they'd have something to look forward to every week, something delicious and fun and sweet. And repetition would engrave it into memory. One happy one, from what otherwise had to have been a pretty damn sad space of time in their lives.

The following weekend, I arrived at Neil's on Saturday afternoon bearing an overnight bag, nightgowns for each of the girls (I was clearly not above bribery), and a puffy pink sleeping bag emblazoned with the whole gaggle of princesses all over the front.

"Who's *that* for?" demanded Clara, after they had each unwrapped their own gift. She was eyeing the sleeping bag covetously.

"Oh, that's for me," I said, shooting an arch smile at Neil. "For my sleepover with your daddy."

It was worth the twenty-nine dollars at Target just to hear his delighted, dirty laugh.

"I brought PJs too," I told him between kisses a few hours later, when we were finally alone in his room.

"You didn't have to; I got you some." He jerked his chin at the bed. Neatly folded on top of the duvet was a set of fuzzy gray pajamas spangled with the New England Patriots logo in red, white, and blue.

"You," I muttered, my voice rippling with the effort not to laugh, "you are a fucking asshole."

"Enemy territory, baby, I told you that," he murmured as he whisked my shirt over my head.

The next morning was as sweet as the one the week before. I was beginning to feel like I had stepped out of my own life and into somebody else's. Eating pancakes in another woman's kitchen, watching her kids giggle as they licked maple syrup off their lips. Having sex with her husband in the bed she had picked out for them from the Crate and Barrel catalog. I felt dirty, like I had stolen something that didn't belong to me, and I was going to get away with it — because the rightful owner of all of it was gone forever under the snowfall blanketing East Lawn Cemetery.

Neil had told me he suspected she would rather have been cremated, but he thought it would be easier for the girls if there was a proper grave. So they could bring tulips to her resting place. And trace their little fingers over the grooves in the stone that spelled the letters of her name, like sightless hands mapping an unseen face. I thought of him, dizzy with grief, having to answer this massively important question that had never occurred to him even two hours earlier. But he'd made the right decision; I was sure that, given the circumstances, Eva would have agreed. So there she was . . . and here I was. Slipping into her life like it was a jacket I'd mistakenly taken from a restaurant coatroom.

I stepped over to Neil, who was pouring a second round of batter onto the griddle, draped my arm around his back, and craned upward to plant a kiss on his jaw. But instead of turning toward me, he flinched away as if my arm were a strand of seaweed that'd clung to him in the ocean. He darted a glance at the girls, who were in their usual spots at the island. Annie was chewing complacently, cheeks stretched around an ambitious mouthful of pancake, but Clara had storm clouds gathering in her small face.

Ah.

I dove toward the refrigerator to hide my burning cheeks between its doors. Of course, I should have realized. Sleepover friend really and truly meant *friend*. Neil, otherwise a remarkably intelligent man, seemed to genuinely expect his kids to believe I was in the exact same category of adult as, say, his best friend, Colin — with the sole (peculiar) exception of my sleeping location.

After breakfast, I dodged into Neil's room to grab my things while he was occupied with the girls. If this had been Adam, I wouldn't have hesitated to speak up; whether I was upset over something real or something stupid, I always knew I could let it fly, and he would give me a fair hearing. Not to mention, love me the same at the end of it.

But I had no desire to discuss what'd happened with Neil. It was going to lead to a Talk involving a lot of things I didn't feel like hearing, things I'd known since the beginning — but I didn't want him to feel he had to say them. As if I needed letting down gently. As if I'd been taking this seriously. At all.

"I should get going," I said when I returned to the kitchen, with a convincingly relaxed smile. "I'll see you at work tomorrow. Bye, girls, have a fun rest of the day!"

Neil's hands paused on the cast-iron griddle he was scrubbing. It had to have been a wedding present, just like my Dutch oven. "You're leaving?"

"Yeah, I've got a lot of housework to catch up on. Glamorous, I know."

"I'll walk you out," he said, setting down the sponge, but I shook my head.

"No, it's okay," I said, as I backed down the hallway toward the door. Past the wall covered with photos of the Crenshaw family. "I'll see you later."

"Stop — just hold on a second."

He got exactly four steps before Clara yelled for him.

"In a moment, Clara."

Then Annie. "Daddy, c'mere!"

He made a "Shit, sorry" grimace and froze.

"You better see to that," I said, still smiling my creepily cheerful smile.

"Why are you in such a rush? Just give me five minutes."

Impatience tightened my voice, and I didn't try to stop it. "Neil, I have a lot to do. I'll see you tomorrow. May the Pats lose badly."

It was my signature parting line, and I said it to demonstrate my good humor. But as soon as the door closed behind me, I gave a groan of pure relief.

Well. So much for my guilt over easing

into Eva Crenshaw's stolen life; her husband didn't even want me touching him in front of their children. He might be screwing me in private, but apparently even the mildest outward gesture of affection was crossing over a line I hadn't realized was there. He was two little people's father, and clearly he was still very much someone else's husband. He always would be.

God, how I missed my own. I missed *my own.*

23

Life is everywhere life, life in ourselves,
not in what is outside us.
— Fyodor Dostoyevsky to his brother
Mikhail Dostoyevsky, December 22, 1849

As the weeks slipped by until my filing date, flicking past and out of view like the landscape outside a fast-moving car, dread congealed in my stomach. It took me a while to identify it, because it was so far from what I was expecting to feel. What I'd expected to feel, what I deserved to feel, was relief. A rising sense of buoyancy at the prospect of severing the last ties between myself and my faithless train wreck of a husband. But that wasn't it. That wasn't it at all.

Meanwhile, I roped my schedule with Neil firmly back to two days a week from where it had somehow slipped to three. I started getting texts like *It's been three days since I kissed you. Can you show me how it works again?* and *It's mighty cold in my bed — I'm concerned about possible health consequences,* but I substituted occasional stolen workday interludes in place of the extra sleepover. Frankly I felt it was better for both of us that way.

I finally confessed about him, piled on my couch next to Ruby under a complex arrangement of blankets while we watched *A Christmas Story* late at night on Christmas Eve. I'd been laughing till I was gasping for breath, and at one point I nudged her irritably in the shoulder.

"Why have we never watched this before? This is basically the best movie I've ever seen."

"Care. I have tried to get you to watch this movie at least thirty thousand times. What is the variable between this year and every other year?"

I sighed, not even having to answer.

"Speaking of whom," said Ruby, "you're barely over a month till your filing date. Are you completely freaking out?"

One of the most perplexing things about Ruby is that in any given delicate situation, she can either be so willfully, mulishly obtuse you want to strangle her with her own hair — or she will abandon all social niceties and grab the proverbial bull, bellowing, by his horns. But it was late, and I was tired.

I stared ahead at the TV screen, where Ralphie's father struggled to reassemble his shattered major award. "Honestly? I'm scared shitless."

Ruby shifted position on the couch, sending one knee into my spleen. "You shouldn't be. This is the right call, and you know it. As your breakup coach, I think what you need to stave off the filing blues is a trip."

This bore every sign of trouble. Also adventure, it was true, but mainly trouble.

"Where are we going, Cancun? We gonna see if we can catch some college kids at the end of their winter break?"

"Close!" she said cheerfully. "We are going to Vegas."

"Rube, are you serious? No. I'm down to go someplace warm, but Vegas is really not my kind of place."

"Which is exactly why I picked it," she said. "Dragging you out of your comfort zone is super fun for me. Merry Christmas! Hope you like your present, 'cause you're sure as hell not getting anything else. Hey, the fire is getting a little low, can you put another log on?"

"God, you're a pain in the ass," I muttered, unearthing myself from the blanket fort to drop another log into the cheerful blaze in my woodstove, doing the requisite poking and turning that Ruby insisted meant I had a better idea of how to maintain the fire than she did. "So, Vegas, really? When were you thinking of going?"

"The weekend after next, and don't even try to act horrified, because I know you don't have any plans. Sorry not sorry," she said, and tipped back her mug of spiked cider.

"I do have plans, actually."

"Caroline."

"I do!"

"Well, they can't be that important. You have two weeks to get yourself in order, including getting a wax in case you run into any eligible gentlemen. I'm assuming your vagina looks like Sasquatch at this point."

I smacked the side of her head. "Screw you! It does not!"

"Baby Sasquatch?"

"My vagina is in excellent condition, thank you very much. I've been seeing somebody."

She lowered her mug in surprise. "Wow. Already?"

" 'Already?' It's been almost five months! And besides, it's not like there's some kind of mourning period; I'm getting a divorce."

She flipped her free hand palm up, like, *Hello.* "Uh, there's totally a mourning period."

"Oh, like you know so much about it."

"You know what? Screw you. My advice isn't automatically invalid because I haven't personally experienced something."

"In this case, it is."

"Got it. Well then, feel free to ignore me. Enjoy your kamikaze rebound. I'm sure the guy will. Poor fucker."

"You don't need to lose any sleep over him, believe me," I muttered into my cider. "At least not as far as I go. He's got more than enough baggage of his own."

"Oh good, even better."

She stared at me, then nudged me with her bony, wool-covered toes, but I ignored her. I did not want to talk about Neil, either the gorgeous stuff or the stuff that made me sad. Or, I suppose if I was being honest, I didn't want to talk about the gorgeous stuff *because of* the stuff that made me sad.

January was a new month, a new year — and, after the requisite "settling in" days after New Year's, a chance to give one last knock at the Diana Ramirez piñata. Neil had suggested a while back that I should

347

make a menu of sorts for our prospective donor, full of tasty, tempting items she might spend her money on, so I started with a template of an older one he gave me and updated the offerings from that. A lot of what was already on it would work — $22,000 to buy some new computers to expand the interactive multimedia lab (she was a techie, so this ought to be a shoo-in); a $15,000 grant to fund a hands-on painting program at Kidspace (who wouldn't want to help introduce kids to art?); $30,000 to subsidize a summer concert series featuring musicians to be mutually agreed upon by Diana and the museum.

The main thing I wanted to add was a direct grant to an artist, through a working residency at the museum. I loved the concept of giving an artist a studio, not a gallery. It was something I had been wanting to try out for a long time, because it introduced museum visitors not just to the finished product of artwork, but the act of making it. It demystified the process in a way that I thought was extremely important. And I knew exactly the artist I wanted to propose.

"Forty thousand dollars for a six-month residence for Farren Walker?" Neil let the list drop to his desk and looked up at me with a tired sigh. "Not Farren again. You know Tom's not going to back you on that one."

"I know he didn't last time, but if I can get Diana on board —"

"Care, tell me what specifically leads you to believe you can get Diana on board with Farren?"

"She was into Farren's work that time at my house. I know she was pretty zoned out when we had her at the museum, but I've been thinking about it, and I think she gets intimidated by big, serious art like the Le-Witts and the climate change installation. She doesn't want to admit it, but it's too abstract for her. She told me that she's interested in the process of making things by hand, so I think she'd really dig a residency where an artist can demonstrate their process and interact with visitors."

"Maybe," he said. "But I bet you could find somebody who would make more of a splash for us, and a splash is a *good* thing. Farren Walker is not going to make a big splash. Honestly? If you can stand it, I think it wouldn't be the worst idea to look at Patrick Timothy."

"No," I said, my voice like the crack of a whip. "Why would you even say that?"

He sighed and rubbed his brow with one

hand. "Because, aside from your completely understandable dislike, the guy is the real deal. You said so yourself."

"He is. But a photographer makes no sense for a working residency. I'm telling you, Diana will love this idea."

"But Patrick's credentials —"

"Oh my god!" I yelled, stamping my foot for emphasis. "Do *you* want to jump into bed with the guy, too? Look, I get it. Farren's not young and media-friendly like Patrick. She's not sexy. But she's an exceptional talent."

"An exceptional talent that no one outside of Massachusetts has heard of."

"Which is exactly the point! Come on, Neil, we're supposed to be shining a light on the best, the most creative, the most groundbreaking. Patrick is fantastic but he's not groundbreaking."

"Maybe not to you, but he does have buzz, and he'll get people in the door."

"Tom's Murakami show is going to get more than enough people in the door. I want to give a spot to someone below-the-radar. And unlike Patrick who sold out his first show at the Haldoran in two weeks, Farren actually needs the money. I want her to have this. She deserves it."

Neil drew his hand slowly over his head.

"I know, but baby . . ."

"Don't 'baby' me," I snapped. "I'm pitching Farren and that's that."

So, I realized as I clipped my way along the resonant wooden floor of the hallway toward my office, that had to be one of the reasons why sleeping with your co-worker was generally held not to be the greatest of ideas. Because, potentially, you might disagree about something work related. At work. And the person you were sleeping with might not be your boss, but maybe he still had a say in what you did and an opinion that had to be paid attention to — and it might infuriate you. For example, when he was saying something that made a lot of sense, professionally, but was completely inconsiderate on a personal level. And he might call you "baby" in his sexy voice and it might piss you off because it made you want to be mellow to him when you knew damn well you ought to stick to your guns.

I put Farren on the menu. I gave a glancing compromise to Neil, in a footnote to the effect that we were open to discussing other artists before finalizing any plans. But I also attached the document I'd written up the last time I pitched Farren, which included a bunch of photos I'd taken of her working in her studio, and a terrific portrait of her beaming Muppet face. It was a misleading photo — she looked innocent in it. "Don't be fooled by the grandma face," I wrote by hand on the page. "The woman is a menace and the most delightfully inappropriate person I know. You should come to her studio to meet her and watch her work." *There's your personal connection, Neil.* I paid Ruby a couple hundred bucks to throw the menu into Illustrator to make it look fancy and print it on the appropriate weight of card stock. I mailed it to Diana with a friendly little note, and then . . . we waited.

"Try not to get into too much trouble in Vegas," Neil said, while an Ella Fitzgerald song drifted in the background the Friday morning before I drove down to the city to meet Ruby for our flight. "Remember the house always wins."

"That sounds like a metaphor for life," I said, winding my hair into its customary chignon. Neil loved to watch me put my hair up in the morning almost as much as he loved to take it down at night. It was very Edwardian of him, and I'd been trying to squash how much I adored it.

He smiled. "I suppose it is."

"I don't think you have to worry about us. Ruby talks a big game, but we're way more likely to end up watching a John Belushi marathon in our bathrobes than we are to join a celebrity entourage."

"We haven't talked about this," he said, "but I'm hoping you won't be interested in any of the invites you're going to get. To other guys' hotel rooms. I'd like to keep you all to myself, if that's all right with you."

My hands stilled briefly on my hair as my body flushed with warmth. "Oh. Yeah. Okay, sure."

He stepped close and got right into my space the way I loved. "Well, then. I guess that makes you my girlfriend?"

Suddenly, hurt spurted out of me before I could slam my fingers over the crack. "I don't know. Does that mean I'd be allowed to touch you in front of your children?"

Neil blew a sigh through his lips and kissed me, one hand gently holding my jaw. "Damn it. I knew you were upset about that. I should have made you talk about it. Look, baby . . . I wasn't rejecting you. I'm sorry I made you feel like that. I just need to be careful toward them. This is the first time I've dated anyone since their mom died, and the most important thing is for them to feel comfortable. I have to take things slow, okay?"

He was right. I knew he was. But the thought pinched at me that I wanted to feel important, too. I deserved to. If nothing else, my marriage had given me that. "I understand that. And I understand what you need out of . . . this. I guess I just thought you would have started to feel ready to open that up to them a little bit by now. It's not like it's only a few months since she died."

"I know. But it's not just the girls, it's my in-laws too, and . . ."

And you. It is actually also you. It will always be you. I gazed up into his lovely face with those deep, understanding eyes, and saw the mistake I'd somehow made. *So this is what this feels like,* I thought.

"So then no, I'm not going to be your girlfriend. It's clearly too much for you."

"Care —"

"And besides," I continued, "how can I be somebody's girlfriend if I'm still somebody else's wife?"

Neil stroked my cheek with his thumb for an instant, then dropped his hand against his thigh and stepped back. "That sounds like a pretty fair question," he said quietly. "You let me know when you figure out how to answer it."

24

During the day you can't see the latitudes and you can't really see a star, but they're both still there.
— Uncle Lynn Martin to Peggy, Dorothy, Chuck and Dick Jones, date unknown

The morning of our flight, Ruby was bitterly resisting getting out of bed. Last night she'd been impossible, careening around her apartment like a trapped pigeon, packing and repacking her monogrammed leather duffel, then staging and restaging the obligatory predeparture photograph of it for her blog. Duffel parked among tangled white linens, the zipper partially open to reveal a spill of dark gray sequins, with her pencil-heeled black satin sandals tossed insouciantly nearby. *Look out, Vegas, we're comin' for ya.*

"Forget the stupid photo," I'd told her. "We have to get up in five hours."

"I'm not tired," she'd said. "I want to get this right. It's important."

"It's *not* important, it's a photo of your freaking suitcase," I'd said, which had earned me a dirty glare.

But now, of course, she groaned when I elbowed her.

"Ruby. Chop-chop."

"Fiiiiiiiiiiiiine."

It occurred to me, as I studied her, slumped open-mouthed against the taxi window half an hour later, that Ruby was the only girl I knew who could make having *actually* just rolled out of bed look good. She had her sheaf of hair swirled into its customary ball on the top of her head, and her heavy black-framed glasses softened the effect of the purple shadows under her eyes. Her throat and chin were invisible under a cream cashmere scarf so thick it looked as if her head were floating on top of it. Tailored burgundy wool trench coat, slim ankle-length jeans, crisp white Chucks . . . my sister was *chic.* When had that happened?

Chic notwithstanding, she did make me feel like I was maneuvering a toddler through the airport; I had to be in charge of both of our IDs and tickets because she was too catatonic to be trusted.

"Can you go and get me a coffee?" she

whispered, eyes closed, as she collapsed into a seat at our gate, the strength required for standing evidently beyond her.

Five minutes later, my phone rang while I was waiting behind several equally bleary-eyed people for the unidentified obstruction at the Starbucks register to clear, and I swiped it to talk without even looking at it: "Oh my god, I'm coming! Somebody's reinventing the American currency system up here. Hang in there, little vampire."

But instead of Ruby grumbling at the delay, all I heard was Jonathan's warm laughter. "Let me guess — Ruby's on her ass 'watching the bags' and you're in line for coffee?"

"Blaster. How did you — what? Are you inside my brain? How did you know we were at the airport? How did you even know I was awake at all?"

"Oh. You said it was an early flight, so I just guessed. Wanted to wish you good luck before you guys took off."

"Ruby said one of her exes told her there's a weird juju thing where clueless newbie girls are known to do well at the craps table," I said, shuffling forward in the line.

"Really? Which ex was that?"

"Damned if I know. Right now I'm focused on remembering every subtle nuance of her coffee order. I gotta go."

"Have fun," he said, laughing.

The reason I'd never been to Vegas before was simply that I knew I'd hate it. Ruby has a natural affinity for the campy, the boldly artificial, and the weird, but I have never been that way; I tend to admire things that deserve it and leave the rest aside. This eruption of glass, concrete, and neon was an eyesore on the wind-scraped desert of Nevada, and the wink-wink wackiness of the mini pyramid and Eiffel Tower felt like Disney in a way having nothing to do with fun.

After arriving at midday, we napped for a while, then snacked on room service in bathrobes (I hadn't been kidding) before launching our preparty ablutions in the enormous brown marble bathroom. I was halfway through my makeup when I heard Ruby's phone ringing once, then again. Which was so hilariously typical. Anyone who knew Ruby knew to call her twice — once to (maybe) get her attention, and then again to reiterate that you actually did in fact want to talk to her.

"Oh crap, can you get that?" she called from the shower, wet face poked around the edge of the curtain. "It might be our restaurant calling back about that time change for the reservation."

"Sure."

"Wait, shit, no," she yelled after me.

"I got it," I yelled back, locating the phone buried under her discarded jeans. I dug it out, already opening my mouth to answer the call with "Ruby Fairley's phone" or something equally awkward, when my hand froze around the phone. The missed call was not from the restaurant, it was a different name entirely. Less a name, really, than what looked like a nickname: Tennessee. And just in case I wanted to tell myself the reference was to a different person — perhaps some dashing fellow named after his mother's favorite playwright whom Ruby had met in the snack aisle at her bodega — right underneath the missed call, two recent texts floated unclaimed on the screen:

Pretty girl, you gotta tell Caroline. I almost blew it this morning.

And,

Have fun. Love you.

"Care, gimme it." Ruby came charging out of the bathroom, one hand extended toward me, the other clutching her hastily wrapped towel. Her skin was damp and flushed from her shower.

Reflexively, I clutched the phone against

my chest. "Hey, Ruby? What is it that my best friend Jonathan wants you to tell me?"

Her lips formed a perfect little O of dismay, but no words came out.

"Okay. Let's try this one. Which I'm pretty sure is actually more to the point. Why is my best friend Jonathan texting you that he loves you?"

She inhaled deeply and squared her shoulders. "Because he does."

The facts snapped into place like a deadbolt sliding home. They were dating. Clearly had been for a while. My best friend. *My* person. My 99.5 percent platonic main guy. Had been hiding a relationship with my own freaking sister.

And then the second wave of it hit me, like an aftershock.

He was going to break my little sister's heart.

"If you hurt her, I swear to Christ I will cut off your fucking dick with your favorite Wusthof knife and run it through a meat grinder while you watch."

I was storming. I was screaming into my phone in the middle of the hotel hallway, and a family passing with two blond toddlers stared at me reproachfully, but I didn't care. Who the fuck even brings toddlers to Vegas?

"Care, I'm not going to hurt her." Jonathan's voice was infuriatingly calm.

"Right. Sure. What are you even doing with her, Jonathan?" I yelled, as I stomped into the elevator and punched the button for the lobby. I didn't know where I was going, I just had to get out of earshot of Ruby. Although admittedly there was a strong possibility she heard the line about the meat grinder. "Why are you messing around with my little sister?"

"I'm not messing around."

"All you ever *do* is mess around. Why Ruby? And anyway, when? How? What the hell exactly is going on here?"

He sighed. "We've been together since the end of the summer."

"What?" My mind flew back to the three of us on the couch on my porch, passing a bottle of Adam's wine back and forth as we drank directly from the nozzle. Jonathan teasing her, Ruby laughing. Ruby always laughed louder and brighter when there was a guy she liked around. How could I have missed it? "So, what, like, since my house?"

"Pretty much, yeah. Listen, we wanted to tell you, but you've had so much stuff going on."

"So you're telling me you have been screwing my sister for *four months* and it's never managed to come up in conversation before now?"

"I'm sorry. We should have talked to you sooner."

"You should have talked to me *first,*" I said, as the elevator doors opened and the noise of the lobby rushed around me, voices bouncing off marble. "That's what a normal person would have done. *Hey, friend of fifteen years, I really like your little sister. Is it cool if I date her? I promise I'll treat her the way she deserves.*"

"Right, but you had just discovered this whole mess with Adam. It didn't seem like the time. You've been in a pretty crappy place the last few months; we didn't want to rub your face in it. And anyway, I am treating her the way she deserves. I love her, Care."

"Do you?" I turned down the hallway that led to the hotel's conference center and slumped onto a bench opposite one of the large windows overlooking the pool.

"Yeah. I really do."

That quiet warmth in his voice, I could hear it. If it were anybody else making him sound that happy, I would have been smiling so hard my face hurt. But Ruby? *My*

Ruby? It didn't even make sense. The two of them had always existed in separate spheres of my life; the thought of them merging into this unnatural two-headed monster was utterly beyond bizarre. Not to mention terrifying.

"Well, please tell me I'm wrong that you haven't told her we kissed. I know she was keeping the relationship a secret but there is no way she could have been chill about that this whole time."

"Yeah. I . . . no."

"Jonathan!"

"I thought about it. Obviously. But it didn't seem necessary."

I leapt to my feet and started pacing again. "Are you kidding me?"

"Not kidding you, no. Why would I have to tell her everything I ever did before we were together?"

"You wouldn't, but a smart man would have told his girlfriend that he made out once with her sister. Especially if the girlfriend was possessive and territorial, and used to be convinced that the man and the sister had a thing for each other."

"That's exactly why I didn't tell her. She would make way too big a deal of it. She has no reason to worry about us, and I don't want her obsessing about something that doesn't mean what she'd think it does. You and I were there, and we know what that was, but Ruby wouldn't get it."

"I don't know. It seems like something she should know."

"Well, she's not going to. I'm not going to tell her, and you're not either." He heard my hesitant noise and barreled forward. "Repeat after me: No, Jonathan, I will not tell my sister that you and I briefly kissed when I was in extreme emotional distress."

"Excuse me, it wasn't that brief," I grumbled.

"Caroline."

"All right," I sighed. "I won't tell her."

"Thank you," he said, voice thrumming with relief.

I was so very glad to hear it. So happy my little sister had someone looking out for her tender heart. And so shot through with pain at how badly I missed meaning that much to someone. I probably never would again.

Ruby was still in her towel when I went back upstairs. "Are you done freaking out?" she said, leaning close to the mirror to sweep a mascara wand through her long lashes.

I stared at her like I'd never seen her before. My sister: *Jonathan's girlfriend?* It's not that she wasn't his type; Jonathan's type had never been more specific than "pretty face, big smile." He liked a dynamic personality, which Ruby had.

But Ruby liked fratty banker types. Decent, basic guys who inspired about the same depth of emotional response as a *Friends* episode. Jonathan was complex and challenging, passionate in many ways but forbiddingly inflexible in others. They'd been dating four months; did she even have a clue yet what an utter pigheaded ass he could be during an argument? At what point would he figure out that pouting in response to criticism was not a behavior she was going to grow out of? And Jonathan could be *critical*.

As I leaned against the doorway, mentally embroidering ever more dire scenarios in which two of the people I loved most in the world steered each other's hearts off a cliff to crash in blooming fireballs, Ruby slapped the mascara tube down on the counter and spun to face me.

"What, Caroline? What is it? You think I'm not good enough for him? I shouldn't get my hopes up?"

"No. Of course not, where are you getting that?"

"It's so obvious you would think that. 'What is perfect Jonathan doing with stupid little Ruby?' "

"Ruby, I don't think you're stupid. That's not fair at all."

"Fine. Not stupid, but flighty. Flaky. Not together enough for him and all his big plans."

I opened my mouth. Okay, it was possible this was one of the reasons why I wouldn't have pegged the two of them as a natural fit. Jonathan was the most fiercely ambitious person I knew; Ruby was . . . not.

"Yeah, see?" she said triumphantly. "You do. Well, if you'd asked, if you'd given one single shit about somebody else's life, I could have told you I have plans too. The blog is doing incredibly well. I'm not going back to advertising, I'm sticking with it. I have some sponsors and collaborations coming in. I'm teaching a styling workshop in February and I had to add more dates because the first one sold out in two hours."

"Peanut, that's *amazing*! Why haven't you told me all this before now?"

"Because you didn't ask. Do you even look at the blog?"

"Of course! Not every single day, but —"

"Well, not too much lately, or else you might have noticed I've been doing a lot more food styling the last few months. Almost like I've been spending a lot of time with a chef," she spat, hurling her hair clip into her toiletry bag with deadly aim. The force with which it landed knocked her jar of concealer loose, spattering pale beige powder across the marble counter.

I rubbed my fingers up and down the center of my forehead (Adam called it my worry line) and sighed. Yes, Ruby was being dramatic, but she was also right. I had been so absorbed in my own life the last few months that I'd been missing out on everybody else's. Ruby's success; her — *incredibly weird* — relationship. Forget my perceived inability to respond positively to her and Jonathan's big news; if I hadn't been so mired in my own drama this summer when they were at my house, I would have been alert enough to wave the requisite racing flags to divert them away from each other in the first place. The only person I know who likes flirting more than Jonathan is Ruby. Interested in each other, they must have been *unbelievably* obvious. They must have been sniffing each other's asses like puppies.

I shoved my worry away and dredged up a smile. I crossed to her and fitted my hands to her slim shoulders. "You're right. I'm sorry I haven't been paying enough attention to you. I've been a crummy sister when you've been absolutely amazing to me. Including this trip. I'm going to be better, I promise."

She gave me a thin one-sided smile and turned back to the mirror to continue putting her face on. Her body motions had lost their righteous ferocity. "We're serious about each other, you know."

I cleared my throat awkwardly. "Yeah, that's — that's what he said. When I called to threaten him with bodily injury," I added, sneaking a glance at her to see if she would crack a smile. She did.

"Construction's starting on the restaurant in March. Soft open at the end of May."

"Wow," I said, focusing my attention on sweeping her navy polish smoothly onto my left thumbnail. Important task. That kept my face down. Useful to hide how disorienting I found it to be hearing information about Jonathan from somebody else. Particularly, for god's sake, from her.

"Soooo," she said, and I looked up. "So, we are going to be moving up to the Hudson Valley by the end of April."

The "we" dripped off her tongue clumsily, unsteadily, a droplet too loaded with information for one single word. And I couldn't even pretend it didn't splatter all over me.

"Wow," I said again, letting my surprise

give it an extra syllable or two as it rolled around my mouth. "Good for you guys."

"You're not going to freak out again?"

With an effort, I shrugged. *Who, me?* "I can't pretend it's not going to take a little getting used to, but I'm happy for you both."

She watched me carefully. I could imagine a hushed phone conversation later, while I slept or danced or barfed up some bad decisions I hadn't even made yet: *Actually, it wasn't too bad. She said she's happy for us. I think she'll come around.*

"Anyway," I said, grinning broadly, "I like you way better than Mariah, that's for sure."

It was a test, and it was a mean one, and I regretted it as soon as I saw her lips tighten. "I know who Mariah is," she said quietly. "If you want to play that game. I even remember her from the time. You were sure she was a cokehead in training. Turns out you were right," she added, with a whisper of a smile.

I carefully capped the nail polish and took a deep breath. "That was shitty of me. Five minutes into my vow to be a better sister." I turned my face and stared at her, imploring her to understand. "Maybe I should stop trying to be cool here, and just be honest. This is really, really weird for me. I know you guys had your reasons, and I know I've

369

been a little checked out lately, but I *really* wish you had managed to tell me you were dating before it got to 'We're in love and oh by the way we're moving in together.' It's a huge piece of information to absorb. I'm having trouble" — I swirled the air in front of my face — "absorbing."

She shifted uncomfortably. "I know. That was my fault. He wanted to tell you a lot sooner, but I knew you would freak out, so I kept dragging my feet."

I could easily believe it. And, I realized, Jonathan hadn't thrown her under the bus even a little bit when he'd talked to me. *We should have talked to you sooner.* He had her back. They were a team. That "we" again.

"You understand that the reason this is hard for me is not because I want him, right? It was never that way when I was with Adam, and it's still not. I've got the only blastproof panties along the Northeast Corridor." Well. For the most part, anyway.

She nodded, smiling.

"We will pass over for the moment the fact that your panties are apparently *highly* susceptible," I said, and she laughed. "I just think . . . until I get used to this — and I will — can you try to skip the parts where you fill me in on details you know full well I didn't know about Jonathan's life? And I will avoid finding ways to remind you how much longer I've known him. Please try to keep in mind that it's weird for me. 'Cause I'm sorry, but it's weird. It's *weird.*"

"It's not as weird as you think, actually. I've had a crush on him since your wedding. We were just never single at the same time."

"Since my . . . for ten years? *Seriously?*" I yelled.

"Yes, Caroline, seriously. God, and you wonder why I didn't tell you." She flounced her arms over her chest and stared at me crossly.

I threw my hands in the air, surrendering. "Okay. I need a drink before we talk about this any more."

"Me too," she muttered. "Go put your boobs in your club-rat dress and let's go to dinner."

"Jesus, I still can't believe you went and got yourself blasted."

Ruby's face lit with a grin, and I knew instantly I had made a severe tactical error. My sister loves to share sex stories. Loves it. Ruby tells sex stories the way other people share travel adventures or their kids' softball victories. My usual response to them was to squeal in feigned shock, laugh generously at the punch lines, and privately feel a pang of either jealousy or horror. I had often found myself sending a brief mental bubble of gratitude skyward for my good fortune in marrying a man who'd figured out at age seventeen where my clitoris was and what to do with it. But sex stories involving Jonathan were an appalling prospect, for several reasons.

"No. Stop it. Don't do it, don't you dare," I said, in an increasingly threatening tone as her grin widened.

"Come on, don't you want to know?" She dipped a chip into our bowl of guacamole and crunched enthusiastically.

I feigned a sudden interest in the dinner menu resting near my arm. "No. I absolutely do not."

"Not even whether it's good or not?"

"You wouldn't be sitting there with that smug-ass grin on your face if it wasn't pretty good."

"Oh god, Caroline, it's *so good*," she groaned, committing gluttonously to the overshare. "I've never had such phenomenal sex in my life. Like, I didn't even know my body could do some of the things he makes it do."

"Gross," I moaned, squinting at her from

between my fingers. "No more."

"You're such a prude," she said. "You should be kicking up your heels, too. Free to frolic after — what — sixteen years with the same guy?"

"Seventeen."

"Exactly. So, loosen up. We're in Vegas! And I'm an awesome wingwoman. You've got your tits out, so now let's get you laid."

"Getting laid is definitely not my problem," I said. And I suspect it's unlikely anyone has ever sounded more prissy when alluding to a highly satisfying sex life. "*Definitely* not," I repeated, for good measure.

"Oh?" said Ruby, crossing her arms over her chest. "Do go on."

I clutched my sangria, cheeks flaming. How could I possibly offer up the details of my laughing, luminous sex with Neil for the salacious appraisal of my sister? *He makes me feel like a goddess, when I so desperately need it* was not the kind of comment Ruby was looking for. "Um."

"Did you get totally crazy? Like, doing it with the lights on?"

You know what? There *was* something. "We've been going to his place on our lunch breaks. A couple of times a week. He lives a few blocks from the museum, and we can be as loud as we want without worrying about his kids hearing."

"Now you're talking," said Ruby, looking suitably impressed.

"Yeah," I said, warming to my topic. "We did it with me sitting on his kitchen island the other day. I always wanted to do that, but Adam was too freaking short."

Ruby raised her sangria in the air and cheered. "Hip hip hooray! To — what's his name again?"

"Neil," I said, blushing.

"To Neil, who is not too freaking short."

I clanked my glass against hers and took a deep drink, buzzing with alcohol and embarrassment and remembered pleasure.

"All right, you don't need to get laid in Vegas, then. But we're gonna take our cute asses to a club and let those boys try."

25

You once found my willingness to love you a beautiful and courageous thing. I still think it was.
— Rebecca West to H. G. Wells,
March 1913

"Before we go any further," shouted Ruby, "you need to pick your Vegas name."

We were standing just inside the entrance of the nightclub portion of TAO, while other newcomers fresh off the queue swirled around us and the thump of the music pounded all the way into my chest. I didn't think I'd set foot inside a nightclub since I went to visit a friend who'd spent a semester in Paris during college, and it seemed like things hadn't changed much. The enormous, high-ceilinged space was crammed with people, all of them holding drinks, talking, laughing, and pushing past one another through the crowd with a "Mind your back" hand on a shoulder.

"My Vegas name?" I bellowed back.

"Yes. You need to choose an alternate identity."

"Why?"

"Because Vegas."

"What's yours?"

"Sangria," she said, grinning.

"Fine, then I'm Michelada," I said, remembering the bizarre drink she had ordered for her second round at dinner. Only Ruby would go to a Mexican restaurant and order something that tasted like the bastard child of a beer and a Bloody Mary.

"All right, let's go." And she grabbed me by the elbow and steered me into the crowd.

Ruby had been right about one thing: We had no shortage of suitors. I was self-conscious at first, knowing I was practically glue-factory age compared to most of the women in the club shaking their booties to Pitbull, but the guys kept coming. Since I had spent nearly all of my life since the onset of puberty in an exclusive relationship, I had never had occasion to test these particular waters, but damn — apparently "big boobs, tight dress, pretty enough face" was something of a golden ticket, at least in Vegas. I said as much to Ruby over my third margarita (we were keeping the Mexican theme going), and she shook her head in disgust.

"Wow, and you're supposed to be the smart one? You have got to be quite literally the *last* person alive to figure that out."

"I mean, I'm not going to do anything, but still. That one guy, Charles? He was pretty hot!"

"Meh . . . he's cute. I'll take me a Tennessee redhead any day."

"Are you doing this to torture me, or are you actually this gross right now?"

"I'm bananas in love, and you're a captive audience. The fact that it tortures you is an added bonus."

I shot a sideways look at her, and couldn't help smiling. She *was* happy — she was sparkling with it, reflecting light and joy in every direction like a human disco ball. In spite of my worries, there was nothing for me to do but step back and let it shine.

At one point, I got a text from Neil: *How's it going? You hit it big at craps yet?*

Ruby and I are at a club, using false identities named after Mexican cocktails, I responded.

Margarita? he wrote.

I glanced at the half-finished drink in my

hand. Clearly we needed to recruit another friend.

OMG! I wrote. *Huge crazy news. Ruby and Jonathan have not only been secretly dating each other since September, but are apparently IN LOVE. (!!!!!!!!)*

Wow! Good for them.

And that was all he wrote. Because, of course, he had never even met Ruby or Jonathan. He knew them from my stories, but he'd never met them in person, let alone known them for years, so how could he possibly appreciate what a weird and shocking development this was? He had no context for it. He wasn't really a part of my life. And what's more, he could not have made it more clear that he never would be.

All of a sudden, a wave of missing Adam crashed over me, threatening to capsize me like a tugboat limping through a storm. Adam would get it. He would understand every single nuance of this long, ridiculous day, and he would shit the appropriate cinder block at the Ruby and Jonathan news. He would say, "I *can't believe* they didn't tell you, that is insanity," and "Yikes, that's gonna be messy. Can you take out some sort of liability insurance?" And then he'd invent some cheesy celebrity couple nickname — Rubathan, probably.

I turned away from Ruby and the guys of the moment and braced my forearms on the bar, panting fast, panicky breaths and staring at the filthy, crushed confetti on the floor while my carefully constructed fantasy of "moving on" collapsed into a sinkhole. It was all wrong, and I should have known it. I didn't *want* to move on. I wanted my marriage back. I wanted my husband back. I wanted everything to be the way it should have been, the way that we had promised it would be, more than ten long years before. I was supposed to make a court filing in less than a month that would end our marriage, and there was nothing I had ever wanted less.

The thing I had forgotten — if I had ever really realized it at all — was that breaking up with Adam didn't only mean removing myself from a source of pain; it meant removing myself from a source of deep-seated joy. It meant actually losing him. Actually being *without* him, every day. Without his arms to welcome me or his laughter to infect me or his faith to bolster me or his understanding to . . . understand. I wanted all of it, every bit of it, even his petty infractions like stealing the blankets from me in the middle of the night or leaving dishes in the sink or being too lazy to refill the Brita pitcher so I had to do it every single time I wanted a cold drink of water. The thought of being mad at him for something stupid instead of something huge — the ability to yell, "God, you are being *so annoying* right now, will you knock it off?" and have him stick his tongue out to taunt me — was suddenly the greatest luxury I could imagine.

He had hurt me terribly, and nothing could erase that. But there was so much, *so* immeasurably much, that we had earned during those thousands of days we spent together — I couldn't just walk away from it. There had to be a way to reboot our relationship, to build it in a more deliberate and conscious and mature way than we ever had before, instead of coasting on the momentum of what we'd started seventeen years ago. To nurture it as a growing, organic thing rather than treating it like a time capsule. There had to be a way to fix us.

Ruby's hand was gentle on my shoulder. "Care? You okay? Do you need to sit down?"

"I need to go," I mumbled. "And I need to call Adam."

"Whoa," she said. "No, you do not. That is the margaritas talking. But yeah, let's head on out of here. Gents, it's been a pleasure." And then my sister hooked me by the arm and led me, first to the coat check and then, through some deserted and off-limits-looking corridors, to the welcome relief of the outside world — even if that world was a night still throbbing with headlights and neon.

"I think I better let you dry out a bit before we go home," sighed Ruby.

"That is entirely unnecessary," I said, but she speared me with a look. Damn it. I was doing it again.

"Bullshit," she said. "And anyway, I've got the munchies. I saw a Denny's near here when we were coming in."

"Jonathan would disown you," I grumbled.

"Jonathan is learning that he can't cure me of my junk food thing. Come on, Michelada, let's march."

With a cunning deepened by intoxication, I waited patiently for the moment I could get my call in to Adam. This was primarily achieved by not mentioning it again to Ruby, though she eyed me suspiciously as we tucked into our food: hers a stack of pancakes, and mine some sort of scrambled egg sandwich.

"How are you feeling?" she said, shoving

her last hunk of pancake into the lake of maple-flavored corn syrup she'd made on one side of her plate. "A little better?"

"I was never feeling bad in the first place. This was completely your idea."

"True," she said, then chewed peacefully for a few moments. "Okay, I'm gonna hit the potty before we leave. You will please give me your phone."

"What?" I squeaked.

She put her fork down and turned her palm up, fingers waving. "Hand it over. I didn't forget the part where you said you wanted to call Adam, and I'm not letting you screw up all the progress you've made at letting go of him. The last thing you should do is call him while you're drunk and sappy. Gimme."

"I'm not going to call him."

"Cool, then you'll have no problem giving me your phone, just so you don't slip and fall and accidentally dial his number."

I scowled at her, and she scowled right back. *Damn it.* Ruby could be a stubborn little shit when she wanted to be.

Sighing, I handed her the phone. She was probably right that I shouldn't call when I'd been drinking. It could wait until tomorrow.

But then, as she scooted out from the booth and took off for the bathroom — her slinky dress and stilettos garnering a few confused stares even in a Denny's located on the Las Vegas strip — I noticed something she'd forgotten. Which was that her own phone, rather than nestled inside her bag where she obviously thought it was, sat forgotten on the table next to her.

I grabbed it and punched in her birthday — no go. Damn it. Ruby's password had been her birthday for as long as I'd been scolding her to pick something less obvious; why the hell had she picked *right now* to finally change it? And what the hell would she have changed it to? She didn't have a pet, or an anniversary —

But I knew what she was obsessed with. J-B-J-B. No. J-B-R-F. *No.* Damn it, Ruby!

Then, in a flash, I remembered what I'd seen on this very same phone, what felt like three days ago by now. T-E-N-N, and boom, there I was: in.

Not surprisingly, considering it was some ungodly o'clock on the East Coast, it took him a long time to answer. I had to let it go to voicemail once. Then, finally, his voice, stumbling from sleep:

"Ruby? Why are you calling me, is Caroline okay? Tell me what's wrong, right now."

"It's me," I said, awash with tenderness at

the naked terror in his voice.

He let out a long, gasping sigh. "Jesus Christ, it's five o'clock in the morning. You scared the living shit out of me. For a second I thought my dad had another heart attack, and then when I saw it was Ruby —"

"I'm sorry," I whispered. This was it: the moment where I could start pouring out every drop of longing, telling him how much I missed him and wanted him to come home. He would come up with a way to fix us.

"Is everything all right? Where are you?"

"I am at Denny's."

"Denny's. Is that so. What are you doing at Denny's?"

"Eating . . . a . . . wait, what was it called? Moons Over My Hammy."

"Sounds nutritious. Where is this Denny's?"

"In Las Vegas, Nevada."

"Vegas? Why are you in Vegas?"

"Liberation," I said. "Furtherance of personal goals."

"You're furthering your personal goals in Vegas."

"It was Ruby's idea," I said. "Oh. By the way, Ruby and Jonathan are dating."

"Wha-a-a-t?" he said, his laughter trembling over the word. "That is . . . *ridiculous.* She's going to drive him nuts in ten seconds."

I didn't like the way he automatically assumed Ruby would be the problem. It wasn't on the list of responses I'd imagined he would give to this piece of news. "They're four months into it. They love each other."

"God help us," he muttered. "That won't be fun to be in the middle of when it melts down. So," he said, and I could imagine him sitting up in our bed, knees bent, getting ready for a story. "What goals are you pursuing in Vegas?"

"Ruby told me it was time I got my tits out."

"Interesting. That sounds like something I'd like to see. So did you?"

"Yes. But *everybody* has their tits out here. And the skirts . . . their skirts barely cover their ass cheeks. I was on the dance floor at this club, and I looked up at the mezzanine where the girls were waiting for the bathroom, and I could see allllllll of their underwear. Blue thong, red thong, pink thong. Pretty sure I even saw straight-up labia. Not that that would interest you," I said. Swerving around to it at last.

"Sweaty club-rat vagina? No. Not appetizing."

"What about mine?" I whispered.

He hissed his breath through his teeth. "Caro . . ."

"I felt so stupid," I said, voice shivering with tears. "Putting on this stupid dress to make drunk guys look at me. When my own husband doesn't want to fuck me anymore."

"Caro, no." There was a rustling sound; probably him rearranging his position in bed. He had this way of focusing his body toward me when I was upset with him, to let me know he was paying attention. "Honey, that's not true."

"Don't lie to me. You already lied too much."

"That's not a lie. I know the words probably don't mean much, but it's not a lie. I screwed everything up, but I've never stopped wanting you. Just like I've never stopped loving you."

"Then why?" I said. "Why wasn't love enough to stop you from making that decision? I called you in the middle of the night from this stupid Denny's because I want to try again. I want you to come home and be my husband and spend the rest of your life with me, like you were supposed to. I can forgive you for concealing yourself as long as you promise to be truthful from now on. But you have to answer this one thing: Why

386

were you willing to hurt me, if you love me so much?"

He was silent for a long time. "There's just something about him and me. I don't know how to explain it to you. Except it's like what I said, the first time you asked me. I felt this . . . pull, and I followed it, even though I shouldn't have."

My mind focused in on one of his words, instantly narrowing everything down to a pinpoint. "So I don't know if you know it, but you just said 'There is' something about you and him. 'There *is,*' present tense, as if whatever that something was is currently active." I waited for him to respond to this, but it was just silence. Again. "Adam. Are you still seeing him?"

"I will stop," he whispered. "I will stop, and I'll come home."

I gave a half sob, half laugh. "Yeah. Sure. I could have sworn you told me it was over back in August, and then again back in November, but clearly I misunderstood you. I see that now you are sincere. So, if I called him in a minute, to tell him you're ending it, where would he be? You know I have his number. I can enter the number" — I rustled in my bag, temporarily forgetting Ruby had kidnapped my phone — "and where would that phone ring? Did you go to the living room so you could talk to me while he sleeps?"

"Caro. Don't do that. Please don't do that." His voice was thready with panic.

"Why not? You want to be the one to do it? Or you don't want to do it at all?"

"Caroline. Sweetheart, please. Just don't."

I could hear my own hitchy, uneven breathing. "You can't stand the thought of it. You don't want to leave him at all."

"I think I'm in love with him," he whispered. And they were his first words in any of this, since it all began, that rang in my ears with the pure sound of truth. "I love both of you. What the fuck am I supposed to do about that?"

"You were supposed to choose. You were supposed to choose *me,* because you promised me you always would. Because you fell in love with me *first.*" There were more sophisticated things I wanted to say, but the alcohol blurred them all away. All I could process, all I could articulate, was that I hurt. Even after this long, it hurt. And I despised myself for reaching out to him in a moment of weakness, and setting myself up for another blow. But at least perhaps, this time, it was the final one.

"I'm still in love with you, too."

"Too bad," I hissed. "You can't come

home to me, because I'm not your fucking home. You do not have a decision to make; you already made it. And guess what I didn't tell you, Adam? I'm sleeping with somebody else. He can't get enough of me. And I can't get enough of him, 'cause let me tell you, he fucks me better than you ever did. And if you think I'm lying? I will be happy to send you a motherfucking *photograph.*"

26

Touch a string, and it will vibrate even if it should long have yielded no tone.
— Bettina von Arnim to Frau Rath Goethe

After seven and a half winters in western Massachusetts, I thought I'd seen the far end of cold, at least as far as the usual range of human experience went. But standing on a plateau on the edge of the Grand Canyon in January, while a desert wind whipped my face and roared in my ears and thrust frigid hands into every hollow place in my body — that was the limit.

"Why are we doing this?" I said to Ruby through uncontrollably chattering teeth.

"You always wanted to see the Grand Canyon."

"Don't recall specifying January," I said. "Or hungover."

"The hangover's your own fault," she said, which was unarguably true. My brain had bounced around my skull all the way to Arizona.

I could have bailed on coming, of course. Sanity would have dictated that I stay in our cushy bed at the Venetian, carefully waiting to move until the sliver of sunlight through the curtains didn't feel so much like a knife blade pressing between my eyes. But that would have meant being trapped in that room with my thoughts.

"Don't let him ruin this for you," Ruby had said, and it was that that got my feet to the floor. That, and the memory of how she'd found me the night before, when she came back from the bathroom: sobbing into my arms on the Formica tabletop of a Las Vegas Denny's. It had not been a high point in my life. But she hadn't said "I told you so," or scolded me for stealing her phone; she just sat down next to me and put her head on my shoulder till I stopped crying.

"Let's go back to the hotel," she'd said. "Do you still want to go to the canyon tomorrow? I think we should go."

I'd nodded, happy to let my little sister mother me. The Grand Canyon thing had been my idea in the first place, and I knew by insisting on it she was trying to buck my spirits up. However, neither of us had been prepared for the cold.

Ruby shuffled closer and hunched her body against me. "It is pretty damn beautiful," she said.

I untucked my chin from the neck of my down puffer and looked around me. We were standing in the (mercifully short) line for the Grand Canyon Skywalk, a cantilevered, horseshoe-shaped glass walkway that had been built on the far western end of the canyon as a destination within driving distance of Las Vegas for family-oriented or party-weary visitors such as ourselves. Clumps of pale gray clouds piled up on the never-ending horizon and in the immense dome over our heads, and in the thin midwinter light, the landscape was a leached sandy beige. The legendary canyon just looked like an enormous dry ditch.

"Can you imagine what it looked like before the Colorado River got dammed to water every lawn in Las Vegas?" I said.

"And the entire state of Arizona. I know."

"It used to be something magnificent."

"You're depressing me," Ruby said, digging her pointy chin into my shoulder through the thickness of my coat. "Come on; the line is moving."

We shuffled forward, into the visitors' center building and then along the route toward the entrance to the bridge. When I saw the open sky spread out before me, I stopped.

I've never been terrific with heights, and the glass-floored Skywalk, dangling from the top of a cliff almost a mile above the canyon bottom, was intentionally made to agitate the stomach contents of people like me. I stepped forward, and stepped back.

"Come on," Ruby said. "It's completely safe. You know it is. They must have built this thing to handle like five times the stress it actually carries."

"I do know it is. I know it here," I said, pointing at my head, "but this part of me has a different idea altogether." I pressed my palm into my belly and tried to feel brave.

"Yeah, but that part of you is wrong. Just come out with me. Here, hold my hand."

Adam wouldn't make me do this, I thought. I'd planned to see the canyon one day with Adam, who knew my fear of heights, and never wanted me to feel scared or uncomfortable.

Adam was also over.

I bit down so hard my jaws ached with strain, and I walked. I walked right past Ruby's outstretched hand, only stopping when I reached the railing. The reassuringly high railing. And then I looked down.

■ ■ ■ ■

"You ran away so fast you almost took out that little old lady," giggled Ruby.

It was evening, and we were drifting on bent legs, half afloat in the warm water of our hotel pool, well fed on burgers and many, many miles from the yawning chasm of America's greatest natural wonder.

I shuddered as I remembered the dizzying view through the floor of the Skywalk. "Korean tourists are inherently hardy," I said.

"I'm glad we didn't have to put that to the test," Ruby said. "You did it, though. You walked out!"

"If you can call it that," I said. "I was having this big 'You go girl' moment with myself and then as soon as I made it I turned around and booked it the hell out of there."

Ruby chuckled again. "Well, I mean, yeah. But you did do it. How come you even wanted to see the Grand Canyon, anyway? If you're so scared of heights?"

"Because it's the Grand freaking Canyon. I'm an American. And it looks beautiful in pictures."

"Beautiful . . . and like a canyon."

"Look, I thought it would be more Caroline-friendly, all right?" I floated backward until I reached the wall of the pool, hooked my arms on the edge, and pedaled my feet slowly through the water. My body looked vulnerable, oddly raw and half-baked, through the green underlit water. "You know what made me walk out there?" I said, after a moment. "Thinking Adam wouldn't have encouraged me to. He knows how scared I get, so he would have said, 'Oh, you stay here, I'll tell you how it was.' And then I wouldn't have done it."

"Good for you, then."

"I'm so tired of him being my frame of reference for everything, Rube. I'm so tired of thinking about him. I'm sure you are profoundly tired of listening to me talk about him."

"That's going to change eventually. It just will. There was no way he wasn't going to be on your mind today, after last night."

"That's true," I sighed, tipping my face back to look at the sky, still filled with light even at nighttime. Loose gray clouds drifted against the blackness above them. "God, I feel so stupid. I feel like I wiped out all the progress I'd made at feeling better, just so I could get slugged in the face with the same shit all over again."

"Here's the thing, though. You've been putting all this emphasis on figuring out why Adam did this to you. Why he lied, why he hid things, why he cheated. And I get that the nature of his sexuality feels like an important part of that, but honestly? I don't think it is. Being bi doesn't mean someone is inherently likely to cheat. If you make a commitment to one partner then you're supposed to stick with it, no matter what sexy bits you like to play with. And he failed. Which means the reason he did it is that he's selfish. I think it is literally as simple as that."

I scooped up a handful of water, then watched as the drips splashed back into the pool from between my loosened fingers. "I guess. I just can't let go of this idea that there has to be more to it than that, because *he* was better than that."

Ruby looked at me for a moment, then one corner of her mouth lifted sadly. "I don't know, Care. I think maybe the hard part here is that you need to accept that he wasn't. He isn't the man you thought he was." She slid closer and leaned against the wall next to me, her hair trailing through the water in a soft swirl around her shoulders. "I saw this thing on the Internet somewhere. It's funny, ninety-nine percent of what you see on the Internet is such horseshit, but I saw this thing a little while ago that stuck with me, and what it said was, 'People can only give you what they have.' And I see you fighting to put what Adam did into some other frame of reference, like there's some deeper explanation that would justify it a little bit. You want it to make sense. You want there to be a reason that will let you still value him, somehow. But the fact is, he failed you because he didn't have the strength to stop himself. It just wasn't there. What he had was love, but not the other stuff. He didn't have the integrity to make the right decision. And that's really all it comes down to. That is the truth at the heart of Adam."

"I tried again to ask him why he did it. And all he could come up with was 'There's just something about him and me' and 'I felt a pull.' He thinks he's in love with Patrick. *In love.* I don't even . . . I don't even know what to do with that."

There was a long pause, partially filled by the dance-lite soundtrack pumping from every speaker surrounding the pool. "Is that all he said?" Ruby's voice was quiet.

"No. He said 'I'll end it,' followed quickly by panic when I threatened to do it for him. Jesus, it was so fucking horrible," I moaned, and sank all the way under the water as if that would let me escape the humiliation and pain. But no; it was down here, too.

When I surfaced again, Ruby was regarding me gravely. "Care, I have to tell you something."

"*Do* you have to?" I said. "I'm a little fragile right now."

"I think I do. I wasn't sure before, but from what you said about Adam being in love with Patrick. . . . Here's the thing. Adam has always liked guys."

My lungs released the breath I'd been holding in one quick puff. For a second there, I'd thought she was going to tell me there was another affair. "No, he said it was a recent thing. A curiosity thing. 'Exploration.' "

"It's not."

"I mean, I know it's not usually, but he said —"

"He's lying."

"Why would you say that?"

"A few weeks before your wedding," she said, and another big breath froze in my chest as I realized this was not merely an opinion. It was a story. A story I had never heard until today.

"A few weeks before my wedding?" I mumbled.

She bit her lip and nodded. "I heard something."

"What?"

"You remember my friend Amy Kerson, right?"

"Sure."

"Well, we were hanging out one night at her Hamptons place. Her brother Brett was there too."

"Adam always hated that kid."

And then I caught it — the faintest pucker of her eyebrows.

"Ruby, please tell me what Brett Kerson had to say."

She licked her lips. "Amy asked me something about the wedding. Brett was . . . surprised. That you guys were getting married. When I asked him why, he said . . . he said Adam was gay. He said, he might think he could manage it now, but it would surface eventually."

My brain, peering around the corner at what she might say next, did not like the view one bit. "Why, he thought Adam was giving him sexy eyes or something?"

She shook her head. So slightly I knew she didn't want to move it at all. "He said they had a relationship, Care. A really intense one, like, they slept together and everything, until Adam ended it. It happened when they were sixteen, the summer before your junior year. The summer before he met you."

It was stunning, how absolutely I accepted it. Even while I drew my breath at that moment, I remember thinking, *I wish I could pretend I didn't believe this,* but it was like looking at a photograph that you don't notice is slightly out of focus, until you see the next frame: The softened edges suddenly crisp. I couldn't disbelieve it, not even for an instant.

Brett had been one of the most popular guys in our grade, the way the drama kids always were at a nerd factory like Stuyvesant. Engaging, charismatic, brilliantly talented. I'd always figured Adam's loathing of him was like the way two magnets with the same charge will repel each other — magnets only have use for the metal that clings to them. But this wasn't like that at all.

Adam had been the metal.

Adam hadn't hated Brett for being competition; he'd hated him for being desirable. I remembered that night at his parents' farmhouse, my trembling breath, my incandescent wonder that we were sharing these amazing things for the very first time, with each other. When in fact, the only first I'd been for Adam was a vagina.

And my sister had known it. Known it, and hid it, for over ten years.

I stared at her, trembling, sick with shock. "You *knew*? You knew this thing about him, this thing that ruined my marriage, and you *kept* it from me? How *could* you?"

My voice had started out as a whisper, but by the time I got to the last sentence I was screaming, and Ruby flinched in the face of it. "Care, I'm so sorry. The thing is, I didn't know. I didn't know *what* I knew. I knew Adam had been with a guy once, but by that point it was seven years before, and you'd never even hinted that it might be a thing with him, and —"

"I hadn't hinted because I had no idea!"

"I know. I know. But just listen to me for a second. I was only eighteen, and I had no idea what I should do. It was three weeks before your wedding, which was the most important thing in our family right then, since the minute you got engaged, so I knew Mom would blame me if I did anything to mess it up. And honestly, I was scared that *you* would blame me, like I was trying to rock the boat on purpose."

"I would never have blamed you. Ruby, I deserved to know! How could you have held this back from me?"

"You're saying that with hindsight, though." She was staying calm, and her calmness was beginning to infuriate me. It wasn't like her. And I wanted to keep screaming. "Can you honestly say that if I'd told you what Brett said back then, you would have believed me? Or would you have accused me of making it up for drama?"

"I wouldn't have accused you of making it up," I said. "And at least then I would have known. I could have talked to him about it. God, I mean, maybe I could have ended it then, and found somebody else who wouldn't have put me through this fucking nightmare I'm in right now!"

Ruby's face was tight and serious. "I'm sorry. I really am. You guys had been together for so long by then, and you seemed so totally happy and so sure about it. There was no doubt in my mind that Adam adored you. I thought I was doing the right thing."

"Fuck your 'sorry,'" I spat. "And fuck your 'right thing.'" I clambered up the steps of the pool, shivering violently as the chilly wind wrapped around my wet skin, and burrowed into my towel. "I guess you've told your precious boyfriend by now," I added, and when I saw the guilty twitch of her face I knew I was right.

"Okay, I did, but —"

"FUCK YOU!" I yelled. "Fuck both of you! You know how much I would hate that, to be gossiped about behind my back like some kind of scandal. 'Oh, let me tell you all my secrets about Caroline. She doesn't even know Adam's always had a thing for guys!' "

"Care, it wasn't like that. We were saying how much it all sucks, and he asked me —"

"If you'd ever picked up on anything. Right? Oh, I know exactly how that conversation went down. And I know you're going to call him as soon as I walk out of here, and whine about how I wigged out when you told me your little secret, so can you just freaking save it, please? Save it. Please let me have a little dignity, and wait until you get home before you pick me apart."

She opened her mouth to say something, then shut it again, shaking her head. "We wouldn't 'pick you apart,' " she said, wading out of the water. "It's not mean to talk about the problems going on with someone you care about. But yes, if it's that big a deal, I promise."

Suddenly, it surged up into my throat — the thing I knew, that Ruby didn't. I felt like a teapot on a stove, boiling with angry steam pressed against my valve. The urge to release it, to watch her nervous little face twist into shock and pain, slammed through my veins so fast that I actually gasped.

"What?" she said. "What's wrong?"

Jonathan and I kissed a few months ago, and it was fucking awesome. I wanted to say it. I wanted to lash out at her, make her hurt the way I hurt. Make *somebody* else hurt. Anybody at all.

"Care, you're freaking me out."

I closed my eyes, dragged in a huge, slow breath, and forced myself to let the fury go.

"Care?"

"Oh, holy hell," I whispered. "I am so very far from over this."

27

I find it hard to understand in my mind what it means to love you after you are dead.
— Richard Feynman to his wife, Arline, October 17, 1946, sixteen months after her death

I could tell Neil knew what was coming as soon as I saw his face. He tucked his sleet-spattered coat on the back of the chair opposite me at Tunnel City Coffee the following Monday after work, and sat down with his forearms braced on the table. His eyes were as warm as ever, but a sad little smile curved one corner of his lips.

"Hey, Care. Something you need to talk about?"

Staring at his big, capable hands wrapped around his coffee cup, I nodded.

"Are you giving things another shot with Adam?"

That whipped my head up. "What? No. Oh god, no. The opposite. No, that is really, truly done. I'm calling a lawyer tomorrow."

"Oh," he said, his shoulders relaxing underneath his thick gray sweater. "Then what's going on? Is everything okay?"

I sighed, and reached for one of his hands with mine. "I think we need to stop seeing each other."

He nodded slowly as he absorbed this, one corner of his lip pinched in his teeth. "Did I freak you out when I asked you to be exclusive?"

"No. I haven't dated anyone else this whole time. It's just . . . I thought I was more ready to move on than I actually am. My marriage is over, there's no question about that. But I've realized I'm a way bigger mess than I thought I was."

"You don't seem like much of a mess to me," he said.

"I think that's because I'm good at rebounding. Honestly, I'm scared that I'm rushing into this too fast. I like you so much. It feels so good to spend time with you — I'm scared it feels too good, you know? Like I haven't given myself enough time to get Adam totally out of my system, and be by myself, and grieve for our marriage and finish letting it go. I'm scared that

406

when I'm with you I'm just transferring that over instead of reaching a real ending point."

He tugged at his earlobe. "Well, yes and no. Dating somebody new after ending a marriage isn't some radical new experience. A lot of the basic functions are the same. You spend time together, you have sex, you cook meals, you talk. The fact that you're doing that with me doesn't mean you're transferring your feelings from your old relationship."

I must have looked skeptical, because he continued. "I know it's different, because Eva has been gone a lot longer than Adam has been . . . exploring. But for me this feels familiar in all the right ways, and new in all the right ways. Familiar, because I'm spending time with a woman I enjoy and admire and am attracted to."

"And what are the right ways that it's new?"

"You," he said, wrapping his hands over my wrists where they rested on the table. "Everything about you. Being with you is kind of like diving into a tray of fresh-baked cookies when you're starving. I don't want to stop seeing you, even if you're still figuring a few things out."

"I don't want to, either," I said. "But I'm

feeling like I probably should."

"Caroline, I really like you," he said softly. "But I still miss her, every day. I will never not miss her. It will never not hurt. I'm just trying to find my way back to something that feels like life. So I don't mind that you're trying, too."

"I know. But the truth is, that's part of this, too. I'm certainly not ready for anything serious right now, but if I ever were . . . I don't think I'd be happy being permanently stuck behind your children *and* your wife."

"Is that how I make you feel?"

"I'm not blaming you. I mean, how could it not be like that? I just don't think it's a situation I should stay in."

"Fuuuck," he sighed, rubbing both hands over his scalp. "That first time we slept together. I'm sorry about that. I told you I was. You have to know it never happened again."

"You didn't tell me, actually. But I believe you. And I honestly don't blame you even one little bit. But I can't put myself into a situation where all I'll ever be is second fiddle to a ghost."

His lips compressed with frustration and he slung backward in his chair, arms crossed over his chest. I could see the impulse to

408

argue with me simmering in his face. But he didn't. Which, coming from Neil, said more than enough.

For a few moments, all there was between us was the hiss of the espresso machine and the clatter of dishes and cash registers. A few tables away, two college-aged girls were on what, judging by their nervous but excited body language, looked like a first date. I wondered whether they'd be in love or hate each other a year from now.

"When I was in Vegas," I said, pulling my eyes away from the girls, "I finally hit the bottom of how far the problems went. It was worse than I'd ever realized, because even the whole time I was begging him to tell the truth to me, Adam would not stop lying. I'm just so . . . angry. I feel like it's poisoning me."

"You think I'm not angry, too?"

"But it's different. You're angry at life, for being miserable and cruel and unfair. I am only angry at *him*. I'm so furious at him for putting someone else in front of me and lying to me and shitting all over our marriage, I'm scared I'm never going to be able to let it go. I don't want to be this bitter, angry person, and I hate that he turned me into this."

"You won't be. Not always."

"I don't know that. I don't know how I'm ever going to trust somebody again. I mean, how? How am I supposed to? It wasn't only the cheating, it was everything he hid from me, including the fact that he has *always* liked guys. Yeah," I said, as Neil's eyebrows flicked northward, "that was the big revelation I got in Vegas. Adam told me he's in love with Patrick, and Ruby finally decided to inform me that my husband apparently had a passionate relationship with another guy from our high school the summer before we got together. Which means I'm not sure I understood *anything* about my marriage correctly. After something like that, how can you ever believe that the next person you want to trust isn't capable of the same kind of deceit?"

Neil sighed and slowly shook his head. "I don't know, baby. That's a doozy, all right. I can tell you I've never hidden anything from you, and I never would, but I understand those words don't mean a lot when the last person who made that promise wound up going back on it."

And the awful thing was, he was right. The words *didn't* mean a lot. Even coming from someone I cared about and trusted as instinctively as I did Neil, there was nothing where my certainty should have been. Nothing at all. He was an honest, good-hearted, wonderful man; but then, I'd thought Adam had been, too.

I turned my face toward the window, where a mix of sleet and rain spat down from a grim white sky, and tiny pellets of ice bounced and danced on the sill outside. All of a sudden, I felt unbearably tired. I had proven everything I could possibly need to prove — I was not only fine on my own, but even recovering some independence I hadn't noticed I'd surrendered. I was desirable, not just to a kind and beautiful man like Neil but, in case I had wondered, to the general population of dudes trawling Vegas for a warm hole to ejaculate in. I had, until the nuclear fight at the pool, grown closer with Ruby than I'd felt since I could remember. I'd done all this proving and growing, and somehow the pain of Adam's betrayal still festered inside me, like a fetid old well in the woods half covered with branches. No matter how badly I wanted to relax into Neil's undemanding warmth, I couldn't contaminate him with the water from that well. It would poison anything we tried to make.

"I wish like crazy that I could change my mind here," I said softly. "I know you're not trying to push me into anything serious, but still, I just . . . I don't think I'm ready. I don't trust myself with you right now. I don't want to make you regret this."

His smile was sad but sweet, and in spite of everything, it made me feel better. It told me he understood that I was trying hard to do the right thing. "Okay. I respect that. And I appreciate it." He half-rose from his seat, cupped my face in one hand, and gave me a lingering kiss that made me lean toward him like a flower. And then he let me go.

He stood, whirled his coat from his chair back onto his arms, and zipped it closed with the decisiveness of motion I enjoyed about him. "Guess I'll see you around," he said, with that one-sided smile, and then he walked to the door, flipped his hood up over his head, and stepped out into the rain.

I'd known that ending things with Neil would make me feel like crap. What I didn't expect is that I would start missing him as soon as he walked away.

The next day was the first time the view of North Adams didn't lift me. In the thin, tentative light of an early winter morning, the landscape looked like a bruise: raw gray-brown mountains, smudged with white and overhung by purple, pewter-tipped clouds.

As I hurried toward the entrance to the museum building, the frigid, smoke-scented wind whipped at my face until my eyes watered. Without consciously deciding to, I stopped in front of *Tree Logic* and looked up.

Ice from the previous day's storm limned the branches of the young trees, accentuating their awkward posture. They looked weighted down and tired. It had been a frigid winter — what if they were dead under there, and we didn't even know? What if maybe planting a bunch of trees upside down just to see what they would do was not so much an artistic expression as it was an exercise in how to slowly kill some perfectly healthy trees?

Inside my office, I dialed the number Jonathan had given me months ago — his cousin Harriet, an attorney who practiced in Brooklyn.

Her tone was brisk and efficient. "Caroline, nice to talk to you. . . . I wish it were under better circumstances."

"Yeah, me too."

"So, I don't actually practice family law myself, but I'm happy to refer you to a colleague who does. I just wanted to check one thing with you first. Jonathan mentioned you live in Massachusetts, but you want to file in New York, is that right?"

"Yeah, we were married in New York."

"Well, the state where you married doesn't have a bearing on where you file the divorce; it should be your state of residence. So if you live in Massachusetts, then you need to file there. And you should consult an attorney who's in the Massachusetts bar. I'm afraid I don't have any connections there at all. I'm so sorry I wasn't able to be of more help."

Embarrassment, and a slick of oily guilt, slid over me as I put down the phone.

I was an idiot. I had done the legal equivalent of self-diagnosing via WebMD. I thought I'd been sensible, going right to the New York state court website back in September instead of to Divorces4Less, but what I'd utterly failed to recognize was that I didn't belong on the New York website in the first place. And if I'd had the common sense to call a living, breathing lawyer at any point before this moment — as both my sister and my mother had repeatedly told me to do — I would have found that out.

Well, at least I'm working with the correct state now, I thought, as I sheepishly typed "Massachusetts divorce" into my browser. Scanning the requirements and the proce-

414

dures, most of which reflected the same legalese terms that the New York pages had, I spotted something that knocked my heart down under my stomach.

Massachusetts had no waiting period to file. I could have started the process as early as I'd wanted to. Had Adam somehow been convinced not to fight me on it, the divorce could have been nearly complete by now. This could almost be over.

28

After all I do only want to advise you to keep growing quietly and seriously throughout your whole development; you cannot disturb it more rudely than by looking outward and expecting from the outside replies to questions that only your inmost feeling in your most hushed hour perhaps can answer.
— Rainer Maria Rilke to Franz Kappus,
February 17, 1903

Something I did, on the formerly rare occasions when I needed a moment at work to clear my thoughts, was to get up and walk into the galleries. I didn't have a favorite place to go, since most of our exhibits were only transitory, so I tended to let my feet wander where they would.

That morning, I found myself in the Alex Lim gallery. The exhibit I had developed with Alex featured a series of works he had done using antique books: He had, with a meticulousness that even I could hardly comprehend, programmed a laser cutter to pierce delicate and impossibly small holes at selected intervals, and varying depths, throughout the thickness of the book. The result was that, when the books were opened to the intended page, the words behind the pierced sections showed through, fitting into and yet altering the meaning of the text on the pages displayed.

I had assembled the exhibit, and written the copy for it, to discuss Alex's concept of creating a physical narrative within a narrative. The artist using his hands to impose a new iteration of the story that had originally been breathed into life by the writer. But that morning, as I stood motionless in front of one of Alex's tiny, perfect, beautiful books, I thought about layers.

Alex had deliberately picked the spots he had lasered out. Having chosen them, he'd known what the finished, altered text would say. But the truth was, he could have chosen any of these hundreds of pages to start with, any others of the pages to drill to, any others of these words to eliminate and reveal. Every page was a layer, and every layer had its own words. They weren't all revealed at once, and each page, each layer, said different things, but they were all part of the same story.

I'd thought I'd read the book of Adam from cover to cover — reread it till it was soft and tattered. Hell, I'd thought I was practically a co-author. But he had only ever let me read certain pages. There were some never revealed, and others where only a few selected words were permitted to show.

And I myself was not much different. There were layers I'd hidden from myself, even in the midst of the decision that was supposed to be the greatest reckoning of my life. I hadn't called a lawyer because I hadn't been ready to say goodbye to my husband. It was, at the end of it, exactly as simple as that. Months ago, I should have looked in the right places, for the right information, and moved forward with what I had told myself, as well as everyone who mattered, that I wanted to do. And yet, I hadn't. I'd been grateful for New York's waiting period, because it had let me procrastinate. And the procrastinating had let me hide. It had taken finally passing through to the other side, where I was truly ready for the marriage to end, before I could set my feet upon the path to do it.

My divorce attorney turned out to be

exactly no more, and exactly no less, than I needed. I had selected him because he had the highest Yelp rating for family lawyers in the western Massachusetts region, which was proof that, despite my initial thought of, *Wait, there are Yelp pages for lawyers?*, people like me were exactly why such things existed. It took us one afternoon meeting to set up all the paperwork, including the statement enumerating the financial arrangements I was requesting: the share I'd paid into our savings and retirement accounts, and a payment plan for the house. It was fair, and reasonable, and I had every hope that Adam would agree to it. The house in particular, I thought he would; his parents had put both our names on the deed, but he'd never wanted to live there in the first place. Letting me gradually buy out a property he didn't want and hadn't spent a dime on seemed to me the least he could do.

As I sat with my pen poised over the complaint form, the strangeness of it gripped me. I was really doing it; there it all was, all the proper information with the proper dates and the proper names. Including the one I was going back to: Caroline Fairley. It beckoned to me, like a long-missed loved one. Miss Fairley felt like a lighter me, a freer me; I was looking forward to being her again.

Four days later, Len the lawyer sent me confirmation that Adam had been served. And the oddest thing was that I didn't hear from him. Even if he had accepted that we had to end this — after all, he'd finally admitted to being, albeit reluctantly, in love with someone else — I'd thought he would at least acknowledge what I had done. Given past precedent, I was expecting a letter. But there was nothing, not even a text.

And in the meantime, I couldn't seem to get away from missing Neil. It was a full, 360-degree sort of missing. Not just for what I'd thought would be the most obvious loss — the pleasure we'd found together — but every single thread he'd woven through my days. His texts; his emails; the thrill of hearing his voice in the hallway at work and thinking, *That's my man, and nobody knows;* his affectionate kisses; his music; his pancakes; his stubborn intellect; his deliberate, thoughtful approach to parenting; his devotion to his daughters; even his daughters themselves.

All of it added up to the fact that I missed his warm, steady presence in my life. Even when I hadn't seen him in a few days, the knowledge that I was about to, or that I could pick up the phone and call him anytime I felt like hearing his voice, had done far more to fill up my loneliness than I had realized. And so had the fact that there was somebody who wanted me and cared about me, who I wanted and cared about, too.

The one thing that made it hurt a little less was knowing that that fact hadn't changed; I was the one who'd thrown the brakes here. But I knew I had to, for his sake as much as my own. And the desolation that roared into the void created when I pushed him away — it told me I'd been right. I needed to feel it. I needed to let the loneliness in.

One afternoon toward the end of January, I was marking up a loan agreement for a piece I wanted to borrow from a collector when the museum's receptionist beeped me to answer a call.

"I have a Diana Ramirez for you, do you want to take her?"

"Oh my god!" I yelped, dropping my pen. "Yes! Yes, I want to take her." God help me, I'd all but forgotten about her.

A moment later, we were connected. "Hi, Diana," I gushed, aware I sounded like the teenage fangirl of a pop star, yet completely unable to stop myself. "So nice to hear from you! How were your holidays?"

"Oh, you know . . . family," she said, with her easy laugh. "This is where I give you the obligatory 'Sorry I haven't called, work work work, blah blah work' routine, so let's just skip over that this time, okay?"

"Sure," I laughed. "Consider yourself excused. What can I do for you?"

"I got the little menu that you sent — that was super cool."

Are you going to pay for any of it? my brain yelled, but all I said was, "Great, I'm so glad you enjoyed it. My sister designed it, actually." Something inside me pinched at the thought of Ruby, whom I hadn't spoken to since the disastrous revelation in Vegas.

"Did she? She did a nice job. I was calling about something you had on there — the residency for that artist, Farren Walker. Is that the woman you were telling me about when I visited? Who used to work at the print shop and then started doing her own art?"

"That's her," I said, gratified that I'd been right: Diana had been paying attention to Farren's work.

"Do you really think she'd be up for hosting me at her studio? I'm thinking about donating some money for her, but I'd love

to see how she works. It sounds interesting."

Diana Ramirez, tech darling and noted
corporate raider, sounded . . . self-
conscious.

"Oh my gosh, Farren would *love* to have
you. And I'd love to take you. I'm overdue
for a visit to her anyway, so this is perfect.
When would you like to come up?"

"This Saturday, maybe? Is that nuts?"

Yes, it is, I thought, but I dug my cell-
phone out of my purse with my free hand
so I could text Farren: *Nice, cool rich lady
wants to come to the studio this weekend and
maybe donate some money for a residency.
Please tell me you're free?*

"Well," I stalled, "I'll need to check with
Farren of course, but —"

*Good thing I just whipped myself up a fresh
Rich Lady pie,* Farren replied. *Got some stuff
in the works I think you're going to dig. Bring
the dame on down!*

I grinned. Farren was a loose cannon, but
I was pretty sure she'd behave herself
around someone who might decide to give
her a job. The woman was crazier than a
bag of cats, but she was sure as hell no fool.

"All right, Diana, you're on. Farren wrote
me back that she's been working on some
great stuff and she'd love to host you this

weekend."

"Oh, that's awesome," said Diana, sounding genuinely excited for the first time since I'd been in touch with her.

I reminded myself that just because Diana was interested, that didn't mean she would ever actually part with the dough. Neil had told me about a donor he'd courted for two *years* before the guy finally coughed up a check — for a whopping $5,000. But still, when I hung up the phone, I was smiling for the first time in a week.

29

You belong in the most secret part of you.
Don't worry about cool, make your own
uncool. Make your own, your own world.

— Sol LeWitt to
Eva Hesse, April 14, 1965

Farren's house was like something out of
Anne of Green Gables: tucked away on a
back road, around a corner, at the bottom
of a hill, half screened by the plumy ever-
greens that loomed above it. Currently surrounded by heavy white drifts as was the
rest of western Massachusetts, the house
was small and of indeterminate age, with
dormer windows and various additions so
tiny as to seem almost pointless poking out
of the structure on every side. Farren's
husband (the second one) had been a
builder before ALS brought him down a few
years back; working on their house had been
his favorite way to spend time until the

disease stole his body.

The lady of the house greeted us at the door in a shirt, apron, and jeans so crusted with paint I could barely see how she folded them — though on second thought, I was inclined to think folding wasn't really much of a thing for Farren. More than anyone else I knew, she reveled in messiness. She wasn't filthy in the way that leaves decomposing food around and accumulates dust rhinoceri instead of dust bunnies — but she was about six inches short of that.

"Well, howdy, dollface!" she yelled, clutching me into a hug so robust I almost toppled over. "Awfully nice to see ya. What's shakin'?"

"Oh, not too much, just divorcing my husband," I said. Being around Farren always brings my own naughty streak out of its usual state of deep cover.

"Damn it, girl. What happened to trying?"

"Long story," I sighed. "And no," I added repressively as I spotted the question brewing in her eyes, "the redhead has nothing to do with it. Anyway, enough about that — let me introduce you to Diana. This is Diana Ramirez; we went to college together."

"Farren Walker," she said, sticking out one paint-smeared paw. When she saw Diana hesitate, she rolled her eyes. "You're fine, it's dry. Come on in, girls, let me fix you up a bite to eat."

Farren, it turned out, really had whipped up a pie. Farren loves to bake, but the difficulty with her offerings is that her creative brain tends to take liberties with the ingredients in ways that yield mixed results of tastiness. From the *Cooking Light* still open on her bright turquoise kitchen counter, I could tell that this pie was meant to be a simple blueberry one, yet what Farren served to us appeared to contain as many sliced canned pineapples, mandarin oranges, and maraschino cherries as blueberries. I knew if I asked her, she'd tell me the pie had needed to be more colorful.

"So, Farren," I said, setting my fork on my plate after I had worried down the pie, "what is this new work you wanted to show us?"

She bounced to her feet and headed for the kitchen door. Diana and I followed, our boots squeak-crunching as we picked our way along a narrow pathway carved into an otherwise unbroken twenty-eight-inch-deep drift of snow. I had a pathway like it at home, myself.

Farren's pathway led to her studio, a building nearly as large as the house itself, which had been built by Farren's husband

to her exact specifications. It was a wonderful space, with high ceilings and paint-
spattered concrete floors, all of it lit by the
massive assemblage of windows that made
up the north-facing wall. As always when I
stepped inside this place, my pulse acceler-
ated at the sprawl of pure creativity: Half-
completed canvases hung from the walls,
and color tests and various inspiration images were pinned thickly to a tackboard near
the door. My favorite part was Farren's supply area, where immense tubs of paint, their
sides drooling with dried spills of color,
squatted next to a rack containing her tools
and her screens.

"Okay, before I show you the good stuff,"
Farren said to Diana, "silk-screening for
dummies: the Farren Walker technique."

With a flourish of her hand, she reached
into her rack and pulled out a large metal
frame with an expanse of mesh stretched
across it, similar to the kind window screens
are made from, but more finely woven. On
the surface of the mesh, a chemical treatment had created a semi-opaque layer,
through which a random scattering of ir-
regularly shaped holes revealed the mesh
itself.

"Now, traditional silk-screening, as a
printing method, is done with liquid ink,"

she said. "It's used to create color and pattern. That was Andy Warhol's thing. But I thought it would be more fun to juice the ink up to a real paint that has some heft to it." Farren plopped the screen onto the dark gray test paper she had set up on a nearby table, then spooned a few ounces of viscous, shimmery paint into the screen. With a squeegee-like tool, she smoothed the paint around the screen, pressing it into the pattern area, then set the squeegee aside. She took the screen by the edges and, with the gentlest possible touch, rocked it gently from side to side, angle to angle; then she slowly lifted it away.

"Et voilà!" Farren said, and I offered a spontaneous burst of applause in response to her showmanship. There on the paper was the image she had created by pressing the paint through the holes in the thickened mesh: a soft, glittering galaxy of stars, not just spots of color but each with a thickness and body all its own. "I made it pretty thick, to show you how it works," she said, "but when I use this screen for artwork I start thin on the paint and slowly build it up to more layers." She pointed over Diana's shoulder, at a piece she'd made using multiple layers of the screen, including some where the paint was transparent and yielded

only texture.

"Oh wow," said Diana. "I see it now. That's so cool how you thought to do that."

"One of the things I think makes Farren's work so special," I said, slipping back into curator mode, "is the way it's more controlled than painting, but more complex than printmaking. And it has depth, but it's definitely not sculpture, either."

"I'm special!" said Farren, wiggling her hands and pirouetting in place. "All right, come on, let me show you the Big Kahuna."

With Diana and me trailing behind, Farren scurried to the center of the room, where a huge canvas sat braced on two sturdy wood tables that had been shoved together for the purpose.

"Wow," I said, stepping closer for a look. It was the largest piece I had ever seen Farren create. Her work had been slowly but surely growing larger over the years, starting with prints about the size of the front of a T-shirt and, as she gained confidence and gave rein to her curiosity, moving out to more traditional artwork sizes. But this new piece was so large I wasn't sure how she'd even gotten it inside the studio.

I stopped short before I drew too close, momentarily overwhelmed by the complexity of it. "It's . . . a map?"

"A maze," Farren said.

The bottom layer of the work looked like an abstracted city map, rendered in tints of gray and white. The "streets" were marked with names, but, sure enough, none of them progressed for any great distance across the canvas; everywhere I looked, the streets turned or stopped, forced into corners, walled in by delicate ridges of paint that must have been made by one of Farren's special screens.

But the map itself wasn't the only thing. Row after row of yellow dots marched across the canvas, following the rigid lines of the streets, but here and there, one was missing. And as I looked closer, I could discern subtle variation among the dots themselves: They were all the same diameter, but the shapes of some were crisply formed, where others were slightly smudged and flattened. Overall, the work was only partially completed; below a certain point, the lines for the maze streets were barely sketched in, and the dots layer was absent completely.

"This is amazing," said Diana, peering close. "What's with the dots?"

"When I started working with the thicker paint," Farren said, "I noticed that it didn't act consistently like ink does. It responds to

431

the presence of the screen in different ways. More or less the same, but with these tiny little differences. The differences are my favorite part."

"And what about the missing dots?"

"They started happening naturally. The paint would cover too thinly and not press through. Or one of the holes in the screen would get clogged without me realizing it. So I made a few more screens with holes missing, to reproduce the inconsistency."

Diana looked at her quizzically. "You didn't want it perfect?"

Farren split a pumpkin seed with her teeth and spat the shell into her hand. "Perfect is boring."

"Spoken like a true artist," said Diana.

"It is. Perfect is no way to live. Perfect isn't life."

"Perfect is the goal," said Diana. "Or, if not perfect, there has to be a predictable result. You made this screen so you can reproduce the effect of these dots in a consistent way, right?"

"They look consistent, but they're not," said Farren, smiling. "What do you do, Diana?"

"Software," Diana said, and Farren clapped her hands together.

"Damn! I would have said engineering or

science. But I was close, though, right?"

"You were."

"Is it engineering software?" Farren said, narrowing her eyes cannily.

"Dating, actually. I developed a group of dating applications for cellphones."

"What, something like that Crush app thing?" said Farren. "I have a couple of fellas I talk to on there."

"It actually is Crush," I said. "Diana is the founder."

"Well, by golly! Imagine that. So you developed software to tell people how to fall in love."

"I developed software to help people *find* each other," Diana said. "What they do once they've met is completely out of our control."

"Aha!" yelled Farren, thrusting her index finger at Diana like a rapier. "And there you go. Honey, aside from love, art is the most subjective thing there is. You're never gonna have a predictable result. Not in how it gets made, or in how people feel about it. So what I like to do is start from a place where I expect that something's going to turn out a little weird. That tension between what the eye expects and what it receives is the coolest thing to me."

"Like those vision trick things?"

"Not even. Just the difference between what looks like perfection, and the imperfection it actually is."

"Well, can you show us on the painting?" I said, needing to steer the conversation back to the artwork.

"Abso-tutely," Farren said, and whipped out from her apron the smallest screen I'd ever seen her use. About the size of an address book, it was more of a stencil than a screen, and as she set it to the canvas and daubed paint onto it I realized why. The maze was too haphazard to be put into a repeating image like a screen would make; Farren only wanted the shape and height of her individual lines to be consistent.

"Are the dots supposed to be the guidelines for the maze?" said Diana suddenly. "I mean, from our perspective we can see that they overlay it, but if you were in the maze and you were walking, and you saw these dots, they would look like the path."

"Nailed it in one," said Farren, not breaking her concentration as she fitted her stencil into place on a new row of the maze. "The dots are the guidelines we think we see. But they're only an illusion, not the thing that marks the path."

"And they're untrustworthy themselves," I said. "Weird shapes, occasionally missing."

434

"They don't take us where we think we're going to go," Diana said. "The maze stops, and turns, and changes course."

"It sure does, doesn't it?" I said quietly, as I stared at the artwork. Farren's husband died before her sixty-third birthday. It would have been the year of their eighteenth anniversary — not their fortieth, as it would have been for Adam and me when we reached that age. Her first husband had left her for her cousin. Two months later, her brother's best friend asked her out on the date he'd wanted for twenty-five years.

Diana was quiet on the drive back to my house from Farren's studio, staring out the window at the snowy hills. I considered trying to draw her out, engage her about Farren and the art, but it seemed too greedy. I wondered, though, what unexpected turns a life like hers could have taken, a life that had led her so young to such spectacular success. None of our conversations had ever yielded mention of a partner, and maybe that was something.

She came back to herself when we reached our destination, though. "Thank you so much for arranging that," she said from behind her scarf, stamping her sleek black boots on my frozen driveway as the wind blew ice crystals across our feet.

"My pleasure," I said. "Can I get you anything before you go? Hot cocoa? Another slice of fruit cocktail pie?"

"No, thank you. I've got to get going. Stupid phone's been blowing up all morning. I had it on vibrate," she added sheepishly. "Sometimes that's the closest I can get to unplugging."

Those corners in the maze didn't always sneak up on you, it occurred to me. Sometimes you could steer yourself right into one with your very own hands.

"Come on in and warm up before you get back on the road," I said. "Half an hour. You did tell me you liked my kitchen."

She laughed. "All right, cocoa sounds great."

"Did you enjoy yourself at Farren's?" I said, while we waited for the kettle to heat up. "I know she was thrilled for the chance to show off."

"She's fantastic," said Diana. "I love people who do their own thing fearlessly like that, you know?"

I cocked my head, evaluating. I was pretty sure it would be all right to ask. "Am I crazy, Diana, or did you not like me in college?"

She met my eyes and smiled ruefully. "I

was jealous," she said. The words slipped out easily, the way things do long after we've stopped giving them importance.

"Good grief, jealous of me? What on earth for?"

She lowered her chin and peered at me from under her brow. "You really have no idea?"

"I really don't. You and I were pretty similar, if you think about it."

"Yeah, except that you were perfect. You had this great boyfriend who adored you and this gorgeous friend who obviously also adored you —"

"Mmm," I said, as I poured the hot water for the cocoa into our waiting mugs. "As I'm sure you heard me tell Farren earlier, Adam and I are getting divorced. He cheated on me for months, and lied to me about all kinds of stuff. Even back in college he was lying." It was odd to remember there had been a time when I was embarrassed to tell her about it. By now, the thought of trying to hide it made me uneasy. It was my life, and I had to own it. Otherwise, I was no better than Adam.

"Oh, wow. That's horrible. I am so sorry to hear that. Really."

"And Jonathan and I still do not want to screw each other."

"I don't know what's wrong with you," she said, with a flicker of humor. Lord, even Diana was one of the legions. "But that was only part of it. You just came off like you had everything all lined up and the waters were going to part on command for you. It drove me nuts. I like you now, though," she added, from behind her cocoa mug.

"Oh, thank you, Diana," I said tartly, before I remembered who I was talking to.

"Hey, you asked," she said, palms spread wide.

"I did. I most certainly did." I circled the island to sit next to her, then realized I'd unconsciously mimicked her elbows-on-counter posture. It made me feel like we were two old cronies at a bar, trading stories. "You know what, though — Adam made that same comment recently. In the middle of the breakup. He'd been doing all this great writing without telling me, because he thought I'd think it was beneath him, and he said the reason why was because I wouldn't understand uncertainty . . . or the concept of someone changing their mind about what they want. I don't know what I did to give the impression that I'm so rigid."

"Not rigid, really, just . . . smooth. Bumpless."

"Now you're making me sound like a shaving cream ad," I said, and she laughed. "I guess I'm not exactly bumpless anymore, though."

She took a long sip of her cocoa, both hands wrapped around the mug. "That's not always a bad thing."

"No," I said. "It is not always a bad thing at all."

From Adam himself, it was still silence. Several times a day, I considered calling him, but set my phone down every time. The truth was, my instinct told me he wasn't ignoring me to be childish. He was either developing the tactics for his very last stand, or — what felt, finally, and astonishingly, like the most likely thing — he was having the papers reviewed as a prelude to signing them. Either way, I figured I could leave him alone a little while longer.

Three days after the visit with Farren, I returned from my lunch break to find an envelope on my desk. For an instant my heart vaulted into my chest at the thought that it might be Adam's papers, but of course he wouldn't have sent them here. The envelope was from Crush, Inc., and I knew what it was by the weight of it. With shaking fingers, I tore it open.

And then I stared. My eyes skipped all over the page, not comprehending the notes scribbled on it. Scrawled in silver marker though they were, the marks didn't change or disappear, no matter how long I looked at them. Neither did the smaller, lighter piece of paper that had slipped out of the envelope along with the menu.

I needed another pair of eyes. In a haze, I walked the now-familiar route to Neil's office . . . and found it empty. A bolt of pain shot through me at the sight of that empty chair, but I sucked in a deep breath and reminded myself that the only reason I hadn't spent last night sleeping with the man's lovely arm around my waist was my own decision. Not a decision that made me feel good, but still the right one.

"It's pretty shocking I haven't killed that plant yet, huh?" said Neil. From right behind me.

Startled, I turned to face him, my mouth opening and closing pointlessly.

"Care. Can I come into my office, please?"

I shuffled aside as he circled his desk and sat down. He was wearing a fitted white dress shirt with the sleeves rolled up his forearms, and it made him look professional and competent and sophisticated and, frankly, offensively hot. How on earth could

440

there ever have been a time when I hadn't noticed him?

"So, what can I do for you?" He swiveled his desk chair to the side, one ankle on the opposite knee.

And, finally, I remembered why I was there. Mutely, I set the envelope on his desk and shoved it toward him.

His eyebrows climbed higher and higher as he read, then he dropped the menu card on his desk and looked up.

"Holy shit," said my professional, competent, sophisticated colleague. "Holy *shit*. All of it?"

Afraid to speak in case it woke me up from a dream, I nodded.

"All of it. Even Farren!"

"Of course Farren," I snapped, ignoring the tiny flash of humor that curled Neil's lips before it vanished. "Diana loved her. Because she's amazing."

"This is awesome, Care. Absolutely awesome. I never expected that she would come through with this much."

"I never expected that she would come through at all," I confessed. "Before she called to ask about meeting Farren, I'd pretty much given up on her."

"Well, you were right that she was interested in the craftsmanship aspect. You nailed it."

I shifted my weight on my feet, not wanting to leave yet but not able to think of a decent reason to stay. "Okay, so I guess . . . you know what to do with that check. Do we send her some flowers or something to thank her?"

"Sure. Yeah."

"And maybe Farren will make her a small piece."

"Yes. By all means ask her."

"Or, hell, I'll give her mine."

"I don't imagine you'll have to do that," he said, with a quiet smile.

For a long moment, we just stared at each other. I felt like I was waiting for him to say something, and he seemed to be waiting for *me* to say something, but there were no more words to be said. I'd been right to end things between us, and we both knew it.

"Well, anyway," I mumbled, "I guess I better get back to work. If I can make myself concentrate instead of floating around my office the rest of the afternoon."

"No kidding," he said. "Good luck with that."

I lingered in his doorway another few moments, just to push it extra far beyond the point of awkwardness, but right as I finally

442

turned to go, I heard him call my name. Instantly I popped my head back into the doorway.

"Yeah?"

"Fantastic job," he said, smiling. I waited another second or two.

But that was all he had to say.

30

All I care about — honest to God — is that you are happy and I don't much care who you'll find happiness with. I mean as long as he's a friendly bloke and treats you nice and kind. If he doesn't I'll come at him with a hammer and clinker.
— Richard Burton to Elizabeth Taylor,
June 25, 1973

There was a certain kind of winter evening that I loved, but which had mostly always proved elusive to me among the demands of work events, family, social life, and Adam's perpetual restlessness. But, in the stillness of Adam's absence, I was free to make these evenings, as often as I liked, and so I had been. It was the best way I knew to carve something out of my loneliness that I enjoyed.

When I got home from work, I would change into my favorite cashmere sweatpants (a gift from Adam, but somehow, I didn't mind anymore), my red shearling slippers that Ruby had given me that Adam teased me about, and my enormous fifteen-year-old Williams sweatshirt that both Ruby and Adam deplored. I would pour a glass of inexpensive Hudson Valley Cabernet that Neil had stumbled on during one of his stab-in-the-dark wine purchases, which I enjoyed in defiance of Adam's long-standing "Anything under fifty dollars is vinegar" guideline. I'd put on some quiet music, set a fire in the woodstove, and curl into the corner of the couch with a book in my hand and my favorite blanket draped over my lap. The blanket was a fuzzy wool plaid whose rich colors reminded me of that time in the fall when all the leaves are down but the snow hasn't come yet: acorn brown and pine needle green and the purple-gray of naked branches.

Sometimes I'd read, but often I'd find myself staring into the fire, mesmerized by its flickering glow and perfectly happy to be that way. If it was snowing, which it seemed to do every couple of days at this time of year, sometimes I'd just stare outside, past the pale reflection of my face, and watch the flakes drift in and out of the spill of light from the window.

It was an evening like this in early February, when I had a fresh glass of wine and a brand-new novel with a beautifully gowned historical lady on the cover, when I heard the thump of a car door outside. There was a hurried stomp of feet up the porch steps, a hesitant knock on the door, and then, as I rounded the corner to the front hallway, I saw him through the narrow windows that flanked the front door — Adam.

When our eyes met, he gave me a sad, one-sided smile, and the kind of wave that's just a lifted palm. *Hi. I used to live here with you. It's cold out, would you let me in?*

"Hey," I said, as he unzipped his coat and kicked the snow from his sneakers onto the sturdy gray welcome mat. Sneakers, in February. Adam never really did give in to the demands of the winters up here. "How come you didn't tell me you were coming? I would have made sure I was here."

He shrugged, not looking at me. "I wasn't sure you would see me. I guess I could have just mailed it, but . . ."

My eyes flicked to the leather messenger bag he had set on the floor. So this was it, then.

"No," I said, my lips trembling with the urge to cry. "No, I'm glad you're here."

He hesitated, and I realized he was staring

446

at his shoes. If he lived here, he would have kicked them off already, knowing how I hated having dirty melted snow tracked across my hardwood floors. But it felt too casual to him, now, stripping down to his socks. Too familiar. It was the dumbest little thing. I never would have guessed a pair of sneakers could break my heart.

"Adam, you can take off your shoes," I said. And then I turned away before I started crying.

In the kitchen, I turned the heat back up on the Dutch oven I'd left to cool on the stove. "I made a braised pork shoulder," I called, as if he were a normal husband home from a late day at the office. "It was pretty good, you want some?"

"Nah," he said, from the other side of the island. "I grabbed something along the way."

I had no idea whether this was true or not, but I wasn't surprised he didn't fancy a nice cozy home-cooked meal. I turned the stove back off. "Some wine, though?"

"Sure," he said automatically.

I poured him a glass. He didn't comment on the label. When he took a sip, he didn't wince. And I didn't make a comment about it. Sometimes, it was so much easier to let things go.

"Do you want to go sit down?" I said, and

he nodded.

"Ella Fitzgerald, huh?" he said, briefly lifting up my iPod as he settled into the couch — his usual end of the couch. "Since when do you listen to jazz?"

Suddenly I remembered that I'd mentioned Neil to Adam that night in Vegas, as a weapon. As an angry, drunken brag. I hated that I'd cheapened my relationship with Neil like that. "My friend introduced me to her."

"Your friend?" Adam said, the faintest pause between the two words. Asking the question as if he hadn't known the moment I said it. Adam knew all of my friends; I would have referred to them by name.

"The guy I was seeing," I said. "Who is still my friend."

The muscles worked around his mouth, but he kept silent. I watched him swallow it down, all of it, drop by drop. I watched him look around, absorbing the fact that I'd spent time with someone else in this house, cooked and dined and laughed with someone else, made love with someone else — under the roof that was supposed to be ours.

For a long time, Ella's wistful voice was the only sound between us. A log shifted in the fire. Adam took a deep sip of wine, and I heard the noise his throat made.

448

"You were partly right, you know," he said at last, tapping his wine glass with one finger while he stared into the fire. "About what you said in your letter — that I was hiding things from you because of my dad's influence. I absorbed a lot from him growing up, about what a man should be, and what a successful writer should look like. And I bought into it all. I think I was . . . obsessed with living this perfectly assembled life: writing the right kind of stuff, being married to the right kind of woman. In my mind, the stuff that contradicted that — I didn't think of it as concealing it from *you,* specifically. . . . I was concealing it from everyone. I had this need, I guess, to control and select what I displayed to the world. Ghostwriting celebrity memoirs wasn't a part of who Adam Hammond should be — I mean, who would ever be proud to write something where they didn't even get their own name in the big type?" His voice was taut with bitterness and disapproval, and though I didn't know if Theodore had ever said those words to his son, I could easily imagine it.

"And," he continued, "wanting to sleep with men *definitely* wasn't part of it. God, I spent so many years telling myself that was just a minor aberration."

"It wasn't just Patrick, was it?" I said quietly.

He sighed, deeply, and turned his face to me. His eyes looked dark in the soft light; his face looked leaner than usual. "No. There were a couple of people in college. And every now and then since we've been married."

Even though Ruby's revelation about Brett Kerson had led me to suspect this might be the case, that didn't make it any easier to hear. "How often is 'every now and then'?" I said, hating the way my voice trembled.

"I don't know. Maybe three or four times. And it's the truth that I'm not sure, because it was the last thing I wanted to think about, once it had happened. But Patrick was the only — Christ, I can't believe I'm saying this — the only real affair. I'm so sorry, Caro," he said, as I turned my face to the ceiling so I could blink back the hurt and disappointment. "I'm so sorry. I know it's meaningless, but I am." He was silent for a long moment, then continued. "This is the thing I couldn't explain to you about all of this. I couldn't even admit it to myself for a long time, because I was still clinging like hell to the idea that I was a straight guy who also liked men every once in a while. So when you pushed me to be honest about it, I just shut down. But that's not really who I am."

"You're bisexual," I said, but he flipped his palm back and forth. Maybe yes, maybe no.

"Yeah . . . but not in the way I kept insisting I was. The honest truth is, I'm on the other side of the Kinsey scale. The reason I kept thinking of myself as, I don't know, straight with an asterisk, is that I'd loved you, and loved sleeping with you, for so long. You were the person I wanted to share my life with, not some guy. But, sweetheart — you're almost the only woman I've ever been attracted to."

While I struggled to assimilate this, he continued.

"That's why I idolized you the way I did. I never told you, but you weren't the first person I had sex with. The summer before —"

"I know," I said, abruptly cutting him off. "Brett Kerson. Ruby told me."

His lips parted with surprise, but then he swallowed. "That's right; she was friends with his sister, wasn't she?"

"Yeah. Evidently Brett was heard to express informed surprise that you were about to get married."

451

"So . . . you knew?"

"Absolutely not. Ruby kept that little tidbit all to herself until a few weeks ago."

He blew his breath out slowly. I knew he had quickly grasped the full range of implications of this; whatever his faults, Adam had always been highly perceptive. "Wow. No wonder she never liked me."

I waved it away with one hand. "That wasn't it. You two were just never each other's cup of tea. She knew about Brett, but I'm sure she never thought —"

"That I was doing exactly what I was doing. God, it's such a cliché," he said, rubbing his hands over his face, elbows jutting into the air. "The guy who can't admit to himself that he's gay, so he cheats on his wife until he takes it too far to keep it secret." He let his hands drop, leaned over, and took my hands in his. "I am so sincerely sorry, Caroline. I hate how much I hurt you. I know that what I've done has damaged you, and even though you are healing up even stronger than you were before, I should have treated you fairly in the first place. I'm sorry I wasn't strong enough to be honest with us both. We didn't have to end up here; it was me that led us."

"Are you sorry you married me?" I whispered.

He shook his head, eyes gleaming with tears. "Never. Everything I said, I meant. I've loved you more than anyone else in my life. I was going to say, before — that summer, with Brett. He was over one time, so we could fool around while Mom and Dad were out of town. Except they got back early. They didn't catch us literally in the act, but it was one stop short of that. I had time to grab my pants but not to put them on, so I remember I just wadded them into my lap to cover my crotch. It was so fucking humiliating. And the way my dad looked at me, Caro — I will never forget it. Just . . . this . . . *disgust.* I doubt you can imagine what it feels like to have your parent look at you that way."

I had my arms around him before he'd finished the sentence, and he clutched me, tears and breath hot against my neck. "I'm so sorry," I whispered, and held him tighter. "Adam, I'm *so* sorry. I hate that he failed you like that."

"It could have been worse," he said, on a shuddering breath. "It could have been way, way worse. He didn't hit me or kick me out of the house or disown me. And even afterward — after the initial shock, they just walked upstairs without saying anything, and Brett left, and I went to my room. They came in after a little while, and he sat in my desk chair and he said, very calmly, 'I don't want anything like that to ever happen again. You're young and confused, but things like that are not appropriate. Do you understand me?' And that was it, Caro, that 'Do you understand me?' Because I did. It was all he had to say."

I understood it too. Adam's father had always been kind to me, but he was a stern and unbending man. Profoundly intimidating to his sixteen-year-old son in a way that the thirty-four-year-old son had still not fully freed himself from.

He took a deep breath and loosened his arms. "And so that's — that's when I started trying to crush it. I'd kissed a couple of girls before, but I'd never wanted to do much more than that, except to satisfy my curiosity. So I figured the problem was that I hadn't found the right girl. I started looking at porn more, and it was definitely interesting," he said, a note of wry humor in his voice. "I decided that I was going to get myself a girlfriend. I didn't like the kind of girls my friends liked, with their giggling and their cliques, but there was this girl in my English class."

I smiled a little, knowing what was coming.

"She didn't talk a whole lot, but when she did, the things she said were so smart that I was completely impressed. She was beautiful, but she didn't draw attention to it like the other pretty girls; it was obvious that her brains were what she valued about herself. And she had this dignity about her, as if she knew full well that high school was nothing but one long embarrassment we all had to get through before we could get on with becoming adults. I liked this girl more and more. So, I asked her out.

"For our first date I took her on a picnic up at the Cloisters, because I knew she liked art. It was one of those fall days that's so perfect you can barely even believe it's real. We sat under a tree that was blooming with gold leaves, and talked and talked and talked, long after we finished our food. And then we lay on our backs on the blanket and stared at the deep blue sky through the leaves, and I reached over and took her hand, and I could feel my whole body come alive." He took my hand, interlacing our fingers. "And then when I kissed her, I knew. This was my girl."

He cupped my face with his free hand. My eyes drifted closed as our lips met, and I leaned into the kiss with a sigh. I kissed him slowly, committing him to my memory once and for all.

Oh, Adam. My beloved storyteller. How I was going to miss him.

"I know I've given you plenty of reason to doubt everything I ever told you," he said, stroking my cheek with his thumb, "but you should never doubt that I loved you. I still do. I always will. You were everything to me. Everything I wanted to be. My dream girl. So much so that I hated the thought of letting you down by showing you all of who I actually was."

I clasped his face and shook my head. "None of it would have disappointed me except the cheating."

He rested his forehead against mine. "And it's really too late to try again?"

"You know it is," I said. "I forgive you, but I could never trust you. And you're in love with Patrick. Something about him reaches you in a way that I never did. You need to follow that."

His smile was infinitely tender, and infinitely sad. "After all of this, you want me to be happy. Do you know how rare that is? To be that generous?"

"You being happy with someone else doesn't take anything away from me, Adam. We're already broken. But I'm always going to love you too, and I want to see you content and at ease with who you are."

He cupped my head and pressed a kiss to my forehead. "I never deserved you."

"Maybe not," I said, getting to my feet. "But I wouldn't necessarily say so. Ruby says that people can only give us what they have. I think probably, you did your best with what you had."

"Are you sorry you married me?" he said, echoing the same question I had asked him before.

"There have been days when I have been," I said. "There were a lot of those days. But today isn't one of them. I'm not sure how I'll feel about it tomorrow, but no; today, I'm not sorry I married you at all."

31

The memories of the blissful moments I have spent with you come creeping over me, and I feel most gratified to God and to you that I have enjoyed them for so long.
— Major Sullivan Ballou to his wife, Sarah, a week before his death in the Battle of Bull Run, July 14, 1861

I knew Adam was gone as soon as I opened my eyes. The house was too still, like the surface of a lake at dawn. Even when Adam was "being quiet," he couldn't be. He dragged a small trail of noise and motion behind him at all times; his idea of being quiet so as not to wake me was to play his music softly. There was no music this morning; no gush of water into the bathroom sink; no creaking floorboard in the hall; no ring of a dropped spoon in the kitchen, followed by a muttered curse.

When I made my way downstairs, the

main room glowed with the kind of pearly morning light that is unique to sunny days in winter. The ashes in the woodstove were gray and cool; the blankets Adam had slept under were neatly stacked on the end of the couch; our wine glasses had been washed and set out to dry, facedown on a towel on the counter. Droplets of water still clung to the bases of the stems.

On the dining table was an envelope with my name on it. The rip as I opened it was loud in the silence, so loud that I flinched. I expected to find a farewell letter from him inside, along with the other thing — it was the Adam thing to do. But no: It was only the papers. Signed.

I guessed we'd said our farewells last night, after all.

The dining chair creaked as I sat down to read. It seemed inconceivable that this document was the one that would end the long tale of our relationship, with all its many stories worn soft from retelling, chapter after fully lived and fully loved chapter. How was it that these words related to me and Adam? *Plaintiff* and *Defendant.* But there were those other words, summarizing the adultery, which had happened. And there, my maiden name that I was returning to. This had become our story, somehow.

But there was something else after all, I found. As I leafed through the pages, checking that everything was there, I saw it: Adam's final gesture of love and kindness in our marriage. Enclosed with the papers was the deed to the house, signed over to me outright, in full. There would be no payment plan required; he was giving it to me. The Hammonds' lawyer could not have been best pleased with this, but Adam had done it anyway, because he was generous. Always so generous with his gifts: the perfect thing, at the perfect time. Exactly what I needed the most.

As I wiped my tears away with my thumb, my mind returned, inevitably, to the question Adam had asked me the night before. Was I sorry I had married him? Also too, that question's conjoined twin siblings: Did I wish that Ruby had spilled her news about Adam and Brett at the time that she'd heard it? And, if I *had* heard it, would I have gone ahead with the wedding?

I sipped my tea, feeling the welcome warmth slide down my throat. The second two questions were far easier to answer than the first. I did wish Ruby had told me; knowing that critical fact about Adam could have saved us both a great deal of pain in either scenario. Whether I had broken off the engagement then, or continued on with my eyes open — knowledge is power, as I believe a few people have remarked. But I didn't think I would have broken things off. I cast my thoughts back to Caroline of ten and a half years ago: eager, determined, and deeply in love. Adam of ten and a half years ago would have told me that an early exploration did not indicate a lasting inclination. He would have told me he thought of no one but me, then enthusiastically demonstrated his attraction to me in our grown-up queen bed, and that would have been it. He'd still have cheated on me in college, and, presumably, also during our marriage.

Maybe there was a limit to the power of knowledge, after all.

The only real question to answer was whether I regretted it. Last night, soft with wine and tenderness, I had told him I did not. But even in the bright chilly light of morning, alone, with my hand resting on the papers that would end our marriage, I couldn't wish the marriage had never happened.

I had been betrayed and lied to and humiliated, hurt more terribly than I'd ever been by anyone or anything before. And it had happened at the very hands of the person I most deeply loved and trusted.

But despite every bit of that, I was still here. Despite my early certainty, I had not expired of pain. I still had my family, and I loved my sister and her astonishing choice of a boyfriend more than ever. I'd grown at work, landing a major donor and securing a residency for an artist who deserved to be seen. Hell, I'd even managed to have a gorgeous fling with a man who wasn't Adam, thus introducing myself to both the best sex I'd ever had, and the sort of kindness two hurting people can share.

Most of all, there was every year before this one. Every year of joy and laughter and love, full of far, far too many memories ever to count. Adam's ritually melodramatic driveway shoveling, full of Shakespearean gestures and proclamations that made me double over with laughter even as the raw wind whipped at my face. The way his hand always seemed magnetically drawn to my butt, dispensing little pats and rubs anytime he was within range. His unapologetic pride at introducing me as his wife. The deep pleasure of making our own home together and filling it with things and people we loved. That sense of belonging to another person, wholly and happily; of being one half of a partnership. The simple peace of having someone to rest my head on when I was tired.

I sobbed once, then the tears caught in my throat. Never had I felt the sheer loss of my marriage more acutely than I did in the moment I asked myself whether I regretted it. Because the answer was no, no, no, never. I could *never* wish we hadn't had what we did. The extent of Adam's cheating didn't sour me the way I would have expected, because it had come from a more complicated place than sheer selfishness; and, aside from Patrick, I knew it had all meant nothing. Hypotheticals were worthless — thinking "Maybe I could have married someone else who wouldn't have cheated" felt as alien and wrong as "Maybe I could have been born to a different family." It was like imagining a different face looking back at me in the mirror.

What was mine was mine, flawed as it might be. Adam had been mine; my marriage had been *mine.* I had chosen it and lived it and loved it.

I nearly knocked over my chair in my haste to reach my phone, and dialed his number with shaking hands.

"I'm driving, so I can't talk long," he said. "Didn't think I could handle saying goodbye to you so I just left. The papers are on the table."

"The answer is no," I said. "I am not sorry I married you. I will never be. I am *glad.*"

Silence, then I heard the huff of breath that meant he was crying. "I love you, Caro."

"I love you too. Get home safe. Take good care of yourself. And be happy."

Ruby greeted my phone call with a protracted groan of protest.

"Quit grizzling," I said. "It's nine-thirty in the morning, not seven-thirty."

"I went to bed late," she whined.

"I bet you did. Saturday's a late night for the culinary industry, I hear."

She gave a little hiccup of self-satisfied laughter, and I knew I had her.

"Look, Rube, I just wanted to say that I'm sorry. You did a really sweet thing, taking me on that trip to try to cheer me up, and I'm sorry I caused such a huge fight when you were only trying to help. I shouldn't have given you such a hard time about the stuff with Adam. It wasn't fair of me to blame you. You were young, and you had no idea what to even make of the information, let alone what to do with it."

"Wow. This is an unexpected topic for an early morning phone call. But thank you.

464

All of these statements you're making are true."

"Yes, they are. So, I'm sorry."

"It's okay, Care. I get it. You have to know I thought it was for the best not to tell you, right? And if I'd heard anything after that, anything at all —"

"I know. You would have said. I totally believe that. The thing is, though," I said, staring at the small stack of papers on the table, "it felt like a huge deal when you told me, but I realized it wouldn't have mattered either way. It would have taken him all of three minutes to convince me there was no reason to worry. I still would have married him. And we still would have ended up in exactly the same place."

"You think?"

"I know." Briefly, I filled her in on my long talk with Adam.

After I was finished, she was quiet for a moment. "Wow. So it's really over, huh?"

"Not *over* over, not until we get the decree, but I'm giving the papers to my lawyer on Monday to file with the county."

"Do you feel okay about it?"

"Yeah. I do," I said, and something slipped loose inside me as I realized I meant it. "We never had a way back up from where we'd landed."

"No, I didn't think you did. Soooooo . . . . what's going to happen with your rebound guy?"

"I broke it off. Specifically because he deserves better than to be the rebound guy."

"Well, yeah, but at some point you will be ready to actually date again."

"Sure, but I don't know when that's going to be. I can't ask him to wait for me."

"I don't know, Care; if he likes you, maybe he already is."

The ache at the impossibility of Neil rolled over me like fog off the ocean, dreary and cold. "Trust me, he isn't. There were bigger issues there than just my rebound. Anyway, can I talk to the Blaster, please?"

After an extremely brief pause that called unavoidably to mind the fact that the two of them had to be naked in bed together, Jonathan came on the line.

"I definitely told you to stop calling me that."

"There is no way that will ever happen. Especially since your latest and hopefully final blast was directed at such a special target."

"You know, I've gotta tell you, you might want to reconsider your assessment of which one of us did the blasting in this relationship," he said, then there was the

466

sound of a sharp smack. "Ouch! Damn it, woman!" I heard rustling, then the sound of Ruby's squeal in the background.

"Oh my god, CUT IT OUT," I yelled. "I'm never calling either of you again if I'm going to have to listen to foreplay. Jonathan, come back here."

"Did nobody teach that girl some manners?" he grumbled.

"Yeah, no, we've been trying for twenty-eight years," I said. "Anyway, just listen for a second. I wanted to tell you I'm happy for you guys. You obviously don't need my permission or my blessing, but I know I freaked out pretty hard when I heard about it, so . . . I'm over it. You don't have to worry about me being a Grinch anymore."

"Oh," he said. "That's all?"

"That's all. Why, what did you think I was going to say?"

"Darlin', I had no damn idea. But, thank you. I get how it could feel weird to you. But me and this little wood rat here, we're good."

I smiled. If Jonathan was giving Ruby an unflattering animal nickname, he definitely loved her. He referred to his own sister as "Porcupine"; though, in Kim's case, that was also down to personality.

After we said goodbye, I set the phone

down on the table with a soft clack. And suddenly I realized there was no one else to call. Adam was, finally, really and truly gone; and Ruby and Jonathan were holed up in their love nest in the city, so neither of them was coming to visit me for a really long time. My local friends weren't close friends, and nearly all of them were couples in whose company I would now be a very ponderous third wheel.

I was going to be alone, and this time it was for keeps. I'd been completely alone for the past few weeks — no Ruby, no Jonathan, no Neil — but somehow the last tenuous link to my marriage that remained had kept me from feeling the full depth of my loneliness. But now that Adam and I had officially said our goodbyes, it was rising like floodwater.

It was just me and the silence again.

32

"Perforation problems" by the way means
to me also the holes that will always exist
in any story we try to make of our lives.
So hang on, my love, & grow big & strong
& take your hits & keep going.
— Iggy Pop to a fan named Laurence,
1995

In the weeks that followed, I learned something about silence that surprised me. Silence doesn't kill you.

Much like the initial shock and pain of Adam's betrayal last summer had gradually dulled to a hollow ache by fall, so, too, did the sharp awareness of my loneliness subside to a more tolerable thing. I kept up my wine-and-book evenings on my couch, and I allowed myself a few more ways to fill the void. I called my parents more. I joined a volunteer group that offered art classes for low-income kids. I was touched and heart-ened to discover that, once I finally told my local friends that Adam and I had split, they invited me over anyway. I spent way too much money on a glorious pair of shoes, even though there was no one to admire me in them, simply because they were beautiful.

Out of faith in the power of exposure therapy, I visited Ruby and Jonathan (!) in the city over the long Presidents' Day weekend, and managed to return home three days later without having experienced the slightest urge to kill either one of them or even myself. It actually felt . . . surprisingly normal. It felt like the three of us hanging out at my house in September. Yes, they were holding hands and saying "we" a lot, but Ruby was clearly on notice to tamp down on her typical level of unrestrained PDA, and I was damn sure Jonathan didn't want me making fun of him for any of the girlfriend-related stuff I usually did.

The strangest thing, really, was being on the outside of a "we." I recognized how exceptionally spoiled it meant I was, to be experiencing that sensation for the first time at the age of thirty-three, but nevertheless it was as unpleasant as I'm certain everyone who had felt it before me could attest. It felt like standing outside someone's house on a snowy night, looking in through their warmly lit windows, with no invitation to come inside. But my sister and my (god help me) brother-in-law-apparent were good comrades, and they didn't make me feel pitied. They just made me feel welcome.

I missed Adam, of course, but it was manageable. A little duller every day. Slowly, it was becoming less about missing him as my husband, and condensing down into just . . . missing *him*. One day after work I flopped down on the couch with my wine and book, and without stopping to second-guess the decision, I called him.

"Hi, Caro," he said, and the guardedness in his voice made me flinch.

"Hi," I said. "It was kind of spur-of-the-moment for me to call you, I guess — but I was thinking about you and wondering how you were."

"Oh. I've been wondering about you, too."

"Well, so," I said, "how are things going?" It was an intentionally open question — he could make his response as general or specific as he wished.

"It's so weird to hear you say that. Know what I mean? I'm getting more used to not having you in my life, but to actually have a conversation where we catch each other up on our lives . . ."

"Yeah, it's completely weird," I said. "But still. Tell me."

"Well," he said slowly, and I had a sudden, vivid memory. Adam and I, at a few points in our marriage, had gone hiking together. Now, two true things about us are that we are both born and bred New Yorkers, and that neither of us has a naturally outdoorsy bone in our bodies. I had no more idea what I was doing on our hikes than he did, but I can truthfully state that he was a hell of a lot more helpless. If the trail was flat and dry, he was fine. But when, every so often, the trail inevitably ran into a source of moisture, he would stop. I would leap ahead like an eager Labrador, gleefully squelching into the goo, but Adam would stand there, for anywhere from thirty to ninety seconds, trapped by the importance of choosing exactly the most squelch-free route on which to place his feet.

It was what he was doing now.

"It's okay. You can tell me. I asked."

"So, how's work?" he said, mimicking a phony small-talk tone, but I could hear a smile in his voice.

"Sure. Start there."

"It's actually great," he said, and the happiness in his voice made me smile in return. "Richie's book hit the *Times* list. Near the

472

bottom, but still."

"That's your second one now, right? You've *got* to tell your parents about it."

"I did."

I sat upright on the couch and tucked my feet under me. "Oh wow! What did they say?"

"My dad was pretty confused, but he read the book, and he actually liked it. And you know he wouldn't have spared my feelings if he thought it was a pile of shit."

"Of course he liked it. It's a great book."

"It really could have gone the other way."

"But it didn't," I said.

"It didn't. It went way better than I expected. Honestly, it opened up my whole life, to be able to let go of what I thought he thought I should be doing."

"That's great, Adam. It must feel so good."

"It's a huge relief," he said. There was a pause in which both of us, on our separate ends of the phone line, peered at the deep and impassable swamp ahead on the trail. "I also told them about Patrick."

"Are you serious?" I whispered.

"And the funny thing is," he said, laughing slightly, "once I started telling people, I couldn't stop. I told my whole family, I told my friends, I told Father Kelly; I even told my agent."

"What, exactly, were you telling?"

"That you and I split up because I had an affair, with a man, and that I am in love with him."

"Wow," I said softly.

"Dad didn't take that quite as calmly as he did the ghostwriting."

"Ugh, Adam, I'm sorry."

"It had to be done. Aside from what happened with you, I was just so *sick* of myself. Thirty-four years old and crushed by my father's opinion. It's no way to live."

"No, it's not."

"So, right now I'm trying to get him to understand that I haven't turned into a different person. I don't listen to Madonna or want to work in fashion or whatever the hell he thinks guys who like guys are into. It's . . . challenging," he said. "I think it's going to be an ongoing process for the rest of our lives."

"Yeah. Sadly, I'd say you're right about that one."

"But honestly? It's actually fine, because I'm figuring out the balance in my own life at the same time. I've never been open about this before, so I've never had to evaluate what it means to me. It's part of who I am but it's not everything. It's not my definition as a human being."

"No, it's not. And maybe this is a weird thing to say, but I'm proud of you. For opening up about it. I truly believe you will be much happier in the long run."

"I do, too. And thank you. It's not a weird thing to say. It means everything to know you still want the best for me."

"Of course I do," I said, staring down at my empty left hand. "It's my instinct to wish that for you. I meant it when I said I'd always love you."

"Me too, Caro," he said softly. "And that's something good."

As I grew accustomed to the silence, I also spent more time with Farren in her studio, while she worked on her maze, and we talked about it. All the corners and the false instructions that had lain in wait for us, and for everyone we loved. Marriages ended for the right reasons, and the wrong ones; too soon and, sometimes, far too late. Jobs led in good directions and bad, to dead ends and long, wide-open straightaways.

Sometimes, life just works like this: You plan to see the Grand Canyon on a romantic trip with your husband, and be moved by its majesty. That is what you reasonably expect, based on the decisions you have made in your life and where they've taken you. And then what actually happens is that you break up with your husband, and you see the Grand Canyon on a bonding trip with your sister, accompanied by a shattering hangover; and your overall impression is that this particular example of nature's majesty is a bit underwhelming and frankly fucking scary. And while the dream was nice, the reality is — well, it's reality. That trip of mine had been the best my current reality could possibly be, actually, and that was pretty damn cool.

It was what I had to do. Enjoy the life I actually had, because the life I'd thought I'd have was gone. The change had the appearance of being my choice, but it wasn't. It had never really been. The old life I'd thought I'd have was based on an Adam who never existed in the first place. So all I could do was walk forward. And keep an eye out for the beauty along the way.

After a while, a day arrived where the calendar said it was a week away from the first day of spring, which, in western Massachusetts, meant it was the kind of raw, bitter, late-winter day that can make you lose your will to keep on living. The only sign of warmer weather was the steady, unstoppable lengthening of the days; so, as I approached my car in the parking lot after work that afternoon, there was enough light left in the sky to let me see right away that someone was leaning on the small burgundy Impreza next to my ancient Volvo.

Neil, leaning on Neil's car, next to mine. He wanted to talk to me. In the relative privacy of the parking lot, after work. Did that mean what I thought it might? What I found myself wishing, *badly,* that it did?

He smiled when he saw me, and I picked up the pace, scuffing my heavy winter boots over the salt-stained pavement. My warm breath dampened the scarf I'd pulled over my face against the cold. Skirting a sooty snow mound that our caretaker had built in an adjacent parking space, I screeched to a graceless halt in front of Neil and shoved my scarf aside, but that lovely smile of his just grew.

"Hey, Caroline."

He was wearing his woolly knit cap with the earflaps, and the unexpectedly adorable effect of a sexy guy in a dorky hat nearly undid me right then and there. "Hey."

"Do you have a minute to talk?"

I let myself have a moment to take him in, to absorb him. To sift through all the layers of what he was to me. My colleague, whose encouragement had led me to achieve things I hadn't known I could. My friend, who had given me kindness and understanding. My lover, whose laughter and tenderness and desire had lit up the darkest winter I'd ever known, replenishing what Adam had taken away from me. I respected this man, I admired him, I enjoyed him, I desired him, I cared about him — and I *missed* him.

Yes, I had a minute to talk.

"Do you want to get in the car so we can warm up? We can go somewhere else if you want. I just didn't want to make a big deal out of this for no reason."

Oh. Maybe it wasn't the kind of talk I had been hoping for. Maybe he was about to inform me he was seeing somebody else and would not be available in case I ever developed any ideas about restarting our — whatever it had been.

I circled his car and sat down on the passenger side. It was, in fact, delightfully warm; and it smelled a little bit like him. Neil pulled his hat off and stuffed it into the console next to a broken purple crayon.

"So, listen," he began, then took a deep breath and released it. This was something he'd thought about beforehand. Whatever it was he wanted to say. "I just wanted to tell you that I miss you," he said. "A lot. And

I'm so goddamn tired of missing people. If you need more time to get your head into a better place, I understand, believe me. Just . . . don't wait forever. It's like people say about having kids: There's never a perfect time, and if you keep waiting for that moment when everything's exactly the way you want, then you'll never do it, because that moment will never come. You don't have to be one hundred percent ready. I know *I'm* not one hundred percent ready, but I like you so damn much, Care. And I trust us to figure it out as we go along. I hate the thought of not trying at all because it might be confusing or it might get a little bit messy."

Oh, glory. This *was* what I'd wanted him to say. This was it, exactly. And yet.

"I'm tired of missing people, too. Definitely including you. I'm just scared that I don't have enough distance yet," I told him. "You deserve to be treated as your own person, not a stand-in. A relationship between us should be its own thing, not me trying to fill the void that Adam left."

He reached his hand across the console, and I met him, circling his warm fingers in my chilly ones. It felt so good to touch him.

"I've never once felt like a stand-in with you. Which is more than you can say for me. That first time we slept together . . . I'm so sorry. I want you to understand it was not intentional; my brain was so out of whack, it was like a muscle memory, it just —"

"It's okay," I said. "It really is. I understood all of that when it happened. I meant it when I said I didn't blame you."

He stroked his thumb across my knuckles. "I figured out after my brother died that loss splits your world into people who get it and people who don't. It's human nature to try to make things not feel as awful as they are, which is why people say garbage like 'Everything happens for a reason.' But you've never done that. You never tried to pretend. Even that night — I'd done something you should have been angry at me for, but instead, you saw that I was hurting and you gave me comfort. You weren't trying to make me talk about it, you weren't telling me it was going to be okay; you were just . . . there with me. It was such a *relief*. You've been so generous to me. The least I can do is offer you the same thing."

I raised my gaze from our joined hands so that I could meet his eyes straight on. "What are you offering, though? What *can* you offer?" It was a question I knew to ask, now.

"A lot more than I thought I could," he

said softly, leaning forward until he could stroke his free hand over my hair. "I've thought about this a lot, and here's the thing. Part of me will always love Eva, and that's the way it should be. But I'm ready to let it not be all of me. I'm ready to let it not even be most of me. Something I never realized before is that accepting that she's gone is not the same as . . . actually letting her go."

His voice quavered slightly, and when I squeezed his hand, he squeezed mine back, hard.

"But what you said to me before, about always playing second fiddle, it made me realize that I *have* to let her go if I want to have any kind of a future. So, I've been making room. Because I want to try this with you, for real. I won't always get everything right, but I'm going to do my best, because you're important to me. I promise I will make you feel that."

Another promise. Another choice. An extended hand I could grasp, or walk past.

"And as for your divorce baggage," he said, voice warm with that humor I adored, "you don't scare me. If you can give me and my loss baggage a shot, then I'm up for whatever weirdness you're worried you might splash around. Lay it on me."

I made a motion as if I was scooping a handful of liquid from my chest and tossing it at him, and he rubbed it into the skin of his throat like sunscreen. For a long moment we just smiled at each other, then he spoke again.

"So, listen. We will take it slow. As slow as you like. All I want from you is to let me take you to dinner sometimes, and make love to you a lot, and cook you and the girls pancakes on Sunday mornings. That doesn't sound like too much to handle, does it?"

"Knowing your pancakes, no."

He slid his fingers slowly between mine. "Only the pancakes?" His voice had the deep, smooth, coaxing cadence of an upright bass.

Oh, god. *Down, girl.* "Also the saxophone," I croaked out.

"The girls were asking about you, you know."

I fixed him with a grim stare. "Neil. Don't lie."

He threw his head back and laughed. "Annie did," he amended.

"Clara hopes I have been permanently relocated to Chattanooga," I said, and he laughed again.

"God damn, I've missed you. Are you in a better place with Adam these days?"

"Yeah. The papers were signed about six weeks ago. I'm expecting the judgment pretty soon, and then there's sort of a last-chance period before it becomes final. But, uh, neither of us is going to be having any second thoughts on this one."

It was Neil's turn to squeeze my hand, this time. "I'm sorry, baby. I know you know it was right, but it must have still been hard to do it."

"It hurt, but it wasn't hard to do it. There was no place else for us to go, and by the end he knew that too. I miss him. But I think we'll be able to be friends before too long."

"If anyone can do it, it would be you."

His voice trailed away into silence, and for a moment, all there was was the hypnotic rub of his knuckles against the back of my hand.

"So. Care."

"Hmm."

"Now that I've unloaded all of that, what do you think? Come back and give it a try?"

And here it was. That choice again. To offer trust, without a guarantee of safety, simply because there was someone asking for it.

As shattered as I'd been by Adam's betrayal, I knew I had no true reason to fear the same from the man in front of me. Neil had kindness, empathy, integrity, and a steadiness I could see now that Adam had always lacked.

He also had a wall full of photographs of his dead wife.

And a child who didn't like me, and in-laws who wouldn't welcome my presence in his life. But the thing was, he also had another child who *did* like me, and I badly missed the flame that lit inside me when I made her laugh. Then there was the way he was looking at me right now, like I was the first daffodil of spring and his favorite part of his favorite song, all rolled up in one. And, most of all, there was the answer I could feel ringing inside me, ringing so loud I was surprised I couldn't hear the sound.

We always make the same choice, don't we? As terrifying and often foolish as it is, we do it over and over and over, because the other way is just too cold to bear. We take a deep breath and square our shoulders and take that left that leads us deeper into the maze.

I stacked my other hand on top of Neil's and locked our fingers. "Of course I will," I whispered.

And when he kissed me, even though it wasn't my first kiss or even *our* first, it still felt like a beginning. I had no idea what the story of my future would be without the man I married in it, but this was, as Neil himself had said last fall, the first of many steps. And I liked the direction I was headed.

ACKNOWLEDGMENTS

The part where I get to thank everyone is my favorite part!

First of all, enormous thanks and love to O Captain! my Captain! Meredith Kaffel Simonoff, who is the wind beneath my wings; and also, of course, to my wonderful editor, Kara Cesare, for loving and guiding this book and for being every bit of a dream come true to work with, every step of the way. Huge thanks as well to the marvelous Random House/Ballantine team, including Nina Arazoza, Emma Caruso, Christine Mykityshyn, Jess Bonet, Misa Erder, Belina Huey, Marietta Anastassatos, Beth Pearson, and everyone else who's given input and assistance on this book as well as my first.

Thank you as always to those poor souls I've pressed into service to give me feedback on my drafts, including Amy FitzHenry, Wynne Newman, and Jess Rogers — your thoughts and advice have been invaluable.

Special shout-out to Jen Kingsley, who was patiently answering my questions about curatorship and museum life while forty weeks pregnant with a nine-pound baby.

To Cory Barber and Melissa Walker — thank you for being your amazing, inspiring, creative selves. If you didn't already know how much I admire you, you should certainly know it now.

My sincere gratitude goes to Shaun Usher, whose wonderful website and book *Letters of Note* I stumbled across while researching correspondence to use in this book. A great many of the letters featured here I discovered through Shaun.

My writer friends have been involuntarily entrusted with my sanity, and you've done a remarkable job of spreading the word, propping me up, and talking me down, as the case has required: Emily Giffin, Taylor Reid, Mary Kubica, Allie Larkin, Liz Fenton, Lisa Steinke, Michelle Gable, Rachel Goodman, Terra McVoy, Joy Callaway, and all the awesome folk of the WFWA.

And, of course, I owe another enormous thank-you to every single one of my readers, for trusting me with your time and entertainment, and for in many cases reaching out to me to share your enjoyment and your own stories. I love every one of you.

The same goes for all my blogger and book-lover buddies, who've been so wonderful with your support and enthusiasm for my work, and so generous with your friendship in general: Jenny O'Regan, Ginger Phillips, Estelle Halick, Jess Martinez, Melissa Amster, Nancy Farrow, Megan "Adios Pantalones" Simpson — you are the actual best.

To all my co-workers who've put up with me, friends who've cheered me on, and family who have supported me in my moments of both triumph and panic, thank you from the bottom of my heart. I couldn't do it without you.

And Allen, you get the last word as well as the first: You make me feel grateful, and joyful, every single day. You're the best parts of Adam and Neil and every love story I'll ever write.

Hello, lovely readers!

Thank you so very much for reading *Results May Vary* — I truly hope you enjoyed it. You are the reason why I, and all authors, write.

I hope you'll reach out and connect with me through one of the means below, because I would LOVE to hear from you! I especially love meeting book clubs via webcam, so please don't hesitate to contact me to join in with your group!

Twitter: @MBethanyChase
Instagram: Instagram.com/bethanychase
  author
Facebook: Facebook.com/bethanychase
  author and Facebook.com/m.bethany
  .chase
Pinterest: Pinterest.com/mbethanychase
Snapchat: mbethanychase
Litsy: bethanychaseauthor

Skype (for remote book club chatting):
bethanychaseauthor
Website: bethanychase.com
Email: m.bethany.chase@gmail.com

Lastly, if you enjoyed the book and can spare a few moments, I would be so grateful if you would consider leaving a review of the book at the retailer or book-sharing site of your choice. Those reviews are a tremendous help to authors, and help ensure that we get to keep writing books for readers to enjoy.

Read on, my friends, for an essay in the Reader's Guide I wrote exploring the theme of trust and vulnerability that's woven through *Results May Vary,* as well as some great questions for book clubs. Let's talk soon!

Xoxo,
Bethany

■ ■ ■ ■

RESULTS MAY VARY

BETHANY CHASE

■ ■ ■ ■

A READER'S GUIDE

AN ESSAY BY BETHANY CHASE

One of the things I found myself grappling with as I wrote *Results May Vary,* and which Caroline struggles with throughout the book, is the delicate nature of trust. In our best and closest relationships, trust is the default setting. If we have good parents, we learn to trust them from the moment we're born — again and again, they protect us and care for us, and we reward that care with love. Friendships and romantic relationships develop gradually into a structure of closeness, with moments of shared experience and mutual support climbing upward and bracing each other like bricks laid in mortar, creating a shelter that becomes ever more solid and reliable with time.

But if someone betrays our trust, what then? The shelter cracks, or maybe it crumbles all the way down. And then, suddenly, there is a choice to make.

What fascinated me as I wrote this story

was Caroline's realization that there has been a break in her relationship, between a past when she trusted her husband without thinking about it and a future in which it will have to be a deliberate and ongoing choice.

Prior to the opening of the story, Caroline never *chose* to trust Adam, because she always had that default setting: She understood, without conscious consideration, that he loved her, supported her, wanted the best for her, would never knowingly hurt her. But after she finds out about his affair, that unthinking sense of security is gone. He *has* hurt her, terribly, and so the trust she has given him is destroyed. And so, she must determine first whether she wants to rebuild it, and then, if she does, *how* to rebuild it.

When someone you love dearly has shown you that they will hurt and mistreat you, how do you rebuild? What steps do you take to replenish what's been lost? Can you trust this person without having to be aware of it, and is it worth it to have to work to trust someone? Doesn't that destroy the very joy of it? Because trust at its most beautiful and rewarding does not have to be consciously built.

I think the partner of trust is vulnerability. One of the primary ways we demonstrate trust toward the people in our lives is to give them access to our raw, tender parts: the insecurities, the painful memories, the innermost emotions, the feelings we yearn to have reciprocated. As trust deepens, we allow our defenses that protect these parts of ourselves to drop away. So surely one of the steps to regaining trust in someone is to slowly — *slowly* — lower those barriers.

In the kayaking scene, Adam very intentionally places Caroline in a position that maximizes her vulnerability, which she recognizes, and she spends most of the day fighting to keep her armor on. She's short with him, and guarded, and won't show him any signs of softness until, at their picnic, he asks her to. And in that moment she asks herself what is more important: to satisfy her savagely wounded pride, or to heal her relationship? So she reaches deep inside herself for the courage and generosity to let a little of her indignation go and start treating her husband like the man she loves again.

Of course, she finds out not much later that there are even more reasons to mistrust Adam than the one she knew at first, the main example of which was born in his own (unfounded) lack of trust in her. And this, finally, is what makes her decide that the relationship is too badly shattered to repair.

And that is a question that anyone in her position has to answer: At what point do you decide the other person has transgressed too much to deserve your good faith? There is a point of no return, and we all have to keep an eye on that in every single one of our relationships, whether with our partners or with our friends or even with our parents. Sometimes, for our own emotional safety, we have to stop being vulnerable and walk away. How do you know what that threshold is? And, when you have been badly hurt in a relationship, how — as Caroline wonders — do you muster the willingness to open up all your raw and tender corners to somebody else?

And the answer is, always, there's no reward without risk. There is no guarantee of safety, but for most of us, the immense rewards of connection make it worthwhile to accept that danger. As frightened as we might be, we just have to keep on trying. We have to take a breath, square our shoulders, and take that turn that leads us deeper into the maze.

QUESTIONS AND TOPICS
FOR DISCUSSION

1. If you were facing the choice that Caroline does throughout much of the book — to forgive your partner for an enormous betrayal and rebuild the relationship, or to walk away — what would you do? Why?

2. If Caroline had reconciled with Adam early on, instead of continuing a separation that let him rekindle his relationship with Patrick, what do you think would have happened in their marriage? Do you think Adam would have kept seeing Patrick if Caroline hadn't left him?

3. One of the questions the book asks is, How well can we ever really know the ones we love? Aside from Adam's affair and lies, which other characters hide bits of information from one another, and why? What

particular secrets would you find hardest to forgive?

4. Jonathan takes a more laissez-faire attitude than Caroline toward people in a relationship withholding small things from each other. How do you draw the line between what is acceptable and unacceptable? What do you do when there's a difference of opinion between one person's "I truly did not believe this mattered" and his or her partner's "Of course it does"?

5. Adam deeply loves Caroline — at least, he says he does — but it does not seem to be exactly the same way in which she loves him. What are the differences between their feelings for each other?

6. What do you think is going to happen with Jonathan and Ruby? Do you think they will make their relationship work and end up together? Why?

7. What Neil says about his wife in the final scene — that he's realized that letting go of her is a step beyond simply accepting that she's gone — is also true of Caroline with Adam. How much do you think she has truly let go of her husband by the end

of the story? Do you think Caroline and Neil are ready to start a relationship that doesn't have two other people in it?

8. On their trip to the Grand Canyon, Ruby explains to Caroline that "people can only give you what they have." Do you agree with her? How can you know if your partner is giving you everything he or she has? When do you know if it is not enough?

9. We come to learn that Adam struggles with his relationship with his father and a fear of disappointing him, which is one of the reasons he has kept so many secrets from Caroline as well. How can fear affect our ability to experience love? How does this speak to the interconnectedness of our relationships? Has there been a time in your life when you felt that the state of one of your close relationships impacted another?

10. Besides her ability to accept and forgive Adam and his betrayal, another of Caroline's personal successes is her ability to entice Diana Ramirez to donate to MASS MoCA and fund a residency for Farren Walker, an artist close to Caroline's heart. How do you think this victory contributes

to her healing process and new sense of self?

11. In describing one of her pieces, Farren explains, "The dots are the guidelines we think we see. But they're only an illusion, not the thing that marks the path." How does this statement resonate with Caroline's own journey throughout the novel? When in your life have you had to rethink the "dots" you thought you knew? How did you navigate the maze in your life?

12. Caroline eventually decides that "maybe there [is] a limit to the power of knowledge, after all," and that, even with everything she knows now, she wouldn't change anything about her relationship with Adam. Do you agree? When is knowledge powerful? When can it do more harm than good? In matters of the heart, is there more value to your knowledge of your partner or to the experience you share?

ABOUT THE AUTHOR

A native of Virginia's Shenandoah Valley, **Bethany Chase** headed to Williams College for an English degree and somehow came out the other side an interior designer. She is the author of the novel *The One That Got Away,* and when she's not writing or designing, you can usually find her in a karaoke bar. She lives with her husband and cat in Brooklyn, three flights up.

Facebook.com/bethanychaseauthor
@MBethanyChase

The employees of Thorndike Press hope you have enjoyed this Large Print book. All our Thorndike, Wheeler, and Kennebec Large Print titles are designed for easy reading, and all our books are made to last. Other Thorndike Press Large Print books are available at your library, through selected bookstores, or directly from us.

For information about titles, please call:
(800) 223-1244

or visit our Web site at:
http://gale.cengage.com/thorndike

To share your comments, please write:
Publisher
Thorndike Press
10 Water St., Suite 310
Waterville, ME 04901

$30.99 ✓

Eisner

J & J

MAY 0 8 2017